For Carolyn

Simon Scarrow's passion for writing began at an early age. After a childhood spent travelling the world he started work on his first novel after university and was able to pursue his great love of history by becoming a teacher, until he became a full-time writer in 2005.

Simon's Roman soldier heroes Cato and Macro first stormed the book shops in 2000, and Simon continues to create one new adult Roman novel each year. His 400-year-old house in Norfolk is in an area colonised by the Romans in the first century AD, and home to the rebellious tribal leader Boudica. The inspiration for his books comes when walking his dogs around the ruins of a Roman town just outside Norwich.

Simon has many other literary projects in hand including a young adult Roman series and THE SWORD AND THE SCIMITAR, an epic tale of the Siege of Malta in the sixteenth century, as well as developing projects for television and film with his brother Alex. He will shortly be creating a further Roman army novel, bringing Cato and Macro to Britannia for new battles in this unsettled land.

To find out more about Simon Scarrow and his novels, visit www.catoandmacro.com and www.scarrow.co.uk.

PRAETORIAN

SIMON SCARROW

headline

First published in 2011
by HEADLINE PUBLISHING GROUP

First published in paperback in 2012
by HEADLINE PUBLISHING GROUP

3

Cataloguing in Publication Data is available from the British Library

ISBN 978 0 7553 5379 8

Typeset in Bembo by Avon DataSet Ltd,
Bidford-on-Avon, Warwickshire

Printed and bound in Great Britain by
Clays Ltd, St Ives plc

Headline's policy is to use papers that are natural, renewable and
recyclable products and made from wood grown in sustainable forests.
The logging and manufacturing processes are expected to conform
to the environmental regulations of the country of origin.

HEADLINE PUBLISHING GROUP
An Hachette UK Company
338 Euston Road
London NW1 3BH

www.headline.co.uk
www.hachette.co.uk

As ever, my first debt of gratitude is to my wife Carolyn who carefully checked through each completed chapter as the novel was written, and who puts up with me when I get totally absorbed in the tale.

CHARACTERS

Soldiers between postings

Lucius Cornelius Macro – A veteran of the Roman legions. Tough, trustworthy and talented with a blade, and the mentor and best friend of

Quintus Licinius Cato – A young officer who has learned his trade the hard way in battles across the empire. He is courageous and quick-witted, which ensures that he gets the most dangerous of missions to carry out on behalf of Emperor Claudius.

In the Praetorian Guard

Tribune Balbus – in charge of the bullion convoy

Centurion Gaius Sinius – an ambitious back-stabber

Tribune Burrus – commander of the Third Cohort of Praetorians

Centurion Lurco – practically part-time commander of the Sixth Century of the Third Cohort

Optio Tigellinus – Lurco's frustrated subordinate

Guardsman Fuscius – a recent recruit who thinks he's a veteran

Prefect Geta – commander of the Praetorian Guard

At the Imperial Palace

Emperor Claudius – a fair ruler, though not always a
  coherent one
Empress Agrippina – his wife and niece, and mother of
Prince Nero – a pleasant boy with artistic ambitions
Prince Britannicus – the son of Claudius, clever but cold
Narcissus – imperial secretary and close adviser to Claudius
Pallas – another close adviser to the Emperor and Empress
Septimus – an agent of Narcissus

In Rome

Cestius – a vicious and ruthless leader of a crime gang
Vitellius – playboy son of a senator, and long-standing
  enemy of Macro and Cato
Julia Sempronia – the lovely daughter of Senator
  Sempronius

ROME IN THE AGE OF EMPEROR CLAUDIUS

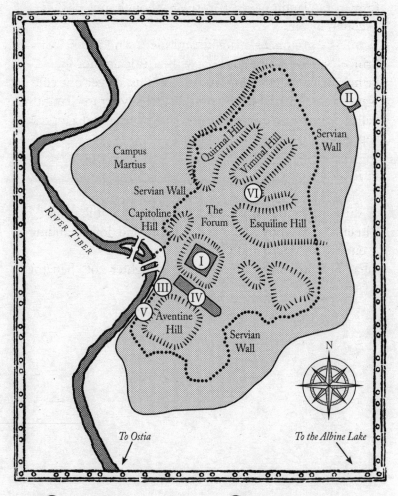

Ⓘ The Imperial Palace Complex   ⒾⓋ The Great Circus

Ⓘⓘ The Praetorian Camp   Ⓥ The Warehouse District

Ⓘⓘⓘ The Boarium   Ⓥⓘ The Subura Slum District

CHAPTER ONE

The small convoy of covered wagons had been on the road for ten days when it crossed the frontier into the province of Cisalpine Gaul. The first snows had already fallen in the mountains to the north that towered above the route, their peaks gleaming brilliantly against the blue sky. The early winter had been kind to the men marching with the convoy and though the air was cold and crisp, there had been no rain since they had left the imperial mint in Narbonesis. A bitter frost had left the ground hard and easy going for the wheels of the heavily laden wagons.

The Praetorian tribune in command of the convoy was riding a short distance ahead and as the route crested a hill he turned his horse aside and reined in. Ahead the road stretched out in a long straight line, rippling over the landscape. The tribune had a clear view of the town of Picenum a few miles away where he was due to meet the mounted escort sent from the Praetorian Guard in Rome – the elite body of soldiers tasked with protecting Emperor Claudius and his family. The century of auxiliary troops that had escorted the four wagons on the road from Narbonensis would then march back to their barracks at the mint, leaving the Praetorians, under the command of the tribune, to protect the small convoy for the rest of the journey to the capital.

Tribune Balbus turned in his saddle to survey the convoy marching up the slope behind him. The auxiliaries were Germans, recruited from the tribe of the Cherusci, large, fierce-looking warriors with unkempt beards thrusting out between the cheekguards of their helmets. Balbus had ordered them to keep their helmets on as they passed through the hills, as a precaution against any ambushes from the bands of brigands that preyed on unwary travellers. There was little chance that the brigands would risk an attack on the convoy, Balbus knew well enough. The real reason for his order was to cover up as much of the auxiliaries' barbaric hair as possible to avoid alarming any civilians they passed. Much as he appreciated that the German auxiliaries could be trusted with guarding the mint, owing their loyalty directly to the Emperor, Balbus felt a very Roman contempt for these men recruited from the wild tribes beyond the Rhine.

'Barbarians,' he muttered to himself, with a shake of his head. He was used to the spit and polish of the Praetorian cohorts and had resented being ordered to Gaul to take charge of the latest shipment of silver coin from the imperial mint. After so many years of service as a guardsman, Balbus had very fixed ideas of how a soldier should appear and if he had been posted to a cohort of German auxiliaries, the very first thing he would have done would be to order them to shave off those wretched beards and look like proper soldiers.

Besides, he was missing the comforts of Rome.

Tribune Balbus was typical of his rank. He had joined the Praetorians and served in Rome, working his way up through the ranks, before taking a transfer to the Thirteenth Legion on the Danube and serving as a centurion for several more years and then applying to return to the Praetorian Guard. A few more years of steady service had led to his present appointment as tribune, in command of one of the nine cohorts of the Emperor's personal bodyguard. In a few more years Balbus would retire with a handsome gratuity and take up an administrative post in some town in Italia. He had already set his sights on Pompeii where his younger brother owned a private bathhouse and gymnasium. The town was on the coast with fine views of the bay of Neapolis and had a decent set of theatres as well as a fine arena, surrounded by taverns selling cheap wine. There was even the prospect of an occasional brawl with men from the neighbouring town of Nuceria, he mused wistfully.

Behind the first five sections of auxiliaries came the four wagons, heavy vehicles drawn by ten mules each. A soldier sat on the bench beside each of the drivers and behind them stretched the goatskin covers, tightly tied over the locked chests resting on the beds of the wagons. There were five chests in each wagon, each containing one hundred thousand freshly minted denarii – two million in all, enough to pay an entire legion for a year.

Balbus could not help a moment of brief speculation about what he could do with such a fortune. Then he dismissed the whimsy. He was a soldier. He had given his oath to protect and obey the Emperor. His duty was to see that the wagons reached the treasury in Rome. Balbus's lips tightened as he recalled that some of his fellow Praetorians had a somewhat more flexible understanding of the concept of duty.

It was less than ten years ago that members of the Praetorian Guard had murdered the previous Emperor and his family. True, Gaius Caligula had been a raving madman and tyrant, but an oath was as solemn a commitment as Balbus could think of. He still disapproved of the removal of Caligula, even though the new Emperor chosen by the Praetorians had proved to be a rather better ruler. The accession of Claudius had been a confused affair, Balbus recalled. Those officers who had murdered his predecessor had intended to return power to the Roman senate. However, once the rest of their comrades realised that no emperor meant no Praetorian Guard, with all the privileges that went with the job, they swiftly cast around for a successor to the throne, and came up with Claudius. Infirm and stammering, he was hardly the ideal figurehead for the greatest empire in the known world, but he had proved himself a generally fair and effective ruler, Balbus conceded.

His gaze shifted to the last five sections of the German auxiliaries marching behind the wagons. While they might not look like proper soldiers, Balbus knew that they were good in a fight, and their reputation was such that only the most foolhardy of brigands would dare to attack the convoy. Anyway, the danger, such as it was, had passed as the convoy descended on to the broad flat valley of the River Po.

He clicked his tongue and pressed his boots into the flanks of his mount. With a brief snort the horse lurched forward into a walk and Balbus steered it back on to the road, passing the leading ranks of auxiliaries and their commander, Centurion Arminius, until he had resumed his position at the head of the convoy. They had made good time. It was not yet noon and they would reach Picenum within the hour, there to await the Praetorian escort if it had not already reached the town.

They were still some two miles from Picenum when Balbus heard the sound of approaching horses. The convoy was passing through a small forest of pine trees whose sharp scent filled the cold air. An outcrop of rock a short distance ahead obscured the road beyond. Balbus instinctively recalled his days on the Danube where the enemy's favourite trick was to trap Roman columns in similar confined settings. He reined in and threw his hand up.

'Halt! Down packs!'

As the wagons rumbled to a standstill, the German auxiliaries hurriedly set down their marching yokes, laden with kit, on to the side of the road and closed ranks at the head and tail of the convoy. Balbus passed the reins into his left hand, ready to draw his sword, and glanced round into the shadows beneath the trees on either side. Nothing moved. The sound of hoofbeats grew louder, echoing off the hard surface of the paved road and the rocks. Then the first of the riders came into view round the bend, wearing the red cloak of an officer. His crested helmet hung from one of the saddle horns. Behind him rode another twenty men in the mud-spattered white cloaks of Praetorian Guard rankers.

Balbus puffed his cheeks and let out a sharp sigh of relief. 'At ease!'

The auxiliaries lowered their shields and the shafts of their spears, and Balbus waited for the riders to approach.

Their leader slowed his horse to a trot and then to a walk for the last fifty paces.

'Tribune Balbus, sir?'

Balbus looked closely at the other officer. The face was familiar.

'What is the correct challenge, Centurion?' he demanded.

'The grapes of Campania are ripe to pick, sir,' the other man replied formally.

Balbus nodded at the phrase he was expecting to hear. 'Very well. You were supposed to wait for us at Picenum, Centurion . . .'

'Gaius Sinius, sir. Centurion of the Second Century, Eighth Cohort.'

'Ah yes.' Balbus vaguely recalled the name. 'So, what are you doing out on the road?'

'We reached Picenum yesterday, sir. Place was like a ghost town. Most of the people had gone to a nearby shrine for some local festival. I thought we would ride out and meet you, and your boys there.' He gestured towards the German auxiliaries.

'They're not mine,' Balbus growled.

'Anyway, we saw you approaching the town, sir, and, well, here we are. Ready to escort the wagons back to Rome.'

Balbus regarded the centurion silently for a moment. He liked soldiers who stuck to the letter of their orders and was not sure that he approved of Sinius and his men meeting them here on the road instead of in the town, as arranged. Clear plans for the delivery of the silver had been made in Rome some two months earlier and all concerned should obey their instructions. The moment officers began to play free and easy with their orders, plans began to fall apart. He resolved to have a word with Sinius's commanding officer when they returned to the Praetorian camp just outside the walls of Rome.

'Centurion Arminius!' Balbus called over his shoulder. 'On me!'

The officer in charge of the German auxiliaries hurried forward. He was a tall, broad-shouldered individual whose scale armour just about fitted his muscular torso. He looked up at the tribune, his beard almost flame-red in the sunshine.

'Sir?'

Balbus nodded to the horsemen. 'The escort from Rome. They'll protect the wagons from here. You and your men can turn back towards Narbonensis at once.'

The German pursed his lips and replied in heavily accented Latin. 'We were supposed to make the handover in Picenum, sir. The lads were hoping to enjoy themselves in the town for the night before we headed back.'

'Yes, well, that's not necessary now. Besides, I doubt the locals will take kindly to being invaded by a small horde of Germans. I know what your men are like when they get some drink inside 'em.'

Centurion Arminius frowned. 'I'll see to it that they don't cause any trouble, sir.'

'Nor will they. I'm ordering you to turn round and march back to Gaul at once, d'you hear?'

The other man nodded slowly, his bitterness quite clear. Then, with a curt nod to his superior he turned and strode back to the convoy. 'Take up your packs! Make ready to march! It's back to Gaul for us, boys.'

Some of his men groaned and one swore a loud oath

in his native tongue, drawing a sharp rebuke from the centurion.

Balbus glanced at Sinius and spoke softly. 'Can't have a bunch of hairy-arsed barbarians imposing themselves on decent folk.'

'Indeed not, sir.' Sinius nodded. 'Bad enough that the Germans have been tasked with guarding the mint and the silver convoys as it is. That should be work for proper soldiers, legionaries, or a cohort of the Guard.'

'Seems that we are not to be trusted by the Emperor,' Balbus said ruefully. 'Too many senior officers playing at politics in recent years. And this is what the rest of us have to put up with. Anyway, there's nothing we can do about it.' He drew himself up in his saddle. 'Have your men form up either end of the wagons. As soon as the auxiliaries are out of the way we can proceed.'

'Yes, sir.' Centurion Sinius saluted and turned away to call out the orders to his men. As the Germans grumpily formed a single column beyond the wagons, the mounted men eased their horses into place and soon the two small forces were ready to part company. Balbus approached Centurion Arminius to issue his parting instructions.

'You're to return to Narbonensis as swiftly as possible. Since I won't be there to keep watch on your men, don't let them cause any trouble in any settlements you pass through on the way back. Understand?'

The centurion pressed his lips together in a tight line and nodded.

'Then you can be off.'

Without waiting for a response, Balbus turned his horse in the other direction and trotted back to the head of the small column where Centurion Sinius was waiting.

He waved his arm forward and gave the order for horse-men and wagons to advance. With a crack of the reins from the drivers, the wagons began to move with a clatter and deep rumble from the heavy iron-rimmed wheels. The clop of the hoofs of mules and horses added to the din. Balbus rode on without looking back until he reached the rocky outcrop. Then he glanced round and saw the rear of the auxiliary column a quarter of a mile down the road, tramping back towards Gaul.

'Good riddance,' he muttered to himself.

The wagons, with their new escort, followed the road round the rocks and the route resumed its straight direction, through another quarter of a mile of pine trees, towards Picenum. Now that he was well clear of the German troops Balbus felt his mood improve. He slowed his horse until he was riding alongside Centurion Sinius.

'So, what's the latest news from Rome?'

Sinius thought for a moment and replied with an amused smile. 'The Emperor's new squeeze continues to tighten her grip on the old boy.'

'Oh?' Balbus frowned at the coarse reference to the Empress.

'Yes. Word round the palace is that Agrippina has told Claudius to get rid of his mistresses. Naturally, he isn't so keen. But that's the least of his worries. You know that kid of hers, Lucius Domitius? She's putting it about that the boy is going to be adopted by Claudius.'

'Makes sense,' Balbus responded. 'No point in making the lad feel left out.'

Sinius glanced at him with an amused smile. 'You don't know the half of it, sir. Agrippina's openly pushing Claudius to name young Lucius as his heir.'

Balbus raised his eyebrows. This was a dangerous development; the Emperor already had a legitimate heir, Britannicus, his son by his first wife, Messallina. Now there would be a rival to the throne. Balbus shook his head. 'Why on earth would the Emperor agree to do that?'

'Maybe his mind is growing weak,' Sinius suggested. 'Agrippina claims that she only wants Britannicus to have a protector and who better for the job than his new big brother? Someone to look out for his interests after Claudius has popped off. And that day ain't so far off. The old boy's looking thin as a stick and frail with it. So, once he goes, it looks like the Praetorians are going to have young Lucius Domitius as their new employer. Quite a turn-up, eh?'

'Yes,' Balbus replied. He fell silent as he considered the implications. As an infant the Emperor's son, Britannicus, had been popular with the Praetorian Guard; he used to accompany his father on visits to the camp, wearing a small set of armour of his own and insisting on taking part in the drilling and weapons practice, to the amusement of the men. But the infant had become a boy and these days attended to his studies. Now young Britannicus was going to have to compete for the affection of the Praetorians.

'There's more, sir,' Sinius said softly, glancing over his shoulder as if to make sure that his men did not overhear. 'If you would care to know it.'

Balbus looked at him sharply, wondering just how far he could trust the other officer. In recent years he had seen enough men put to death for not guarding their tongues and he had no wish to join them. 'Is there any danger in hearing what you have to say?'

Sinius shrugged. 'That depends on you, sir. Or, more accurately, it depends on where your first loyalty lies.'

'My first and only loyalty is to my Emperor. As is yours, and all the men in the Praetorian Guard.'

'Really?' Sinius looked at him directly and smiled. 'I would have thought a Roman would be loyal to Rome first.'

'Rome and the Emperor are the same,' Balbus replied tersely. 'Our oath is equally binding to both. It is dangerous to say different, and I'd advise you not to raise the issue again.'

Sinius scrutinised the tribune for a moment and then looked away. 'No matter. You are right, of course, sir.'

Sinius let his mount drop back until he was behind his superior. The convoy reached the end of the pine trees and emerged into open country. Balbus had not passed any other travellers since dawn and could see none ahead in the direction of Picenum. Then he recalled what Sinius had said about the festival. A short distance ahead the road descended into a slight fold in the landscape and Balbus stretched up in his saddle as he caught sight of movement amid some stunted bushes.

'There's something ahead,' he said to Sinius. He raised his arm and pointed. 'See? About a quarter of a mile in front, where the road dips.'

Sinius looked in the direction indicated and shook his head.

'Are you blind, man? There's clearly something moving there. Yes, I can make it out now. A handful of small carts and mules among the bushes.'

'Ah, now I have them, sir.' Sinius stared into the dip a

moment and then continued, 'Could be a merchant's train in camp.'

'At this time of day? This short a distance from Picenum?' Balbus snorted. 'I don't think so. Come, we need a closer look.'

He urged his mount forward, clopping down the road towards the bushes nestling in the dip. Sinius beckoned to the leading section of horsemen to follow him and set off in the wake of his superior. As Balbus drew nearer he realised that there were several more carts than he had first thought and now he could see a handful of men crouching down between the bushes. The anxiety he had felt shortly before returned to prick the back of his scalp with icy needles. He reined in a hundred paces from the nearest of the men and their carts to wait for the others to catch up.

'I don't like the look of this. Those scoundrels are up to no good, I'll be bound. Sinius, ready your men.'

'Yes, sir,' the centurion replied in a flat tone.

Balbus heard the rasp of a sword being drawn from its scabbard and he took a tighter grip of his reins as he prepared to lead the mounted guardsmen forward.

'I'm sorry, sir,' Sinius said softly as he plunged his sword into the tribune's back, between the shoulder blades. The point cut through the cloak and tunic and on through the flesh and bone into the spine. Balbus's head jerked back under the impact and he let out a sharp gasp as his fingers spread wide, half clenched like claws, releasing his grip on the reins. Sinius gave a powerful twist to the blade and then ripped it free. The tribune collapsed forward between his saddle horns, arms hanging limply down the flanks of his horse. The animal started in surprise and the movement dislodged the tribune from his saddle. He fell heavily to the ground, rolling on to his back. He stared up, eyes wide open as his mouth worked feebly.

Sinius turned to his men. 'See to the drivers of the wagons and then bring them up to the carts.' He looked down at the tribune. 'Sorry, sir. You're a good officer and you don't deserve this. But I have my instructions.'

Balbus tried to speak but no sound escaped his lips. He felt cold and, for the first time in years, afraid. As his vision began to blur, he knew he was dying. There would be no quiet life for him in Pompeii and he felt a passing regret that he would never again see his brother. Swiftly the life faded from his eyes and they stared up fixedly as he lay still on the ground. Further down the road there were a few surprised cries that were quickly cut off as the wagon drivers were ruthlessly disposed of. Then the wagons and the mounted men continued towards the waiting carts. Sinius turned to a large man close behind him and indicated the tribune's body. 'Cestius, put him and the others on one of the wagons. I want two men to ride ahead and keep watch. Another two to go back to the bend in the road and make sure those auxiliaries don't pull a fast one and turn round to take some unofficial leave in Picenum.'

The men with the carts emerged from the bushes and formed them into a line beside the road. Under Sinius's instructions, the chests were quickly unloaded from the wagons, one to each of the carts. As soon as they were secured, they were covered with bales of cheap cloth, sacks of grain, or bundles of old rags. The traces were removed from the mule teams on the wagons and the animals were distributed among the carts to haul the additional burden. Once empty, the wagons were heaved deep into the bushes and their axle caps knocked out and the wheels removed from the axles so that they collapsed down, out of sight of the road. The bodies were taken further into the scrub and tossed into a muddy ditch before being covered over with brush cut from the bushes. Finally the men gathered around the carts as Sinius and a handful of others cut some more brush to cover the gaps in the bushes where the wagons had passed through and to sweep the tracks in the grass. Thanks to the frost there were no telltale ruts in the ground.

'That'll do,' Sinius decided, tossing his bundle of twigs aside. 'Time to change clothes, gentlemen!'

They hurriedly removed their cloaks and tunics and swapped them for a variety of civilian garments in a range of styles and colours. Once the uniforms were safely tucked away in bundles behind their saddles, Sinius looked the men over. He nodded in satisfaction; they looked enough like the merchants and traders who regularly passed along the roads between the towns and cities of Italia.

'You have your instructions. We'll leave here in separate groups. Once you get beyond Picenum, take the routes you have been given back to the warehouse in Rome. I'll see you there. Watch your carts carefully. I don't want any petty thieves stumbling on the contents of these chests. Keep your heads down and play your part and no one will suspect us. Is that clear?' He looked round. 'Good. Then let's get the first carts on the move!'

Over the next hour the carts left the dip in the road singly, or in groups of two or three at irregular intervals, intermixed with the horsemen. Some made for Picenum, others branched off at the road junction before the town, passing to the west or east and following an indirect route to Rome. Once the last cart was on its way, Sinius took a final look around. There were still some tracks left by the carts and the hoofs of the mules and horses, but he doubted that they would attract attention from travellers on their way to or from Picenum.

With a brief nod of satisfaction, Sinius steered his horse on to the road and walked it unhurriedly towards the town. He paid his toll to the guards on the town gate and stopped at a tavern to have a bowl of stew and a mug of heated wine before continuing his journey. He left the town's south gate and took the road to Rome.

It was late in the afternoon when he saw a small column of horsemen in white cloaks riding up from the south. Sinius pulled the hood of his worn brown tunic up over his head to hide his features and raised a hand in greeting as he passed by the Praetorian guardsmen riding to meet the convoy from Narbonensis. The officer leading the escort haughtily ignored the gesture and Sinius smiled to himself at the prospect of the man having to explain the disappearance of the wagons and their chests of silver when he reported to his superiors in Rome.

CHAPTER TWO

Ostia, January, AD 51

The rough sea was grey, except where the strong breeze lifted veils of white spume from the crests of waves as they rolled in towards the shore. Above, the sky was obscured by low clouds that stretched out unbroken towards the horizon. A light, cold drizzle added to the depressing scene and soon soaked Centurion Macro's dark hair, plastering it to his scalp as he gazed out over the port. Ostia had changed greatly since the last time he had been there, a few years earlier on his return from the campaign in Britannia. Then the port had been an exposed landing point for the transhipment of cargo and passengers to and from Rome, some twenty miles inland from the mouth of the River Tiber. A handful of timber piers had projected from the shore to provide for the unloading of imports from across the empire. A somewhat smaller flow of exports left Italia for the distant provinces ruled by Rome.

Now the port was in the throes of a massive development project under the orders of the Emperor as part of his ambition to boost trade. Unlike his predecessor, Claudius preferred to use the public purse for the common good, rather than absurd luxuries. Two long moles were under construction, stretching like titanic arms to embrace the waters of the new harbour. The work continued without let up through every season of the year and Macro's gaze momentarily rested on the miserable chain gangs of slaves hauling blocks of stone across wooden rollers out towards the end of the moles where they were pitched into the sea. Block by block they were building a wall to protect the shipping from the water. Further out, beyond the moles, stood the breakwater. Macro had been told by the owner of the inn where he and his friend, Cato, were staying that one of the largest ships ever built had been loaded with stones and scuttled to provide the foundations of the breakwater. More blocks of stone had been dropped on to the hull until the breakwater had been completed and now the lower levels of a lighthouse were under construction. Macro could just make out the tiny forms of the builders on the scaffolding as they laboured to complete another course.

'Sooner them than me,' Macro mumbled to himself as he pulled his cloak tighter around his shoulders.

He had taken this walk along the shore every morning for the last two months and had followed the progress of the harbour construction with less and less interest. The port, like so many ports, had its complement of boisterous inns close to the quays to take advantage of the custom of freshly paid sailors at the end of a voyage. For most of the year there would have been plenty of interesting characters for Macro to enjoy a drink with and swap stories. But few ships put to sea in the winter months and so the port was quiet and the inns frequented by only a handful of characters in need of drink. At first Cato had been willing enough to join him for a few cups of heated wine but the younger man was brooding over the knowledge that the woman he intended to marry was a day's march away in Rome and yet the orders they had received from the imperial palace strictly forbade Cato from seeing her, or even letting her know that he was staying in Ostia. Macro felt sympathy for his friend. It had been nearly a year since Cato had last seen Julia.

Before arriving in the port, Macro and Cato had been serving in Egypt where Cato had been obliged to take command of a scratch force of soldiers to repel the invading Nubians. It had been a close-run thing, Macro reflected. They had returned to Italia in the full expectation of being rewarded for their efforts. Cato had richly deserved to have his promotion to prefect confirmed, as Macro deserved his pick of the legions. Instead, after reporting to Narcissus, the imperial secretary, on the island of Capreae, they had been sent to Ostia to await further orders. A fresh conspiracy to unseat the Emperor had been uncovered and the imperial secretary needed Macro and Cato's help to deal with the threat. The orders given to them by Narcissus had been explicit. They were to remain in Ostia, staying at the inn under assumed names, until they were given further instructions. The innkeeper was a freedman who had served in the Emperor's palace in Rome before being rewarded with his freedom and a small gratuity which had been enough to set him up in business in Ostia. He was trusted by the imperial secretary to look after the two guests, and not ask any questions. It was imperative that their presence was kept secret from anyone in Rome. Narcissus had not needed to name Julia Sempronia. Cato had taken his meaning well enough and contained his frustration for the first few days. But then the days stretched into a month, then two, and still there was no further word from Narcissus and the young officer's patience was stretched to the limit.

The only information that Narcissus had volunteered was that the plot against the Emperor involved a shadowy organisation of conspirators who wanted to return power to the senate. The same senate which had been responsible for leading the Republic into decades of bloody civil war following the assassination of Julius Caesar, Macro thought bitterly. The senators could not be trusted with power. They were too inclined to play at politics and paid scant regard to the consequences of their games. Of course there were a few honourable exceptions, Macro mused. Men like Julia's father, Sempronius, and Vespasian, who had commanded the Second Legion in which Macro and Cato had served during the campaign in Britannia. Both good men.

Macro took a last look at the slaves working on the breakwater and then pulled up the hood of his military cloak. He turned and made his way back along the coastal path towards the port. There, too, was evidence of the redevelopment of Ostia. Several large warehouses had sprung up behind the new quay and yet more were under construction in the area where the old quarter of the port had been razed to make way for the new building projects. Macro could see that it would be a fine modern port when the work was done. Yet more proof of Rome's wealth and power.

The path joined the road leading to the port and the iron studs on the soles of Macro's army boots sounded loudly on the paved surface. He passed through the gate with a brief exchange of nods with the sentry who knew better than to demand the entrance toll from a legionary. One of the perks of being a soldier was exemption from some of the petty regulations that governed the lives of civilians. Which was only fair, Macro thought, since it was the sacrifice of the soldiers that made the peace and prosperity of the Empire possible. Apart from the idle tossers in cushy garrison postings in quiet backwaters like Greece, or those preening twats in the Praetorian Guard. Macro frowned. They were paid half as much again as the men in the legions, yet all they had to do was dress up for the odd ceremony and see to the efficient disposal of those condemned as enemies of the Emperor. The chances of any active service were slight. That said, Macro had seen them in action once, back in Britannia during the Emperor's brief trip to claim credit for the success of the campaign. They had fought well enough then, he admitted grudgingly.

The blocks of apartments lining the street, three or four storeys high, crowded the already wan daylight and imposed a chilly gloom along the route leading into the heart of the town. Reaching the junction where the streets radiated out to the other districts of Ostia, Macro turned right into the long thoroughfare that ran through the heart of the port where the main temples, plushest baths and the Forum crowded upon each other as if jostling to be the most prestigious establishment. It was market day and the main street was busy with merchants and municipal officials hurrying about their business. A line of slaves, chained at the ankle, on their way to the holding pens of the slave market shuffled along the edge of the street under the watchful eye of a handful of burly guards armed with clubs. Macro passed through the

Forum, which extended across both sides of the street, and then turned into a side street where he saw the imposing columned façade of the Library of Menelaus where he had agreed to meet Cato. The library had been gifted to Ostia by a Greek freedman who had made his fortune importing olive oil. It was well stocked with an eclectic range of books that were arranged on shelves in an equally eclectic manner.

Macro eased his hood back as he stepped up from the street and ascended the short staircase to the library's entrance. Just inside the doorway a clerk sat at a plain wooden desk, warmed by the flames of a brazier. His eyes narrowed suspiciously at the sight of a soldier.

'May I be of any assistance, sir?'

Macro wiped the moisture from his brow and nodded. 'Looking for someone. A soldier, like me.'

'Really?' The clerk arched an eyebrow. 'Are you certain this is the place, sir? It is a library.'

Macro stared at him. 'I know.'

'Might I suggest, sir, that you would have better luck looking for your comrade in one of the inns close by the Forum. I believe that those sorts of establishments are more popular with soldiers than this library.'

'Trust me, my friend arranged to meet me here.'

'Well, it's not where soldiers usually meet, sir,' the clerk persisted, tersely.

'True, but then my friend is not your usual military man.' Macro smiled. 'So, have you seen him? Just answer the question, eh? No need to look down your nose at me, not if you like it the way it is.'

The clerk realised that this stocky, tough-looking visitor was not going to be fobbed off. He cleared his throat and reached for a stylus and waxed slate, as if to imply that he had been interrupted in the process of carrying out some complex and vital bureaucratic task. 'I only came on duty a short while ago, sir. If your friend is here, he must have already entered because I have not seen him and have no idea where he might be. I suggest you go and look for him.'

'I see,' Macro replied evenly. He stood his ground for a moment and then leant forward across the desk and let the hem of his cloak drip down on to the clerk's tablet. The clerk froze, then looked up anxiously.

'Sir?'

'A parting thought,' Macro growled. 'There's no need for the surly treatment, my lad. You try it on again and I might mistake your nice neat little library for a very rough and ready inn, if you take my meaning.'

The clerk swallowed. 'Yes, sir. My apologies. Please feel free to enjoy the facilities of the library as you wish.'

'There!' Macro leant back with a pleasant smile. 'Just as easy to be polite as to act like a complete cunt, eh?'

The clerk nervously glanced about to see if any of his colleagues were in view, but he was alone. He looked warily at the soldier in front of his desk. 'Yes, sir. As you say.'

Macro turned away and rubbed his hands together to warm them up. He had an abiding hatred of the petty officials of the world who seemed to serve no other purpose than to hinder those who actually had useful acts to perform.

The library had a large entrance hall with two doors leading off either side and another directly opposite the entrance. After a brief pause, Macro made for the middle way, his footsteps echoing off the high walls. He entered a long room lined with shelves which were filled with scrolls. The ceiling, rising some thirty feet from the tiled floor, had been painted with nautical scenes which were lit by narrow windows high up in the walls. A line of tables and benches ran down the centre of the library's main room and since it was still early on a cold morning, there were only three men present, two older men hunched over a scroll as they engaged in a muted discussion, and the unmistakable slender figure of Cato in his military cloak. He sat at the far end of the room, where a faint shaft of light provided barely adequate illumination for the broad sheets of papyrus that lay before him.

The loud clatter of Macro's boots caused the two old men to break off their discussion and look up with a frown at the new arrival who had disrupted the usual quiet of the library. Although Cato must have heard the sound of his friend's boots, he continued reading until Macro was almost upon him and then placed his finger on the papyrus to mark his place and looked up. His face was gaunt and he regarded Macro without a flicker of expression as he sat down on the bench opposite Cato. The younger officer had received a severe wound to his face while they were in Egypt and now a white line of scar tissue stretched from his forehead, across his brow and down his cheek. It was quite a dramatic scar but it had not really disfigured his features. A mark to be proud of, Macro thought. Something that would distinguish Cato from the other fresh-faced officers serving the Emperor, and one that would single him out as the seasoned veteran he had become since joining the Second

Legion as a weedy recruit some eight years earlier.

'Found what you're looking for?' Macro nodded at the sheets in front of Cato, then gestured to the laden shelves lining the walls. 'More than enough reading matter to keep you busy, eh? Should help to pass the time.'

'Until what, I wonder.' Cato raised his spare hand and lightly rubbed his cheek where the scar ended. 'We've heard nothing from Narcissus for nearly a month now.'

Cato had sent a message to the imperial secretary via the innkeeper, requesting to know why he and Macro had to remain in Ostia. The reply had been terse and simply told them to wait. Cato's boredom at the enforced stay in the port alternated with acute anger that he was being kept from seeing Julia. Even so, he was tormented by the prospect of her reaction to his scar. Would she accept it and take him into her arms again? Or would she recoil in disgust? Worst of all, Cato feared that she would pity him and offer herself to him on that basis. The thought sickened him. Until he saw her again he could not know her response. Nor could he prepare her for the encounter since Narcissus had forbidden him from contacting her.

'What are you reading there?' Macro broke into his thoughts.

Cato focused his mind. 'It's a copy of the gazette from Rome. I've been catching up on events in the city over recent months to see if there's any hint of what it is that Narcissus needs us for.'

'And?'

'Nothing that springs out. Just the usual round of ceremonies, announcements of appointments and births, marriages and deaths of the great and good. There was a mention of Senator Sempronius. He was commended by the Emperor for putting down the slave revolt in Crete.'

'No mention of our part in that, I suppose,' Macro mused.

'Alas, no.'

'Well, there's a surprise. Anything else of note?'

Cato glanced down at the sheets in front of him and shook his head. 'Nothing significant, unless . . .' He shuffled through the sheets, scanning them briefly, then pulled one out. 'Here. A report dated two weeks ago announcing that one of the Guard's officers had been waylaid by brigands and killed near Picenum. The brigands have not been found . . . He leaves behind a grieving widow and young son, et cetera.' Cato looked up. 'That's all.'

'Doesn't sound like it has anything to do with our being here,' Macro said.

'I suppose not.' Cato sat back and stretched his arms out as he yawned widely. When he had finished, he leant on his elbows and stared at Macro. 'Another day in the wonderful town of Ostia then. What shall we do for entertainment? Nothing on at the theatre. It's too cold to go to the beach and swim. Most of the bathhouses are closed until trade picks up in the spring and our friend, Spurius the innkeeper, refuses to light a fire to warm his place until the evening.'

Macro laughed. 'My, you are in a miserable mood!' He thought a moment and then his eyebrows rose. 'Tell you what. According to Spurius there's some new stock at that brothel down by the Baths of Mithras. Want to go and see what's on offer? Something to keep us nice and warm. What do you say?'

'It's tempting. But I'm not in the mood.'

'Bollocks. You're saving yourself for that girl, aren't you?'

Cato shrugged. The truth was he did not relish the prospect of visiting the disease-riddled whores who served the townsmen and passing sailors. If he caught anything off them then it would ruin his prospects of any happy union with Julia. 'You go, if you really want to. I'm heading back to the inn for a bite, then I'm going to settle down for a read.'

'A read,' Macro repeated blankly. 'What have you got in your veins, lad? Blood, or thin soup?'

'Either way, I'm staying in our room and reading. You can do what you like.'

'I will. Just as soon as I've eaten something to get my strength up.'

The benches scraped back as the two soldiers rose to their feet. Cato swept the gazettes together and returned them to a shelf before he and Macro marched out of the library, their footsteps disturbing the other two men once again.

'Shhh!' One of them raised a finger to his lips. 'This is a library, you know!'

'Library!' Macro sneered. 'It's a whorehouse of ideas, that's what. The only difference is that a library will never leave you with a nice warm glow inside, eh?'

'Shocking!' the man expostulated. He turned to Cato. 'Sir, please be so good as to remove your companion from the premises.'

'He needs no urging, believe me. Come, Macro.' Cato tugged his arm and steered his friend towards the doorway.

★

Spurius's cook, an antique sailor who had lost his leg in an accident, served them a thin stew of barley and chunks of meat that might have come from a highly seasoned lamb shank, but it was hard to be certain as it had lost any flavour it had once had and was the texture of damp tree bark. But it was warm and managed to assuage the soldiers' appetite. When Cato asked for some bread, the cook scowled, stumped off, and returned with a stale loaf which he set down on the table with a thud.

'Here! Spurius!' Macro bellowed, startling the four other customers of the inn. Spurius was at the bar arranging his cheap clay cups on the shelves behind the counter. He turned round irritably and hurried over to the table.

'What is it? And do you mind keeping your voice down?'

Macro gestured towards the bowl of stew, which was still a third full. 'I may be hungry enough to eat this swill but I draw the line at bread that I would not even force a bloody pig to eat.' He picked up the loaf and slammed it down on the tabletop. 'Hard as a rock.'

'So soak it in the stew. It'll soften up soon enough,' Spurius suggested in a helpful tone.

'I want good bread,' Macro replied firmly. 'Freshly baked. And I want it now.'

'Sorry, there's none available.'

Macro eased his stool back. He continued in a lower voice to make sure that the other customers would not overhear. 'Look, you've been told to look after us and no doubt you're being paid well enough to put us up and feed us.'

'I'm being paid a pittance for the pair of you,' Spurius grumbled. 'Or at least I will be when you leave and

Narcissus settles up. Meanwhile you're eating into my profits.'

Macro smiled. 'That snake Narcissus never gives up more than he has to and is as likely to cheat you as he is to honour his word, as we've found out to our cost on more than one occasion.'

'Macro, that's enough,' Cato warned him. 'We don't talk about our business.'

Macro turned to stare hard at him, and then his expression softened. 'All right. But I don't take kindly to being left high and dry in Ostia with only this dive for food and shelter. It ain't right, Cato.'

'Of course not, but there's nothing we can do about it.' Cato turned to the innkeeper. 'Now then, I know you resent us being foisted on you. We don't like it either. But in the interests of us getting on with each other and not causing any trouble, I suggest you do something to improve our rations. To start with, I suggest you get my friend the fresh bread he asked for.'

Spurius took a calming breath and nodded slightly. 'I'll see what I can find. If you promise not to cause any trouble with the other customers.'

Cato nodded. 'We promise.'

The innkeeper returned to the counter and had a quiet word with his cook. Cato smiled sweetly at Macro. 'See what a little bit of reason can achieve?'

Macro sniffed. 'It has its place. But then I have to say that I have found that the application of force can be equally effective at producing results from time to time.'

'Not if you don't want to draw attention to yourself.'

Macro shook his head. 'I could do with a little attention, Cato. This place is driving me mad. It's bad enough that we have to sit and wait at Narcissus's pleasure. But the bastard hasn't advanced us more than a fraction of the back pay we're due and we can't even afford decent food or more comfortable lodgings.'

Cato was silent for a moment. 'No doubt that's intended to help make us compliant.'

Before Macro could respond there was a rattle of cart wheels in the street outside and then the sound died away abruptly as the vehicle drew up outside the inn. Spurius hurried to the door, eased it open a fraction, then quickly ducked outside, shutting the door behind him. Macro and Cato heard a brief muted exchange before the cart continued round the building to the rear where there was a small yard with stalls for the horses of travellers stopping at the inn.

'New customers for this dump,' Macro mused. 'Do you think we should warn them off?'

'Just leave it,' Cato said wearily. He stared down into his bowl for a moment before reluctantly picking up his spoon to consume some more of the stew. Shortly afterwards, the cook reappeared, looking flustered as he limped over to the table and presented them with a fresh loaf. Macro sniffed and looked at Cato in surprise. 'Freshly baked!'

He picked it up, tore it in half and thrust a chunk towards Cato before tearing into the warm doughy mass with relish. From the back rooms of the inn came the sound of voices and the scrape of furniture and it was a short while before Spurius emerged through the low door behind the counter. He glanced round at the other customers and then crossed the room to Macro and Cato's table.

'What now?' Macro muttered. 'I'll bet the bastard wants to move us out of the room to make way for his new guest.'

'I don't think so.'

Spurius leant towards them and spoke very quietly. 'Follow me.'

Cato and Macro exchanged a quick glance before Cato responded, 'Why?'

'Why?' Spurius frowned. 'Just come with me, sir. It'll be clear enough in a moment. I can't say anything else.' He made a slight nod towards his remaining customers. 'If you understand me.'

Macro shrugged. 'No.'

'Come on,' said Cato. 'Let's go.'

They left what remained of their meal and rose to follow the innkeeper across the room towards the door that led to the back. The other people in the room could not help eyeing them curiously as they passed by, Cato noted with a faint smile of amusement. Spurius went first, followed by Macro, with Cato last, who had to stoop under the door frame. There was a narrow room beyond, lit by a single oil lamp. By its weak glow Cato could see that the walls were lined with jars of wine and baskets of vegetables, and a net of fresh bread hung from a hook, close to two joints of cured meat. Clearly the innkeeper ate well, even if his customers didn't. At the far end of the room a door stood slightly ajar and the frame was brightly lit by a fire burning in the next room. Spurius entered the room, followed by Macro who immediately uttered a curse. The room was generously proportioned with a wide table at its centre. A freshly stoked cooking fire crackled beneath the iron grill and provided the room with a rosy light. Seated on the far side of the table was a slender figure in a plain cloak. He looked up from the cheese and bread that had been laid before him and smiled as he saw Macro and Cato.

'Greetings, gentlemen. It is good of you to join me!' Narcissus waved them towards the bench opposite him. 'Or rather, it is good of me to join you.'

'What are you doing here?' asked Macro. 'I had begun to fear that you were going to keep us sitting on our arses forever.'

'It is a pleasure to see you too, Centurion,' Narcissus responded smoothly. 'The waiting is over. Your Emperor needs you again. Now more than ever . . .'

CHAPTER THREE

Cato responded to the imperial secretary's greeting with a cold stare. Despite being born into slavery in the imperial palace, Narcissus had worked hard and been set free by Claudius in the years before he had become Emperor. As a freedman Narcissus had a lower social status than even the humblest Roman citizen, but as one of the closest advisers to the Emperor he had power and influence far beyond that of any aristocrat sitting in the senate. It was Narcissus who also controlled the spy network dedicated to sniffing out threats to his master. In this role he had made use of the services of Cato and Macro before, and was about to again, Cato reflected sourly.

Once the innkeeper had brought a jar of wine and three cups, Narcissus dismissed him. 'That will do for now, Spurius. Make sure that we are not interrupted, nor overheard.'

'Yes, master.' Spurius bowed his head and then turned to leave. He paused at the door. 'Master?'

'What is it?'

'About my daughter. Is there any news of her?'

'Pergilla, wasn't it? Yes, I'm still trying to persuade the Emperor to grant her freedom. These things take time. You keep your end of the bargain and I'll do all I can for her.' Narcissus waved his hand. 'Now leave us.'

Spurius hurried out and Narcissus waited until the sound of footsteps faded and the door at the far end of the linking room closed behind the innkeeper.

'He's a good and faithful servant, but he can be rather demanding at times. Anyway, enough of him!' Narcissus leant forward and nodded at the jar. 'Macro, why don't you pour us all a drink. We should celebrate this reunion of old friends.'

Macro shook his head. 'The last thing you are is a friend of mine.'

Narcissus stared at him for a moment and then nodded. 'Very well then, Centurion. I'll do the honours.' He leant forward, pulled out the stopper and poured a dark red wine into each of the cups. Then he set the jar down and raised his cup. 'At least join me in a toast . . . Death to the enemies of the Emperor.'

Macro had been looking longingly at the wine and with only a brief show of reluctance he picked up the nearest of the cups and repeated the toast. He took a sip and made an appreciative noise. 'So this is what that tight bastard Spurius has been keeping back from us.'

'You've not been entertained well then, I take it?' asked Narcissus. 'Spurius was instructed to make you comfortable.'

'He did his best,' said Cato. If the innkeeper was to be believed then he had not been compensated for the imposition of two guests for as many months. Moreover, if Narcissus was using Spurius's daughter to enforce his will on the innkeeper, Cato was not going to add to the man's problems. 'We were given a clean room and fed regularly. Spurius has served you well.'

'I suppose he has.' Narcissus glanced at Macro's surprised expression and then cocked an eyebrow. 'Though you don't appear to agree that he has served *you* particularly well.'

'We're soldiers,' Macro replied. 'We are used to worse.'

'So you are. And it is time for you to serve Rome once more.' Narcissus took a small mouthful of wine and licked his lips. 'Falernian. Spurius is trying to impress!'

'I imagine you will be in a hurry to return to the palace,' said Cato. 'Best that we get straight to business.'

'How considerate of you, young Cato,' Narcissus responded in an icy tone. He set his cup down with a sharp rap. 'Very well. You recall our last meeting?'

'On Capreae, yes.'

'I raised the matter of a new threat posed by the Liberators. Those scum will never rest until the Emperor is disposed of. Naturally, they claim to act in the interests of the senate and people of Rome, but in reality they will plunge Rome back into the dark age of tyrants like Sulla and Marius. The senate would be riven by factions fighting for power. We'd have a civil war on our hands within months of the fall of Claudius.' Narcissus paused for a moment. 'The senate had its uses in an age before Rome acquired an empire. Now, only a supreme authority can provide the order that is needed. The fact is that the senators cannot be trusted with the safety and security of Rome.'

Cato laughed drily. 'And you can be, I suppose.'

Narcissus was silent for a moment, his narrow nostrils flared with disdain. Then he nodded. 'Yes. I, and those who serve me, are all that stand between order and bloody chaos.'

'That may be true,' Cato conceded, 'but the fact is that the order you claim to protect is almost as bloody from time to time.'

'There is a price to pay for order. Do you really think peace and prosperity can be maintained without the shedding of a modicum of blood? You two soldiers, of all people, must know that. But what you don't know is that the wars you wage for Rome don't end when the battles are over. There is another battlefield, far from the frontier, that goes on, never ending, and that is the fight for order. That is the war that I wage. My enemies are not screaming barbarians. They are smooth-talking creatures lurking in the shadows who seek personal power at the expense of the public good. They may dress their base ambitions up in the robes of principle, but believe me there is no evil they would not countenance to achieve their ends. That is why Rome needs me, and why she needs you. Men like us are her only hope for survival.' Narcissus paused and helped himself to some more wine, and licked his lips.

'It's funny,' said Cato. 'When other men act out of self-interest you call it evil. When we do it, we're patriots.'

'That is because our cause is just. Theirs is not.'

'A difference of perspective.'

'Don't dignify our enemies with your philosophical abstractions, Cato. Just ask yourself whose Rome you would prefer to live in. Ours, or theirs?'

Macro clicked his tongue. 'He has a point.'

'There!' Narcissus beamed. 'Even Centurion Macro can see the sense of what I say.'

Macro frowned and cocked an eyebrow. '*Even* Centurion Macro . . . Thanks.'

Narcissus gave a light laugh and topped up Macro's cup. 'I meant no offence. Just to say that the right and wrong of it is abundantly clear to a man of action, such as yourself.'

While Macro reflected on this the imperial secretary moved on hastily. 'In any case, Cato, there is really very little choice in the matter. While I respect your right to express an opinion, however poorly thought through, you have to do as I say, if you and Macro want to advance your careers, and especially if you want to marry that rather nice daughter of Senator Sempronius.'

Cato lowered his head and slowly ran his fingers through the dark curls of his unkempt hair. Narcissus had them exactly where he wanted them. More than anything, he and Macro wanted to return to the army. Cato needed a promotion that would carry with it membership of the equestrian class. Only that would make his marriage into the family of a senator acceptable.

'Well, lad,' Macro interrupted his chain of thought. 'What about it? Anything to get us out of this place. Besides, it can't be too bad a job. Nothing more dangerous than we've faced already, surely?'

Narcissus pursed his lips but did not say anything.

With a weary sigh Cato raised his head and looked directly at the imperial secretary. 'What do you want us to do?'

Narcissus smiled slowly, with the air of a man accustomed to having his way. 'I'll begin by explaining something of the background to the situation.' He leant back and folded his fingers together. 'As you already know, the regime was nearly brought down by the conspiracies perpetrated by Messalina. That woman was pure poison. There was no debauchery that was beneath her. The only thing that matched her wanton lack of morals was her ambition. She knew exactly how to wrap Claudius round her finger. Not only him, but many others, including one of the Emperor's other advisers, Polybius.'

'I know the name,' said Cato. 'Didn't he commit suicide?'

'That's what he was ordered to do. In the Emperor's name. There wasn't even time to appeal to Claudius before he was visited by some Praetorian guardsmen who rather pressed the issue.'

'Murdered?'

'The line between murder, execution and suicide has become a little blurred in recent years. Death, one way or another, resolves a political difficulty, or a desire for revenge, or simply comes on a whim from those with the authority to order it. Which is why Messallina could not be permitted to remain in a position where she could exert more influence over the Emperor than his closest advisers. So when she decided to use the Emperor's absence from Rome to divorce him, marry her lover and then seize power, we had to act. Claudius was here in Ostia, to inspect the progress of the harbour development. That's when the news reached me. I could see the imminent danger clearly enough and spoke to those who were closest to the Emperor, Callistus and Pallas. It took all our powers of persuasion to get Claudius to accept the truth about Messallina. Then he denied it all, saying it couldn't be true.' Narcissus visibly trembled at the memory. 'So we encouraged him to drink some wine to soften the blow. That was when we presented him with a warrant for her arrest and execution, among a handful of other warrants issued for the arrest of her allies.'

'You dog!' Macro commented admiringly. 'What did the Emperor do when he came to his senses?'

'He grieved for a month. While the three of us disposed of the other members of Messallina's conspiracy. The point of all this is to make you aware of how easily the Emperor is gulled, and that makes him, and Rome, vulnerable.'

'So what's the story with his new wife?' asked Macro. 'Agrippina. She's his niece, if I recall right.'

'Oh, yes. And that caused a fine scandal when Claudius announced his choice of new bride to the public. I had to battle to get the senate to pass a measure to remove such a marriage from the incest laws. Fortunately one of the leading senators was keen to ingratiate himself with the Emperor. He picked up the job and pushed the new law through. Even then it was no easy feat, I can tell you.'

Cato had been thinking during the exchange. 'Whose idea was it to suggest Agrippina?'

There was a brief pause before Narcissus replied in a venomous tone, 'Pallas. He said we'd have a better chance of avoiding a repeat of the Messallina episode if we chose a bride from within the family. Besides, Pallas has some influence over her. We calculated that we would be able to keep her in line and ensure that Claudius continued to take advice from us.'

'And has it worked? Is the new Empress taking to her role with the required degree of compliance?'

Narcissus tilted his head to one side. 'She's not been much trouble. The only problem is that she came to the marriage with some rather awkward baggage.'

'Baggage?'

'Her son. Lucius Domitius Ahenobarbus. At least that is what he used to be called, before she talked the Emperor into adopting him. Now he's known as Nero Claudius Drusus Germanicus. Claudius's natural son is not taking to the new arrangement. Britannicus refuses to acknowledge his stepbrother and won't call him Nero. So there's no love lost there. Those two are going to be scrambling to succeed Claudius when he goes into the shades, or wherever it is that deified emperors go.'

Macro shook his head. 'Sounds like there's going to be a right old carve-up when the time comes.'

Cato thought for a moment before he spoke again. 'But Britannicus is the Emperor's heir, so surely he is first in line to succeed?'

'If only it was that clear cut,' Narcissus replied. 'Nero is fourteen, four years older than his stepbrother. Britannicus has the additional disadvantage that his mother was Messallina and that puts him under a bit of a cloud as far as his father is concerned. If he should become Emperor then I fear for the enemies of his mother. He's the kind of boy who would make a priority of revenge.'

Macro smiled. 'So, there is some justice in life. That prospect must be causing you a few restless nights.'

Narcissus's expression suddenly hardened. 'Centurion, if you knew only a fraction of what burdens my mind I doubt whether you would sleep at all. The Emperor is vulnerable to threats from all sides. His health is starting to fail and I must do everything in my power to protect him and ensure that peace and order endure.'

'And when the old boy dies? What then?' Macro asked shrewdly.

'Then we must ensure that the right successor is chosen.'

'Who do you have in mind?' asked Cato.

'I'm not yet certain. Nero and Britannicus are young and each has his own virtues and flaws. When the time comes I, and the Emperor's other advisers, will make our choice and point Claudius in the right direction when he names his successor.'

Cato pursed his lips briefly. 'I don't see what all this has to do with Macro and me. There's nothing we can do to influence events.'

'I told you, I felt it necessary to brief you on the wider picture, so that you understand the full gravity of the situation when I tell you what I must ask you and Macro to do.'

The two officers looked at each other quickly then Cato gestured to Narcissus to continue.

The imperial secretary collected his thoughts and spoke in a subdued tone. 'With the palace divided, the Liberators have decided to act. The key to any change of power in Rome is to have control of the Praetorian Guard. It was the support of the Praetorians that made Claudius's accession possible. When the Emperor dies, they are the final arbiter when it comes to the question of who wins the throne. Now, if the Liberators can win control of the Praetorians then the question of which of the Emperor's two sons will succeed him becomes academic. They will be cut down, along with the rest of the imperial family, their servants and allies.' He paused to let his words sink in. 'That is why the command of the Guard is split between two prefects and the Emperor's immediate bodyguard is made up of German mercenaries – men he can trust. However, one of the prefects has been ill for several months, which leaves the Praetorians under the command of the other, Lusius Geta, who is more of a concern. Lately he has been increasing the training of the men, working them hard with regular route marches, weapons exercises and mock battles. Recently the battle training has shifted emphasis. He is now drilling them in street fighting and siege techniques.'

'Sounds like a conscientious commander to me,' said Macro. 'I would be working the men just as hard in his place.'

'I'm sure you would. But this is not the custom of previous prefects. More worrying still is that most of his officers seem to be fiercely loyal to Geta and hold him in high regard.' Naricissus opened his hands. 'You must see that I have reason to regard the man with a degree of suspicion.'

Macro shrugged, but Cato nodded slightly.

'There's more. Last month one of the tribunes of the Guard was killed on the road.'

Cato nodded. 'Balbus.'

'That's right. How did you know?'

'I read of it in the gazette. Not much else for me to do with my time. I gather Balbus was killed by brigands.'

'That's the version that was put out. What the report did not mention is that he was in command of a bullion convoy sent from the mint in Narbonensis. The search party found his body stripped by the side of the road, no doubt to make Balbus look like the victim of a robbery. It didn't take them long to locate the remains of the wagons from the convoy. But the bullion chests were gone. About two million denarii lost in all.'

Macro whistled.

'Quite. A vast sum, and the thing is, only a handful of men, imperial servants and Praetorians, knew about the convoy. This was an inside job. No question of it. I've had those in the know questioned, and some of them put under torture, but my interrogators got nothing out of them. Either they are innocent, or they are tough enough not to crack under pressure.'

'Perhaps word of the convoy leaked out,' Cato suggested. 'Someone overheard or saw something that gave it away.'

'It's possible. But I trust my men to be discreet. They know the price for disappointing me will be severe. So that leaves the Praetorians. Either their security is slack, or there are traitors in their ranks. That's how it seemed to me until a few days ago. Then we had a stroke of good fortune. One of the Praetorians got drunk and started a fight in some drinking hole close to the Great Circus. He was confined to quarters. On closer investigation it was discovered that he had been spending money all day buying drinks for comrades and passers-by. He had also lost a small fortune in silver at the races, and yet he had not drawn any money from his savings at the barracks. I gave orders for him to be released and his centurion put him on fatigues for a month. Two nights ago I ordered my agents to snatch him and take him to a safe house outside the city for questioning. He proved to be a tough customer and more rigorous methods of interrogation were necessary, alas. Before he died he confessed to being involved in the attack on the convoy and he gave up one name. A centurion who is serving in the cohort entrusted with guarding the imperial palace, Marcus Lurco. According to the man, Lurco is one of the leading conspirators. So now we know that there is a faction of traitors in the Praetorian Guard.'

'Did the Praetorian mention any link to the Liberators?' asked Cato.

'He did.' Narcissus took a breath. 'The situation is serious. There's only one reason why they would be after such a fortune. They're amassing a war chest. Once they have enough, it's my belief that they'll use the money to bribe the Praetorian Guard to back them when they attempt to overthrow the Emperor.'

There was a brief silence. Macro drained his cup and poured himself another while trying to look thoughtfully engaged. 'All of which is very interesting, but what's this got to do with us?'

'It's simple. I need some men on the inside who I can trust completely. I want you and Cato to join the Praetorian Guard, penetrate the conspiracy, identify the leaders and then, if necessary, eliminate them. Oh, and locate and return the stolen bullion.'

Macro stared at him and then laughed. 'Easy as that. Surely you have agents who are used to all this cloak-and-dagger bollocks? We're soldiers and wouldn't have a clue about how to go and stab a man in the back. There has to be someone better than us you can use.'

'Oh, I have a small circle of men I can rely on. A very small circle, and men I can ill afford to lose. Besides, for this job I need men who can pass as soldiers.' Narcissus paused and smiled thinly. 'Let's not beat about the bush. You two are expendable. Besides, I know you will accept. How can you do otherwise?'

Macro shook his head. 'We'd be mad to accept such a task.'

'You have no other choice, given that what you desire is within my power to grant – or withhold, as I see fit.' His gaze switched to Cato. 'Is that not so?'

Cato nodded reluctantly. 'He's right, Macro. If we want to return to the army and if I'm to have my promotion, what else can we do?'

'Precisely.'

'No,' Macro replied. 'Think about it, Cato. We're soldiers. We're trained to fight. Not to spy, not to play the part of some imperial agent. They'd see through us in an instant. I'm not going to end up with my throat cut and my body dumped in the Great Sewer. Not me. I won't do it. Nor will you if you have any sense.'

'This is not some scheme I dreamed up on the road from Rome.' Narcissus spoke with icy intensity. 'I have considered the matter carefully and I am certain that you two have a far better chance of succeeding than my agents. You are experienced soldiers and will fit in with the Praetorians where my men would stick out like sore thumbs. You are also virtually unknown in Rome, whereas my men are familiar faces. If I use anyone else then I will have to hire men in from outside the capital, men whose ability I don't know, and who I have no idea how far I can trust. The truth is, we need each other. If you see this through, I give you my word of honour that you will both be generously rewarded.'

'I'm not sure your word is good enough,' said Macro.

'How do you plan to get us into the Praetorian Guard?' Cato intervened. 'If a pair of officers turn up and start asking questions, the opposition are bound to be suspicious.'

'Of course, that's why you will be joining the Praetorians as rankers. Two veterans of the Second Legion just returned from Britannia. Your appointment to the Guard is a reward for gallant service against the barbarians. It's a credible cover story, and it's close enough to your experience for you not to have to act much. All that will be different is your rank. It shouldn't be too hard a role to play.'

'Easy for you to say,' Macro grumbled. 'What if we run into anyone we've met before?'

'It's unlikely. It's over three years since you were last in Rome, and then you were renting rooms in the Subura while you were on half-pay. No one in the Praetorian Guard knows you. Apart from a handful of my clerks who might remember your faces, you shouldn't be recognised by anyone at the palace.'

'What about Senator Sempronius?' Cato asked. 'And Julia? If we encounter them our identities will be exposed.'

'I've thought of that.' Narcissus smiled. 'I've arranged for the senator to conduct an inventory of the Emperor's estates in Campania. I've instructed him to take his daughter with him so that she can enjoy the social scene. It's a light enough task, but one that will keep them out of the way until spring. By which time I trust that you two will have unearthed the traitors in the Praetorian Guard and any of their accomplices in the city.'

'There are others who will recognise us. Senator Vespasian for example.'

Narcissus nodded. 'I'm aware of that. Vespasian has been elected one of the consuls this year and will be busy in the senate.'

'Vespasian is a consul?' Macro smiled. 'Good on him.'

'While I share your regard for his abilities, I have to say that Vespasian's elevation to the consulship is something of a concern. He may be more ambitious than I previously gave him credit for.'

'Oh, come on!' Macro shook his head. 'You can't be suspicious of Vespasian. After all that he has done for the Emperor? Why, if it wasn't for him then I dare say the campaign in Britannia would have been a disaster. And there was that business with the pirates. He served Claudius loyally.'

'I know. But it is my job to look for danger signals. Any displays of ambition have to be carefully scrutinised. So, Vespasian is being watched closely.' Narcissus paused before he continued. 'It would be most unwise to take the risk of our being seen together, so you will report to me via one of my agents, Septimus. Aside from me, he'll be the only one in the know. You can meet him at the Vineyard of Dionysus in the Boarium in two days' time.'

'How will we know him?' asked Cato.

Narcissus pulled a ring from the little finger of his left hand and passed it to Cato. 'Wear this. My agent will have its twin.'

Cato held the ring up to examine it and saw that a design had been artfully carved into the red stone: a depiction of Roma astride a sphinx. 'Nice.'

'Of course I'll have that back once it's served its purpose.' Narcissus looked at them both. 'Well then, any further questions?'

'Just one.' Macro leant forward. 'What happens to us if we decline your kind offer of employment?'

Narcissus fixed him with a cold stare. 'I haven't

considered that yet. For the very good reason that I cannot imagine you would be so foolish as to refuse the job.'

'Then you had better start considering.' Macro sat back and folded his arms. 'Find some other mugs to do your dirty work. I'm a good soldier. There'll be an opening for me sometime or other. I can wait.'

'For how long, I wonder? Perhaps not for as long as I might wish to keep you rotting here.'

Macro's expression darkened. 'Fuck you. Fuck you and your nasty little schemes.' Macro bunched his hands into fists and for a moment Cato was afraid his friend might take it into his head to pulverise the imperial secretary. The same thought occurred to Narcissus who flinched back. Macro glowered at him for a moment then stood up abruptly. 'Cato, let's go and get a drink. Some other place. The air's foul here.'

'No,' Cato answered firmly. 'We have to do it. I'm not staying in Ostia any longer than I can help it.'

Macro stared down at his comrade for a moment and then shook his head. 'You're a fool, Cato. This snake will get us killed. Why should we succeed in uncovering the Liberators when the Emperor's agents have failed all these years?'

'Nevertheless, I'll do it. And you'll come with me.'

'Bah!' Macro threw up his hands. 'I thought I knew you. I thought you were smarter than this. Seems I was wrong. You're on your own, Cato. I'll have no part of this.'

Macro strode to the door and wrenched it open, slamming it behind him. Cato heard his footsteps receding with a sinking feeling in his heart. Macro was right about the dangers, and Cato realised that he had little confidence that he could see such a mission through without the tough and dependable Macro at his side. For the first time in many months, he felt a pang of fear. The prospect of facing the Emperor's shadowy enemies on his own was daunting.

'I shouldn't worry about him.' Narcissus chuckled. 'Now he's had a chance to unleash his anger at me, he'll come round soon enough.'

'I hope you're right.'

'Trust me, I can read almost any man like a scroll. And our friend Macro is a somewhat less challenging read than most. Am I wrong? You know him well enough.'

Cato reflected for a moment. 'Macro is capable of surprising turns of thought. You should not underestimate him. But yes, I think he'll come with me. Once he's had a chance to simmer down and reflect on the fact that you might make his life very difficult. I take it you meant that.'

Narcissus's thin lips twisted into a faint smile as he rose to leave. 'What do you think?'

'Fair enough. But I have one piece of advice for you, if you want this mission to go well.' Cato paused. 'Never ever call him a friend to his face again.'

CHAPTER FOUR

The surface of the Tiber was dotted with flotsam and patches of sewage as the barge approached Rome late in the afternoon. A team of mules was towing the vessel against the current and their driver, a skinny, barefoot slave boy, flicked his whip once in a while to keep the pace up. Ahead a thick pall of woodsmoke hung over the city as the inhabitants struggled to stay warm through the dreary winter months, adding the output of the communal fires they were permitted to the smoke of the tanneries, smiths and bathhouses that plied their trade in the capital.

Cato wrinkled his nose as a foul odour swept across the surface of the river, blown by the stiff easterly breeze.

'You forget how bad the place stinks,' Macro muttered sourly at his side as they stood on the small foredeck of the barge. They were the only passengers. The rest of the available space was piled with jars of olive oil from Hispania. So heavily laden was the barge that there was scarcely a foot of freeboard above the glistening sweep of the Tiber.

'Oh, it ain't so bad!' a cheery voice sounded from behind them and the two soldiers turned to see the captain of the barge approaching them round the jars. The man's thin frame was evident even under his tunic

49

and thick cloak. A felt cap was jammed on his head from which protruded straggles of dark hair. He smiled, revealing a jagged display of teeth that reminded Cato of a cluster of long-neglected and stained tombstones. 'They say you get used to it soon enough when you live here. Course, I don't, seeing as me and the lad there make the trip up from Ostia only five or six times a month.' He gestured to his son on the steering oar at the rear of the barge, gangly like his father and no more than ten years old. 'Ostia smells like a bloody perfume market by comparison.'

'You don't say,' Macro responded drily.

'Too right.' The barge captain nodded. 'So, what are you visiting Rome for, my friends? Soldiers on leave, eh? Back from the provinces?'

Macro's eyes narrowed suspiciously. 'What we are and what our business may be is none of yours – friend.'

The other man raised his hands defensively, but continued smiling. 'No offence! Not meaning to pry, like. Just a polite question. I could see you was soldiers, soon as you boarded in Ostia. Like I said to my son, them's soldiers. You can see it in the way they hold themselves. Proud and erect like. Warriors. You can see it from their scars too, I said. It was obvious. So, no offence meant, sirs.'

'None taken.' Cato smiled back. 'And you're right, we've just come back from campaigning in Britannia.'

'Britannia?' The man scratched his cheek. 'Think I've heard of it. Where's that then?'

'Across the sea from Gaul.'

'Oh yes, I have it now! That was the place there was all that rumpus about when the Emperor celebrated a triumph some years ago.'

'Yes.'

'So what's this about the campaign still going on? We was told the place was conquered.'

'We've beaten the most important tribes. The army's just mopping up the remnants,' Cato explained smoothly. It had been nearly four years since they had been in Britannia and although he had heard fragments of news about the progress of the campaign, it was clear that the barge captain knew far less. Narcissus had promised him a detailed report, along with their documents appointing them to the Praetorian Guard, and forged letters of commendation from the governor of the new province, when they met their contact in Rome. 'In fact, my comrade and I fought in the decisive battle. We led our legion in the charge and captured a Celt chief. That's why we're here. The governor recommended us for an appointment in the Praetorian Guard as a reward.'

The barge captain's eyes widened and he shook his head. 'Who'd have believed it? Two bloomin' war heroes on me barge. Wait till the lad hears this! He's always wanted to be a soldier when he grows up. I always thought it must be a good life. Nice pay. Looked after well. And there's the uniform! Turns the ladies' heads, does that. Then there's the good outdoor life and the chance for glory and spoils, eh? Isn't that right?'

'Oh yes.' Macro smiled. 'It's a great life all right. One long party I thought when I signed up. Never imagined I'd be fighting hairy-arsed barbarians in a frozen, bog-strewn wasteland. Strange how things turn out.' He winked at the captain. 'The only thing that keeps me up at night is worrying how I'm going to spend all that money I'm paid.'

'Ignore my companion,' said Cato. 'He got out of bed the wrong side this morning. Literally. He had a skinful last night and smacked his head on the wall when he woke up.'

'Very funny,' Macro growled. 'I had a reason to get drunk, didn't I? A bloody good reason. I already think I should have stayed where I was.'

The barge captain looked astonished. 'What, and miss out on being a Praetorian?'

Macro eyed him coldly. 'I can assure you, if I could avoid it, I would with all my heart.'

Cato intervened quickly. 'That's just the hangover talking. I'm sure he'll get over it. He just needs a little bit of peace and quiet.'

'I can see that clear enough!' The barge captain roared with laughter at Macro's fragile expression. 'Still, I'd get used to it, if I was you. I've seen them Praetorians drink in some of the inns close to the wharves. They don't half go at it, and they can be a right handful when they're in their cups, I can tell you!' He paused and frowned. 'And heavy handed with it of late.'

'Oh?' Cato looked at him inquiringly. 'There's been trouble?'

The barge captain nodded. 'A fair bit these last months. The grain supply has been running low, what with that business in Egypt last year. Price has been rising steadily. The mob don't like it one bit and there's been a few shops looted and some grain merchants beaten up. So the Praetorian Guard started cracking heads together. Well, more than that. They've gone and killed some people.' He looked at the two soldiers warily. 'Had to, I suppose. I mean, you've got to have order, haven't you?'

'Yes,' Macro said tersely.

'Anyway, we don't want to keep you from your duties.' Cato nodded towards the rear of the barge.

'Oh, don't worry about that. The lad can handle it all right up until I heave the mooring ropes ashore.' He smiled cheerfully. 'No need to break up the party.'

'There's no party,' said Macro. 'Now go about your business.'

The barge captain looked surprised, then a little hurt, and he turned and unhurriedly made his way back to the stern.

Cato sighed. 'Was that necessary?'

'What? Me getting rid of the chirpy sod? I thought so, before you blabbed every detail of our affairs. The man's got a mouth as wide as the Tiber. Half of Rome is going to know we've arrived before the day is out.'

'And what's the problem with that?' Cato glanced back towards the stern where the captain had taken the steering oar from his son and was staring ahead intently. 'What's he going to say? Just that he carried two soldiers upriver from Ostia and that they were on their way to join the Praetorian Guard. That's not going to harm us in any way. On the contrary. If anyone starts to check up on us then he will be able to confirm the cover story. And anyone who speaks to him is going to realise at once that he's too guileless to spout a line that he has been told to deliver.' Cato paused to let Macro think it through. 'Relax. You have to try not to think like a spy otherwise you'll stop behaving like a soldier. If that happens the enemy will see through us in an instant.'

'Enemy?' Macro puffed his cheeks out. 'What a fine to-do this is. Here we are pretending to be Praetorians so that we can hunt down and kill some other Roman citizens who just happen to have a different set of political values. At the same time they're busy plotting the murder of their Emperor and anyone who stands between them and that aim. And all the while the frontier of the empire is teeming with real enemies who would like nothing better than for us to turn on each other. Forgive me for sounding naive, Cato, but isn't this all just a little fucked up?'

Cato was silent for a moment before he replied. 'Yes. It's a mess. But that's not our concern. We're here to do one job. Whatever you may think, this isn't that different from our duties as soldiers. We're here to scout the enemy out, then infiltrate their position and take them on. Macro, it isn't the job of soldiers to think beyond that. We don't get to debate the whys and wherefores of the campaigns we fight for Rome. It's the same with the job at hand. Right or wrong, we swore an oath to the Emperor and that makes anyone who decides to be his enemy, our enemy. Besides, Rome could do worse than have Claudius on the throne, a lot worse.'

Cato eased himself down on to the foredeck and stared towards the vast sprawl of palaces, temples, theatres, markets, bathhouses, private homes and teeming apartment blocks that covered the hills of Rome. Macro's bitter expression faded and he chuckled to himself.

'What's so damned funny?'

'Just thinking. When we first met I was the one who was stuck on the certainties of duty, and you who was forever putting the other side of things. By the gods, it used to drive me mad.'

'People change.'

'I don't think so. At least, not that much. No, I think

I understand you well enough, Cato. This is all about getting that promotion, so that you get Julia. Funny how a man will try to justify with reason the desires of his heart.'

Cato glared back at him, angry with himself for being so transparent. Then he relented. The thing was, he was shocked to discover that he had half believed what he had said to Macro. The only shred of comfort was that Macro, above all people, knew him well enough to see through his argument. He would have to hope that he played his part well in the coming days. If not, then he would surely be found out and killed.

The barge eased towards the vast warehouses that stood at the foot of the Aventine Hill. In front of the warehouses was the river port where hundreds of barges and smaller craft crowded a wharf that stretched along the bank of the Tiber. In the distance, where the river bent to the west, Cato could see the Sublician Bridge where the swift current flowing beneath the wooden trestles of the footbridge effectively ended the upriver commercial traffic for the barges from Ostia. Dusk was not far off and already some of the details of the city were merging into indistinct grey shapes in the distance.

The mule team reached the terminus at the start of the wharf and the slave untied the yoke and handed the tow cable to a gang of burly men who were waiting to haul the barge on to a mooring. The captain released the steering paddle and then he and his son took some thick timber poles to fend the barge off the vessels that were already moored alongside the wharf. Sometimes the boats were tied up two or three deep so that gangplanks were laid across the sides and the cargoes loaded or unloaded across the intervening hulls. The captain glanced ahead and seeing that there was little sign of a berthing space for some stretch he indicated a single craft a short distance away.

'There!' he called, pointing out the spot to the men pulling on the tow rope. Their leader nodded and shortly afterwards the barge was tied up alongside. Cato and Macro picked up their kitbags and marching yokes and waited until the gangways were tied securely before they made to quit the boat.

'Best of luck with the new posting!' The captain beamed as he ushered his son towards them. 'This is my boy. Come to meet the heroes of the campaign in Britannia. Say hello, lad.'

The boy looked up shyly and whispered a greeting that was drowned out by the shouts and cries of the gangs of porters on the wharf. Cato smiled down at him and gently squeezed the boy's shoulder.

'Your father says you want to join the legions. Do you think you are tough enough?'

The boy shook his head quickly. 'Not yet.'

'I'm sure you will be one day. You should have seen me when I was your age. Nothing but skin and bones, and I turned out all right.'

Macro looked at him with feigned shock, but Cato ignored his friend and continued, 'Work your body hard and you could be a hero one day, and make your father proud.'

'Or,' Macro spoke under his breath, 'you could end up as the dogsbody of a scheming imperial freedman . . .'

The barge captain's smile faded a little. 'I'm proud of him already.'

'Of course you are,' Cato replied quickly. 'Come on, Macro, let's be off.'

Swinging his kitbag up on to the fork at the end of the marching yoke, Cato carefully picked his way along the gangplank extending over the next boat and then up on to the wharf, feeling greatly relieved to have solid ground beneath his boots, even if it was covered with filth. Macro joined him and both men looked around for a moment to get their bearings.

'Where did you say we were to meet that contact of Narcissus?' asked Macro.

'An inn called the Vineyard of Dionysus, on the north side of the Boarium. From what Narcissus said, it should be over that way.' Cato indicated the civic buildings rising up beyond the end of the warehouse complex and they set off along the wharf. After the relative quiet of the streets of Ostia, the empire's capital was a seething turmoil of noise and sights and the sweaty stench of people mingled with acrid woodsmoke. Gangs of slaves, some chained together, struggled under the burden of bales of exotic materials, jars of wine and oil and smaller sealed pots packed in straw-filled cases that contained perfumes and scents from the east. Others carried ivory tusks, or lengths of rare hardwoods. Around them skirted the captains of the barges, merchants and petty traders and the air was filled with voices, in a smattering of tongues: Latin, Greek, Celtic dialects, Hebrew and others that Cato had never heard before. The dusk was thickening in the dark winter air. Amid the gloom, fires flickered in braziers and cast pools of lurid red light across the paved wharf strewn with mud and rubbish. A few dogs and feral cats darted through the crowds, sniffing for food. Beggars squatted in archways and in front of locked doors, rattling wooden or brass bowls as they cried out for spare coins.

Cato edged through the press and Macro followed closely, careful to keep a firm grip on his yoke. Every so often he glanced over his shoulder to make sure that his kitbag was safe from petty thieves. He had heard stories of sharp knives being used to cut open the goatskin containers, so that a swift hand might pluck something out without the victim knowing until it was too late.

'Shit, it's like being stuck in the middle of a battle.'

'Without the danger,' Cato replied tersely then added, 'or the blood, the bodies, the screams and the great big icy hand of terror clamped round the back of your neck. But otherwise, yes.'

'Funny.'

The crowd thinned out a little as they neared the arched entrance to the Boarium market. Like the warehouses, it was built on a grand scale with a columned entrance, above which loomed a pediment topped with statues of statesmen from the republican era, their original paint now obscured by a patina of grime and bird shit. The tang of blood and meat from the butchers' stalls filled the air. On the other side of the entrance a wide vista opened out, large enough to camp a legion in, Cato estimated. The temporary stalls were already being dismantled and packed, with the traders' goods, on to small handcarts to be taken to the secure stores at the side of the Boarium. Elsewhere the permanent stalls were being closed up for the night. Around the edge of the Boarium was a two-storey colonnade. The ground level was used for shops and inns, while above were the offices of those officials who collected duties and the rents of the traders.

Many of the city's bankers rented premises on the second level as well, aloof from the bustle below as they counted their profits.

The Vineyard of Dionysus was easy enough to find. A large painted placard had been fixed over the entrance to the premises. A crudely painted man with a big grin was holding a brimming drinking horn against a backdrop of heavily laden grape vines, amid which, in a fascinating variety of positions, amorous couples were going at it hammer and tongs. Macro paused outside with a quizzical expression.

'That one there, that's just not possible.'

'It is after you've had your fill of our wines!' announced a cheery voice. A thickset man with heavily oiled hair detached himself from the pillars either side of the entrance and beckoned them inside. 'The wares of the Vineyard of Dionysus are famous across Rome. Welcome, friends! Please step inside. There's a table for all, a warm fire, good food, fine wines and the best of company,' he winked, 'for a modest price, sirs.'

'We need food and drink,' Cato replied. 'That's all.'

'For now,' Macro added, still scanning the illustrations above the door. 'We'll see how we go, eh?'

The tout waved his customers inside before they could move on and then followed them. The interior was larger than Cato had expected, stretching back some sixty feet. A counter was set halfway down the side of one wall, flanked by alcoves, two of which had their curtains drawn. A thin, heavily made-up woman with wiry red hair sat in another alcove with a bored expression, her head propped on her hand as she stared blankly across the room. The place was filled with the first of the evening trade – men from the Boarium who had packed up their stalls or finished their business for the day. Most were having a quick drink before returning home for the night. There were a few old soaks among them, bleary eyed and with stark veins on their noses and cheeks, who were only just starting a long evening drinking themselves into oblivion.

The tout who had picked them off the street called out to the innkeeper who nodded and chalked up two strokes on the wall above the wine jars to add to the tally of those that the tout had already brought in.

'Here's your table.' The tout gestured to a plain bench with four stools a short distance inside the door. Cato and Macro nodded their thanks and squeezed past the other customers and set their yokes down against the wall before sitting.

Macro glanced round and sniffed. 'Narcissus chose well.'

'Yes. The kind of place where men can get lost in the crowd. Nice and discreet.'

'I was thinking it was well chosen because it was my kind of place. Cheap, cheerful and waiting for a punch-up to start any moment.'

'There is that,' Cato replied offhandedly. He scanned the room for any sign of their contact. Only a handful of customers seemed to be drinking on their own but none seemed to return his gaze in any meaningful way. A moment later the innkeeper threaded his way over to them.

'What would you like, gents?'

'What have you got?' asked Macro.

'It's on the wall.' The man pointed to a long list of

regional wines that had been chalked up on a board behind the counter.

'Mmmm!' Macro smiled as he ran his eye down the wines. 'How's the Etruscan?'

'Off.'

'Oh, all right. The Calabrian?'

'Off.'

'Falernian?'

The innkeeper shook his head.

'Well, what have you got?'

'Today it's the Ligurian or the Belgic. That's it.'

'Belgic?' Cato raised an eyebrow. 'I thought they made beer?'

'They do.' The innkeeper scratched his nose. 'They should stick to beer in my opinion.'

'I see.' Cato shrugged. 'The Ligurian then. One small jar and three cups.'

'Yes, sir. Good choice.' The innkeeper bowed his head and turned back to the counter.

'Is he trying to be funny?' Macro scowled. 'Anyway, Ligurian? Never heard of it.'

'Then tonight should be something of an education for us.'

The innkeeper returned with the wine and the cups and set them down on the table. 'Five sestertii.'

'Five?' Macro shook his head. 'That's robbery.'

'That's the price, mate.'

'Very well,' Cato cut in, fishing the coins out of the small sum that Narcissus had advanced them. 'There.'

The innkeeper swept the coins off the top of the table and nodded his thanks.

Cato picked up the jar and sniffed the contents. His

61

nose wrinkled at the sharp acidic odour. Then he poured them each a cup of the dark, almost black, wine. Macro raised his in a mock toast and took a mouthful. At once he made a face.

'By the gods, I hope there's better inns close to the Praetorian camp.'

Cato took a cautious sip and felt the sour, fiery flow all the way down into his guts. He set the cup down and leant against the wall behind his back. 'Just have to hope our contact turns up soon.'

Macro nodded. They sat and waited in silence, while around them the locals drank copious amounts of the only available wine, seemingly oblivious to its rough flavour. There was a cheerful atmosphere, except at the table where the two soldiers sat, waiting with growing impatience as night fell outside. At length Macro stirred, drained his cup with a wince, and stood up. He gestured towards the woman still sitting in the alcove.

'I'm, er, just going over there.'

'Not now, Macro. We're waiting for someone. Another time.'

'Well, he ain't showed up yet, so I might as well enjoy myself.'

'We shouldn't risk drawing attention to ourselves.'

'I'm not.' Macro nodded towards the drawn curtains. 'Just fitting in with the locals, as it were.'

As he spoke, one of the curtains covering the alcoves was gently drawn back and a tall sinewy man with short dark hair eased himself out of the alcove. He had already pulled on his tunic, and held a neck cloth in one hand. Behind him a woman was slipping on the short tunic that signified her trade. He turned and tossed a few coins on to the couch and then made his way out into the middle of the room.

'There,' said Macro. 'No one's paying him any attention.'

Cato watched as the man glanced round and then saw the two empty stools at their table. He came over. 'May I?'

Cato shook his head. 'No. We're waiting for a friend.'

'I know. That's me.' The man smiled and then sat down opposite the two soldiers. He raised his hand so that they could see his ring and then laid it down close by Cato's hand so that he could see that the designs were identical. Cato looked at him carefully, noting the dark eyes, smoothly shaven cheeks and the small tattoo of a half-moon and star on his neck, before it was hidden by the strip of cloth he arranged loosely about his neck. Cato felt a stab of mistrust even as the man lowered his voice and spoke. 'Narcissus sent me.'

'Really? Then what's your name, friend?'

'Oscanus Optimus Septimus,' he said in a low tone that Cato could just make out. 'And I'll have that ring back, if you don't mind.' He held out his hand.

Cato hesitated a moment before he took off the ring and handed it over. 'I assume that's not your real name.'

'It serves. And as far as anyone is concerned from here on in, you are Guardsmen Titus Ovidius Capito and Vibius Gallus Calidus, is that clear? It would not be wise to reveal your real identities to me.'

The names were neatly written on the documents that Cato had been given; he had taken the identity of Capito, and Macro had that of Calidus, both veterans of the Second Legion.

'That mark on your neck,' Macro commented. 'I take it you served on the eastern frontier.'

Septimus narrowed his eyes slightly. 'I might have.'

'In the legions or the auxiliary cohorts?'

Septimus was silent for a moment and then shrugged. 'Not that it matters, but I did a stint in a cavalry cohort before I was recruited by Narcissus.' He gestured towards his neck. 'That was the cohort's emblem. Most of the lads have the tattoo. Bit of a pain now as I have to keep it covered up in my line of work.'

'I can imagine,' said Macro. He took a deep breath and exhaled impatiently. 'Anyway, you're late. Kept us waiting while you saw to your woman over there.'

Septimus frowned. 'My woman? Hardly. I was using her as a cover.'

'Whichever way you like it.'

Narcissus's agent scowled at Macro. 'If I had a woman, it wouldn't be one like her. Anyway, her alcove provided a good place to keep an eye on you when you turned up. And the other customers. Just to make sure you weren't being watched, or followed. Sorry for the wait, but I had to be sure. This business is too dangerous to take any chances. Right, the introductions are over. Let's go.'

'Go?' Cato leant forward slightly. 'Go where?'

'To a safe house. Where we can talk without any risk of being overheard. It's also a place where we can meet and where you can drop off any messages safely. You shouldn't have any trouble getting to and from the Praetorian camp – the soldiers pass in and out of their barracks freely. That's how we'll communicate for the most part.' Septimus looked round warily. 'Follow me. But let's make it look casual. Better finish our drinks first.'

He poured himself a cup and raised his voice. 'For the road!'

Macro and Cato followed suit and forced down what remained in their cups, then reached for their packs and stood up. By now the inn was filling with customers and they had to push their way to the entrance. Outside the tout was still looking for further custom. He smiled as he saw them. 'Leaving so soon? The night is barely beginning, sirs. Stay awhile and drink your fill.'

Macro stopped in front of him. He drew a breath and spoke loudly enough so that passers-by could clearly hear him. 'Anyone who drinks their fill of the slop in this place is going to be staying for more than a while. It's poison.'

The tout tried to laugh it off and clapped Macro on the shoulder as he turned to join Cato and Septimus. In a flash, Macro spun round and slammed his fist into the tout's stomach. As the man collapsed, gasping for breath, Macro backed off with a look of bitter satisfaction.

'That'll knock the wind out of the bugger. Stop him peddling his wares for a bit.'

Septimus glanced nervously at the people who had stopped to witness Macro's action.

'Macro,' Cato hissed. 'Let's go before you attract any more attention, shall we?'

They strode unhurriedly along the edge of the Boarium and left by the wide street that passed between the Palatine Hill and the Capitoline. To their right the edifices of the imperial palace complex covered the hill; torches and braziers lit the columns and statues that looked down on the rest of Rome. On the left loomed the mass of the Temple of Jupiter, built on a rock with sheer sides in places and accessed by a wide ramp that zigzagged up to the temple precinct. They entered the Forum and crossed in front of the senate house. A party of finely dressed youths came the other way, talking loudly as they boasted of their ambitions for the night's entertainment. They quietened down a little as they passed the two soldiers and the imperial agent then continued as before when they were a safe distance beyond. On the far side of the Forum another street led past the Temple of Peace and up into the Subura, one of the poorer quarters of the city where crime was rife and the buildings so poorly constructed that hardly a month went by without one of the ramshackle tenement blocks collapsing or burning down.

'Narcissus isn't putting us up in the bloody Subura, I trust,' Macro said quietly to Cato. 'Had enough of it the last time we had to stay in Rome.'

Septimus glanced back. 'It's not far now. On the edge of the Subura, as it happens. So that it's convenient for you to get to from the Praetorian camp. Don't worry. The apartment is in one of the better tenement blocks. At least that's what the landlord said when I took it.'

'And you believed him?'

'Doesn't concern me. I don't have to live there.'

The street began to incline and they passed between the first of the tall brick structures where most of the city's inhabitants lived. The tenements crowded the street and towered high above so that the dim gloom of the night sky provided almost no illumination. A few lamps burned in the entrances to the buildings but the streets were in darkness. Which was no bad thing, Cato reflected as the foul air filled his nostrils. He did not want to know what he was stepping in. Around and above them, they could hear voices. Some laughter, some quiet conversations, occasional angry shouts or the crying of infants and the splatter of slops being emptied into the streets.

'Here we are,' Septimus announced, climbing a few steps up from the street into a narrow entrance. An oil lamp flickered in its bracket and revealed a muscular man in a plain tunic sitting on a stool just inside the doorway. He took a good look at Septimus and nodded before he lit a taper from the lamp and handed it to the imperial agent. There was a short corridor with a narrow staircase at the end of it. As he led the way up the stairs Septimus raised a hand in front of the taper to protect the flame. On the fourth floor he stopped in front of a door and opened the latch. He led the way inside and Macro and Cato lowered their packs on to the floorboards.

'Just a moment, I'll light a lamp,' said Septimus and he reached up on to a shelf. The pale flicker of the taper flared for a moment and then the flame settled into a steady glow and he removed the taper and blew it out. 'There.'

He placed the lamp back on the shelf and turned round. By its wan glow Cato could see that the room was empty except for two bedrolls. It was barely ten feet across and another doorway led through into a similar-sized room.

'Not much in the way of creature comforts,' complained Macro, prodding one of the bedrolls with the toe of his boot.

'We like it that way,' said Septimus. 'There's nothing to steal. In any case, the watchman keeps an eye on the place most of the time.' He reached inside his tunic for a small pouch and took out a small bundle of scrolls and two sets of waxed slates, and handed them over. 'The rest of your documents and the report on Britannia. You can sleep here tonight and then make your way up to the Praetorian camp in the morning. If you need to leave me a message then put it over there beneath the shelf. The floorboard is loose and there's a small space underneath. Make sure that you come up here and check as regularly as you can. If there's a message, then turn the lantern towards the door. Otherwise point it away. If it's pointing any other way then we'll know that the apartment has been compromised.'

'Compromised?' Macro chuckled. 'What's that? Secret agent talk?'

'We understand,' said Cato. 'I assume we can use this place to hide if we need to. Or conceal something.'

Septimus nodded. 'And if you need to meet me for any reason. Just make sure that you are never followed here. If the enemy manages to do that then they can keep tabs on the visitors and trace me back to Narcissus. Watch your back at all times and don't take any chances.' He looked at Macro. 'Is that clear?'

'I'll be fine, you'll see. It's him you need to look out for. Cato.'

'No!' Septimus thrust up his hand. 'Only use your cover names from now on. At all times. Whoever you were before today must be left behind. From now on it's Capito and Calidus.' He stared at them a moment and then made towards the door. 'Get some sleep. Tomorrow you join the Praetorian Guard.'

CHAPTER FIVE

Early the next morning Macro and Cato passed through the Viminal Gate on the city wall and into the suburb where the Praetorian camp had been constructed during the reign of Tiberius. A light rain was falling and formed puddles in the expanse of the parade ground that stretched from the city wall to the camp. They strode across the open space to the main gate and presented themselves to the optio on watch in the guardhouse. He was a short, well-built man with neatly trimmed hair that had receded some way. Macro and Cato had lowered their yokes and stood to attention as the rain dripped from the hems of their cloaks.

'What do we have here then?' the optio asked goodnaturedly.

Cato reached into his side bag, drew out the document appointing them to the Praetorian Guard and handed it to the optio. 'Transfer from the Second Legion, sir. Legionaries Titus Ovidius Capito and Vibius Gallus Calidus. We've been appointed to the Guard.'

'Oh really? Capito and Calidus? Sounds like a bloody mime double act.' The optio took the flattened scroll and unravelled it. He quickly scanned the document and looked up. 'It says here, "For meritorious conduct in the field". Did you two take on the barbarian army by yourselves then?'

Cato felt a fleeting desire to tear a strip off the optio, but suppressed the impulse. They were back in the ranks and needed to behave accordingly.

'No. Optio.'

'No? Then I'd like to know what you two heroes did that warrants a transfer to the Praetorian Guard. But that'll have to wait.' He looked round them and pointed to one of the men standing by the gate. 'Over here!'

The Praetorian came trotting up and stood to attention. Cato glanced at him. He was young, barely out of his teens. Like the Praetorians who had briefly appeared during the early stages of the campaign in Britannia, he wore an off-white tunic and cape. Beneath the cape glinted a vest of scale armour of the same issue that some legionaries still favoured. The rest of his kit – sword, dagger, boots, groin guard and helmet – were standard issue. Only the shield was different, oval rather than the rectangular design used in the legions. A large scorpion decorated the front. The symbol had been chosen by a previous prefect, Sejanus, to flatter his master, Emperor Tiberius, who was born under that star sign.

The optio folded the scroll and handed it back to Cato. 'Escort these two beggars to headquarters. Centurion Sinius is in charge of recruiting, training and transfers. Take them to him.'

'Yes, sir.'

'Off you go, lads. Oh, and welcome to the Praetorian Guard. You'll find it somewhat different to life in the legions.'

'Yes, sir. Thank you, sir.' Cato nodded.

They shouldered their yokes once again and followed the Praetorian out of the guardhouse and into the shelter of the arched gateway. He waited until they had their yokes comfortably positioned and then set off down the wide avenue leading into the heart of the Praetorian camp. On either side were two-storey barracks which ran back from each side of the route for a hundred paces. The plaster covering the walls was clean and looked to have been painted recently. In the same way the paved road had no litter and was obviously swept regularly.

'Your run a tidy camp,' said Macro.

'Oh, that's down to Geta,' the young Praetorian replied. 'He's a stickler for high standards. Keeps us on our toes all right. Surprise barrack inspections, calls to arms in the middle of the night and regular kit checks are the order of the day here, mate. Don't know what things are like in the legions, but you'd best play it his way when you're here in Rome, or else.'

Cato looked at the youth. 'I take it you weren't transferred from a legion.'

'Me? No. Many of the lads are recruited from central Italia. What with all the perks of the job it ain't easy getting in, but a letter of commendation from a local magistrate usually swings it. Unfortunately I was a few years too late to qualify for the donative the Emperor handed out when he took power. Five years' pay, that's what he gave each man! Bloody fortune. Still, Claudius ain't going to last forever and whoever comes next will have to cough up again, if they know what's good for them.'

Macro coughed. 'Your loyalty to the Emperor is most touching.'

71

The Praetorian glanced at him with a quizzical expression and then smiled when he realised that Macro was mocking him. 'I'm loyal enough. Without an emperor to protect, where would the Praetorian Guard be? Disbanded and sent to join the legions, that's where. On half of the pay, stuck in some forsaken frontier outpost surrounded by barbarians waiting to cut your throat at the first opportunity. Not much of a life.' He paused and looked at the other men closely. 'No offence meant.'

'None taken,' Cato replied lightly. 'Tell me, are all the Praetorians as cynical as you? No offence either, but you strike me as, well, a bit mercenary.'

'Mercenary?' The Praetorian considered the suggestion. 'I suppose some might see it that way. It's certainly a cushy number for the most part. Generous pay, comfortable accommodation, good seats at the games and not much chance of active service. And you've arrived at a fortunate time, as it happens. It's the Accession games in ten days' time.'

'Accession games?'

'On the anniversary of the day that Claudius became Emperor. He puts on a parade here in the camp, some gladiator fights and a few other events and caps if off with a feast. He doesn't forget who put him in power and he makes sure he keeps relations with the Praetorian Guard sweet. So you can get used to the imperial treats. That said, it ain't all a holiday. Geta drills us hard and if we're called on, we can put up a decent fight.'

'We've seen the Praetorians in battle,' said Macro. 'That was back in Britannia. They did well enough.'

The Praetorian's expression brightened. 'You were there? At Camulodunum?'

Macro nodded.

'I've heard from those who accompanied the Emperor that it was a hard battle.'

'It was. But it shouldn't have been. The enemy laid a neat trap for us. If Claudius hadn't been so keen to charge in and have his great victory then we wouldn't have been caught on the hop. As it was, the Second Legion saved the day, and the skins of the Praetorians and the Emperor.'

'You were with the Second Legion, I take it.'

'We were. And proud of it. The Second Legion Augusta is the best legion in the army. You should have seen us, boy. Battle after battle we tore them Celts apart. Not that they were soft, mind. The Celts are big men, brave, and they'd sooner fight than do anything else in life. It wasn't an easy campaign. I know some in Rome say that it was. But they weren't there. I was, and I know what I saw, and I speak the truth. Ain't that right, Ca—'

Cato coughed loudly and glared furiously at Macro. The latter flushed and cleared his throat before continuing. 'Just ask Capito there, when he's got over his coughing fit.'

The Praetorian looked at Cato and then turned his attention back to Macro. 'Look here, Calidus, a word of advice. I'd watch what you say about your legion in front of some of the other lads here. They tend to think that because we're the Emperor's own, it makes us the best soldiers in the army.'

'And what do you think?'

'I've only ever known the Guard. I think it would be rash of me to offer an opinion about things I have no experience of.'

Macro smiled. 'Wise boy.'

They had reached the heart of the Praetorian camp and Cato and Macro saw for the first time the colonnaded front and pillared entrance to the headquarters. Macro let out a low whistle.

'Bloody hell, looks more like a temple than a military building.'

They passed through the gateway, looking up to marvel at the carvings on the ceiling that arched overhead. Inside the entrance was a large open space, a hundred feet on either side, Cato estimated, which was lined by another colonnade. Directly opposite the gates was another entrance, this time to the headquarters offices which formed the far side of the square. A handful of clerks, wrapped in cloaks, scurried about their duties and a section of guardsmen stood watch outside the offices. The Praetorian explained his order to the optio in charge of the section and then lowered his shield and unbuckled his sword and dagger belts and left them with the other weapons surrendered by visitors on a table inside the entrance.

The optio nodded to Cato and Macro. 'Leave your yokes and kitbags here. Any weapons on you?'

Cato pointed to the kitbags. 'In there.'

'In there, *sir*,' the optio snapped.

Cato stiffened. 'Yes, sir.'

'I don't know what discipline is like in the legions, but the Praetorians are sticklers for it,' the optio continued, as Macro hurriedly stood to attention beside Cato. The optio curled his upper lip as he looked over their worn cloaks and tunics. 'Same goes for your kit. Prefect Geta likes his men well turned out. You two look like tramps. Don't show your faces here again unless you are neat and clean. Is that clear?'

'Yes, sir,' Macro and Cato chorused.

'Right, lad, get these two in front of Centurion Sinius.' He smiled coldly. 'I dare say that the centurion will be equally unimpressed by you. Go.'

They followed the young Praetorian into the entrance hall and then right into a long chamber with offices on one side and long tables where clerks sat between piles of waxed slates and baskets of scrolls. Long slits high up on the walls provided barely enough illumination for the men to work and Cato saw some squinting at the smaller details of the records in front of them. He was still smarting from the frosty reception that he and Macro had received since arriving at the camp. Cato had grown too used to the automatic deference of the lower ranks in recent years and it was an uncomfortable jolt back to the first days of his army service to be treated as a common soldier once again. No longer was he Prefect Cato, he was merely Guardsman Capito, and he must live and breathe the part he was forced to play. The same was true for Macro. Glancing to his side as they strode past the first office doors, Cato saw that Macro looked unperturbed by the small dressing-down they had just received. That was a surprise, Cato thought. He would expect Macro, of all people, to rankle at such treatment.

'Here we are,' the Praetorian announced. He indicated the nearest door. Unlike most of the other offices in the chamber, the door to this one was closed. 'Centurion Sinius's office.'

He paused briefly to give the new arrivals a chance to compose themselves and then knocked.

'A moment!' a muffled voice called from inside. There was a short delay. 'Come in!'

The young soldier lifted the latch and swung the door inwards. He stepped into the doorway, stood to attention and bowed his head. 'Beg to report that the optio of the watch on the main gate ordered me to escort two recruits to headquarters, sir.'

Cato, being taller than most men, was able to see over the Praetorian's shoulder into the office. The centurion closed a waxed tablet and tidied it away into a small document chest on the side of his desk. Sinius looked to be in his late twenties or early thirties, too young to have won promotion from the ranks; Cato guessed he must have been directly appointed to the centurionate. A member of a wealthy equestrian family who had relinquished his social privileges to join the Praetorian Guard. Unusually for a Roman the officer had fair hair, with a light wave that was carefully combed in an attempt to hide the premature onset of baldness. He was a slender man, sinewy with a hard face. However, when he looked up he smiled warmly.

'Very well, show them in.'

The youth stood aside and Macro and Cato marched in and stood a respectful distance in front of the centurion's desk, shoulders back and chests out. The office was generously proportioned – fully fifteen feet across. A shuttered window was behind the desk and light entered from two openings higher up the wall, just underneath the eaves outside. The wall to the left was shelved and filled with carefully arranged wax tablets, sheets of papyrus and scrolls. A gleaming breastplate and an ornately decorated helmet, with a red feather plume, hung on a frame standing against the opposite wall.

Sinius glanced at the two recruits briefly and then

nodded to the Praetorian. 'You may go. Close the door behind you.'

The youth stepped out and there was a light clatter as the latch dropped back into place. Sinius regarded the new arrivals carefully. Cato did not return his look but stared directly ahead, fixing his eyes on the small bust of the Emperor that stood on a pedestal next to the rear wall.

'Let's get the preliminaries over.' Sinius leant forward and held out his hand. 'Your appointment document-ation, please.'

'Yes, sir.' Cato took out the folded papyrus and the letter of recommendation and placed them in the centurion's hand. Sinius read through the documents steadily, and tapped the imperial seal at the bottom of the transfer notice, as if to ensure that it was genuine.

'You two come highly commended. Your former commander speaks very well of you. He calls you both exemplary soldiers. That remains to be seen, as a somewhat higher standard applies in the Praetorian Guard compared to the legions. In any case, your paperwork is in order and the imperial palace has approved your appointment, so guardsmen you are.' He glanced again at the document. 'So which one is Capito?'

'Me, sir,' said Cato.

'And Calidus.' The centurion smiled quickly at Macro. 'You're both welcome. Despite what I said about standards, the Guard can always use experienced soldiers. We are not called upon to fight very often, but when we are, the burden of expectation weighs heavily on our shoulders. In that case, the more veterans we have in the ranks, the better. The other side of the coin is that you must accept that your new duties require absolute adher-ence to established protocols. Your appointment specifies that you are to serve in Centurion Lurco's century of the Fifth Cohort. Lurco is on leave at the moment, so you'll be reporting to the cohort's commander.' He paused. 'Apparently the Emperor was so taken by your brave example that he requested that you be assigned to protect him and his household. That's why you're in the cohort assigned to protect the palace.'

'We are honoured, sir,' Cato responded.

'So you should be. Such a role is usually only conferred after some years of service in the Guard. Even then, our men have to be aware of the precise manner in which they are to perform their duties. There is a very rigid hierarchy within the imperial palace and all guardsmen are expected to know it and address members of the household strictly in accordance with their station. As the officer responsible for recruiting, training and the manning of the Guard cohorts I will do my best to prepare you, although I've only been holding this office for a little over a month now. I'll have someone who knows the ropes explain the details.' He smiled again. 'You will have to make allowances for me, as I will have to for you, eh?'

'Yes, sir,' Macro and Cato replied.

'The palace cohort is commanded by Tribune Burrus.' Sinius picked up a stylus and made a hurried note on a waxed tablet.

'*Tribune* Burrus, sir?' Macro raised an eyebrow.

'That's what I said,' Sinius replied sharply, then suddenly his expression softened. 'Ah, I understand. The tribunes of the legions are staff officers, aren't they? It's different in the Guard. The cohorts are each commanded by a tribune who usually holds the post for one year, before retirement. That's not the only difference. The cohorts of the Guard are twice the size of those in the legions. In fact, there are nearly ten thousand Praetorians on the rolls. Some are on detached duties, but most are here in camp, giving the Emperor over nine thousand men to draw on if there is any emergency. Tends to make the mob think twice before they cause any trouble.' He paused briefly. 'Of course, we're not the only ones charged with keeping order. There are the urban cohorts and the vigiles, who do a decent job of patrolling the main thoroughfares and breaking up drunken brawls and so on. The Praetorians are really there as a last resort. So when we go in, the people know we mean business.'

'Does that happen often, sir?' asked Macro.

'No. But trouble is brewing,' Sinius's tone became serious. 'Thanks to the disruption of the Egyptian grain supplies last year the stocks in the imperial granary are running very low. The dole has already been cut, and people are going hungry as the price of grain rises. We've already seen some small riots. It's a funny thing,' he mused. 'Here we are in the greatest city in the world. We have fine bathhouses, theatres, arenas, goods and luxuries from every corner of the world, the best minds toil away in our libraries and one emperor after another has overseen the construction of vast temples and public buildings. Yet we are never more than a few meals away from unrest and the collapse of order.'

Cato and Macro made no comment and continued staring ahead.

Sinius sighed. 'At ease. I've been through the

formalities. Now I'm curious to know a little more about you. I have a few questions.'

The two men relaxed their posture and glanced at each other. Cato cleared his throat and answered for them. 'Yes, sir.'

'Firstly, you've come from Britannia?'

'Yes, sir.'

'Where the campaigning continues, despite the fact that Claudius celebrated a triumph awarded by the senate for the conquest of Britannia some years ago.'

'We control the heart of the island, sir. We're pushing our enemies back into the mountains bordering the new province. It's only a question of time before the legions have finished the job.'

'Really? I have a cousin who serves in the Ninth Legion. He writes to me from time to time, and I have to say he rather lacks your confidence in such steady progress. According to him we're struggling to crush those who still resist us. The enemy raids our supply lines constantly and fades away the moment we show up in force.'

'That is their new manner of fighting, sir,' Macro intervened. 'Forced on them after they had given up facing us in pitched battles. It is the strategy of the defeated. All they're achieving is buying a little more time before they eventually bow to Rome.'

'I only wish my cousin shared your phlegmatic nature, Calidus. However, he is not the only soldier who seems to think that the campaign is not going as well as the imperial palace would have us believe. Perhaps there is a different view among the rank and file. After all, common soldiers, such as yourselves, lack the wider perspective, as it were. Tell me, what are the men of the legions thinking? What is their . . . mood?'

Cato considered the question carefully. It had been some years since he and Macro had served in the Second Legion. Even then, the campaign had taken its toll on the men's spirits. But that was to be expected. The issue now was how to use this opportunity to test the centurion sitting in front of him.

'There are some who are not best pleased with their posting, sir.' Cato spoke in a cautious tone.

'Go on.'

'It's not really for me to speak for them.'

'I understand, Capito. Look here, this is an informal conversation. You're in the Guard now, nothing can change that. I'm just curious about the situation in Britannia. Trust me.'

Cato shot a quick look at Macro who was too uncertain about the direction the conversation was heading to respond. He just shrugged his heavy shoulders.

'Well, sir,' Cato continued. 'When we left, the feeling in the ranks was that the campaign was getting nowhere. To be sure, we control the south and east of the island, but beyond that the tribes are in control. They hit our supply convoys and smaller outposts and run for it. They know the ground and move fast, so we have next to no chance of catching them.' Cato paused. 'If you want my opinion, the new province will never be secure. We'd be better off cutting our losses and withdrawing, sir.' Cato was struck by a sudden inspiration and continued. 'I even overheard some of the officers of the legion discussing it one night, sir. While I was on sentry duty. They're as keen as the rest of us to get out, and one of 'em said that the only reason we were there in the first place was because Claudius needed to play the all-conquering hero. And that once he had had his triumph, the army in Britannia was forgotten.'

'I see.' Sinius pursed his lips. 'Doesn't sound like there's much love lost for the Emperor among the legions in Britannia.'

Cato looked at him nervously. 'That's just what it looked like when Calidus and I left the Second, sir. The situation may have changed.'

'Of course, that's possible. Thank you for being frank with me, Capito. Rest assured, our little conversation will go no further than these walls.'

Cato nodded. 'Thank you, sir.'

Sinius waved a hand dismissively. 'Think no more of it. Our business here is concluded. You'll need to draw your kit from the stores then join your cohort. Tribune Burrus's men are in the barracks in the south-western corner of the camp. Hand this waxed slate over to his clerk when you sign in there, and you'll be enlisted in Centurion Lurco's century.'

'Yes, sir.'

'It just remains for me to say welcome to the Praetorian Guard. Perform your duty and keep your noses clean and you'll find this an excellent posting. The biggest challenge you are likely to face is fighting off all the women who fancy the uniform and the pay and status that go with it. That's not just the women on the street. There's more than a few wives of senators who take a fancy to Praetorians.'

Macro could not help smiling at the prospect.

The centurion paused for a moment before he

continued in a lower voice. 'A word to the wise. Avoid any temptation to get overly familiar with any member of the Imperial family, if you take my meaning. You have been warned. Off you go.'

The two men left the room and closed the door behind them. Centurion Sinius stared thoughtfully at the door for a moment and then opened the document chest and took out the waxed tablet he had been examining. He picked up a stylus and made a few notes then replaced it in the chest. He rose from his desk and left headquarters to give some instructions to one of his followers.

CHAPTER SIX

M acro held up the plain white toga and shook his head. 'This is no good for a soldier. We're supposed to wear this over the left shoulder and arm, right?'

On the other side of the section room Cato nodded.

'It's madness,' Macro continued. 'You can't swing a sword properly with this on. You'd trip over it and do yourself an injury long before you could take down an opponent.'

He bundled the toga up, tossed it on to his bed and sat down with a disgusted expression before glancing over the rest of the kit they had been issued from the camp's stores. The toga was the formal uniform for the Guard when on duty in the city. A sop to those inhabitants of Rome who still clung to the values of the old Republic when the presence of armed men on the streets was held to be a threat to their liberty. For a similar reason, Claudius had taken to wearing an unadorned toga on many ceremonial occasions, without even the narrow purple stripe of a junior magistrate. The display of humility played well with the mob and the more easily impressed members of the senate. As far as Macro was concerned, the toga was wholly impracticable for those soldiers who were supposed to be guarding the imperial palace.

'What about the German bodyguards?' Macro looked at Cato. 'Do they have to wear this?'

'No. But then they're barbarians, from Batavia, I believe. It would offend public sensibilities for them to be seen in togas.'

'Bollocks,' Macro mumbled. His gaze returned to the rest of the issued items. In addition to functional armour, there was a brass cuirass, an attic helmet with a decorated crown and slim cheekguards that served little practical use, and almost no neck guard. Then there were the off-white tunics and light-brown cloaks that would readily pick up the dirt and grime of Rome's streets and require constant cleaning. At least the short sword, oval shield and heavy javelin looked like proper soldier's kit. Cato had already folded his toga, tunics and cloak and placed them neatly on the shelf above his bed. With a sigh, Macro began to follow suit.

'What was all that about the failing spirits of the lads in Britannia?' he asked.

Cato hissed, then stood up and crossed to the door. He glanced outside. They had been assigned a comfortable room on the upper storey with another two men from the Sixth Century of the Third Cohort, the unit presently assigned to protect the imperial palace and the Emperor's entourage whenever Claudius emerged on to the streets to visit the senate or enjoy the entertainments of the theatre, arena or racetrack. In the legions the soldiers were obliged to bunk eight to a room, or share a tent on campaign, crowded together. Here in the Guard there were four men to a room, which was airy and well lit by the shuttered window on the wall. Out in the corridor Cato could see a few figures some distance away, leaning on the rail overlooking the avenue of trees that approached the Praetorians' bathhouse. Even that was on a grand scale compared to the usual offering of a legionary fortress. A suite of chambers was arranged to one side of a sand-covered exercise yard, all contained within a low plastered wall. The other Praetorians ignored him. A few of the doors were open along the corridor but the conversations of those within were impossible to overhear. Cato returned to his bed and sat on the edge.

'Keep your voice down when we talk. And we have to make sure that we use our assumed names at all times.'

'I know,' Macro grumbled, finishing folding the last of his tunics and cloaks. He sat down opposite Cato. 'I'm sorry about earlier. It's just that I don't hold with this going undercover business.'

'Well, you'd better. We're spies for the present, and there's nothing we can do about it until the job is done. If we fail, Narcissus will throw us to the wolves. That's if we survive the tender mercies of the Liberators.'

'I know, I know,' Macro responded wearily. 'I'll keep my mind on the work in hand, I swear it. But tell me, Capito,' he could not help smiling a little at using the assumed name, 'why did you feed Sinius that line about the situation in Britannia?'

'I had to tell him something, to make sure he believed our cover story. But then it occurred to me, if I spoke of their discontent, it had to be of interest to the other side. Even if Sinius has nothing to do with the conspiracy, there's a good chance he'll talk about what we've said with the other officers. That puts our names about and hints that we might be amenable to an approach from those who are opposed to the Emperor.' Cato puffed out his cheeks. 'Anyway, that's what I thought.'

Macro nodded. 'Sounds good. As ever, you have a devious turn of mind, my friend. No wonder Narcissus likes you so much.' He gave Cato a searching look. 'Before too long I imagine you'll be taking over his job in the palace. You'd be good at it.'

Cato stared at him and responded in a deliberate low, hard voice. 'I might just do that.'

For a moment they stared at each other and then Macro slapped Cato on the shoulder. 'You nearly had me there!'

Macro roared with laughter, and Cato joined in. They were still laughing when the sound of footsteps approached and a figure appeared in the doorway. Cato looked round to see a thin man with a narrow face watching them coldly. His skin was badly pockmarked and his hair was streaked with grey. Cato guessed that he was a few years older than Macro. He stood up and offered his hand to the man.

'The name's Titus Ovidius Capito. Late of the Second Legion, before I was transferred to the Praetorians.'

'Capito.' The man nodded. 'Glad to see you're in high spirits. You're also in my section, as it happens.' He jerked his thumb at his chest. 'Name's Lucius Pollinus Tigellinus. Optio of this century, second-in-command to Centurion Lurco. Your friend there is the other new boy?'

Macro stood up. 'The friend can talk for himself. Vibius Gallus Calidus. Also of the Second.'

Tigellinus sniffed. 'An undistinguished unit as far as I recall. You may have impressed your superiors in Britannia but you're going to have to start all over again to impress me, and Tribune Burrus.'

'We'll do our best,' said Cato.

'Good, then you'd better get your service tunics on and report to the Tribune.' Tigellinus pointed at their legion issue. 'Best get rid of those rags. Sell 'em in the market, you won't need 'em again, and I won't allow them to clutter up my shelves. I'd move yourselves. The tribune hates slackers.'

He turned away and strode off down the corridor. An instant later a fresh face appeared at the door and entered the room. He was a young man, possibly the same age as the Praetorian who had escorted them to headquarters, but to Cato's eyes he seemed too fresh faced to be a soldier. The thought caught him by surprise as he realised that he was only a few years older than the young Praetorian standing before him. A few years of experience that made all the difference, he reflected.

The Praetorian looked round to make sure that Tigellinus was not within earshot before he spoke. 'Don't worry about him. Tigellinus gives all the new arrivals a hard time. Says it does 'em good to keep them on their toes. Should have seen how he used to treat me.' He smiled. 'Fuscius is the name.'

Macro smiled back. 'I'm Calidus and the lanky one there is Capito. Transferred from the legions.'

'I guessed as much when I saw the . . .' His words trailed off as he pointed at the scar across Cato's face. 'How did you get that?'

'Sword cut,' Cato explained flatly. 'Last year in . . . Britannia. Took it when we were ambushed by some Durotrigan tribesmen.'

Fuscius stared at him for a moment longer in frank admiration, then realised that he must look foolish and flushed with embarrassment. 'I'll wager you have quite a few tales you could tell about Britannia.'

'How much will you wager?' Macro asked drily. 'If you want decent stories then you come to me, young 'un.'

'Oh?' Fuscius did not know how to proceed without offending either man so he just mumbled something as he squeezed past and made for one of the beds either side of the window. 'Anyway, it's good to have someone else in the room. Tigellinus isn't much of a talker. Well, he does talk, but mostly to complain about things.'

'So we've noticed,' said Cato as he pulled his red tunic off and slipped on his newly issued Praetorian tunic. 'Come on, Calidus, better hurry.'

'When you've done for the day, some of the lads and I are going out for a drink tonight,' Fuscius said. 'Fancy joining us?'

'Sounds good,' Cato replied as he smoothed the tunic down and fastened his thick military belt round his middle. 'Calidus?'

'Why not? Could use a decent drink after that filthy muck we drank when we arrived.'

'Good, then let's find the tribune.'

Tribune Burrus was an aged veteran. From the number of scars he bore on his face and arms, he had served a good many years in the legions before being appointed to the Praetorian Guard. Aside from a fringe of white hair, he was bald. One eye had been lost and a leather patch covered the socket, tied in place with a thin strap. He was tall and thickset and Cato realised that he must have been a formidable figure in his time. Now, though, he was serving his last few years in the Guard before he took his gratuity and left the army. He might use his elevation to the equestrian class to take up an administrative job in Rome, or one of the other cities and towns in Italia, but Cato guessed that the man would prefer the company of old soldiers to bureaucrats. The tribune would end his days in some military colony, respected by men who knew his quality, even as he grew stooped and frail.

'Well, don't just dawdle by the bloody door!' Burrus snapped.

When Cato and Macro were standing to attention in front of him, the tribune scrutinised them for a moment before he continued, 'Proper soldiers at last! About damn time. I've seen too many of these soft city boys joining the ranks of late. Especially after the casualties we took in Britannia. But you'll remember that battle outside Camulodunum. It was your legion that saved us from that trap. My, but those bloody Celts were devious bastards. Fought hard, too, and brought out the best in the Praetorians, even though we were roughly handled. So,' he concluded, 'it's good to have two veterans join the cohort. Though I see that one of you is still a bit on the young side, eh? Which one are you?'

'Capito, sir.'

'Age?'

'Twenty-five, sir.'

'You'll have served seven years then.'

'Nearer eight, sir. I joined about the time I turned seventeen.'

Burrus frowned. 'That's against regs. Eighteen is the minimum age.'

'I was sent to the army by my father as soon as he thought I was ready for it.' Cato spoke tonelessly as he gave his cover story.

'He must be a proud man indeed. You've done well for yourself.'

'Thank you, sir.'

Burrus turned his attention to Macro. 'What's your story? From the look of you, you're an old sweat. How many years have you served, Calidus?'

'Twenty-three years, sir.'

'Good gods, and still only a legionary? You should have been killed off or promoted to centurion by now, optio at the very least. What's your excuse?'

Macro swallowed his bitterness and answered directly. 'I'm a ranker first and last, sir. Didn't see any reason to go and get myself promoted. I like plain soldiering. I fight hard and have put down a good many of Rome's enemies in my time.'

'A good fighter's one thing, but do you think you can cope with the demands of being a Praetorian? You will be constantly before the eyes of the senators and the people. There's more to being a good soldier than killing enemies. If you fuck up and embarrass the Praetorian Guard then you'll embarrass the Emperor and, worse, far worse, you will shame me. If that should happen I will jump on you like a mountain of shit, is that clear, Calidus?'

'Yes, sir.'

There was a pause while the tribune let his warning sink in, then he cleared his throat and continued in a more moderate tone. 'I'll tell you what I tell every recruit at the moment. You've joined us at a difficult time. The

Emperor is getting on and won't last forever, even if some fool of a senator gets him voted a divinity. It's a shame because as emperors go he's been one of the better ones. However, he's flesh and blood, and he will die. Our job is to make sure that is down to natural causes. Now, I know the old joke about natural causes in the imperial family include a host of unusual ailments such as poisoning, a knife in the back or a sword in the guts, being smothered by a pillow, and so on. That will not happen during my time in command of the palace cohort. So you will keep your eyes open when you're on duty. I don't trust those German pricks in the personal body-guard any further than I could spit 'em. Our job is to stop anyone getting close enough to Claudius for those Germans to have to earn their money. As far as I am concerned, my men are the first and final line of defence. If either of you have to throw yourselves in front of an assassin's knife to save the Emperor then you'll do it without hesitation. If not, then there's no place for you in my cohort. Clear?'

'Yes, sir,' Cato and Macro replied at once.

'Good. As I said, it's a difficult situation. There are various factions in the palace who are already making their plans for the succession. Some are backing Britannicus, others the upstart Nero. Besides that, there's the bloody freedmen who advise the Emperor, Pallas, Narcissus and Callistus, shifty little grafters every one of 'em. They'll be looking to make an alliance with their chosen candidate for the purple. That's fine by me, just as long as they don't do anything to try and accelerate the process. Watch for threats from within as well dangers from without. Any questions?' He looked at each of them. 'No? Then I'll have Tigellinus go through the basic protocols with you tomorrow. You better be fast learners, as I'll have you on duty the day after that. It's a case of swim or sink, lads. Dismissed!'

CHAPTER SEVEN

'Bloody bunch of toy soldiers is what the Praetorians are,' said Macro as they walked down the lane leading to the inn that Fuscius had named earlier. Night had fallen and both men had taken their cloaks to ward off the chill of a winter night. On either side of the thoroughfare the dark masses of the cheaply built tenement blocks reared up, pierced by the loom of occasional lamps and tallow candles glimmering within. The foetid stink of sweat, sewage and rotting vegetables filled the air. Macro exhaled sharply. 'They do nothing but prepare for parades.'

'I thought you liked that aspect of the job,' Cato replied. 'You used to tell me that drilling was the reason why the Roman army was successful.'

'Yes, well, it can be overdone,' Macro admitted grudgingly. 'The point is that the drilling is for battle, not for endless parades and ceremonies. They're supposed to be soldiers, not useless bloody ornaments.'

'I wonder. They have a certain élan about them and I dare say that when they have to fight the men will not dishonour the reputation of the Guard.'

Macro looked sidelong at Cato, and stumbled over the body of a dog. 'Oh, shit! Fucking guts are all over my foot . . .' He paused to scrape his boot on the side of a wall.

'What I was going to say was that there's as much chance of seeing the Praetorians in action as there is of seeing the vestal virgins at an orgy. It happens but not often.'

'We're not here for a fight. I don't want to be in the Praetorian Guard any longer than I have to. We're here for one purpose only.'

'I know, to find and kill the traitors.'

'Actually, I was thinking to get all that's due to us from that snake Narcissus.'

Macro laughed and clapped his hand on his friend's shoulder. 'How right you are, lad!'

Cato smiled. Much as he resented having to earn his promotion to prefect over again, it felt good to be restored to the same rank as Macro. There had been moments of tension between them when Macro had to defer to Cato's higher rank, and Cato had regretted the loss of the easy give and take of their relationship in earlier years. That would change once the present task was over, Cato reflected with a degree of sadness. If Narcissus held to his word then he would be confirmed as a prefect and would have an auxiliary cohort of his own to command. In all probability Macro would be appointed to a legion and they would part company. Assuming that their mission was successful, Cato reminded himself.

'I think this must be the place.' Macro pointed down the street to where a small square opened out around a public fountain. A strong breeze had picked up during the early evening and had swept away most of the pall of smoke that hung over Rome and now the stars glinted coldly from the heavens, bathing the city in a faint glow, picking out the roof lines of the tenement blocks further down the Esquiline Hill. As the two soldiers entered the square, they saw to their right a large door with a sign hanging above it with the neatly painted wording: The River of Wine. The sound of shouting and laughter spilled out into the square and the door opened briefly as a man staggered outside, and threw up in the warm glow cast by the lamps and candles that burned within.

'The mouth of the river, no doubt,' Cato suggested.

'Very funny. Let's go to the source. I'm parched.'

Cato held his friend's arm to restrain him a moment. 'By all means drink. But don't get drunk. We can't afford to slip up.'

'Trust me, I'll stay as sober as a vestal virgin.'

'That is not an encouraging comparison, according to some accounts.'

They crossed the square and carefully stepped round the man doubled over in the gutter as he continued heaving up from the pit of his stomach. Stepping through the entrance, Cato saw that the inn was large and extended much of the way beneath the tenement block above, which rested on the thick support columns that divided the room. It was already filled with the evening trade and the warm air was thick with smoke from the lamps and candles and the acrid odour of cheap wine. The flagstone floor was covered with a loose layer of straw and sawdust. Cato estimated that there were over a hundred men and a few women squeezed into the space and all the tables were filled so that some customers sat slumped against the walls. There were small clusters of off-duty guardsmen as well as men from one of the urban cohorts. The rest were civilians.

'Hey! Over here!'

They turned towards the voice and saw Fuscius beck-oning to them from the corner not far from the entrance. He was sitting at a long table with some other guardsmen. Several jars of wine stood before them.

Cato and Macro made their way over to the table and Fuscius, with several cups of wine under his belt, made the introductions.

'Lads! Here's the two new boys I told you about. Well, maybe not boys, eh?' He wrapped an arm round each of the new arrivals' shoulders and breathed over Cato's face as he turned to grin blearily at him. 'This one's Capito. And this here's Callus.'

'That's Calidus,' Macro corrected him evenly. He looked round at the other men and nodded a greeting. There were nine of them, three who looked like veterans and the others fresh faced and young, like Fuscius. Most seemed to have had as much to drink as Fuscius, though the veterans were better at holding their drink and still seemed to have their wits about them.

'Have a seat,' Fuscius continued and glanced down and saw that there wasn't a bench at that end of the table. He turned round to the next table where three scrawny youths were sitting with a fat whore, plying her with wine.

'Get up!' Fuscius ordered. 'Oi, on your feet! I need your bench.'

One of the youths looked round and muttered, 'Piss off! Find your own fucking bench. This one's taken.'

'Not any more. When a Praetorian tells you to jump, you bloody jump. Now get up.'

'You going to make us?' The youth smiled coldly and his hand slipped down towards his belt.

Fuscius stepped aside to reveal the table where his comrades were sitting. 'Only if you force us to.'

The Praetorians glared at the youths. They took the hint and hurried to their feet, roughly lifting the woman who groaned in protest. She was so far gone her limbs were loose and her companions struggled to drag her away through the throng. Fuscius pulled the bench over to the table and waved Cato and Macro down.

'There you are. Head of the table. Have a drink.' He pulled the nearest jug over, saw that it was empty and reached for the next before filling two cups to the brim and pushing them towards Cato and Macro, spilling a measure of the contents.

They picked up their cups and raised them to toast the other men. Cato made a show of drinking a deep draught and squirted most back into the cup which he lowered to his side and discreetly tipped on to the floor. Macro had taken a good swallow and now wiped his mouth on the back of his hand.

'Ahhh, not bad!'

'Of course.' Fuscius grinned. 'They keep the good stuff for the Praetorians because we pay well, and they dare not give us second-best.'

'I see.' Cato pursed his lips, then raised his cup again and pretended to take another sip.

'So what do you make of the new posting so far?' asked one of Fuscius's companions. 'Is it, or is it not, the best job in the army?'

'There's a world of difference between the Praetorian Guard and the real army,' said Macro. 'Yes, it's a good job, but it ain't proper soldiering.'

Cato winced as he saw the expressions of the other

men around the table freeze for a moment. Then one of the older guardsmen blew a loud raspberry and laughed and the others joined in.

'Typical bloody legionaries!' another one of the veterans called down the table. 'Think they own the army. Then they come here with their high and mighty airs. Bollocks. Give 'em a year in the Guard and they'll forget they ever were legionaries.'

Macro leant forward and pointed his finger at the man. 'Now see here. You don't know what you're talking about. You show any disrespect for the legions in front of me and Capito and we might take it to heart just enough to beat the living shit out of you. Ain't that right, Capito?'

'What?' Cato shot a furious glance at Macro.

'I've had it up to here with these preening ponces. Going on about spit and polish as if it was all that mattered.' He took another mouthful of wine and continued, 'Taking twice the pay of a decent soldier and sitting pretty while the same soldier goes out and risks his life for Rome . . .'

'So?' the veteran at the other end of the table responded. 'You've served your time on campaign, like me, and this is the long overdue reward we've always promised ourselves. What's your problem with that?'

Macro stared hard at him, then drained his cup and set it down with a sharp rap, and blew a raspberry. 'Not a bloody thing! Now fill the cup again.'

The men round the table roared with laughter and Fuscius poured more wine into Macro's cup. He glanced at Cato but the latter shook his head with a quick smile.

'Tell me,' said Cato. 'What's with all the training that

I hear you've been put through? I thought the Guard was an easy posting. Seems like Prefect Geta is preparing the Praetorians for war, from what I've heard.'

'Fucking Geta!' one of the younger men spat. 'Ever since Crispinus went off on sick leave, Geta's been making us work like dogs. Route marches, sword practice and those bloody false alarms night and day. I'm sick of it. I think you're right. He wants to persuade the Emperor to send us off to some damned war.' The man looked down into the dregs of his cup. 'Knowing my luck, the Praetorians will be sent back to Britannia to clear the mess up.'

'Ha!' Fuscius clapped his hands together. 'Small world! Friend Capito here has just returned from Britannia. And Calidus.'

'Oh?' One of the older Praetorians struggled to focus his attention on the new arrivals. 'What's the word then? Are we winning?'

Cato pursed his lips. 'Define winning.'

'Define winning?' The man frowned. 'What bollocks is that? Either we're winning or we ain't. Which is it?'

'You'll have to forgive my friend,' Macro intervened. 'He thinks he's a philosopher. Truth of it is that the Celts are tougher beasts than the Emperor thought. We can beat 'em on the battlefield easily enough, so they've taken to ambushing our lads then running like hares. Cowards they may be, but they're whittling us down, man by man. If you want my opinion, Rome's better off without those bog-hopping barbarians. The Emperor should bring the troops home.'

'What about them Druids?' asked one of the younger Praetorians.

'What about 'em?'

'If we don't crush 'em in Britannia, we'll only have to fight them again in Gaul, and then everywhere else they can get to. At least that's what I've heard.'

'Then forget what you've heard,' Macro said harshly. 'I'm telling you, the Druids are broken. Retreated into the mountains. They're finished. That line they spun about having to invade Britannia to save the empire from the Druids is a bloody black lie. There's only one reason the legions are in Britannia, and that's to make the Emperor look like a proper general. Any halfway decent emperor would never have put his men's lives at risk in order to look good in front of the mob.'

Cato had been watching the men's reactions as his friend spoke and could see most of them nodding with approval. The discontent with the imperial policy towards Britannia was evident. The implication of Macro's last sentence was not lost on them.

'He won't last forever,' someone muttered.

'Then what, you fool?' the veteran snapped. 'You think we'll find a better emperor than Claudius waiting in the wings?'

'Could hardly be worse. That lad, Nero, has a good heart, and he likes the Guards. He gets round the camp. He'll look after us.'

'I've seen it all before. Young Gaius Caligula was just the same, and look how he ended up.'

At that moment there was a loud chorus of shouts as a gang of tough-looking men in grimy tunics entered the inn. They had clearly had some drink and were in good spirits – until their leader, a giant of a man, saw the Praetorians and held his arms out to stop his followers.

The other customers glanced over and the conversation rapidly began to die away.

'Well look over there, lads!' he called over his shoulder. 'We've been honoured by the Emperor's toy soldiers tonight! Look at 'em. Filling their guts with wine. Just as they stuff themselves with good bread and fine cuts of meat.'

'Who on earth is that?' asked Cato.

'Cestius,' Fuscius replied. 'He's the leader of the Viminal gang – a pretty tough crew. They drink in here from time to time.'

'He looks a tough enough proposition all on his own.'

'He is. Used to wrestle in the arena. Broke two men's necks with his bare hands.'

Cestius folded his massive arms and glared at the Praetorians for a moment before he continued. 'Oh yes, they do well enough, while the rest of Rome goes hungry. I've never seen such a bunch of pansy layabouts in my life. All spit and polish and full of bullshit. There's not a real soldier amongst 'em. I've seen harder-looking men begging in the gutters.'

Some of the customers had risen from their tables and were making for the exit as unobtrusively as possible. More followed and the Praetorians at the other tables got to their feet unsteadily and backed towards the table where Cato, Macro and the others were still sitting.

'This looks like a nasty situation,' Cato muttered.

'Perhaps.' Macro nodded. 'But we'll see what these Praetorian lads are made of.'

'Frankly, I'd rather they, and we, stayed in one piece.'

Cato stared at Cestius as the gang leader began to make his way through the rapidly emptying inn towards them.

Over by the counter the innkeeper was frantically retrieving as many jars and cups as possible before the storm broke. He dumped the first load behind the counter and dived out for some more while there was still a moment's grace. Cestius and his thugs crowded towards the Praetorians, and Cato saw that some of them were brazen enough to defy the law and carry knives in their belts. Others had heavy leather saps. Cato had no weapons with him and a quick glance around revealed that only a handful of Praetorians had come out armed, mostly with small knives they used to cut meat and bread.

'There's a law against going armed within the walls of the city,' Cato announced as boldly as he could. There was a brief pause as everyone looked at him in baffled amusement.

Cestius stood a short distance from the soldiers. 'This inn is on my turf. My turf, my rules. I'm afraid you're going to have to leave, boys,' he said with false civility. 'Right now.'

Fuscius looked round at the other Praetorians and his hand reached for his cloak, until Macro swatted it away.

'We're just having a quiet drink, friend.' Macro smiled at Cestius. 'As you can see, there's plenty of space for both of us, thanks to your entrance.'

The corner of Cestius's mouth lifted in a half smile, half sneer. 'Ah, but a quiet drink is exactly what I want, and a mob of loudmouth Praetorians is going to spoil the mood.' He jerked a thumb over his shoulder. 'So you get out.'

Macro looked disappointed. 'There's no need to be so touchy.' He paused and sniffed. 'Besides, you and your lads stink like you just crawled out of some sewer. No offence, but you do. Now, for the sake of a quiet night, let's have no trouble, eh? You and your lot can drink over there, in the far corner. You can have the first round on us, since, as you say, we can afford it. Come!' He reached for the nearest jug and filled a cup. Then he turned towards Cestius, took a pace towards him and offered up the cup. Cestius's gaze was instinctively drawn to the cup. That's when Macro smashed the jug into the giant's face. There was a splintering crack as the jug burst in a rush of red wine. Cestius staggered back a step, blood streaming from his crushed nose. Macro threw the handle down and his parade-ground bellow filled the inn.

'GET STUCK IN!'

Snatching up a stool, Macro hurled himself towards the gang members. One, with more presence of mind than his comrades, leaped in front of his leader and stood in a crouch as Macro's stool arced towards his head. Those Praetorians who had not yet had too much wine scrambled forward, swinging punches, while the others lurched into action clumsily. The man in front of Macro threw his arm up to try to ward off the blow but his forearm smashed into the side of his head and there was a crunch as a bone broke, and a cry of agony. Cato bunched his hands into fists and looked for an opponent.

'What are you waiting for?' Macro called over his shoulder. 'An invitation? Hit someone!'

Both sides were matched in terms of numbers and the brawl began to spill out across the floor of the inn.

'Noooo!' cried the innkeeper as he snatched a jug from a table just as it went crashing over under the impact of two men wrestling as they tried to grab each other's throats. More tables and benches went over, together with the remaining pottery cups and wine jugs, and dark jets of wine exploded across the floor. Cato stepped forward, fists raised. In front of him one of the Praetorians stumbled to one side, exposing a stocky man with a shock of dark hair. His mouth was open, revealing only a handful of crooked teeth. Cato lunged forward and threw his right fist at the man's face. The blow connected on the chin, snapping the jaw shut, and the man fell to his knees. At once Cato pressed his advantage, striking each side of the head before the man slumped on to his side, dazed.

A quick glance revealed that Macro was still attacking Cestius, slamming fist after fist against the man's head and body in a flurry of powerful blows. Incredibly the gang leader was weathering the assault and had raised his fists to block Macro's punches. Cestius shook his head in an attempt to clear his vision and then went for Macro with a deep growl that Cato heard above all the other groans, grunts, cries and crashes that filled the inn. Cestius lashed out with his left, a boxer's punch that caught Macro on the shoulder and knocked him back a step. The right swung out and round in a sweeping blow that Macro had plenty of time to duck and get an upper cut of his own in. Cestius's head juddered but he stepped forward and punched Macro again, this time catching him full in the ribs with the first and striking him below the left eye with the second, snapping his head back. Macro reeled away, against the table he had been sitting at shortly before. The cups and jugs shot off the top of the table and crashed to the floor. Macro was dazed, blinking wildly, as the giant loomed over him. Cestius grinned cruelly and punched him again in the stomach and then on the mouth, splitting his lip.

Cato realised that unless he moved quickly Macro was going to be severely beaten. He thrust aside one of the Praetorians as he desperately tried to make his way to his friend's side. Cato never saw the blow, but his head jerked to one side and he instantly had double vision. Instinctively he lowered his head and raised his fists protectively and the next punch glanced off his elbow. Ahead he saw Fuscius had downed an opponent and was beating the man with the leg from a shattered stool.

'Fuscius!' Cato shouted. The young guardsman looked up and Cato shouted, 'Save Macro!'

Fuscius frowned and Cato felt a cold tremor of fear in his guts as he realised what he had said. He drew a sharp breath and cried out again. 'Look out for Calidus!' He raised his arm and pointed to make sure his instruction was clear. Fuscius turned and saw the gang leader throw another punch; he tightened his fist round the stool leg and came up behind Cestius, raising the leg high over his head.

'Watch it, chief!' someone cried and Cestius began to turn. But it was too late and the stool leg cracked down on the top of his head. His jaw dropped in a groan and Fuscius hit him two more times. Blood streamed down, plastering his hair to his scalp. Fuscius changed tactics and now rammed the end of the leg into the giant's stomach, doubling him over.

'That's it!' Cato called out, crouching as he backed towards Macro. He exchanged a few blows and kicks with two of the gang and then he was beside Macro. Meanwhile Fuscius kneed his opponent in the face and then struck him about the head a few more times until the gang leader tumbled on to his back, arms flailing as he took two men down with him in a sprawling heap of limbs.

'Look out!' a voice cried. 'Someone's called for the urban cohort! Let's get out of here!'

The first of the gang members peeled away from the brawl and headed for the entrance. Others, bowed and staggering, struggled after them.

'The chief! He's down. Here, you, help me!'

Two of the gang hurried to their dazed leader and grasped him under the arms. Fuscius went to hit the downed giant again, then paused, as if unsure of the ethics of hitting a defenceless man. By the time the desire to take advantage of the situation had won out, the gang leader had been dragged halfway to the door and his boots were scrabbling for purchase as he tried to stand. By now both sides had mutually decided to break up the fight and were warily drawing apart, leaving tables and benches knocked over amid the shards of broken pottery and puddles and splatters of wine. The innkeeper covered his face with his hands and shuddered.

Cato knelt down by his friend's side. Macro was slumped against a pillar, eyes flickering as blood coursed from cuts to his brow, nose and lip.

'Hey, Calidus?' Cato said loudly. 'You hear me?'

'Wheerrrgghh.' Macro licked his split lip and winced, then spat out a gobbet of blood. 'What the fuck happened? What hit me?' His eyes opened wide and he recognised Cato. 'Lad! We're under attack! To arms!'

'He's lost it.' Fuscius chuckled as he knelt beside Cato. 'Knocked senseless.'

Cato nodded. He was afraid that in his dazed state

Macro might say something that would give them away. 'Fuscius, get me a jug of water. Now.'

'Right.' The guardsman rose up and made his way over to the innkeeper to make his request. While the innkeeper sighed and went to do as he was bid, Cato leant close to Macro's ear and whispered, 'You've been in a fight and were knocked down. But you're all right. Just remember the mission. Don't say a word until you can think straight. Got that? Macro! Did you get that?'

'Yes . . . Fight. Keep much shut.'

'Good man.' Cato sighed and patted him on the shoulder. He stood up as Fuscius returned with a pitcher of water and handed it over. Cato stepped back and took aim before slinging the contents of the pitcher in Macro's face. The torrent of water caused Macro to jolt up and splutter. His eyes opened wildly and he looked as if he might attack the first thing he saw. Then he recognised Cato and opened his mouth to speak, frowned as he remembered his friend's warning and clamped his jaw shut instead. He breathed deeply for a moment before he spoke thickly. 'The other bloke?'

'Is out for the count. Thanks to Fuscius here. Otherwise you'd be on the way to the Underworld by now. Fuscius, help me get him up on his feet. Before the urban troops arrive.'

But it was too late. The sound of boots drumming on the paved street echoed round the square. The Praetorians were helping their injured up when the first of the troops entered the inn. An optio with a long staff strode in and looked around. 'What's this then? What's going on here? I was told it was a brawl.'

'No,' Cato protested. 'We were just having a drink

when the Viminal gang charged in and started beating the place up.'

'A likely story!' The optio snorted. 'Bloody Praetorians think you can pull the wool over my eyes.'

'It's true, man!' Cato shouted at him. 'They've only got a short start on you. They'll be making for the bottom of the Viminal. If you go now and stop wasting bloody time, you can still catch 'em.'

'You catch 'em!' the innkeeper cried out to the optio. 'Someone's got to pay for all this!'

'And it won't be us,' Cato said firmly. 'Not if the Emperor has anything to say about it. He'll not take sides against his Praetorians. Better to go after the gang.'

The optio bit his lip and then turned and left the inn.

'Come on, boys!' Cato heard him call out and then the sound of their boots hurrying off filled the air.

Cato eased Macro up on to his feet and slung his friend's arm across his shoulder. Fuscius took the other side.

'Praetorians!' Cato called out. 'We are leaving!'

They stumbled outside and then in a loose column headed out of the square and up the street in the direction of the Praetorian camp.

'Thanks for helping him out,' Cato said to Fuscius through gritted teeth. 'You probably saved Calidus's life.'

'Yes, I did, didn't I?' The young guardsman's voice filled with pride. 'Do you think he'll be all right?'

'He will. Trust me, he's had worse in his time.'

'Good.'

They went on in silence for a moment before Fuscius spoke softly. 'By the way, who's Macro?'

Cato felt his heart miss a beat. 'Macro? Must have had

109

a bit too much to drink. Macro was a mate of ours back in Britannia. Slip of the tongue. That's all.'

'Oh, right,' Fuscius responded vaguely. 'Slip of the tongue then.'

CHAPTER EIGHT

'Right then, since you two have got such a nice shiner each, you're bound to draw attention to yourselves. If any of the imperial family speak to you, be ready to respond with the appropriate form of address.' Tigellinus sighed impatiently as the century, dressed in their duty togas, crossed the Forum towards the palace gates two days later. 'One more time. The Emperor?' He was marching beside Macro and Cato and had been running through some of the basic protocols since they left the camp.

'We call him "sir" outside of the palace, and "your imperial majesty" inside,' Cato replied.

Tigellinus nodded, and then added quietly, 'And some can call him whatever they like behind his back.'

Cato turned to look at him with a surprised expression. Tigellinus smiled thinly.

'You won't be so shocked when you've been here for more than a month, Capito. You'll see for yourself the truth of the situation. Claudius has always been ruled by his freedmen and his wives. Messallina had him eating out of her hand, until she made a play for the throne and got the chop. Her replacement's a sharp one.' Tigellinus's smile warmed for a moment. 'Agrippina knows exactly how to tweak his strings. His or any other man's. Now then, what about the Empress?'

'"Imperial majesty" in the palace and in public,' Cato replied. 'Since she does not have to worry about public opinion.'

Tigellinus turned to him sharply. 'That's enough, Capito. You're a bloody ranker. You don't get to comment on such matters. Just the correct form of address from now on. Clear?'

'Yes, Optio.'

The column stopped at the gate to relieve the section on duty and then continued up the broad staircase to the main entrance hall of the imperial palace. Cato had been raised within these walls many years ago and felt a peculiar tingle in his scalp at the thought of all that he had seen as a child on the fringes of the imperial court. For a moment he wondered how many of the slaves he had been raised with were still serving in the palace. He had been a fresh-faced youth when he left, but now he was older, his hair was a military crop and he bore the scars of his years in the army. He would not be recognised even if he did encounter someone from his past.

At the head of the column of four centuries marched Tribune Burrus and at each station of the first watch he barked the orders to relieve those who had been on duty during the night. There were three watches in all, the first running from first light to noon, the second from noon to dusk, and the third – the least popular – guarding the palace through the night. The night watch operated with only two centuries since they simply had to guard the entrances and patrol the public precincts of the palace. The private suites were protected by the German bodyguards.

At length, it was the turn of Tigellinus's section as the column passed through the palace and into the gardens of the imperial family, built on a terrace, surrounded on three sides by a colonnade. The fourth side had a marble balustrade and overlooked the Forum. Tigellinus and his men took up their positions around the garden, with Cato and Macro being assigned to the entrance of a small hedged area around a fountain. Marble benches, with red cushions, were arranged near the fountain. Due to the height of the garden there was little residual water pressure from the aqueduct that supplied the palace and only a small jet of water emerged from the fountain to tinkle pleasantly into the surrounding pond.

'Nice.' Macro nodded as he looked round the neatly kept garden. 'A very restful spot indeed. With the kind of view you could get killed for.'

'It's been known to happen,' Cato replied as he adjusted his toga. It was a cumbersome thing and he kept getting the interior folds snagged on the handles of the sword he wore underneath.

'What are you doing?' Macro stared at him. 'You look like you've picked up a particularly nasty itch off some tart.'

'It's this stupid toga.'

'Lad, you are pretty hopeless sometimes.' Macro shook his head. 'Here, let me sort you out before the whole bloody thing gets tangled.' He stepped over to Cato and pulled a length of the cloth up, over the shoulder and then folded it across his friend's left arm. 'There. See how that goes?'

'Thanks . . . Still feels ridiculous.'

'Well, if anyone can make it look ridiculous, you can.'

Macro continued looking round the garden again. Tigellinus and the others had taken up their stations and wandered along their beats, as if they were civilians come to take in the pleasant surroundings. 'So this is what we do? Just swan around up here for the next five hours? How is that going to get us any nearer to exposing this conspiracy that Narcissus is so keen to uncover?'

'I don't know. We just keep our eyes and ears open.'

The sun rose higher into the sky, accompanied by a gentle breeze that ruffled the topmost boughs of the trees in the garden and carried off the smoke from the fires burning in the city. Despite the pleasant day and the peaceful scene, Cato's mind was troubled. While there were unmistakable signs that the Emperor's authority was slipping, there was little direct evidence of a conspiracy. Prefect Geta's tough training regime was no more than what was expected of any good commanding officer. And they had seen no sign of sudden wealth among the ranks since they had arrived at the Praetorian camp. Today was the first day they were to put into practice what they had learned about their duties from Tigellinus. Cato paused to think a moment about the optio. Tigellinus, he had discovered from the other guardsmen in Lurco's century, had been with the Praetorians for just over a year, after having been recalled from exile, along with a number of other people who had fallen foul of Messallina. Most were friends or servants of Agrippina who had been persecuted by her predecessor. Quite what Tigellinus had done to be sent into exile no one could say.

Cato's thoughts were interrupted by the sound of voices and he turned towards the colonnade to see a stooped silver-haired man in a cloak, leading two boys towards the hedged enclosure around the pond. One of the boys looked to be a teenager, long limbed and with a fine head of curly dark hair. The other was younger by a few years and was solidly built, with fair hair. He looked down as he trailed the others, and held his hands behind his back, as if deep in thought.

The old man glanced back and called out in a thin reedy voice, 'Keep up, Britannicus! Don't dawdle.'

'Ha!' the older boy called out with a ready smile. 'Come on, little brother!'

Britannicus scowled but increased his pace nevertheless.

'Heads up,' said Cato. 'We've got company.'

They quickly stood to attention, just inside the enclosed area either side of the entrance, and stared straight ahead. The light patter of footsteps on the paved path gave way to the soft crunch of gravel as the man and two boys passed through the opening in the neatly clipped hedge. They ignored the two guards as they crossed to the pond. The old man eased himself down on to a bench and indicated that the boys should sit on the edge of the pond.

'There. Now let me collect my thoughts.' He wagged a gnarled finger. 'Ah, yes! We were going to talk about your responsibilities.'

'Boring,' said the older boy. 'Why can't we discuss something more important?'

'Because your adopted father wishes you to think on your obligations, Nero. That's why.'

'But I want to talk about poetry.' His voice was plaintive and slightly husky. Cato risked a look at the tutor and his two students now that their attention was on each other. The boy, Nero, was effeminate-looking with a weak jaw and a slight pout. His eyes were dark and expressive and he regarded his tutor with an intense gaze. A short distance from him Britannicus sat resting his head in his hands as he stared down at the gravel, apparently uninterested. The tutor looked vaguely familiar and then in a flash Cato remembered him. Eurayleus. He had been one of the palace tutors when Cato was a child. Eurayleus had been tasked with the education of the children of the imperial family. As such he had little to do with the handful of other tutors who taught the sons of the palace officials and the children of the hostages that Rome kept in comfort while their elders were required to maintain treaties or apply pressure in Rome's interest. As Cato recalled his childhood he could well remember the aloof manner in which the tutor had regarded the rest of the palace staff. Their paths had only crossed once, when a young Cato had been running up and down the corridor outside the tutor's door and had received a beating.

'We will talk about poetry another time,' Eurayleus said firmly. 'Today's subject for discussion has been decided by the Emperor and neither you nor I can challenge his decision.'

'Why?' asked Nero.

'You can ask that question when you become Emperor,' the tutor replied tersely.

'If he becomes Emperor,' said Britannicus. 'Ahenobarbus is only the adopted son. I am the natural son. I should be first in line of succession.'

Nero turned to his stepbrother with a frown. 'My name is Nero.'

Britannicus shrugged. 'That's what some say. But in

your heart you will always be what you were first named. And to me, too, you will always be Ahenobarbus.'

Nero glared at him for a moment before he spoke. 'Always quick to try and cut me down to size, aren't you? Well, you may be the natural son of the Emperor, but your mother was most unnatural. So I wouldn't set too much store by the Emperor's affection for you, little Britannicus.'

'My mother is dead. She died because she was a fool. She let the power of the imperial palace go to her head.' Britannicus smiled faintly. 'How long do you think it will be before your mother does the same? Then what will become of you? At least I have common blood with my father. What do you have?'

Cato could not help looking at the younger boy, surprised by the confidence and knowingness in the tone of his voice.

'Boys! Boys!' the tutor broke in with a wave of his hand. 'That's enough. You must stop this bickering. It is not worthy of the Emperor's heirs. What would he say if he could see you now?'

'S–s–stop it!' Nero mimicked and let a little bit of spittle dribble from his lips as he stuttered, and then giggled.

The tutor frowned at him and held up his hand to quieten the boy. 'That is ungracious of you. Let there be no more digressions from today's lesson, do you hear?'

Nero nodded, struggling to stifle a smile.

'Very well. The subject today is responsibility. Especially the responsibility of an emperor to his people. Now, I could lecture you on the matter, but being Greek, I prefer to deal with this by way of protracted dialogue.'

Cato heard a long soft hiss of expelled air come from Macro at the tutor's words.

'Let's start with you, Nero, since you are in high spirits today. What do you think are the primary responsibilities of an emperor?'

Nero folded his hands together and thought for a moment before he spoke. 'His first duty is to make Rome safe, obviously. Rome must be defended from its enemies, and its wider interests must be protected. Then the emperor must look after his people. He must feed them, but not just with food. He must give them his love, like a father loves his children.'

Britannicus sniffed derisively, but Nero ignored him and continued.

'He must teach them the important values: love of Rome, love of art, love of poetry.'

'Why these things?'

'Because without them we are nought but animals that scratch a living and then die unmissed.'

Britannicus shook his head. The movement was caught by the tutor.

'You have something to say?'

'I do.' Britannicus looked up defiantly. 'Ahenobarbus is too influenced by that new personal teacher of his, Seneca. What is poetry to the common people? Nothing. They need food, shelter and entertainment. That's what they want from their emperor. He can do his best to give some of them that, but not all. So what is his duty? It's simple. His duty is to uphold order and fight chaos. He needs to defend Rome from those within as much as from the barbarians who live beyond our frontiers.'

'That is a very cynical line of thought, young Britannicus,' the tutor commented.

'I am young. But I am learned beyond my years.'

'Yes, your precocity has been noted.'

'And not approved of.' Britannicus smiled coldly.

'There is a wisdom that comes with age and no other way. Until you have walked in the boots of other men, you are not wise. Only well read.'

Britannicus regarded the man with a world-weary expression. 'Perhaps if you had walked in my boots you would understand my cynicism. I have a family that is not a family but a colony of killers. I have a father who no longer treats me like a son. I have no mother, and I have a . . . brother who will surely kill me if ever he becomes Emperor.' The boy paused. 'Walk in those boots, Eurayleus, and see if you do not have to live on your wits.'

The tutor stared at him with a sad expression and then drew a deep breath. 'Let us continue. Nero thinks that the common man can have poetry in his life.'

'Yes, I do,' Nero said fervently.

'Does he have this capacity innately? Or must it be taught to him?' The tutor turned to Macro and Cato as if noticing them for the first time. 'Take these two men. Soldiers. They know little but the art of destruction, which is the opposite of knowledge. They know weapons and drill, and spend their leisure time in mindless bouts of drinking, womanising and visits to the arena. Is that not so, soldier? You there!' He pointed at Macro. 'Answer me.'

Macro thought a moment and nodded. 'Pretty much sums it up, sir.'

'You see? How can you expect to teach such men to appreciate the finer sentiments of poetry? How can you induce them to know the subtle shades of expression upon which the finest literature turns? They are a class apart. Why, look at them. See those black eyes? Not content with their dullard existence of the mind, they compound their denigration by engaging in brawls. What hope is there of them finding their way to the great works of the finest thinkers? I doubt that they can even read. You there, the other man. Tell me, have you ever read the works of Aristotle?'

'Which, sir? *The Poetics*, *Politics*, *Ethics*, *Metaphysics*, *Nicomachean Ethics* or *De Anima*?'

The tutor stared at Cato for a moment, nonplussed.

Britannicus chuckled. 'Please continue, Eurayleus. Your line of argument is most intriguing.'

The tutor struggled to his feet and gestured to his pupils. 'Come, let's find somewhere more, er, private, to continue the discussion.'

He walked straight between Cato and Macro without meeting their eyes. Nero followed him, pausing only to wink at Cato and pat him on the shoulder before he left the enclosure. The smaller boy was slower to get up and he came and stood before Cato and stared up at him.

'What is your name, Praetorian?'

'Capito, sir.'

'Capito . . . You are rather different to the other Praetorians, aren't you?'

'I'm not sure what you mean, sir.'

'Yes you do. I shall watch you. I don't forget a face. I may need you one day. Tell me, Capito, if you could choose your new emperor when Claudius dies, who would it be? Me or Ahenobarbus?'

'The choice is not mine to make, sir.'

'But you are a Praetorian, and when the time comes, the Praetorians will have to make a choice, as they did when my father became Emperor. So who would you choose?'

Cato was stuck. He dared not provide an answer for the boy. Moreover, he was surprised by the mature depth to his eyes and the shrewd, knowing manner of his speech.

Britannicus shrugged and kicked a small stone towards the pond, and for a moment looked just like any other boy his age. Then he spoke again. 'When the time comes, you will have to make a choice. For me there will be no choice. I must try to kill Ahenobarbus before he kills me.' He looked up at Cato again, staring into his eyes without any trace of self-consciousness. 'I'm sure we will run into each other again, Praetorian. Until then, farewell.'

He folded his hands behind his back again and walked off quickly on his short stocky legs to catch up with his tutor and stepbrother. As the sound of footsteps faded, Macro turned to Cato and puffed his cheeks out.

'Phew, he's a strange one, that Britannicus. An old man in a boy's body. Never seen the like.'

Cato nodded. There had been something very unsettling about the boy. Something that had left Cato feeling quite cold. He had about him an air of ruthless calculation and Cato had no doubt that Britannicus had meant what he had said about killing Nero when the time was right. The child would have his backers too – men like Narcissus who wanted to ensure that they retained their positions of influence when Claudius passed into the shades. However, it was clear to Cato that the imperial secretary would be dealing with a boy emperor possessing far greater intelligence than the present incumbent. Britannicus would be his own man. But what kind of man? Cato wondered. There was some truth in what Eurayleus had said. Intelligence was one thing. But unallied to wisdom and empathy it could easily result in a cruel tyranny of reason every bit as damaging to Rome as Caligula's madness had been. Even at his present age, Britannicus was something of a force to be reckoned with.

'What do you make of the other one?' asked Macro. 'Nero.'

'He seemed harmless enough. Head seemed a bit lost in the clouds but his heart's in the right place.'

'That's what I thought. And he's popular with the lads in the Praetorian Guard.'

'Yes.' Cato could see that Nero had an easy charm about him. In the inevitable struggle for succession, that would be a considerable advantage over his more intelligent but cold stepbrother. Cato felt a leaden sense of foreboding weigh down his heart. Neither boy was ready to succeed the Emperor. It would be some years before they had the experience to rule wisely. For that reason, it was vital that Claudius survived long enough to see the order and stability of his reign continue for as long as possible. If Rome fell into the hands of either boy then she would face a danger every bit as grave as that posed by the barbarian hordes biding their time beyond the empire's frontiers.

CHAPTER NINE

The day before the Accession games were to be held was taken up with preparations. A temporary arena had been under construction on the parade ground outside the camp for several days. When the workmen had packed up their tools and departed, one of the Praetorian cohorts was tasked with painting the timber stands and decorating the imperial box with fresh garlands of oak leaves. A large purple canopy was erected over the seating area of the imperial box to shield the Emperor and his family from the elements. On the front of the box some of the Praetorians, with more artistic skills than the rest of their comrades, painted a large mural depicting Claudius being acclaimed by the guardsmen on the day he had become Emperor. Another mural showed the Emperor handing out gold coins to the soldiers in order to remind them of the special beneficence that he showed to his Praetorians, and the loyalty that they owed him in return.

All was complete by the evening of the twenty-fifth day of January. The arena was large enough to seat every soldier in the camp behind the low barrier wall. There was a wide gate opposite the imperial box to admit the participants of the games, and two small exits at each side for those injured or killed to be removed from the freshly spread sand that covered the parade ground. At head-quarters the halls and colonnades had been filled with tables and benches ready for the following evening's feast. Wagons laden with bread, cured meat, cheese, fruit and wine had trundled into the camp, from the surrouding countryside, where their contents were unloaded into the storerooms under the watchful eyes of junior officers to ensure that there was no pilfering.

As night settled across the Praetorian camp, Macro and Cato sat in the hot room of the bathhouse. After exchanging a few pleasantries with their new comrades they had taken one of the benches in the corner where they would not be overheard by the other men scattered about the sweltering chamber. Some of them were engaged in conversation but most sat with sweat coursing down their bodies, relishing the heat.

A drop fell from Macro's heavy brow and made him blink. He wiped his forehead clear on the back of his forearm and glanced at Cato. His friend sat deep in thought, staring at the tessellated floor in front of him. Earlier in the day Cato had visited the safe house and found a message from Septimus demanding a progress report. They were to meet him there in two days' time.

'Sestertius for your thoughts,' Macro said softly.

'Eh?' Cato looked round.

'I know the look. What's bothering you?'

'Lack of progress. I just don't see how we are supposed to do what Narcissus wants. It's not as if the Liberators are advertising for new members, nor have we uncovered anything particularly sinister.'

'What about Sinius?' asked Macro. 'He seems like a suspicious character.'

'True. But we have no proof of his involvement in any conspiracy.' Cato chewed his lip. 'Which begs the question; is Narcissus jumping at shadows? What if those who ambushed the bullion convoy were just after the silver?'

'It's possible,' Macro conceded. 'But what about that man Narcissus had tortured? He said he was working for the Liberators, and he gave up a name.'

'That's no surprise. The interrogators know their craft and can break any man. How reliable is the information given under torture? After a while I imagine a man would say anything to try to put an end to his torment.'

Macro thought a moment and nodded. 'All right. But let's suppose the information is accurate. We should concentrate our attention on Centurion Lurco when he gets back to the camp. Follow him and see who he talks to. If he's a ringleader of the conspiracy then we'll soon know about it.'

'I suppose so.' Cato sighed. 'In any case, he's the only real possibility we have right now.'

They stayed a little longer before using the brass strigils to scrape off the grime that had sweated out of their skin. Then they moved through to the cold room and jumped into the pool where the shock of the chilled water made them gasp. Cato struck out briskly, swimming two lengths of the pool before he climbed out and hurried out to the changing area where he rubbed himself down with one of the towels drying over the rack above the hypocaust flues. Macro joined him and they began to dress.

'You know,' Macro began, 'if there is no conspiracy and we're looking for a gang of thieves then that's going to make things much harder for us. A conspiracy needs supporters to achieve its ends. Anyone involved in a simple theft is going to want to keep it close to their chests.'

Cato nodded.

'In which case,' Macro continued, 'we're pretty well stuffed, since Narcissus isn't going to reward us for failing to produce the results he wants. Insane as it sounds, we'd better pray that there is a conspiracy to unearth.'

As they reached the entrance to the barracks, Tigellinus was waiting for them. He jerked a thumb towards the centurion's quarters.

'Lurco is back. He wants to see you.' Tigellinus smirked. 'He sent for you over an hour ago. Shame I couldn't find you – the centurion is not a man who is inclined to tolerate delay.' The optio gave a dry laugh before he sauntered off to the squad's room. 'Good luck.'

Macro's lips pressed together as he waited until Tigellinus was out of earshot, then he hissed through clenched teeth, 'Bastard. He knew where we were. He's set us up.'

Cato shrugged. 'Nothing we can do about it now. Come on.'

They made their way to the door of the small office adjoining the centurion's private quarters and saw that it was open. Lurco was standing at the window, looking out across the wall of the camp and over the city, illuminated by the twinkling sparks of torches and lamps. He stood quite still as he stared in the direction of the imperial palace, his back dimly lit by the single oil lamp glimmering on his desk. Cato gestured to Macro and they stood directly outside the door frame. Taking a deep breath, Cato rapped on the wooden frame.

'You sent for us, sir?'

Lurco turned quickly and Cato saw that the centurion was younger than he had been expecting, in his mid-twenties. His hair was dark and artfully arranged in oiled curls above a finely featured face that was on the pretty side of handsome. His good looks hardened into a frown.

'Are you the new men? Capito and Calidus?' he asked in a thin, high-pitched voice.

'Yes, sir.'

'Don't just stand there. Enter.'

They strode in and stood before their commander's desk. He was taller than Cato and by tilting his head back slightly he gave even more of an impression of looking down on the other men.

'Where have you been? I sent for you ages ago. Why weren't you in the barracks?'

'Beg your pardon, sir, but we were in the bathhouse,' Macro explained.

'Shirking some duties no doubt.'

'No, sir. We're veterans. We've been excused fatigues.'

'Veterans?' Lurco sneered. 'So, you think the world owes you a living? You think you're better than the rest of us no doubt. Just because you've got some mud on your boots, and a few scratches.' He flicked his hand dismissively in the direction of Cato's face. 'I don't care if you're veterans. The men of my century are all the same as far as I am concerned. And now it seems you all depend on me so much that I have been ordered to cut my leave short and return to the camp for tomorrow's tedious little show put on for the Emperor. I could have been at a party in the city having a good fuck with some senator's wife or daughter, but no, I'm stuck here in the camp. So if I have to give up my friends to be here, then the bloody least you can do is have the damned good grace to come when you are summoned.'

Cato felt an instinctive dislike of the man, and was suddenly painfully conscious of the scar that had ruined his own face. Lurco, with his finely arranged good looks, was the kind of young officer who would be a success with the capital's ladies. Possibly the kind of person that a woman like Julia might encounter and take a fancy to. It was a foolish thought, Cato told himself, angry that he had relaxed his hold on the feelings he had been struggling to suppress.

'We came as soon as we were told you wanted to see us, sir,' said Macro.

'Well, that's not soon enough,' Lurco snapped. He stared at them, his nostrils flared. 'Well, now we know each other, and you know what I stand for. In future when I give an order I expect you to obey it at once. Fail to do so and I will see to it that your veteran status is revoked, and I'll have you up to your necks in shit doing latrine fatigues for the rest of the year. Do I make myself clear?'

'Yes, sir,' Macro and Cato replied.

Lurco stared at them. 'Tomorrow we play host to the Emperor. Our cohort will be placed either side of the imperial box. That means I want a good turnout. My century will be the smartest unit in the entire Praetorian Guard, or I'll know the reason why. Don't you dare let me down. Got that?'

'Yes, sir.'

'Then leave me. Go. Get out of my sight.'

They saluted, turned, and Macro led as they strode out

of the room. They made their way to the stairs and Macro's breath escaped with a hearty sigh. 'What a complete bloody arsehole. I'll bet the uppity bastard has been turned down by some woman. Now he's taking it out on us. As for that bollocks about veterans . . . Damn! The man owes us a little more respect.' He fumed for a moment before continuing, 'It's all down to Tigellinus. He knew where we were. He was in the room when we left for the baths. I'll have words with the optio, so help me.'

'Better not,' Cato responded. 'Not if we want to avoid being punished for insubordination.'

'I was thinking of something a little more forceful than insubordination,' Macro said darkly. 'He needs seven shades kicked out of him. I know his type. He'll set us up at every opportunity. He's the kind of optio who will do all he can to pull the ladder up behind him now that he's sitting pretty waiting for his appointment to the centurionate.'

'Forget it,' Cato said calmly. 'We're not going to be here long enough for him to make our lives a misery. So, we'll ignore him and keep our minds on the job, yes?'

Macro grunted. 'If it turns out that our dear optio is part of any conspiracy then I shall be sure to offer my services to anyone who gets to interrogate him.'

At dawn Tribune Burrus gave orders for his cohort to assemble outside the barracks. The sky was overcast and the air felt damp and clammy as the soldiers formed up in the centuries and stood at ease. Macro and Cato were among the first to fall in and watched as the other guardsmen stumbled out of the building, some still fastening their belts about their tunics. Centurion Lurco was one of the last to emerge, bleary eyed and pale faced.

Cato leant towards Macro. 'He's been drinking.'

'Poor lad must have had his heart broken,' Macro responded without a trace of sympathy.

Tigellinus, positioned two paces in front of the first rank, turned his head and bellowed, 'Silence! Next man who utters a single fucking word is on a charge!'

Lurco winced at the sound as he shuffled into place in front of the optio and the century's standard bearer. When the last men of the cohort were in place, there was a short silence before the sturdy figure of Tribune Burrus stepped out of the main entrance of the cohort's barrack block. The senior centurion of the cohort, the trecenarius, drew a deep breath and called out, 'Commanding officer present!'

The men stood to attention with a loud crash of nailed boots on the paving stones. Burrus strode out to stand in front of his command, hands clasped behind his back as he puffed his chest out and ran his good eye over the lines of men standing in their centuries.

'Most of you know the drill. There's quite a few who have joined our ranks since the last Accession games. I'll spell it out so that we all know what is expected of us. The Emperor, his family and selected guests of the imperial court will be spending the day with the Praetorian Guard. As the unit that will be in closest proximity to the imperial party we are the standard by which the rest of the Guard will be judged. You are on your best behaviour and I will have the balls off any man who gets drunk or acts in any way that discredits the honour of the Praetorian Guard.' He paused a moment and then continued in a less harsh tone. 'As we know, the Emperor has his funny ways. He is inclined to stammer and when he gets excited he has a tendency to slobber at the mouth. It is not the most edifying of sights, I grant you. However, Claudius is the Emperor and we have all sworn an oath to honour and obey him. So there will be no laughing, nor even the faintest of tittering, if the old boy gets going. Is that clear? I can assure you it will be no laughing matter for any man I catch mocking the Emperor.' Burrus turned and paced a short distance before turning back.

'There's one other thing. The new Empress will be joining the games for the first time. Now, I am certain that some of you are still a little surprised, shocked even, by the fact that the Emperor has decided to marry his own niece.'

There were discreet murmurs from some of the guardsmen and Cato was aware of the men stirring uncomfortably on either side of him. Burrus raised a hand to silence them.

'Whatever your feelings, the marriage was sanctioned by the senate and so it is lawful. The morality of the situation is not our concern. We are soldiers and we obey orders, right or wrong, and that is the end of it. So, if any of you harbour any misgivings about the Emperor's new wife, keep them to yourselves. That is an order. I don't want to hear one word of discontent pass your lips.' He paused again to let his words sink in. 'One last thing. Today is supposed to strengthen the ties between the Emperor and the Praetorian Guard. Claudius is paying for the entertainment and the feast that follows it. Therefore it would be polite of us to express our gratitude at every occasion. You will cheer for him and his family as if your lives depended on it. That should please the old boy no end. A happy emperor is a generous emperor. Every time you applaud him, it's money in the pay chest. Or will be, whenever he gets round to presenting the next donative to the Guard . . . The imperial party is expected to arrive at the camp two hours after sunrise. Every man is to be in his seat before then, suited and booted. That's all!'

As the tribune turned back towards the entrance to the barracks, the senior centurion bellowed, 'Cohort, dismissed!'

As the command echoed back from the walls of the barracks, the men stood at ease and then began to fall out of formation. Macro was staring after the retreating tribune.

'Well, that was pithy and to the point.' He looked up at the sky. 'Might be an idea to fetch our cloaks before we get some decent seats.'

By the time they had climbed the stairs at the back of the temporary arena, hundreds of men had already settled in their places. Burrus and his men had been assigned the seats flanking the imperial box which rose above the northern side of the arena to take whatever warmth was offered by the sun. Unlike the raked seating erected for the Praetorians, the imperial box was constructed on a platform level with the rearmost seats. Cato pointed them out.

'Up there.'

'But if we want a good view of the entertainment we should go to the front,' Macro protested.

'It's the Emperor and his party we want a good view of. That's the best spot.'

Macro muttered something under his breath, took a sorrowful look at the empty seats right by the arena and then turned to follow his friend up the steep stairs between the rows of seating. At the top Cato looked into the imperial box and then shuffled a short distance from it to allow the curve of the seating to afford a better view of the imperial party. Satisfied, he sat down. Macro looked at the rapidly filling ranks of benches stretching out in front of him and sighed.

'Nice view,' he said flatly.

'It's good for our purposes,' Cato replied, pulling his cloak on and easing the hood back so that his head was exposed.

Around them the Praetorians streamed in through the entrances and hurried towards the best of the remaining seats. The air swelled with good-natured conversation as the light slowly strengthened. The sky was still overcast, but a lighter patch marked the position of the sun as it struggled into the heavens and shed a little more warmth over the city and the surrounding countryside. The officers were among the last to enter, picking their spots in the front row and displacing the rankers who were already seated there. Macro smiled at the sight, instinctively enjoying their disappointment. Directly below them Tribune Burrus and his centurions took their places and behind them sat the optios and standard bearers. Cato watched Lurco settle down close to the imperial box, but not so close as to be out of sight of those sitting at the fringes of the Emperor's entourage. He wore an eye-catching gold bracelet on his left arm and no doubt hoped to draw the attention of a prospective patron to further his career. Tigellinus was sitting behind and to one side of his centurion and Cato could read the contempt in his expression as the optio turned to regard Lurco.

At the appointed time the uneven tramp of boots from the direction of the Viminal Gate announced the approach of the imperial party. Mounted German bodyguards led the way, and then came the first of the litters bearing the Emperor's guests. Slaves, neatly dressed in fresh tunics, laboured under the load of the carrying spars, while those inside the litters chatted freely. A section of eight more German guards on foot came into view through the city wall, their bushy beards and strange armour making them appear barbaric. Then came the litter carrying Agrippina and Nero, and behind that the litter bearing the Emperor himself, accompanied by Britannicus. More litters followed carrying the rest of the party: Narcissus, Pallas, Seneca – Nero's new tutor, recently recalled from exile – and lastly those senators and their wives honoured with an invitation to join the Emperor.

The column halted outside the entrance to the imperial box and the lowest-ranking guests hurried from their litters to take their places before the Emperor and his family took their seats. The prefect of the Praetorian Guard, Geta, emerged from the imperial box and bowed to the Emperor as he sat in his litter. The prefect exchanged a few words with Claudius before joining the other guests in the box.

Many of the guardsmen in the highest seats turned their heads to watch the arrivals. Cato and Macro saw Narcissus look up briefly at the faces overhead but if he saw them he gave no sign of recognition before he disappeared from view. At last the imperial party was ready to enter and Nero hopped down from his litter and held his mother's hand to help her out.

'A dutiful son,' Macro commented wryly. 'And look how he adores his stepfather and brother.'

Having seen to his mother Nero had turned to the last litter with an icy stare. Britannicus stepped out of the litter and then bowed his head respectfully as the Emperor struggled up from his embroidered purple cushions. Holding his son's hand, Claudius limped forward, head twitching, until he stood at the entrance. He smiled as he gestured for Agrippina and Nero to join them and then waited as ten of the German guards formed up ahead of the family and began to climb the stairs into the imperial box. The Praetorians watched expectantly. The bodyguards formed up at the sides and rear of the seated guests so as not to obstruct the view of the arena. Then there was a short pause before Narcissus discreetly gestured with his hand and the occupants of the box rose to their feet.

At once the Praetorians followed suit and let out a deafening cheer, rising to a crescendo as the gilded wreath on the Emperor's head bobbed into view. Claudius climbed the last few steps and walked awkwardly on to the dais where two large chairs sat side by side. Agrippina joined him and the two boys stood at each side. Claudius kept his expression neutral, struggling to contain his tic as he turned his head slowly to acknowledge the acclaim from all sides. At last he eased himself down and when he was seated, Agrippina sat, followed by the rest of the guests.

'She's a looker, all right,' Macro spoke loudly into Cato's ear. 'You can see why the old goat went for her.'

'There was more to it than her looks,' Cato replied. 'She has influence, brains, and comes with a healthy son who might be a useful heir to Claudius should Britannicus fall from favour.'

The crowd's cheering began to subside as the Praetorians started to sit down. Cato and Macro joined them and soon there was an excited hubbub as the editor of the games conferred with his officials to make certain that all was ready. Satisfied, the editor looked over the rail at the front of the imperial box and gave the nod to the four soldiers waiting on the sand below, holding their long brass horns. They raised the instruments and blasted out a series of ascending notes. At once the Praetorians fell silent and at the front of the imperial box the editor raised both his arms.

'His imperial majesty Tiberius Claudius Drusus Nero Germanicus bids his comrades of the Praetorian Guard welcome!' The editor had a finely modulated voice that carried across the arena and could be clearly heard by everyone present.

'In accordance with his desire to assure his brave soldiers that their loyalty to him is returned in kind and with great affection, his imperial majesty, in honour of the day on which the gracious citizens of Rome entrusted him with their welfare, herewith presents a day of entertainments . . .'

The editor ran through the programme, drawing appreciative rounds of applause as each item was mentioned. While he spoke, Cato's attention was focused on the imperial box. The Emperor was sitting as still as his tic allowed, his full attention on the editor. He nodded his thanks at every round of applause. Beside him

Agrippina propped her elbow on the arm of her chair and rested her head on her hand. She looked utterly bored with the preliminaries and after a while turned to look around the imperial box until her gaze fixed on the small cluster of seats where the Emperor's advisers were sitting. Narcissus was engaged in a quiet conversation with one of his companions. The other man was nodding, and then he became aware that the Empress was looking at him and he flashed a quick smile over Narcissus's shoulder. Narcissus noticed and glanced round just as the Empress looked away. There was the briefest of pauses before he continued his muted conversation.

Cato's attention turned to the other members of the box and he saw Britannicus standing stiffly by his father's side, left arm hidden under the folds of his small toga. That he wore a toga was significant. Claudius clearly wished to indicate that his son was soon to be accorded titles and honours beyond his years, just as his adopted son, Nero, had been. The latter, also dressed in a toga, had taken his mother's hand and now raised it to his lips and kissed it, lingering over it for a moment, until she drew her hand away from him.

'Did you see that?' Macro hissed. 'What does he think he's playing at? Trying to start a scandal?'

Cato looked round at the soldiers but there seemed to be no reaction to Nero's effrontery.

'Perhaps people are used to such displays,' Cato suggested. 'Let's face it, the imperial family has form. It might be innocent. It might not. Wouldn't be the first time that members of the imperial family tinkered with incest.'

Macro's lip curled in disgust. 'Perverts.'

The editor wound up his speech to another deafening cheer and Claudius smiled and raised an arm in salute to his soldiers. There was no further preamble before the first event; a boxing match between two Numidian giants. Their skin had been oiled and they gleamed like ebony as they squared up and began their bout. In the audience the Praetorians quickly fell to making wagers over the outcome and shouting the odds to each other. The fight went on for some time and the sand around the two men was flecked with blood as the leather bindings wrapped round their fists tore and gouged. Eventually a knock-down blow was landed to a mix of groans and cheers from the spectators. There followed a display of archery by a dark-skinned man in eastern robes who shot his arrows with breathtaking accuracy, even around his boy assistant as the latter stood against a straw target with his arms outstretched. Afterwards there was a short break before the editor announced the 'Trojan Pageant' – a display of horsemanship put on by the sons of Roman aristocrats. There was tolerant applause from the Praetorians.

A score of riders entered the arena wearing gilded helmets that hid their faces. Behind them came some of the guardsmen carrying target posts and straw dummies which they set up in lines across the arena. When the preparations were completed, Claudius stood up to acknowledge the salute of the leader who rode a pure white mare.

'You may b-be-be-begin!' The Emperor's head shook then he sat down heavily.

The boys took turns charging down the line of posts, slashing at the straw targets with their swords. Then they were handed light javelins and began to gallop down the line of targets, picking one to hurl their weapon at. A stiff breeze had begun to blow, making them work hard to compensate for it as they took aim. Those who missed were dropped from the competition and left the arena. Soon only three remained and the range was increased. After another pass, one more left the competition. The last two, one of whom was the leader, were fine shots and once more a furious round of betting began as the boys matched each other and the range increased. At length the leader's rival missed his target and there was another cheer from the crowd as the winner punched his fist into the air and turned his mount towards the imperial box, reining in with a spray of sand.

'Quite a rider,' said Cato. 'I wonder who he is.'

Macro shrugged. 'Just another bloody spoilt brat showing off.'

The rider raised his hands to undo the chinstraps and then quickly lifted the helmet to reveal his face. There was a surprised gasp from the crowd and then a tumultuous cheer split the air as they saw that it was Nero.

Cato glanced at the Emperor and dimly recalled seeing his stepson drift towards the rear of the box a while earlier. Nero's mother was on her feet clapping her hands with delight while the Emperor beamed. The Praetorians' cheering gradually synchronised into a repeated roaring of his name. 'Nero! Nero! Nero!'

The boy made a slow circuit of the arena, sitting haughtily in his saddle as he revelled in the cheers. Macro nudged Cato and pointed to the imperial box.

'There's one who is not so happy.'

On the dais, beside his father, was young Britannicus;

his expression hardened into a cold scowl and his right hand balled into a tight fist. He only relaxed when his rival finally left the arena and the Praetorians ceased cheering. Noon had passed and the editor announced a short interlude while the targets were removed and the arena prepared for the main entertainment of the day, ten gladiator bouts culminating with a fight between a secutor known as the 'Dove' – the current darling of the mob – and the 'Neptune of Nuceria', a retiarius. A handful of those in the imperial box hurried down the steps to relieve themselves or take refreshment in the area beneath the box.

'I'm going for a quick piss,' Macro announced, standing up.

Cato nodded as his friend squeezed past and made his way down the stairs and along to the head of the staircase leading out of the arena. Cato's mind was still preoccupied with the expression he had caught on Nero's face just before he had left the arena. There was no mistaking the light of ambition that burned there. It had been a calculated performance in front of the Praetorians and for the moment he was their darling.

Macro shook himself off and lowered his tunic. The latrine block was filled with men who were taking advantage of the intermission. He made his way outside towards the gate giving out on to the parade ground. He picked his way through the litters and the slaves squatting silently beside them until he came to the enclosure beneath the imperial box. Two German guards stood either side of the heavy red curtain flaps that covered the entrance. As Macro approached, one of them held out his hand and spoke in his harsh tongue.

'Easy there, Herman,' Macro growled. 'Just passing by. Don't get your beard in a bloody twist.'

At that moment a gust of wind whipped back the curtains and Macro had a clear view of the man Narcissus had been sitting next to in the imperial box. One of his arms was wrapped round a woman as he kissed her arched neck. His other hand was under the folds of her stola, between her legs, and her mouth gaped in ecstasy. They looked round sharply as the curtains flapped and their eyes met Macro's for what seemed a long moment. Then as abruptly as it had come, the gust died and the curtains dropped back into place. Macro had not moved and the German called out another warning.

'I'm going,' he muttered before hurrying back inside the arena. A cold tremor of anxiety ran down his spine. The woman he had just seen in the throes of ecstasy was Agrippina. The last thing he wanted was to be a witness to the infidelity of the Empress. This was dangerous knowledge. Agrippina was sure to have learned from her predecessor's mistakes and would realise the need to remove anyone who could denounce her to the Emperor.

Macro climbed the steps to rejoin Cato and sat down quickly, leaning back on his bench to make sure that he could not be seen from the imperial box.

'What's the matter with you?' asked Cato. 'You look as white as a toga.'

'I'm fine . . . fine.'

'What is it?' Cato had rarely seen his friend look so worried.

Macro shook his head. 'I can't tell you now.' He indicated the men sitting in front and on either side of them. 'Not here.'

Down in the arena the first pair of gladiators had made their salute to the Emperor and now squared off, lowering themselves into a poised crouch as they waited for the signal to begin. The editor milked the tension for as long as he dared before shouting the command, 'Engage!'

The smaller, more lithe of the two fighters charged in and launched a ferocious attack on his opponent and the sounds of blades clashing and the thud of sword strokes on shields echoed around the arena. Then both men parted and began to circle each other warily. Cato smiled at the small piece of theatre the gladiators had used to open the fight with a flash of excitement. Around them the Praetorians were avidly watching, muttering comments about the two gladiators' physiques and fighting styles as they placed bets. Cato leant towards Macro and spoke as loudly as he dared.

'It's safe to speak now. Everyone's concentrating on the action.'

Macro glanced round Cato to look into the imperial box. No more than thirty feet away the Empress had resumed her seat and was staring down into the arena, her face composed. The man who had been groping her was not in view. Macro quietly related what he had seen.

'Are you sure they saw you clearly?' asked Cato.

'Well enough to recognise me if they saw me again.'

'Shit.' Cato frowned. 'That's not helpful.'

'Well, pardon me,' Macro growled.

Cato scratched his chin as he tried to think through the implications. If Agrippina had already taken a lover from among the Emperor's retinue then she was playing a dangerous game indeed. Unless she was using the man to further some other purpose. But what? And did it have any connection with the conspiracy that Narcissus was attempting to uncover and defeat?

As Cato sat in contemplation, Macro saw Narcissus approach the Emperor and bend down close to his ear. Claudius listened and then turned in his seat and looked up at Narcissus in concern. There was a brief conversation before the Emperor nodded and waved him towards Prefect Geta. Moments later, guardsmen hurried out of the pavilion to carry messages to the officers in the arena. Many of the Praetorians close to the imperial box were watching curiously as Tribune Burrus stood up and cupped his hands to his mouth. 'Sixth Century! Form up outside the arena at once!'

Lurco quickly rose from his bench and beckoned to Tigellinus and then hurried across to the entrance. His men began to follow.

'What do you think this is all about?' asked Macro. 'Is it to do with what I saw?'

'We'll know soon enough.'

As they descended the stairs, Cato took a last look into the box. The Emperor and his family had already left their seats, and Narcissus and some others went after them. The rest of the guests remained where they were, trying to look unflustered as the fight continued in the arena.

The men of the Sixth Century gathered around Lurco, while a short distance away the litter slaves were on their feet, ready to take up their burdens the moment the order was given. As Macro, Cato and the last of the men came out of the arena, the centurion called out loudly so that he could be heard over the noise from the arena.

'The Emperor is returning to the palace. He has just received a report that a food riot has broken out in the

Forum. The urban cohorts have the matter in hand but the Emperor wants to take command of the situation in person. Prefect Geta has decided to reinforce the Emperor's bodyguard with the Sixth Century. This is not ceremonial. Our orders are to protect the Emperor, his family and advisers at all costs. If anyone tries to block our path we're authorised to use whatever force is needed to get the litters through.' Lurco paused to draw breath. 'Fetch your weapons and armour from barracks. Then get back here ready to march. At the double!'

CHAPTER TEN

A thick pall of smoke from the direction of the Forum billowed into the afternoon sky as the column of litters and soldiers made their way down the Viminal Hill towards the centre of the city. Even though news of the riot had spread through the streets, many people were still going about their business and hurried out of the way of Centurion Lurco and the two sections leading the party. The Germans closed ranks around the litters carrying the Emperor, the Empress and the two boys. The rest of the Sixth Century filled in the gaps between the remaining litters and brought up the rear.

Cato, Macro and fourteen other men were under the command of Tigellinus as they marched behind a litter shared by Narcissus and two other advisers, including the man Macro had seen with Agrippina. They were marching four abreast, with Fuscius to Macro's right and a surly youth beyond him. After a quick look to make certain that the optio was facing forward, Macro spoke softly to Fuscius.

'See the men in the litter directly ahead of us?'

'Yes.'

'I recognise Narcissus, but who are the others?'

'The one opposite him, the one with the good looks,

is Pallas. One of those bloody freedmen the Emperor insists on surrounding himself with. The other one's Seneca, Nero's tutor and adviser.'

'I see.' Macro glanced to his left at Cato and cocked an eyebrow before realising that it was pointless beneath his helmet. 'Pallas, eh? I wonder what he's up to?'

'Up to?' Fuscius turned his head to Macro. 'What do you mean?'

'Nothing.'

Before they could say another word, Tigellinus glared over his shoulder. 'Silence in the ranks! Keep your bloody mouths shut and your eyes and ears open!'

They progressed in silence and as they drew closer to the Forum the street ahead of them began to empty. A few small groups of anxious-looking civilians hurried by, squeezing past the column with barely a comment or look of surprise as they glimpsed the imperial litter with its barbarian escort. The roar of the mob was clearly audible now, and soon they could discern distinct shouts of anger and even a shrill scream of terror. The smoke was dense and acrid. Wafts reached the column as it entered the square where Cato and Macro had been involved in the brawl a few nights earlier. Cato looked over towards the inn and saw its owner closing the shutters of a window that looked out on to the public fountain, before scurrying inside and closing the doors. A thin and frail-looking woman sat on the edge of the fountain nursing a crying infant with bulging eyes and skeletal arms. She watched the soldiers and litters passing by for a moment before struggling to her feet and limping across to them, holding her free hand out.

'Spare a sestertius for me baby?' Her voice was weak

and strained. 'For the love of Jupiter, spare a coin. We ain't fed for days, sir.' She made to intercept Tigellinus but the optio turned on her with a snarl.

'Clear off, you slut! Take your brat with you. Before I use this!' He brandished his optio's staff at the woman and she cowered back with a screech of terror.

Macro gritted his teeth in contempt for the optio and muttered, 'Glad to see that our optio's got the guts to stand up to a half-starved woman.'

'Shhh!' Cato warned him.

They left the square and continued down the road. A short distance further on, the column came across the first body. An overweight man lay sprawled in the gutter. He had been stripped of all but his loincloth and the mangled stumps on his hand showed where ring fingers had been cut off. His skull had been crushed by frenzied blows. A short distance away was a bakery that had been smashed and looted. The column was passing through the fringes of the Subura, a district of the city that was notorious for its poverty and crime. The crowded tenement blocks reduced the gloomy light further and the rank air caught in Cato's throat as their footsteps echoed off the grimy walls.

As they reached the foot of the hill, there was a sudden outburst of shouting from the front of the column and Cato craned his neck to see Centurion Lurco confronting a small crowd of men who had spilled out of a side street into the path of the Emperor and his retinue.

'Clear the way there!' Lurco shouted, his high voice carrying above the shouting. 'Make way for the Emperor!'

'It's Claudius!' a voice responded. 'Stand firm, boys. Let's put our grievances to the Emperor.'

Lurco threw up his arm 'Column, halt!'

There was little co-ordination possible among the Praetorians, Germans and slaves carrying the litters and the column shuffled to a disorderly stop. Over the heads of the men in front of him Cato could see that many of the men in the crowd were armed with staves, axes and clubs. Lurco warily stepped forward to confront the crowd as more people joined it, shouting and gesturing angrily.

'You will clear the way for the Emperor, now! There will not be another warning!'

'Claudius!' the ringleader bellowed. 'Your people are starving! Feed us!'

'Get out of the way!' Lurco bellowed then looked back over his shoulder. 'Draw swords!' he ordered.

There was a metallic clatter as the soldiers pulled their swords from their scabbards and held them ready. The ringleader stepped forward and Cato recognised him at once.

'Cestius.'

Macro looked up at Cato. 'The big bastard from the inn?'

'Yes.'

'Shit. He's trouble.'

Cestius approached the head of the column and called out loudly enough for all his followers to hear clearly, 'What's this? A party on its way to a banquet, I'll be bound.' He turned back to the crowd. 'While we go hungry, while our children slowly starve to death, this lot stuff their fat faces with delicacies, then throw it all back up, just so they can feed again!'

Some men in the crowd shouted angrily and waved their fists. Cestius turned towards the soldiers. 'We're not moving. We want to put our demands to the Emperor. We want bread and grain at a price we can afford. You, Centurion, get out of our way. We demand to speak to Claudius!'

As the mob roared their approval, Lurco withdrew into the front rank of his men and drew his blade. 'Protect the litters! On my word, advance at the slow step! Optio, call the pace! Shields front!'

The decurion in charge of the Germans formed his men up around the Emperor's litter while the Praetorians surrounded the others. They angled their shields to screen those huddling down in the litters and held their short stabbing swords level to the ground, elbows bent and weapon ready to thrust. Cato felt his heart beating quickly and the chill in his guts and limbs that always came upon him before a fight. Then he was aware of movement at the periphery of his vision and glanced to the side just in time to see the dim shapes of men filtering down an alley to his right. He looked quickly to the other side and saw more coming from the other direction, and yet more, further back, sprinting across an intersection as they cut round the column to try to surround it.

'Look there!' He pointed them out to Macro with his sword. 'It's a trap.'

Before Macro could respond, there was a shout from ahead. 'Advance!'

'One! Two!' Tigellinus called the pace and the leading Praetorians moved forward, shield to shield. Behind the first sections came the Germans and the imperial litter, then Narcissus and the advisers, followed by Tigellinus and his men. For a moment the crowd fell silent and then Cestius roared, 'Kill! Kill them!'

A brick hurtled over the gap between the soldiers and the mob and glanced off a shield before thudding on to the thick fabric covering the Emperor's litter. There was a cry of terror from within. More missiles filled the air: bricks, fragments of paving and lumps of filth scooped up from the gutter. More came from the sides, hurled from the alleys at the flanks of the column caught in the narrow street. Step by step they moved forward. Ahead of them the mob held their ground until the last moment and then began to press back, but those behind who could not see the Praetorians did not move and blocked their retreat. Men scrambled to the side of the street in panic and pressed into the arches and doorways of the tenements. Some managed to escape down the side alleys but a number were caught in the path of the Praetorians.

'Don't stop for anything!' Lurco shouted.

With Tigellinus steadily calling the pace, the Praetorians reached the mob and thrust forward with their shields, battering the nearest men. Then the first sword stabbed out, tearing into the side of a struggling figure. He screamed in agony before slumping down on to the street. At last those at the rear of the crowd realised the danger and began to fall back. But it was too late for those at the front. The Praetorians pushed their shields forward relentlessly, stabbing into the flesh of those before them. Some of the wounded fell to the ground where the soldiers trod over them, others were caught tight in the suffocating press of bodies and were stabbed again and again, screaming with pain and terror.

Over the top of his shield Cato saw the tall figure of Cestius push his way through to an alley where he disappeared with several of his men. Ahead, the mob at last began to break up, leaving several dead and injured bodies in its wake. Those who had had enough fled from the scene to find shelter, or easier pickings. But over a hundred remained, staying beyond reach of the swords as they hurled whatever came to hand at the imperial party. The missiles thudded and cracked off shields and helmets, but the slaves carrying the litters had no protection and already four of them had been felled. One was knocked cold by a blow to the head and blood gushed from a long tear in his scalp. Two of the others had also received head wounds. They released their hold on the litters and staggered to the side of the street before collapsing. The last was clutching his smashed elbow and groaning through clenched teeth. The remaining slaves were struggling under their increased burden and their way was impeded by bodies sprawled across their path. Then one of the slaves carrying the imperial secretary's litter stumbled and the litter thudded down, almost pitching Narcissus into the gutter. Cato saw that the slaves could not hope to make any speed along the street.

'Get out of the litter!' he ordered Narcissus. 'You and the others. You have to abandon the litter. Keep your heads down and stay behind the Praetorians.'

Narcissus nodded and the Emperor's advisers slithered off the cushioned interior and their expensive boots squelched down into the filth-caked street.

'Who gave that order?' Tigellinus yelled from the other side of the litter.

'Me, sir. Capito.'

'Are you the bloody centurion, Capito? You don't

give orders, you obey them.' Tigellinus ducked down to peer through the other side of the litter at the freedmen. 'Best get back in. I'll have some of my men make up the slave numbers.'

Narcissus shook his head. 'They'd only go the same way as the slaves. Your man is right, we have to abandon the litters. I'll tell the Emperor.'

Tigellinus shot a furious glance at Cato and then nodded. 'As you wish, sir.'

'You, Capito, and the short fellow.' Narcissus beckoned. 'I need protection. Cover me with your shields. Let's go.'

With Cato and Macro on either side, holding their shields over the imperial secretary, Narcissus emerged from the ring of Praetorians and the three men made their way the short distance to the Germans screening the imperial litter. Cato winced as a brick struck his shield. At their approach the Germans parted to let them through. Cato saw that five of the twelve slaves carrying the ornately decorated litter had already fallen, and the others could barely keep the litter off the ground. He turned to Narcissus. 'You have to get the Emperor and the others out, or we won't be able to move.'

'I understand.' Narcissus nodded nervously, ducking as a turd flew close overhead. He drew back the curtain to reveal the Emperor protecting Britannicus in his embrace. Next to him sat the Empress cradling Nero's head in her lap. Claudius looked up anxiously and his head twitched.

'Sire, the Praetorians say we have to continue on foot.'

'On f–f–foot?'

'Yes, sire. We won't be able to get the litters much further. It would be dangerous to try.'

'But there are madmen out there!' Agrippina protested. 'Just drop the curtain and get us back to the palace. I order it.'

'I regret to say that there is no choice in the matter, your imperial majesty. Either we move now or we will be stuck here, at their mercy.'

'Where are the urban cohorts?' demanded Agrippina. 'They should be dealing with those scum. They'll find us if we stay here.'

Narcissus shook his head. 'They probably don't even know what's happening.' He turned to the Emperor. 'We have to continue on foot, sire. Now.'

Claudius turned to his wife. 'The soldiers know best, my d–dear. Come, let's not show any fear in front of the m–m–mob.'

Narcissus helped his Emperor out and then handed out Agrippina and the two boys. Claudius put a protective arm round his wife and faced Cato and Macro.

'You two, guard the children.'

'Yes, sire.' Cato bowed his head and then gestured for Nero to join him. 'Calidus, you take the smaller boy.'

Macro nodded. 'Over here, young 'un.'

Britannicus frowned. 'That is not how you address me, soldier.'

'It is right now.' Macro gently took his shoulder and drew him behind his shield.

The decurion of the German bodyguards called to his men to form a cordon round the Emperor and then Narcissus cupped a hand and shouted towards the leading sections a short distance ahead. 'Centurion! Centurion!'

Lurco heard the shout, glanced back and then ordered

his men to hold their position before he made his way to the other party, hunched close into his shield.

'We're leaving the litters behind,' Narcissus explained. 'Gather your men together and we'll make our way across the Forum to the palace. It's not too far now.'

Lurco shook his head desperately. 'It would be safer to return to the camp. We have to escape. Before it's too late.'

'No, sir,' Cato interrupted and pointed his sword back up the street. 'Look!'

A hundred paces behind them another small crowd had gathered in the shadows between the tenement blocks and was already beginning to edge towards them.

'Shit . . . shit,' Lurco muttered, his lip beginning to tremble.

Cato made to say something, but Macro acted first. He thrust himself towards the centurion, sheathed his sword and grasped the officer's shoulder. 'Pull yourself together, sir,' he said harshly. 'Your Emperor's life is in your hands. All of our lives are. Get the men together, shield to shield, and get them moving, or we're fucked.' He saw the dazed look in the officer's face and shook him hard. 'Sir!'

Lurco blinked, then his eyes flickered towards the imperial family and he swallowed. 'Yes, of course. Right.' He raised his head and called to Tigellinus. 'Optio!'

'Sir?'

'Bring the rest of the century forward. Form up by the Germans!'

While the men guarding the Emperor's advisers trotted towards them, Lurco turned to Macro and Cato. 'You guard those children with your lives. Understand?'

'Yes, sir.' Macro nodded. 'They'll be safe with us.'

Once Pallas and Seneca had joined Claudius and his family, the soldiers closed up behind their shields, protecting the slaves as well, and Lurco gave the order for the makeshift formation to advance. The leading sections waited until the rest caught up and then they continued as one body. Meanwhile the crowd behind them had grown bold enough to come closer and hurl insults before following those up with the first stones and broken roof tiles drawn from a pile of rubble at the corner of one of the alleys. Cato and Macro held their shields up and bent forward to use their bodies to protect their charges. Cato had sheathed his sword and had his right hand on Nero's shoulder so that they would keep in step. He felt the boy trembling beneath the folds of his toga.

'It's all right.' Cato spoke in a comforting tone. 'We'll have you back in the palace as soon as we can.'

Nero didn't reply for a moment and then Cato just caught his words. 'I'm scared.'

'My friend and I have been in far worse situations.'

Nero looked up at him. 'But I haven't.'

'Then look on this as a chance to be brave. It is a good thing to learn while you are young.'

Nero nodded uncertainly and took a deep breath to calm his nerves as they picked their way forward. Around them the Germans began to call out a battle chant in their harsh tongue and rapped the guards of their swords against the inside of their shields. Cato straightened up for a moment and saw that there were no more than fifty paces to go before the street gave out on to the open space in front of the Temple of Minerva, on the edge of the Forum.

'Not far before we're in the open, lads,' Macro called out encouragingly.

There was a shout from above and an instant later a roof tile exploded on the ground beside Macro. Britannicus let out a startled cry as a shard gashed his hand. Macro drew the boy in closer and called out a warning.

'Some of the bastards are in the buildings. Keep your heads covered!'

More tiles came down from above and risking a quick look Cato glimpsed a figure lean out of a window, take aim and hurl a tile on to the head of one of the Germans. It struck him on the helmet, driving his head away at an angle, and he pitched over to the side. At once two of his comrades sheathed their swords and picked him up under the arms and dragged him along with the formation. With missiles clattering in from all directions, the soldiers instinctively increased their pace and those at the front began to pull away as they sought to get away from the danger from above.

'Not so fast there!' Tigellinus yelled. 'Stay together, damn you!'

He pushed his way to the front, brushing by Centurion Lurco, and used the flat of his sword to smack the shields of those who were moving too fast. 'No man goes by me! I set the pace and you follow!'

By the time they reached the end of the street, another two men had been struck down among the defenceless slaves huddled together at the rear of the party. One was dead and lay stretched out in the street. The other's foot had been smashed and he limped along, falling out of formation and desperately struggling to keep up. Then the crowd caught up with him and they showed him no pity, even though he was simply a slave and quite blame-less. His screams cut through the air and chilled Cato's blood before they were mercifully cut off and the mob surged forward once again.

As the party reached the precinct of the temple, the full scale of the riot was apparent for the first time. Several stalls in the Forum close to the senate house were ablaze and the breeze swirled the flames and smoke so that the fire writhed like a wild animal chained to a stake. The avenue leading into the Forum was littered with bodies, many still living, and their piteous cries filled the air. Cato noticed some wore the uniform of the urban cohorts. Many more market stalls had been smashed to pieces and only scattered remnants indicated the trade of the stall's owner. A handful of ragged beggars and street children were looting the bodies for whatever valuables they could find. At the sight of the clusters of men who preceded the imperial party, most of the looters hurried into the safety of the Subura's alleys.

As soon as they were out in the open, the optio picked up the pace and the rioters moved out of their way, keeping a wary distance from the soldiers and their swords. Ahead, in the heart of the Forum, the din of the rioters was much louder, amplified and echoing off the temples and palaces that surrounded the Forum. Cato saw that Nero was terrified by the sights and sounds that surrounded him, yet they still had to cross the Forum and gain the entrance to the palace, assuming the mob had not broken through the gates and sacked the complex. With luck there would be some elements of the urban cohorts on hand who would rally to the Emperor and his bodyguards and escort them to safety.

The avenue narrowed between the Markets of Caesar and the Temple of Janus, and then there was a short stretch of colonnade before the main Forum.

'Not far now!' the optio called out to the others. 'Stay together and keep your eyes open.'

The walls on either side closed in and the last of the rioters who had tormented them fell back and only a few more missiles were thrown. After the harsh battering of shields and armour, the scraping thud of the soldiers' nailed boots suddenly seemed very loud. Cato was aware of the heavy breathing of the German bodyguards and the Emperor was muttering something incomprehensible as he limped along beside his wife, his weak legs making him look like a wet spider dragging himself from a puddle.

The attack came just as they reached the end of the colonnade.

With a roar, men streamed out from between the towering stone columns and threw themselves at the soldiers. Unlike the other rioters, these men were armed with a mix of spears, axes, swords, clubs and daggers, and well prepared for a fight. They drove into the shield cordon from both sides, trying to rip away the shields and strike at the soldiers. Cato pulled Nero closer in to his shield.

'Stay with me.' He spoke into Nero's ear. 'Whatever happens!'

He looked round and saw that the attackers were concentrating on the front and rear of the column, where the Praetorians were positioned. As yet the Germans had not been engaged and they crouched expectantly, round shields up and their longer swords held at the ready. Then

Cato saw a stream of men running from the shadows inside the temple. These were armed with swords and at their head was the now familiar face of Cestius. His expression was fixed in determined hostility as he leaped down into the narrow avenue and made directly for the Emperor and his family. Cestius's men formed a narrow wedge on either side as they plunged in among the Germans. Cato saw Cestius duck a clumsy sword cut and clamp his hand round the bodyguard's windpipe and crush it in one quick move. He thrust the gasping man aside and looked round quickly until he saw the two boys. Macro was closer and turned to face the threat, still trying his best to protect Britannicus.

With a savage roar Cestius rushed forward, knocking aside another German. Macro's sword came up and thrust out. At the last instant Cestius parried it aside with a ringing clash of blades and smashed into Macro and knocked him flat on his back. Britannicus stood alone and defenceless but Cestius spared the boy only a brief glance before sweeping him aside and charging on towards Cato, his teeth bared.

There was no time to think and Cato went down on one knee, angling his shield as he pushed Nero to the ground. A look of surprise flashed across Cestius's face the instant before he tripped and fell heavily across the shield, flattening those beneath. Cato felt the hot rush of expelled breath from the other man's lungs. He pushed into the shield, straining with all his might, and Cestius rolled to one side, coming up on his knees, sword raised. His spare hand grabbed at the edge of the shield and he ripped it away to reveal Nero dazed and winded. The giant's eyes filled with triumphant zeal as the point of his sword descended.

'No!' Cato shouted, throwing his body over the boy. The sleeve of his tunic caught the tip of the oncoming blade and there was a sound of ripping material and then a burning streak across his right bicep.

'Bastard!' Cestius snarled, drawing back his arm. Then he glanced up and saw Macro looming before him an instant before the boss of Macro's shield struck him square in the face. Cestius fell back with a groan, his sword clattering to one side. He trembled for an instant and then lay still, his breath rasping.

'Lad, are you all right?' Macro called anxiously as he crouched beside Cato. He saw the rent in the tunic and the bright scarlet spreading across the exposed flesh of Cato's arm and shoulder.

'Nero?' Cato turn to look for his charge and saw the boy struggling up into a sitting position, unharmed. The wave of relief lasted only a moment before the burning agony from his wound struck Cato.

'Cestius is down!' a voice cried out nearby. 'Cestius is down! Fall back!'

As quickly as the men had attacked, they broke off, retreating from the soldiers before turning and running back into the colonnade, the sound of their boots echoing off the temple walls. Macro helped Cato to his feet. The swift attack had been deadly enough. Several of the Praetorians and Germans had been struck down, as well as a similar number of the attackers. The Emperor was swallowing nervously and Agrippina's eyes were wide with terror, but neither they nor their children had been harmed.

'Pick up the wounded!' Tigellinus ordered. 'Close up!' He looked round for his centurion and saw Lurco rising up from the street with a sheepish expression. 'We should move on, sir. Quickly, in case those men come back.'

'Yes.' Lurco nodded. 'Of course.' The centurion cleared his throat. 'The Sixth Century will advance!'

Once again the column re-formed its shield wall round the freshly wounded, the surviving slaves and civilians and moved out into the Forum. Macro picked up Cato's sword and replaced it in his friend's scabbard and then pulled the torn tunic aside to examine the wound. 'You're bleeding badly but it looks like a flesh wound. Painful, but you'll recover.'

'Since when were you a bloody surgeon?' Cato replied through clenched teeth as he adjusted his grip on the shield and held it up to protect Nero again. Then he quickly turned back to Macro. 'Cestius?'

'What about him?'

'We should have taken him with us.'

Macro chuckled. 'You mean we should have killed him.'

'That was an ambush.' Cato lowered his voice so that only Macro might hear. 'There's more to this than there seems. We need to question Cestius.'

Macro looked round. Several men had already emerged from the colonnade to carry off the bodies of the dead and wounded from the brief skirmish. Cestius had disappeared. 'It's too late.'

Cato thought quickly. He could tell Centurion Lurco to turn back and try to recover Cestius before he was taken away, but Lurco was badly shaken and wanted nothing more than to reach safety without delay. The only way Cato could stop him would be to expose his true identity and try to pull rank on the other officer.

Narcissus would have to vouch for him. And by the time that was established it would be too late to send men back for Cestius.

'What's so important about this Cestius?' asked Nero.

'Nothing.'

'Nothing?' Nero gasped. 'That man tried to kill me.'

Cato stared at him briefly then looked up as he kept pace with the other soldiers. The entire length of the Forum was littered with evidence of the severity of the riot. Scores of bodies lay on the ground. The doors of some of the temples had been forced and discarded loot lay on their steps. Several handcarts had been turned over or simply stripped of their contents. To the right, the fire in Caesar's Market was still raging but a company of fire-fighters was already attempting to contain the blaze, with lines of men passing buckets of water from the public fountains. Elsewhere the men of the urban cohorts had almost cleared the Forum, except for a few running battles with gangs of men throwing rocks around the Temple of Venus to the east. Slowly the tension in the small party eased as they realised that the crisis had passed and they were safe.

A century from one of the urban cohorts was guarding the entrance to the palace and hurriedly drew aside as they saw the Emperor. The column passed through into a small courtyard where Lurco gave the order for his men to fall out. Both the Praetorians and the Germans were shaken by the ordeal and leant on their spears and shields to recover their breath. Now that they were all safe, the normal hierarchy reasserted itself. The surviving slaves were ordered back to their quarters and Claudius was composed as he stood by his wife and called the boys to him. Britannicus clutched his father's arm. Narcissus hurried over to the Emperor.

'Sire, are you hurt?' he asked anxiously.

Claudius shook his head. 'N-no. Quite all right.'

'Jupiter be praised!' Narcissus rejoiced, then turned to the Empress. 'Your majesty?'

'Unharmed.' Agrippina smiled coldly.

Narcissus turned to Britannicus and quickly looked him over to satisfy himself that the boy had received no injuries other than that to his hand. Then he saw Nero and with a flicker of anguish approached the boy who still stood beside Cato.

'I saw the man attack you. I thank the gods that you were spared.'

Nero nodded towards Cato. 'This man saved my life.'

Narcissus looked up and met Cato's gaze without a hint of recognition. 'Very well, I shall see that he is rewarded.'

'You do that,' Macro added quietly.

Nero turned to Cato and looked him in the eye. 'I am in your debt, soldier. What is your name?'

'Titus Ovidius Capito, sir.'

Nero's gaze switched to the blood-soaked tear in the tunic on Cato's shoulder. 'Get your wound attended to, Capito. I shall not forget this. I never forget a face. One day, I shall repay you.' He lowered his voice so that only Cato could hear. 'One day I shall be Emperor. If you ever need my help, then it is yours. I give you my most sacred promise.'

He grasped Cato's hand and squeezed it firmly before he released his grip and turned away to join his mother and the Emperor. Narcissus watched him go then turned to fix Cato with an icy stare before he scurried back to comfort his master.

CHAPTER ELEVEN

Four days later Cato was sitting on his bed when Macro and the others returned from their patrol in the city. Following the food riot the Emperor had ordered the Praetorian cohorts on to the streets alongside the soldiers of the urban cohorts, leaving the palace under the protection of his German mercenaries. There were checkpoints at all the major junctions of avenues and streets and even the smallest gatherings of men in public places were swiftly broken up. Rewards had been offered for the ringleaders of the riot and their descriptions had been posted on the streets surrounding the Forum. So far only a handful of minor rabble-rousers had been arrested and disposed of, their heads mounted on stakes outside the entrance to the imperial palace. Cestius was still at large, despite the small fortune offered to anyone who could lead the authorities to his hiding place. Such was his fearsome reputation that none of the inhabitants of the Subura dared to admit they had even heard of Cestius when questioned by patrols.

Cato's wound had been cleaned and stitched up by one of the surgeons in the hospital at the camp who had excused him from duties for ten days to give the wound time to heal. Cato had only ventured out of the camp twice, to visit the safe house and leave a message for

Septimus, requesting a meeting to make his report, and then again a day later to see if there had been a reply. There was none and Cato had decided to stay in camp for a few more days before looking again, just in case his excursions drew unwelcome attention.

'How's that tiny cut on your arm today?' asked Macro as he leant his shield against the wall by the door, and started to remove his sword belt and armour.

'Stiff, but the pain's bearable, thanks.'

'As I said, a flesh wound. Little more than a scratch really.' Macro struggled out of his chain-mail vest and laid it on the floor by his shield before slumping down on his bed. 'Still, it's a good way of ducking out of duties.'

'It has served its purpose.' Cato smiled briefly before his expression became serious again. 'How are things in the city?'

'Quiet. The Emperor has stamped down on it. He's also sent word to every town and city within a hundred miles to send wagons of grain to Rome. The granaries of the Praetorian Guard are going to be used to eke out what little is left in the imperial store. Which means we will be on half rations from tomorrow. Not the smartest of moves.' Macro shook his head. 'We'll need to keep our strength up if we're to keep order on the streets. But if it helps appease the mob, then I guess it will serve its purpose for a few days at least. Beats me how Claudius ever let us get into this situation in the first place. He must have known the situation in Egypt was going to disrupt the supply for a while. So why didn't he plan for it?'

'Maybe he did but someone sabotaged the plan.'

Macro cocked his head. 'What are you suggesting?'

'I'm not quite sure yet.' Cato reached his left hand up and lightly stroked the dressing over his wound, his fingertips sensing the lumps where the stitches had closed the gash. 'Have you been keeping an eye on Centurion Lurco?'

'I have. He's a useless fart if ever there was one. Frankly, Cato, if he is involved in any conspiracy then I'd say the Emperor has nothing to worry about.'

'That's my impression too.' Cato nodded thoughtfully then continued, 'But it's interesting how things are drawing together, wouldn't you say? The theft of the bullion, Narcissus uncovering a plot, the riot, and then that ambush on us the same day.'

'No doubt you think there's a connection between it all,' Macro suggested wearily.

'I'm not sure, but at the very least, it's all pretty suggestive.'

Macro sighed. 'To your mind, yes. For the rest of us, it's just a question of the shit being piled on. That or the gods have decided to give us some grief, for whatever reason. Either way, I think you're jumping at shadows now.'

Cato was silent for a moment before he responded. 'Maybe it's the shadows jumping at us.'

'What is that supposed to mean?'

Cato tried to explain the thoughts that were troubling him. 'Something's going on. I can feel it. There's too much happening to dismiss it as coincidence. All of this makes some kind of sense. Or would, if I could piece it together somehow. Right now I can only speculate, but I'm sure the conspiracy is real.'

'Not very helpful.' Macro eased himself forward and

folded his legs. 'Of course, it could be nothing more than the usual mess. The palace has screwed up the grain dole and some greedy bastards have pinched the silver. As for Narcissus's conspiracy, well, when haven't the Liberators been plotting the removal of the Emperor and the return of the Republic? We're on a wild-goose chase, Cato my lad.'

At the mention of his name, Cato growled. 'Careful!'

'We're alone. What does it matter?'

'It matters because you said it without thinking.'

'Just like you did back at the inn, eh?'

Cato flushed with shame. 'Exactly. We can't afford to make another mistake until this is all over.'

'Come the day,' Macro said wearily.

They were interrupted by footsteps and then Fuscius and Tigellinus entered the room and began to remove their kit.

'Still skiving, Capito?' asked Tigellinus.

'Am I ever, Optio?' Cato forced a grin as he stretched out on his bed. 'This is the life for me. Resting up while you lot tramp up and down those shit-filled streets of the Subura.'

'Ain't that fun?' Tigellinus put his hands behind his back and rubbed the bottom of his spine. 'It doesn't help that the centurion is a bag of nerves. He thinks everyone he sees on the streets has got it in for us. He's stopped and searched almost every man we've run into, and given them a good slapping into the bargain at the slightest excuse. The mad bastard is going to end up causing another riot if he's not careful.' He paused. 'He should never have been appointed to the Guard. Classic case of the stupidity of direct commissions to the centurionate. A centurion needs experience. And guts. You get that the hard way. It ain't right that he's our centurion. Should be someone else.'

'Like you?' Cato suggested.

'Why not? I've paid my dues.' The optio gave Cato a cold look. 'You're in my good books, Capito. Don't ruin the moment.'

'Why am I in favour?'

'For what you did to save the boy. I saw you throw yourself in the way of that sword. That's good soldiering. It's what Praetorians are for. You're all right by me. And you've won yourself some favour with the Empress and her boy.' He smiled. 'That may serve you very well indeed some day.'

'Oh?'

'Of course. Think it over. Claudius ain't going to live forever. Looks to me like young Nero has a good chance of succeeding him, and he owes you. Play your part and you'll come out of it all smelling of roses. In the meantime, remind me to buy you a drink sometime. Now, I've got a report to write for that useless bastard Lurco.'

Tigellinus left the room and they listened to the sound of his boots receding. Fuscius looked at Cato and raised his eyebrows. 'That's the first time I ever heard him offer someone a drink. Maybe old Tigellinus has a heart after all.'

'Then he'll never make a good centurion,' said Macro.

'Really?' Cato struggled to suppress a smile. 'And what would you know about that, Calidus?'

'Trust me, I've seen plenty of them come and go in the legions. The best of them are as hard as nails and there's not a grain of pity in their souls. Of course, there are others.'

'Like Lurco?' Fuscius suggested quietly.

Macro nodded. 'One or two. But they never last. They die quickly. That or they get bucked up to prefect to keep 'em out of trouble. Has Lurco got influence that you know of?'

The young guardsman looked anxiously towards the door, as if the centurion might be eavesdropping. He leant closer to his comrades and whispered, 'I heard him boast that the Empress has taken a fancy to him.'

'Why not? He's a pretty boy.' Macro gave Cato a knowing look. 'In any case, she's got form and almost everyone knows it.'

'But not since she married Claudius. She doesn't want to end up like Messallina.' Fuscius drew his finger across his throat. 'If she's being unfaithful, then she has to be very careful.'

An image of the Empress in the arms of Pallas flitted through Macro's mind. Agrippina took her risks, but how careful she was in covering her tracks remained to be seen. Macro's helmet had obscured his face when he had escorted her through the riot and neither she nor Pallas had given any indication that they had recognised him. For the moment he appeared to be safe.

There was a light knock on the door frame as one of the headquarters clerks looked in. 'You got Guardsman Capito in here?'

'That's me.' Cato raised his hand.

'Centurion Sinius wants to see you.'

'Now?'

The clerk pursed his lips. 'When an officer doesn't say

when it's generally because he means right now. I'd move my arse if I were you.'

'Thanks.' Cato stood up and hurriedly put on his boots and military belt. It had started to rain outside so he picked up his cloak and trotted out of the barracks to catch up with the clerk.

'Did Sinius say what he wanted?'

'No. And before you ask, I didn't.'

Cato glanced at the clerk, an overweight soldier with a round, pudding-like face. 'Are they all as helpful as you at headquarters?'

'Oh no,' the man answered in a sour tone. 'Most of them are complete bastards.'

'Lucky for me they sent you then.'

The clerk glanced at Cato and shrugged. 'Sorry, mate. I'm just a bit pissed off that we're going on half rations.'

'I can understand that,' Cato responded with a quick glance at the man's gut. 'Someone's messed up and it's the rankers who pay the price, eh?'

'You said it, brother. The Emperor's been losing his grip these last months. Spending too much time fondling that niece of his. That ain't right or decent and no good will come of it. Pity that boy of hers isn't a bit older. Nero's got promise, if you ask me. And he favours the Praetorian Guard. Give him a few more years and he'll do fine as the new Emperor.'

'Assuming the job doesn't go to Britannicus.'

The clerk snorted with derision. 'Claudius will be in his grave long before Britannicus is old enough to take the reins.'

'Then it might be useful if someone encouraged the process along, I'd say.'

The clerk looked at him. 'I might agree with you, brother, and there are plenty in the camp who would too, but I wouldn't go and shout it about the place, eh?'

'Just thinking aloud.'

'And that's all very fine now, but words have a way of prompting actions.' The clerk winked at him. 'But no more of it.'

They continued to headquarters in silence and the clerk showed him to Centurion Sinius's door before returning to his duties. Cato had no idea why he had been summoned and thought it might have something to do with his shielding Nero from harm a few days earlier. Perhaps some kind of reward. He stepped up to the door, paused a moment and then knocked.

'Come!'

Cato lifted the latch and entered. Sinius was sitting on a stool beside the small brazier that warmed his office. He looked at Cato and then gestured towards the door. 'Close that and come over here.'

'Yes, sir.' Cato did as he was told and then crossed the room to stand at ease in front of the centurion. There was a pause before Cato cleared his throat. 'You sent for me, sir.'

'Yes, I did.' Sinius regarded him silently for a moment. 'You're an interesting man, Capito. Centurion Lurco's report of the other day's events makes for interesting reading. Apart from saving the Emperor's stepson, it was you who took the initiative in abandoning the litters, I understand. He gives you credit for that at least, the rest he claims for himself. But I have already spoken to your optio and discounted most of Lurco's boasting. You and

Calidus are quite a pair. Very cool headed under pressure, it would appear.'

'We've had our share of skirmishes and battles in the legions, sir.'

'So I imagine. Your actions got the Emperor and his party out of a very dangerous situation. How very loyal of you. You must be very fond of the Emperor.'

'I just did what I was trained to do.'

'Perhaps, but to me it would seem that the pair of you make for good junior officer material, so it's all the more surprising that you were still just common legionaries before you were transferred to the Praetorian Guard. Why was that, I wonder? Care to explain yourself?'

Cato felt an icy stab of anxiety in his guts. 'I have no idea, sir. I guess our faces didn't fit.'

'Explain.'

'There's not much to add to what I said when we spoke before, sir. Calidus and I never saw the point of trying to conquer Britannia. We didn't hide our feelings. Nor did many others.'

'I know. I gather there was a brief mutiny in Gesoriacum before the soldiers boarded the invasion fleet.'

'That's right, sir.'

'And you had nothing to do with that, of course.'

Cato hesitated before he replied. He could see where the centurion was trying to lead the discussion and realised there was an opportunity to test Sinius in turn. 'I didn't disagree with the ringleaders of the mutiny, sir. I just think they mishandled the situation.'

'I see. Mishandled. You would have led the mutiny differently if you'd had your way.'

'I didn't have anything to do with it, sir. Nor did

Calidus. But, since you're asking me, then yes, if I had been in charge I would have been more ruthless. The senior officers had to be removed. It was a mistake to let them remain free. It was the officers who organised the arrest and execution of the ringleaders. It ended as I knew it would.'

'And since then your superiors have been reluctant to promote you and Calidus.'

'That's how it seems, sir.'

'Hardly fair, since you took no part in the mutiny. Men like you deserve better. You deserve better leaders, and that starts at the top.'

'Sir?'

There was another silence, broken only by the light crackle of flames from the brazier. Then the centurion continued in a quiet voice.

'You know what I'm talking about, Capito, though you are smart enough not to admit it. When a leader has failed his followers, or when a succession of leaders have failed us, then a reasonable man – a patriotic man – might well ask if there needs to be change. Wouldn't you agree?'

Cato said nothing, his gaze fixed on the centurion. Sinius let the silence stretch out for a moment.

'Fair enough. Then let me do the talking. You resent your lack of promotion. You resent being ordered to take part in a campaign that has little purpose. You condemn those who had the chance to reverse that policy but failed through lack of resolution. You want change. You want what is due to you. Am I right?'

Cato did not move for a moment and then barely nodded.

Sinius smiled. 'Very well. Then let me put a proposal

to you. There is a group of individuals who feel as you do. I am one of them. The difference between us is that I am in a position to bring about the change that we both desire. If my associates and I succeed in our ambitions, there will be rewards for us as well as rendering good service to Rome. And why shouldn't there be? The risk is ours and we should be compensated accordingly. If I were to offer you the chance to join us, what would you say?'

'I'd say you were a fool, sir. Why should you trust me?' Cato paused for an instant before he risked his next comment. 'For all you know I could be a spy.'

'That's true. And that is why I have had you and your friend under observation by one of my men since you arrived in the camp. If you were spies, then I'd know about it.'

Cato felt his heart lurch. He had been to the safe house twice and Sinius appeared to know nothing of it. He had taken precautions to ensure that he was not being followed but a skilled tail would not have been thrown off the scent that easily. He did not speak for a moment, to give the impression that he was carefully considering the centurion's offer.

'How do I know you're not an agent, sir? You could be testing my loyalty.'

'And why would I do that?' Sinius smiled. 'Do you think the imperial palace really has the time and inclination to test the loyalty of every new recruit to the Praetorian Guard in this manner?'

Cato pursed his lips. 'I suppose not.'

'No indeed. They have their hands full with rather more important matters, I should imagine. Like the business of the food shortage. Well, Capito, what is your response to my offer?'

'Firstly, you mentioned rewards.'

'Yes.'

'I want promotion, for me and Calidus.'

Sinius's eyes narrowed a fraction. 'Calidus is a separate matter.'

'No, sir. He is of the same mind as me in nearly all things. I trust him with my life.' It was easy to say because it was the truth and Cato's sincerity had its effect on the centurion.

'Very well, my offer extends to you both.'

'Thank you, sir. I also want money. Gold. A great deal of gold.'

'That I cannot give you. But I can offer you silver. Quite a fortune, in fact.' Sinius turned and pointed to the document chest beside his desk. 'Open that. There is a false bottom with a catch at this end. Inside is a box. Bring it to me.'

Cato did as he was bid. The chest contained scrolls, some blank sheets of papyrus, pens, ink pots and several waxed slates. He cleared them aside from the near end and found a small catch painted to blend in with the dark wood of the chest. The lid lifted to reveal a cavity twice the size of a mess tin. It was almost filled by the box Sinius had described. Cato grasped the handle and picked it up carefully, slightly surprised by its weight. He crossed the room and handed the box to the centurion. Sinius placed it on his lap and flicked the catch and opened the lid. The contents were in shadow for an instant before the orange glow of the flames in the brazier reflected in the sheen of freshly minted silver coins.

'There's a thousand denarii there, Capito. It's yours if you join us, and there's more where that came from.'

Cato looked down at the coins. They were surely part of the fortune stolen from the bullion convoy. He made himself smile and reached out a hand. 'May I?'

'Of course.'

Cato took a coin at random and raised it up to inspect it closely.

'They're genuine,' said Sinius, and chuckled. 'Unless the Emperor has been debasing the currency.'

With a nod of satisfaction, Cato replaced the coin and gave the officer a searching stare. 'If I – if we – agree to join you and your friends, then you'll just give me this money? There has to be a catch.'

'Not a catch. More of a test. You do as you are asked and the silver is yours.'

'What kind of a test?' Cato asked suspiciously.

'The kind that puts your loyalty to us beyond doubt, and at the same time furthers our aims.' Sinius gently closed the lid of the box and looked steadily at Cato. 'It's simple enough. I want you to kill Centurion Lurco. He is to disappear without trace. Within the next ten days. Do that and you will be welcomed by my friends. Fail in the act and we will not trust your competence. Fail to even attempt it and we will be obliged to treat you as a threat.'

'I see.' Cato smiled grimly. 'Kill or be killed.'

'That's right. The credo of all soldiers, regardless of the circumstances. Should be an easy enough decision for you to make. I give you until dawn to let me know.'

CHAPTER TWELVE

'What are we going to do?' asked Macro as they shut the door of the mess room behind them. They had been playing dice with some of the other men of the century in order to keep up the appearance of being common soldiers. Cato had been careful to lose by a small margin and laugh it off, in order to win the good will of their comrades. Macro, on the other hand, had played to win, and had lost rather more than Cato and was consequently a little bitter as he steered the conversation back to the pressing issue. 'Lurco is a liability, but I draw the line at doing in one of our own. Even if he is a Praetorian.'

'We agree to Sinius's test,' Cato replied. 'What else can we do?'

Macro looked shocked. 'You can't be serious. Kill a fellow officer? No.'

'Of course we don't kill him. But we have to find some way to make him disappear. That's going to be the tricky bit.'

They made their way up on to the wall of the camp and began to stroll slowly along a section overlooking the city. Sentries were posted in the corner towers and gatehouses of the camp and several other small groups of men were walking along the wall, exchanging cheery greetings with Macro and Cato as they strolled by. Cato wondered if any of these men had been tasked by Sinius with spying on them. When they were clear of the last group he continued his conversation with Macro.

'At least we know that the bullion is here. If not in the camp, then somewhere in Rome.'

'Oh, that's a comfort,' Macro replied drily. He gestured towards the city where a million people lived. 'Bound to be easy to find.'

'It's a start. In any case, we have to report to Narcissus. He needs to be told about the silver, and the rest of what we've discovered.'

'Fine. And how are we supposed to get to the safe house if we're being watched?'

'I've been thinking about that. I've made two trips there and Sinius doesn't seem to know about it. The only way that's possible is if his man was on patrol while I left the camp. The patrols have been going on different watches. Now, it might be a coincidence but both times I left the camp was when Burrus's cohort was sent into the city. It's more than likely that Sinius's man is in our cohort.'

Macro thought through Cato's line of reasoning and nodded. 'It's even more likely that he's in our century.'

'I agree.'

'Shit.' Macro hissed through his teeth. 'It could be anyone, even Tigellinus or Fuscius. Or both.'

'Then we'd better start by suspecting them, and be on our guard.' Cato frowned. 'The thing is, we must get in touch with Narcissus as soon as possible. We're out on our own here. If anything happens to us he needs to be aware of all that we've uncovered. So we're going for a drink tonight. Somewhere close to the safe house.'

'The River of Wine?'

Cato nodded. 'It's as good a place as any. We know the layout.'

Macro scratched his cheek. 'And after the other night they know us. I doubt there'll be a warm welcome.'

'We're not looking for a fight, and we can be sure that Cestius and his friends won't be showing their faces there, if they've got any sense. The River of Wine will serve our need perfectly. Come on.'

They signed out with Centurion Lurco's clerk and left the camp and passed through the city gate. Taking the same street as they had used before, they made their way down the Viminal Hill. They spoke in low tones as they walked. Once in a while Cato looked back, but Sinius's agent knew his job well enough to remain out of sight.

'What if we're not being followed?' asked Macro. 'I don't like this pretending that we're just out for a stroll. It ain't natural.'

'Good. If we acted normally then that in itself would look suspicious. Trust me, we're doing fine. And we are definitely being followed. Sinius's man will be watching us like a hawk.'

Ahead, the street bent slightly and ran on for another hundred paces before it reached the square where the inn stood. Cato took a deep breath. 'Let's pray this works.'

They strode into the square and made towards the inn. The place had not yet filled up with the usual evening customers and there were several tables free. As soon as they entered, the innkeeper's face fell and he hurried over to them before they could sit down.

'I'm sorry, gentlemen, but you're not welcome here. Please leave. Now. Please.'

Cato raised his hand. 'Don't worry, my friend. There's just the two of us. Here for a quiet drink. We won't cause any trouble. Just to put your mind at rest . . .' Cato reached into his purse and drew out five sestertii and slapped them on the table. 'Have this on account. What we don't drink you can keep. How's that?'

The innkeeper looked at the coins with a torn expression and then nodded. 'You can stay. But I'll have my eye on you. The first sign of any trouble and I'll send my woman for the urban cohort. Now, sir, what'll you have to drink?'

'Make it the best wine in the house,' Macro cut in quickly as he eased himself on to a bench. 'And for five sestertii it had better be good.'

The innkeeper made a sour face as he scraped the coins into his palm and scurried away.

'What now?'

Cato sat down opposite Macro and then looked round the inn. A small party of men, ten of them, in worn tunics and cloaks sat to the side of the inn, away from the entrance. Cato nodded towards them. 'That's what I need.'

Macro twisted round for a quick look. 'Them? What for?'

'A way for me to get out of here and to the safe house without our shadow following me. Wait here. If I get them to help us, I want you to go to the bar and order something to eat. Make sure you are visible through the entrance.'

'You'd better tell me what you're up to, lad,' Macro grumbled.

'You'll see soon enough. If I go, wait here for me.

Keep an eye on the entrance and see if any familiar faces turn up. I'll be all right. Trust me.'

Cato rose to his feet before his friend could protest any further and made his way over to the workmen. They stared suspiciously at the Praetorian.

Cato smiled. 'No need to worry. I'm not looking for trouble. I just want to ask a favour.'

'A favour?' A short muscular man with cropped dark hair raised his eyebrows. 'What kind of favour?'

'One I'm prepared to pay for.' Cato took out his purse and jingled the coins inside. 'I'm supposed to be meeting a woman friend tonight, but her husband has got wind that she's found herself a lover. He's outside with some friends, waiting for me. They followed me here from the camp. I need to get out of here without them knowing. So, if I could swap cloaks with one of your party who stays with my friend there,' Cato indicated Macro, 'and leave with the rest of you, there's twenty sestertii for your trouble.'

'For that price she must be quite a woman,' one of the other men mused.

'Trust me, she is.' Cato smiled.

The short man pursed his lips. 'You want to screw another man's wife, and you want us to help you. That's a dirty business, friend. Why should we help you?'

'Because the woman's husband is a tax collector.'

'Why didn't you say?' The man grinned. 'Of course we'll help – for thirty sestertii.'

Cato's expression hardened. 'Thirty? Twenty-five, no more.'

'So, she's not so good that you won't haggle over her, eh?'

Thirty sestertii was more than a month's wages for a labourer. Cato frowned, as if struggling over the price, and at length he nodded. 'Thirty then. Fifteen now and the rest when I'm in the clear.'

'Fair enough, soldier.'

He counted half the money out and then the stocky man turned to one of his mates, a tall skinny rake, in his fifties. 'Porcinus, you're the same shape. Give him your cloak.'

'Give him yours,' the thin man snapped back.

His colleague turned towards him and pointed a stubby finger at his chest. 'You'll do what I say if you know what's good for you.'

Porcinus opened his mouth to protest, then thought better of it and nodded sullenly. He undid the pin that held the neck of his cloak together and handed it to Cato, taking his in return. As Cato put on the man's cloak, his nose wrinkled at the scent of urine. 'You're fullers, I take it.'

'That we are.' The stocky man grinned. 'Best toga cleaners in the city. Can't help it if piss is the main ingredient of the process. I dare say your woman might not agree with your choice of rescuers tonight.'

'I'll have to take that risk.' With a reluctant sigh, Cato pulled the hood up over his head. 'Let's get going then.'

The men drained their cups and stood, some of them pulling up their hoods like Cato, so that he would not stand out. The man with his Praetorian cloak put it on and went to sit with Macro, his back to the entrance. Macro poured him a cup of the wine that had been placed on the table a moment earlier. The fullers headed for the doorway and noisily made their farewell to the innkeeper.

Then, with Cato in their midst, they strolled outside into the square and made for a small alley leading up into the Subura district. That suited Cato well enough, and he joined in their banter, laughing along when someone made a crude joke about the innkeeper's wife. All the while he kept shooting quick glances at the doorways and side alleys leading off the square. Nothing moved except for a mangy dog trotting from one pile of refuse to the next. Cato stayed with the group of fullers as they left the square and walked up a narrow alley squeezed between the crumbling tenement blocks of Rome's poorest district. Then, as the alley turned a corner, he patted the stocky man on the shoulder and muttered, 'I'll take my leave of you here.' He handed over the rest of the coins. 'My thanks to you.'

The fuller's face was all but invisible in the dark alley as he replied, 'Give my regards to that lady of yours.'

'That I will.'

'And you can hand back Porcinus's cloak to me as well.'

Cato doubted that Porcinus would ever see his cloak again if he surrendered it now. 'I haven't finished with it yet. I'll give it back to him when I return to the inn.'

'All right then,' the fuller responded quietly. 'Come on, lads.'

Cato backed into an arched doorway as the sound of footsteps padded off over the dirt and refuse that coated the alley. He stood quite still, hardly daring to breathe, until the sound of the fullers faded away against the background noises of the city: occasional shouts and the shrill wail of hungry infants and the clatter of window shutters. He waited longer, to be sure that no one had followed them into the alley. At length Cato eased himself out of the doorway and cautiously made his way to the street where the safe house was. He stopped a short distance from the block and waited again, until he judged that no one was watching the entrance, from the outside at least. Then he crossed the street to the entrance and ducked inside the narrow doorway.

The rank odour of sweat and boiled vegetables filled the darkened stairwell. He trod as lightly as he could on the wooden steps but they creaked alarmingly as he climbed. He heard muted voices from behind some of the doors, and inconsolable sobbing from another. Then he was approaching the fourth storey. Cato slowed, his heart pounding from the climb, and the tension. A thin ray of moonlight shone through an opening in the wall, piercing the gloom and provided faint illumination. There seemed to be no movement on the landing and Cato went to the door and reached for the latch. And froze.

It was the faintest of sounds, like cotton rasping lightly on wood. The sound of a breath being drawn. Cato fumbled with the catch as his right hand dropped to his side and stealthily drew out the dagger from the sheath beneath his cloak. There was a rustle and a rush of footsteps on the stairs above. Cato spun round, throwing back his hood with his spare hand while the other thrust the dagger forward, ready to strike. He caught a dull gleam in the shaft of moonlight and realised that the other man was armed as well. He had his back to the light and his face was in darkness as he stumbled to a halt a short distance beyond Cato's reach.

'Stay back!' Cato hissed. 'Drop the knife!'

There was tense silence for a beat and then the other

man lowered his blade and returned it to its sheath with a soft click. He descended the last two steps to the landing and into the faint light.

'Septimus...' Cato let out a deep sigh and his shoulders sagged in relief. 'Bloody scared the shit out of me.'

Narcissus's agent chuckled nervously. 'You didn't do too badly yourself. Now let's get inside.'

Once the oil lamp had been lit the two men sat on the bedrolls either side of the pale yellow flame. Septimus had brought some bread and sausage with him wrapped in a fold of cloth and stuffed in his side bag. He offered some to Cato and the two ate from time to time as they talked.

'I got the message that you wanted to make a report,' said Septimus, gesturing to the hiding place beneath the floorboards. 'There's been a few developments at the palace that Narcissus thinks you should know about. That's why I'm here. Been waiting for nearly two days.'

'Why were you waiting on the stairs?'

'Never pays to shut yourself in a room without any way out. Now, what did you have to report?'

Cato related the details of the meeting he had had with Sinius earlier on and Septimus frowned. 'He wants you to kill Lurco? But why? He's one of their men. One of their ringleaders, according to the man we interrogated. It doesn't make sense.'

'Unless Lurco has done something to compromise their plans.'

'Yes, that's true. It's never a bad thing to cut out the weak links in the chain.'

Cato could not help smiling at the euphemism. Septimus was clearly the creature of the imperial secretary, and just as ruthless. He brushed the thought aside and decided to voice his doubts.

'I've had some time to study Lurco and I can't say that he strikes me as the conspirator type. He lacks the nerve to see something like that through.'

'Then he's a cowardly traitor,' Septimus sneered.

'But do the Liberators strike you as being cowardly? They may hide in the shadows but it takes courage to oppose the Emperor. They stand to lose everything if they are discovered. That takes guts. More guts than I think our Centurion Lurco has.'

Septimus was silent for a moment. 'So what are you suggesting?'

'That the man you questioned gave up the wrong name. To put you off the scent. I'm not surprised. I'd have tried to do the same in his position.'

'Lurco is innocent then?'

'I don't know for certain. All I'm saying is that I find it hard to believe he could be working for the Liberators. Let's assume that the man you interrogated was attempting to wrong-foot you. He was trying to hide the name of his true master, so he names Lurco instead, to protect Centurion Sinius.'

'That would make sense.' Septimus frowned. 'But that still doesn't explain why Sinius wants you to kill Lurco.'

'He said it was a test.'

'There are better ways to test you. Why pick a senior officer? Why not a ranker, someone who would not provoke nearly so much interest?'

'Unless that's the point,' Cato suggested. 'To increase

the stakes and ensure that Macro and I are irrevocably committed. That said, I can't help feeling there's something more to the choice of target. They want Lurco out of the way for a reason, I'm sure of it.'

'Why?'

Cato shook his head. 'I have no clear idea. Not yet.'

Septimus folded his arms together and leant back against the cracked plaster on the wall. 'What do you think we should do about this test of yours?'

'I don't see that we have a choice,' Cato replied. 'Not if we want to get any further in uncovering the plot. We have to do as Centurion Sinius asks.'

Septimus's eyes widened. 'You mean to kill Lurco?'

'No. Of course not. But Lurco has to be removed. In such a way that it looks to Sinius that he has been killed. There's something else you need to tell Narcissus.'

'Oh?'

'Sinius offered to pay me and Macro to do the job. He showed me a small chest of newly minted denarii.'

Septimus leant forward. 'From the stolen bullion?'

'I think so.'

'Then there *is* a link between the robbery and the Liberators, as we'd feared.'

Cato nodded. 'Narcissus is going to have his hands full. First the conspiracy, then the food riot, and that attempt on the lives of the imperial family.'

A brief look of surprise flitted across the other man's expression. 'What do you mean?'

It was Cato's turn to be surprised. 'He didn't tell you? When the Emperor was on his way back to the palace from the Accession games, he was ambushed close to the Forum. A gang of armed men attacked the party and a handful broke through the ring of bodyguards. One of them made an attempt on Nero before they were thrown back.'

'Oh, yes. I heard there'd been an . . . incident,' Septimus said uncertainly. 'Narcissus has men out on the street looking for the perpetrators.'

'I take it that Cestius has not been found yet?'

'Cestius?'

'He was the man who led the attack and nearly managed to kill Nero. There's a good chance there's some connection between him and the Liberators.' Cato thought briefly. 'They've made one attempt. There may be others.'

'I'll warn Narcissus.' Septimus was silent for a moment. 'Is there anything else to report?'

Cato shook his head. 'What was it that Narcissus wanted you to pass on to us?'

Septimus shifted and rubbed his back. 'As you know, Claudius agreed to the betrothal of his daughter Octavia to Nero last year. He didn't want to make the arrangement too quickly in case it seemed like the ground was being prepared to name Nero as his heir. However, the Empress pushed him into it. Then, several days ago, the Emperor told his advisers that he was thinking of conferring the title of proconsul on Nero.'

'Proconsul?' Cato could not hide his astonishment. The title was assumed by the gilded few in the senate who had completed their year as consul. Even though the rank had become largely honorific since the end of the Republic, it was still a bold decision to award the consulship to a boy of fourteen. 'That's going to put a few noses out of joint in the senate.'

'Indeed. Narcissus tried to persuade the Emperor to abandon the notion, but Pallas backed the Emperor and Narcissus lost the argument.'

'Pallas?' Cato had not yet revealed what Macro had seen below the imperial box on the day of the Accession games. He had no more desire to be embroiled in the personal relations between the Emperor and his wife than Macro. Nevertheless, Pallas was up to something. Cato scratched his chin and continued. 'Do you know if the idea to confer the title came from Claudius?'

'I doubt it. It is not the kind of decision that he would be confident of taking on his own.'

'Then he was prompted by someone. Most likely Agrippina. Positioning her son for the succession.'

'That's what Narcissus thinks.'

'And Pallas? What is his involvement in this?'

Septimus was silent for a moment before he replied. 'Pallas is a confidante of the Empress, as well as being one of Claudius's closest advisers.'

Cato smiled. 'Something of a conflict of interests there, I'd say.'

'Unless he, too, is preparing a place for himself in the succession.'

'Is that what Narcissus thinks?'

'The imperial secretary sees it as a possible course of action he needs to be aware of,' Septimus replied warily. 'As long as Pallas does nothing to, ah, accelerate the succession of the Emperor then Narcissus cannot act openly against him.'

'But I dare say he is prepared to act against Pallas in a covert manner, if he isn't already doing so.'

'That is not for me to say, and it is not within your

remit to even think about it,' Septimus said coldly. 'Your job is to gather intelligence and only act as Narcissus directs you to. Is that clear?'

'Of course. Nonetheless, Centurion Macro and I prefer to be aware of the wider situation. We have our reasons to be wary of your master.' Cato paused and then leant forward slightly. 'Macro and I will leave Rome when our task is complete, but you will remain here. I'd be careful not to tie my fortunes to those of Narcissus if I were in your place.'

'You are speaking out of turn, Cato. I am loyal to Narcissus. It's a rare quality these days, I know,' he said drily, 'but at least some of us know what it means to be loyal, and follow our orders without question.'

'Fair enough.' Cato shrugged. 'It's your funeral.'

The other man glared at him, tiny darts of reflected flame glowing in his eyes. Then Septimus lowered his gaze and cleared his throat and spoke in a less impassioned manner. 'What are you going to do about Lurco?'

'I've got an idea. But we're going to need to bring him here. Then I'll need you to get him away from Rome, until the business with Sinius and his friends is over. Can that be arranged?'

'I'll see to it. The centurion can have a quiet holiday at the empire's expense. Can't vouch for the quality of the accommodation though,' Septimus added, and then was silent for a moment. 'I'd better get back to the palace and report to Narcissus. I'll come here every evening from now on. I get the feeling we're running out of time as far as the conspiracy is concerned.' He stirred and eased himself on to his feet with a grunt. 'I'll leave first. Give me a while before you follow, just in case the entrance is being watched.'

He crossed to the door, gently eased the latch up and left the room as quietly as possible. Cato heard some of the steps creak faintly and then there was silence in the stairwell. Cato pulled the borrowed cloak tighter about his shoulders, his nose wrinkling with distaste at the reek of urine. He sat still for a while as he pondered the situation. Macro was right. This was no business for a pair of soldiers to be involved in. The two of them were far more use to Rome out on the frontiers fighting barbarians. That was simple thinking, Cato chided himself. The empire faced enemies from all sides and it was the duty of a soldier to deal with any threats. Besides, Narcissus had promised to reward them if they successfully carried out the task he had set. Thought of that set Cato's mind towards Julia.

He had been trying not to think of her, but she was a distraction that was hard to ignore, like a permanent ache in his heart. The moment he let his mind wander, it was likely to turn to memories of Julia and the anxiety over the prospect of not spending the future with her. They had not seen each other for over a year. While Cato had been involved in the hunt for the fugitive gladiator, Ajax, and the campaign against the Nubians in Egypt, Julia had been living in Rome, enjoying the society of the rich and powerful. She was young and beautiful and bound to attract attention.

Cato's anguish welled up painfully as he recalled just how beautiful she was, and how she had given herself to him, heart and body, in the months they had been together in Syria and Crete. The fact was they had been apart longer now than they had spent together, and though his feelings for her had been constant, nourished by the prospect of reunion, he had no idea if she still felt the same about him. His instinct said she did, but Cato was distrustful of himself. It could just as easily be naive wishfulness. The rational part of his mind coldly determined that it was more than likely her affections had faded. What was the memory of a young soldier to her now when she was surrounded by the refinement and glamour of Rome's high-born society?

Cato reached up a hand to his face and traced his fingertips across his cheek, as she had done when they first made love. He closed his eyes and forced himself to recall every detail of the setting, every sound and scent of the small garden beneath a Syrian moon. His mind painted her into the scene with every embellishment that he could summon, far beyond the skills that the rough hand of nature used in fashioning the real world. Then his fingertips brushed over the hard lumpy skin of the scar and his heart burned with disgust and fear. Cato's eyes flickered open. He breathed deeply for a moment before picking up the lamp and rising to his feet. He placed the lamp back on the shelf and blew out the flame.

Outside in the street he glanced around but there was no sign of movement so he turned back towards the main street running down the Viminal Hill. As he approached the square, Cato stopped for a moment and thought quickly, picturing the entrance to the inn where Macro sat waiting. There were two alleys a short distance apart that offered the best view of the River of Wine. Cato approached the square from the far end of the alley nearest to the inn. Resting one hand on the handle of his dagger, he crept forward, feeling his way along the rough wall and carefully testing each footstep as he went. There was a shallow bend a short distance before the alley gave out on to the square and as he reached it, Cato held his breath and peered round the corner. At first he saw nothing, but then the faintest loom of mist curled gently from behind a buttress close to the end of the alley. It came again and Cato realised that someone was breathing. From where he was he could not see anybody, so he steeled himself and continued forward slowly, until he had a view of the profile of a man watching the inn across the square. Cato stood quite still and waited. At last the man shifted his position slightly and afforded Cato a quick three-quarter view of his features. Cato smiled thinly as he recognised the man beyond any doubt.

He slowly worked his way back round the corner and up the alley. There he pulled the hood of the cloak up and continued until he came to the junction with the next thoroughfare. He made his way to the edge of the square and affecting a drunkard's gait he half walked, half staggered across to the entrance of the inn, being careful not to glance towards the alley from where Sinius's spy kept watch. Cato stumbled through the door and veered off towards the table where Macro and Porcinus were sitting. As soon as he was out of sight of the alley, Cato stood straight and flicked the hood back.

Macro smiled with relief. 'You've been quite a while. Done what you needed to?'

'Yes.' Cato undid the pin fastening of the foul-smelling cloak and tossed it to Porcinus.

'You finished with me then, sir?' asked the fuller. 'I can go?'

'Yes. Better catch up with your mates before they spend all the money I gave 'em.'

'Too bloody right.' Porcinus hurriedly swapped Cato's cloak for his own and nodded a swift farewell before he hurried off. Cato took his place on the bench opposite Macro.

'I've told Septimus everything I can. He'll report back to Narcissus. Now we need to decide what to do about Lurco. We'll need to work fast.'

'Why? What's the rush?'

Cato thought for a moment. 'The Liberators have made one attempt on the imperial family. They failed last time, and they'll be planning something else. The sooner we work our way into the conspiracy the better. Oh, and there's one other thing.'

'Yes?'

'I know who Sinius is using to watch us. He's in an alley across the square. It's Tigellinus.'

CHAPTER THIRTEEN

The morning air was cold and clammy as the century stood to attention on the small parade ground between the barrack blocks. Macro and Cato held their shoulders back and thrust their chests out as Centurion Lurco and his optio marched down the front rank scrutinising the uniforms and equipment of his men. They were wearing their off-white tunics under their armour and were armed with shield and javelin as well as their swords and daggers. It was kit that the Praetorian Guard rarely had cause to use, but the recent riot had obliged the elite formation to turn out ready for action every day.

Macro and Cato were positioned at the end of the front rank, on the right flank, with the other men from Tigellinus's section. They stood, legs braced, shield gripped by their left hand while their right held the javelin shaft, just below the swelling of the iron weight designed to give the weapon greater penetration when it was thrown. They, like the rest of the men on parade, were staring straight ahead. The centurion stopped a short distance from them and scowled at one of the men in the next section.

'There is what looks like a turd on your boot.'

'Yes, sir.'

'You do not come on parade dressed in shit.'

'No, sir. Must have been one of the wild dogs, sir. Got into the barracks.'

'You-do-not-make-excuses!' Lurco shouted into his face. 'Clear?'

'Yes, sir.'

Lurco turned briefly to his optio. 'Tigellinus, mark him down for ten days on latrine duty since he has developed a taste for shit.'

'Yes, sir.' Tigellinus made a quick note on his waxed slate.

The centurion looked the man over for further signs of fault. He reached for the guardsman's sword handle and gave it a pull. There was a slight grating sound as the weapon left its scabbard.

'There's rust on this. Make that twenty days.'

'Yes, sir.' Tigellinus amended his note.

The two officers continued down the line and stopped in front of Macro. Lurco inspected him closely. Finding no fault, he nodded and then turned and strode a few paces back along the line before he called out, so that all his men could hear.

'Thanks to our fine effort the other day the Emperor has requested that my century guards his imperial majesty and his family for the next month. A signal honour, as I am certain you will all agree. To which end I demand a perfect turnout by you men. Until the situation is settled in Rome you will not be wearing the toga. Instead you will appear as you are kitted out now. As it happens, the Emperor is quitting the city for a few days to inspect the works in Ostia and also the draining of the marshes around the Albine Lake, to the south-east of the city. It will be our duty to escort him on these excursions. He leaves tomorrow. So we will be smart and create a fine impression on any civvies that come out to cheer the Emperor. If any of you let me down, you will suffer the consequences.' He turned to Tigellinus. 'Optio, take over.'

'Yes, sir!' Tigellinus snapped his waxed tablet closed and hurriedly placed it in his side bag along with the stylus. As the centurion strode off, making for his quarters at the end of the nearest barrack block, Tigellinus gave the order for the men to fall out, and then strode off in the direction of the camp's headquarters.

Cato and Macro relaxed their posture alongside the other men. Then Macro glanced at Cato. 'What was that about the Albine Lake? Any idea what's going on there?'

Cato recalled that the lake was a large body of water in the foothills half a day's march from the city. He had passed by it a few times as a child and did not relish the memory. The lake was surrounded by low-lying boggy ground infested with mosquitoes and other insects, which made the land useless for farmers, as well as forcing travellers to make lengthy diversions around the affected area. Draining it was a long-awaited project, finally being realised under Claudius.

'Another of the Emperor's big civil projects,' Cato replied. 'Seems there's been more than a few changes in Rome since we left. First a new port, now the lake, and a new wife and stepson.'

'But still the same old Narcissus,' Macro muttered sourly. 'Pulling strings behind the scenes. Some things never change.'

They followed the other men leaving the parade ground and returned to their section room. Fuscius was already there, carefully placing his cleaned armour and weapons back on their pegs. He nodded a greeting as the others lowered their shields and began to follow suit.

'Bloody footslogging,' Fuscius complained. 'It's been bad enough with all the patrols we've had to mount in the city. My bloody boots are giving me blisters.'

'Hah, you're too soft, lad,' Macro replied. 'Wait until you've had to do some proper soldiering, like Capito and me. Then you'd know what real marching is like.'

Fuscius stared at him. 'Spare me the back-in-my-day routine, Calidus. I'm just pissed off with those bloody rioters in the city. Now they've gone and made my life even more difficult because the Emperor wants to divert their attention to the great works he's doing for the benefit of the people. Pah, it's a goodwill stunt and nothing else. I'll be glad when things have settled down again.'

'Assuming that happens,' said Cato.

'Oh it will,' Fuscius replied. 'I've heard a rumour that the Emperor's diverted some grain from Sicilia. Once that reaches the city, it'll keep the mob quiet while other supplies are organised.'

'And where did you hear that?'

Fuscius tapped his nose. 'Friends of friends.'

Macro snorted and shook his head. 'Like *you* have highly placed contacts . . .'

Cato pursed his lips. 'Well, I hope you're right. The Emperor needs to buy some time.'

Fuscius hung up his sword belt. 'There's a dice game in the mess. You two want to come?'

'Sure,' Macro answered. 'Soon as we're done here.' He patted the purse hanging at his side and smiled. 'Time to spend some of the pay that headquarters advanced us.'

'Or lose the lot.' Fuscius laughed. 'I'd be careful to check the dice before you play. Some of the lads are not above trying to put one over on new recruits.'

'I wasn't born yesterday.' Macro raised a fist. 'Besides, let 'em, if they dare.'

Once Fuscius had gone, Macro turned to Cato. 'What are we going to do about Lurco? You said you had a plan.'

Cato glanced towards the door to make sure no one was within earshot before he replied. 'Centurion Lurco is a keen party boy. More often than not he spends the night away from the barracks. It's a question of following him and trying to catch him alone.'

'And then?'

'Then we have to tell him the situation.'

Macro snorted. 'That's great. He gets accosted by two of his men, rankers, and you think he'll sit down quietly for a chat? Let's assume, for argument's sake, that he doesn't listen to us. Then what?'

'Then we use force and take him to the safe house and get Septimus to arrange for him to disappear, until the conspiracy is crushed.'

'And when shall we do it? Tonight?'

'No. We wait until we get back from escorting the Emperor. If Lurco goes missing tonight then there's a danger that a different century will be assigned to guard Claudius while there is a search for Lurco. We need to stay close to the Emperor. Our first duty is to protect Claudius from any further attempts on his life.'

They joined the dice game in the mess hall. Some tables and benches had been dragged aside so that the men could gather round the action. The standard bearer over-saw the cast of the dice and the raucous placing of bets between throws. Cato leant close to Macro and cupped a hand to his friend's ear. 'I need to drop a message off. Tigellinus may still be at headquarters, if he hasn't returned to the barracks. Try and find him and keep an eye on him. If he leaves, you follow him. Agreed?'

Macro nodded. 'Be careful.'

Cato smiled, and then waited until there was a roar of delight and frustration at the latest roll and the winners crowded round those taking the bets to claim their winnings. Using the chaos to cover his exit, Cato slipped out of the hall and fetched his old army cloak that he had worn in Egypt. He had decided that it would be best not to wear a cloak issued from the Praetorian stores if he was to blend in on the streets. When he reached the safe house he wrote a brief note to Septimus explaining his intentions for Centurion Lurco once the century returned to Rome after escorting the Emperor. He placed the waxed tablet in the cavity beneath the floorboards, turned the lamp towards the door as agreed to signal a message, and then left. Back on the street Cato pulled his hood up and headed towards the square where the River of Wine stood. Even though it was late in the morning the streets and alleys were far quieter than usual. The men of the Praetorian Guard and urban cohorts were still patrolling the city and breaking up any gatherings, as well as stopping and questioning anyone acting in such a way as to provoke their suspicion. Cato assumed that most of the Subura's inhabitants were too nervous to venture out for anything other than food and water.

He was making his way down a dim alley when he

saw a figure approaching from the other direction. Like Cato he was wearing his hood up and kept his head bowed. He wore an expensive embroidered tunic beneath the flaps of his cape. There was something about him that sparked a vague sense of recognition in Cato. Something in the way he carried himself as he paced down the alley, the swagger of a fighting man. As they passed, his shoulder caught Cato and he mumbled something that might have been an apology or a warning and continued on his way without breaking his stride.

Cato felt a cold tremor ripple down his spine as he walked on, not daring to look back immediately. It was Cestius. Cato was certain of it. He waited until he was a safe distance before slowing and glancing over his shoulder. The gang leader was already some thirty paces away, and then he turned abruptly into a side alley sloping down towards the Forum. Cato doubled back, ran to the tight junction and peered round the corner. Cestius was walking steadily on, head bowed. He passed an open door where a haggard woman sat on a step with a wailing infant clutched to her small, sagging breast. She muttered something and held out her hand, but Cestius swept by without a word. Cato let him build up a decent lead and then followed him down the alley, hurrying past the woman. He spared her a sidelong glance, just long enough to see her pinched face and large eyes. The infant's arms were thin and spindly and the skull clearly defined under the pale skin. Beyond her he saw other children on the floor of the room, sitting listlessly as the family starved.

'A coin, sir.' She made to clutch at the hem of his cloak and Cato just had to time to swerve beyond her grasp. He increased his pace to get past her and then slowed to keep his distance from Cestius. The big man continued heading down into the heart of the city, emerging a short distance from the Temple of Venus and Rome. Then he turned towards the Tiber, keeping away from the centre of the Forum as he passed along the palace wall. A semblance of normality had returned to Rome, for some at least, and parties of officials and a handful of senators and their retinues crossed the Forum on their way to or from the senate house. A few of the usual market stalls were set up in the porticoes of the basilica, but there was not the usual loud throng of traders and shoppers that normally filled the Forum. Soldiers stood at almost every junction, scrutinising passers-by. Cestius kept clear of the soldiers as far as possible and left by a narrow unguarded alley, heading towards the Boarium market and the warehouse district.

As Cato kept up with the man, his mind was whirling anxiously. Why was Cestius courting danger by taking to the streets when a reward had been placed on his head? Where was he going? Cato scrutinised the other man's clothing. The cloak and tunic were expensive items and Cestius had replaced his heavy boots with a soft leather pair that extended halfway up his calf, the kind of boots that Macro would have derided as effeminate.

Cato continued following Cestius, down towards the Tiber, between the mass of the Capitoline Hill to their right and the palace on the left. The Boarium had suffered the same decline in activity as the Forum and no more than a third of the stalls had been erected. There were fewer soldiers in evidence, mostly clustered outside the offices of tax collectors and money lenders, many of whose premises had been looted during the riot. Cestius continued through the Boarium until he came to the bank of the Tiber, where the Great Sewer emptied into the river, then he turned left towards the warehouse district.

A terrible stench of human waste filled the air as the dark stream of shit, piss and refuse merged into the flow of the Tiber. The hummock of a human body had caught around the bows of a moored barge and a pair of rats were busy chewing through soaked cloth to get at the rotting flesh beneath. Already a boatman was rowing out to the body to retrieve it to add to the small pile of corpses that had been fished out of the river close to the exit of the sewer – the usual harvest of careless drunks, murder victims and accidents. It was a sight Cato had been familiar enough with as a boy when he had come down to the wharf with his father. He recalled that when enough corpses had been gathered to fill a wagon, they would be carried off to a mass grave outside the city walls.

He turned away from the grisly sight just in time to see Cestius exchange a few words with a stout bald man in a bright yellow cloak and green tunic. Two muscular men with heavy clubs stood silently behind the bald man as he talked with Cestius. The bald man smiled and patted Cestius on the arm before they parted company. Cato discreetly scrutinised the man as he approached and noted the gold chain round his neck and the jewels in the rings on his fingers. Clearly a man of some wealth, and not afraid of displaying his fortune in public, as long as he was accompanied by a pair of bodyguards who looked as if they would pulverise anyone who even considered grabbing their master's purse.

Cato steered aside so that they passed each other by a safe margin and continued following the gang leader. Cestius continued for a short distance before he looked round quickly. Then, seemingly satisfied that no one was watching him, he made for the guarded entrance of one of the warehouse compounds. He nodded a greeting to the man at the gates, who heaved one open to admit his visitor and then drew it shut once Cestius had disappeared from sight. Cato felt a surge of panic at the prospect of losing his quarry. He stopped on the wharf opposite the gates and squatted down and retied the lace of his boot as he looked over the gateway. A sign was painted on the wall next to the heavy timbers of the gates announcing that the warehouses were rented out by Gaius Frontinus. It invited interested parties to apply at his offices in the Boarium.

Cato drew a deep breath to steady his nerves and strode up to the gates. The guard stirred and moved to block his way. He was a thickset man with a scarred face and Cato guessed that he must be one of the many former gladiators who turned up in such roles after they had won their freedom, or been discarded by their trainers.

'What do you want?' the guard demanded without any preamble.

'I'm supposed to meet my master here, sir,' Cato replied. 'I saw him enter just a moment ago.'

'Really? So what's his name then?'

Cato opened his mouth and caught himself just in time. If Cestius was in disguise then there was a strong possibility that he was using a false name as well. If Cato tried to use his real name the guard would refuse him entry. Worse still, he might mention it to Cestius on the way out and thereby alert him to the fact that he had been followed.

The pause was long enough for the guard to reach a decision. 'Thought so. You're a chancer. Now turn away and piss off. Before I make you.' He patted the studded club swinging from his belt.

Cato knew that there was no sense in provoking any disturbance. He backed off a few paces and then turned and walked back towards the Boarium. Then it occurred to him that there was still something useful that he could discover and he broke into a run. He pushed his legs hard, looking for the man in the yellow cloak and his two bodyguards. There was no sign of his easily distinguishable cloak on the length of the wharf, and Cato ran on into the Boarium. Even though the market was not filled with its usual dense press of bodies, there were enough people to obscure Cato's view. He pulled himself up on to the pediment of a statue of Neptune and hung on to the shaft of the trident as his gaze swept over the market. Then he saw the yellow tunic, on the far side, close to the hall of the grain traders.

'Oi! You! Get off!'

Cato looked round and saw a soldier from one of the urban cohorts striding towards him. Cato clambered down and made to leave the spot but the soldier blocked his path.

'What do you think you're doing?'

'Looking for a friend.'

'Trying to cause trouble more like.' The soldier growled and slapped the side of Cato's head, making it ring. Cato blinked as he staggered to one side.

'Acer!' a voice cut through the air. 'That's enough!'

An instant later an optio stepped up and glared at the soldier. 'We're here to keep the peace, you bloody fool. Not to start another fucking riot.' He turned to Cato. 'You! Get on your way!'

Cato nodded, and staggered off through the market, heading towards the halls of the merchant guilds on the other side of the Boarium. People who had witnessed the confrontation stared warily after him, as if he carried some kind of frightening mark. It was a sign of the nervous tension that still hung over the city. No one wanted to be associated with any man who fell foul of the military. Cato's head quickly cleared and he slowed to a steady pace as he crossed the market. He could no longer see any sign of the yellow cloak outside the hall of the grain merchants and feared that he had lost his man. As he reached the portico, topped by a pediment and statue depicting Ceres holding a thick sheaf of wheat, Cato paused and looked round. There was no sign of the bald man, so he continued inside.

After the daylight outside it took a moment to adjust to the gloomier lighting of the hall. There was a large open space in the centre filled with tables and benches. Along each wall stood two storeys of offices from which the merchants conducted their trade. At the far end was an auction podium in front of a large board on which the grain cargoes were chalked up for sale. Only it was clear today, and the merchants were in a depressed mood. Cato saw the man emerge from the colonnade at the side of the hall. He crossed to the clerk sitting on the step beside the podium and began to address him. Cato pulled down his hood and turned to one of the merchants standing close at hand. He indicated the bald man and asked for his name.

'Him?' The merchant squinted briefly. 'Why, that's Aulus Piscus. Why do you ask?'

Cato thought quickly. 'My uncle owns a bakery in the Subura. He sent me down here to see if there's any grain to be had.'

'You'll be lucky!' the merchant snorted. 'There's been nothing for days. Your man Piscus snapped up the last cargo.'

'I see.' Cato stared at the bald man. 'I assume Piscus is one of the big dealers in the guild.'

'Only in the last few months. Before then he was just a small-time trader.'

'Looks wealthy enough now.'

'Oh, he's done all right for himself.'

'How's that?' Cato pressed.

'Well, either he came into a fortune, or he's acting as a front for someone who has. Whichever, the lucky bastard's done well out of it. Well enough to pay for those two thugs that guard his back.'

Cato nodded, stepping away. 'Thanks. I won't take up any more of your time.'

'Time's a luxury I can afford right now.' The merchant smiled thinly. 'There's not much the likes of me and your uncle can do until the grain supply flows again, eh?'

Cato shook his head and then moved away. He crossed the hall and approached Piscus and the clerk, overhearing the end of their exchange.

'You let me know the moment the first grain ship reaches Ostia, you hear?'

'Yes, master.' The clerk bowed his head.

The bald man leant closer. 'See that you do, and I won't be ungrateful. Understand?'

The clerk nodded wearily, as if he had heard the same offer several times already that day. He looked up as Cato approached and the bald man turned round with a quick look of anxiety.

'Can I help you?' Piscus asked curtly.

'As a matter of fact, you can, sir.' Cato smiled and politely bowed his head. 'I'm looking for a friend. I missed him in the Boarium a moment ago and then saw him on the wharf, when he stopped to speak to you.'

'A friend? You?' Piscus looked at Cato in his worn cloak with undisguised contempt. 'I don't think so. Why would a wealthy merchant like him have anything to do with you? Be on your way.' He clicked his fingers and his bodyguards stepped forward menacingly.

Cato bowed his head and stepped back. 'My mistake, sir. Perhaps it wasn't my friend.'

He turned and left the hall, moving off along the paved area in front of the guild halls, deep in thought. What was Cestius up to? The gang leader from the Subura clearly had another identity, or there was another man in Rome who could have passed as his twin brother. Cato discounted the idea at once. The man he had followed looked, moved and sounded just like Cestius. In which case why was he passing himself off as a merchant? And what was he doing down in the warehouse district? There was one way to try to find out. Cato made for the small basilica given as the address of the man who leased the warehouses. Entering the building he saw that it was on a much less impressive scale than the grain merchants' hall. A score of open-fronted offices lined the walls. He found the sign of Gaius Frontinus easily enough. Below it, the office was fronted by a plain stone counter. A clerk sat on a stool behind it, working through a ledger.

Cato coughed. 'Excuse me.'

The clerk lowered his stylus and looked up. 'Yes . . . sir?'

'I'm looking for Gaius Frontinus.'

'He's not here, sir. May I help?'

'Perhaps. I'm inquiring about leasing some storage space down on the wharf.'

The clerk took in Cato's poor appearance. 'We don't lease lock-ups. Just warehouses.'

'That's what I'm after.'

'Then I can't help you, sir. We let them two months ago. There's nothing available.'

'I see.' Cato frowned. 'Who did you let them to? Perhaps I could talk to the man and get a sublet.'

'I am not at liberty to say, sir. In any case the master dealt with that contract personally.'

'Then can I see Gaius Frontinus? To discuss a contract when the present one expires?'

'The master is not here, sir, as I've already told you. He left Rome on business a month ago.'

'Did he say when he would be back?'

'No, sir. He just left me a letter telling me to take charge in his absence.' The clerk coughed self-importantly. 'Now, if you don't mind, sir, I have work to do. You might try one of the other leasing offices. I'm sure you'll find what you're looking for with one of the smaller concerns. Good day.'

Cato nodded and walked off slowly. He felt the familiar tingle of cold dread grasp the back of his scalp. There was more to the conspiracy than Narcissus had realised. The Liberators, or whoever else it was, were preparing the ground on a far wider scale than the imperial secretary had guessed. Cato could link only a few elements of the puzzle together but one thing was for certain. The enemy was well organised and their plan was already being put into effect.

CHAPTER FOURTEEN

The sun was shining fitfully through the scattered clouds as the Praetorians took up their positions around the stage that had been set up for the Emperor to address his summoned guests. Most of the senators and their wives had been carried out on litters to the side of the Albine Lake. The lower ranks of Roman society had made the short journey in carts, on horseback or on foot, and were to stand behind the seating areas that had been arranged for the senators. March was coming to an end and the ground was firm and free of the glutinous winter mud that had hampered the work of the engineers. They were tasked with digging the channel that would drain off most of the lake, and the surrounding marshes, into a tributary of the Tiber.

Centurion Lurco's men were footsore after the previous day's march from Ostia, and the march to Ostia from Rome two days before that. Claudius had made a quick inspection of the progress on the new harbour and gave a series of short speeches around the town to reaffirm his love of his people and to promise them the rich rewards that would flow from the increase of trade passing through the port. The Emperor had also provided a banquet for the leading politicians, merchants and administrators of the port. Having appeased the people of Ostia, he and his court had moved on to the engineering works at the Albine Lake to attempt to win over the people of Rome. Claudius was due to make a public announcement and the men of his escort had been speculating on its nature all morning.

'Has to be a spectacle,' said Fuscius. 'That or a distribution of food. Maybe both.'

'As long as he doesn't reduce our rations to supply the mob,' Macro grumbled. The Praetorian Guard had been on half rations for three days and his stomach was beginning to growl. Despite the imperial order for other towns and cities to send their food reserves to the capital, only a handful of wagons were entering the city each day and most of the stock was bought by those wealthy enough to pay the premium prices demanded. Supplies earmarked for the public granary were diverted by corrupt officials and pilfered by those entrusted with guarding what little grain remained. Many of the poorest and weakest had already starved to death and as the supply wagons rumbled into the capital they passed the carts carrying the dead to the open graves outside the walls of Rome. The cries and wails of lamentation echoed through the narrow streets of the slums and Macro wondered how long it would take for the grief to turn once more to anger. When that happened, only the Praetorians and the urban cohorts would stand between the Emperor and the mob.

Cato had been listening to the exchange. 'If there's no bread then Claudius is going to have to depend on circuses to keep the mob happy. If he is going to stage a gladiatorial event then he'll have to do something special.

Even then, he may have satisfied their bloodlust but their bellies will still be empty.'

Fuscius shrugged. 'I suppose. But it might buy him a few more days in which to find some food. Just as long as he doesn't take any more of ours. If he does, then there'll be consequences,' the young Praetorian added darkly.

'Consequences?' Macro spat on the ground with contempt. 'What consequences? Claudius is the bloody Emperor. He can do what he likes.'

'You think so?' Fuscius cocked an eyebrow. 'He's Emperor just for as long as the Praetorian Guard says so. We made him. We can just as easily put someone else in his place, if he forces us to.'

'Who's this "we" you're talking about? You and a few disgruntled mates?'

Fuscius looked round and lowered his voice. 'Not so few of us, judging from word going round the barracks. If the time comes, I'd make sure you're on the right side, Calidus.'

'Maybe, but until then, I'd keep my mouth shut if I were you. You're talking treason, lad.'

Cato smiled thinly. 'You know the saying, treason is just a question of timing. Fuscius has a point. Best to see how things work out *before* you pick a side.'

Macro shook his head in disgust. 'Politics . . . Good soldiers should never get involved in it.'

'Oh, I agree with that, sure enough,' Cato replied. 'Trouble is that sometimes politics can't help getting involved with soldiers. Then what's a man to do?'

As he asked the question, Cato watched Fuscius for his response. The younger Praetorian was silent and his expression suddenly became fixed and unreadable as he glanced over Cato's shoulder.

'What's all this then?' Tigellinus barked. 'Gossiping like old ladies? Fall in, the Emperor's coming.' He jerked his thumb in the direction of the tents further along the side of the lake. The German bodyguards were stirring and the slaves hurried forward with the imperial litters. The men of Lurco's century raised their shields and javelins and began to form up around the stage. Half of the men stood either side of the approach to the rear of the stage while the others, including Cato and Macro, provided a loose screen around the sides and front. Meanwhile the last of the senatorial families had arrived to take up their seats.

'Shit . . .' Macro muttered and Cato glanced sharply at him.

'What?'

'To the right, close to that red litter, see that party of hooray Horatios. Try not to be obvious.'

Cato casually turned his head to survey the Emperor's audience until he saw the party that Macro had indicated – twenty or so young aristocrats in expensive tunics beneath their rather more austere togas. They seemed to be gathered around one individual. He was a tall but manifestly overweight individual whose jowls shook as he talked. At first Cato could not recognise him from that angle, but then the man slapped his thigh and laughed loudly enough for the sound to carry clearly over the hubbub of the other senatorial guests, several of whom turned in his direction with expressions of disapproval. The man turned and glanced towards the stage and Cato felt a chill seize his heart.

'By the gods,' he muttered. 'Vitellius . . . Bastard.'

'Who is he then?' asked Fuscius.

Cato shot a warning glance at Macro before the latter replied. 'He was senior tribune in the Second Legion a few years back.'

Fuscius made a wry smile. 'Doesn't sound like you approve of him.'

'He nearly got us killed,' Cato said flatly, as he considered how much it was safe to say. He was cross with himself, and Macro, for their reaction to seeing Vitellius again. The former tribune had been involved in a plot to assassinate the Emperor while Claudius was in Britannia. Even though Cato and Macro had foiled the attempt, Vitellius had managed to deftly exculpate himself. 'Vitellius is the kind of man who puts himself first, above all other considerations. A word of advice, Fuscius. Never step in his way. You'd be crushed under his heel with no more regard than if he had trod on an ant.'

'I see.' Fuscius stared towards the loud group of aristocrats for a moment. 'Still, seems like a popular lad.'

'He has charm,' Cato admitted, recalling all too painfully how the tribune had seduced Cato's first love, and then killed her when there was a danger that she might expose his plot to kill the Emperor. 'Bastard,' he repeated.

'I just hope he doesn't see us,' said Macro. 'We didn't exactly part on good terms, Fuscius,' he explained.

Cato watched as Vitellius turned away again, engrossed in conversation. 'We should be all right. He can't possibly recognise us under all this kit.'

A brassy blast cut through the air to announce the approach of the Emperor. The Praetorians quickly snapped to attention, shields held in and spears grasped perpendicular to the ground. The public fell silent and stood respectfully. Behind Cato the imperial litters made the short trip from the tents and then their occupants waited until the German bodyguards had taken their place at the very foot of the platform. The Emperor and his coterie of close advisers climbed out and advanced down the short avenue of Praetorians, and up on to the stage. Out of the corner of his eye Cato could see that Claudius was doing his best to disguise his limp and suppress his tic and look dignified before his guests. He made his way up on to the dais and sat on the gilded throne. There was a pause as he surveyed the audience with an imperious tilt to his head and then he waved those that had them back to their seats. Narcissus and Pallas stood discreetly behind the dais, as befitted their status. Though they wielded far more power than any senator, consul or proconsul, as freedmen they technically ranked lower than the poorest freeborn Roman citizen presently starving to death in the most squalid districts of Rome.

'Remember, sire, keep it clear and keep it short,' Cato heard Narcissus say.

'I kn-kn-know,' Claudius replied tartly out of the corner of his mouth. 'I'm no fool, you know.'

He cleared his throat with a rather unpleasant guttural sound and drew a deep breath.

'My friends! Rome has endured much hardship in recent months. Our b-b-b-beloved city is troubled by social unrest. The failure of the grain supply has vexed our p-p-people. I have done all in my power to scour Italia for food to feed the capital. However, I believe we are close to solving the g-g-gr-grain shortage.'

Cato's ears pricked and he sensed Macro stir beside

him. Finding a reliable supply of food was the key to ending the strife in the city. Once that was dealt with, the people would be grateful to their Emperor and his enemies would no longer be able to exploit the discontent. Claudius had better be right, Cato thought. If he raised hopes only to dash them, it would only inflame the anger of his people.

The Emperor was about to continue when Narcissus leant forward slightly and spoke in an undertone. 'Remember, pause for effect.'

Claudius nodded, staring at the audience for long enough for a few uncertain coughs to break out. Then he launched back into his prepared speech. 'Until the people's bellies are filled again, it is only ri-ri-right that the Emperor offers Rome the com-comfort of enter-tainment to help them through the c-cri-crisis. If their stomachs are empty, then let their hearts b-be-be filled instead!' He thrust his arm into the air with a dramatic rhetorical flourish.

'Pause for applause,' Narcissus prompted and there was a brief delay before those in the audience who had been primed clapped their hands. The sound quickly spread and swelled and Narcissus smiled cynically, while his master bathed in the adulation of his audience. Narcissus allowed it to go on for a while and then made a cutting action with his hand. The applause died away, rather too soon for the Emperor's taste and his brow creased into a frown before he continued, with a gesture towards the channels and dams that had been constructed to link the lake with the Tiber's tributary.

'By the end of next month, my engineers will have completed their work here and once the lake is dr-

drained, we will, b-b-before the end of the year, have increased the farmland close to R-r-rome by several thousand iugerae. More land means more grain. Never again will Rome go h-hun-hungry!'

This time Narcissus did not need to prompt the applause. It was freely given by those who were relieved at the prospect of pacifying the mob.

'Before the lake is dr-dr-dr-drained,' the Emperor continued, 'it is my intention to use the natural arena of the Albine lake to stage the gr-gr-greatest gl-glad-gladiatorial spectacle in history.'

The current of excitement that swept through the crowd was palpable and it was a while before the muttering died away enough for Claudius to resume.

'Two fleets, crewed by ten thousand gladiators, will fight on the lake, b-be-before the eyes of the entire pop-population of Rome! For generations to come, people will remember the reign of Cl-cl-claudius not because of food riots but because of our gladiators and the spectacular N-nau-naumachia they provided. Our heirs will look on us with envy. Th-thin-think on that, and pass the word into every street and alley of Ro-rome!'

Claudius thrust out his arms, as if to embrace the thousands who stood cheering before him. Cato caught a look of smug gratification on the face of Narcissus as he turned to Pallas. The latter looked furious, but held his position, and a moment later forced himself to join in the celebration with muted applause.

'Bloody hell.' Macro shook his head and muttered to Cato, 'Where's he going to find ten thousand gladiators? He's mad.'

'No,' Cato responded quietly. 'Just desperate.'

Claudius turned away from his audience and arched an eyebrow at his two closest advisers. 'Well?'

'A fine speech, sire!' Narcissus clapped his hands together. 'The Naumachia is just what your people need.'

'Indeed,' Pallas agreed. 'Your speech was so good that one grieves over its brevity.'

Narcissus glanced daggers at the other freedman and then smiled brilliantly at the Emperor. 'Ah, yes! But brevity is an art that few in history have mastered as well as you, sire.'

'Yes, quite.' Claudius nodded vigorously. 'And when w-word of the games reaches the vulgar mo-mo-mob they'll forget that they were ever h-h-hungry. Speaking of which, it's time to return to the palace. I need to eat. I have a craving for mush-mushrooms.'

With a last gracious wave to his audience Claudius left the dais and limped down from the stage back to his litter. Pallas followed quickly, trying to steal a lead on his rival. Narcissus let him go and then, as he passed by Cato and Macro, he seemed to catch his boot and trip over his toga. His arms flailed as he fell against Cato. Cato felt the imperial secretary's hand thrust something into the palm of his shield hand.

'Are you all right, sir?' Cato asked, as he helped Narcissus back on to his feet.

'I'm fine,' Narcissus snapped. 'Unhand me, soldier.' He shook off Cato's grip and hurried to catch up with Pallas.

'Charming man, that,' said Macro.

'He's a freedman,' Fuscius hissed. 'Shouldn't be allowed to treat a Praetorian that way. It ain't right.'

As the Emperor climbed into his litter, those summoned to hear his brief announcement began to shuffle back towards their own litters and horses, anxious to get back on the road to Rome before the route became clogged with traffic. Centurion Lurco cupped a hand to his mouth and bellowed the order to his men. 'Sixth Century! Fall in behind the imperial litter!'

'You heard him!' Tigellinus shouted. 'Move yourselves!'

The Praetorians began to hurry over to form up behind the German bodyguards surrounding the litter. Cato hung back and when he was sure that he would not be observed, he opened his hand and saw a small, neatly folded sheet of papyrus. He thumbed it open and saw a few words written in fine print. He crumpled it up and closed his fist before he took up his station beside Macro near the front of the column and muttered to his friend, 'Narcissus wants to meet us in the safe house as soon as we return to Rome.'

The imperial secretary looked up anxiously as Septimus opened the door to Cato and Macro late in the afternoon. The shutters were open and pale shafts of light illuminated the room. Narcissus was leaning against the wall, his arms crossed. He waited until the door was shut before he spoke.

'You've taken your time.'

'We came as soon as we could,' Cato replied.

'Are you sure that no one saw you come here?' Narcissus asked earnestly.

Cato nodded. 'Tigellinus was called to headquarters to get tonight's watchword. We left before he got back to barracks.'

'What if the Liberators have other men watching you?'

'We doubled back and stopped a few times to check. We're safe.'

'Safe?' Narcissus laughed humourlessly. 'No one is safe at the moment. Not you, not me, and not the Emperor.'

Macro cocked his head to one side. 'Somehow, I think vulnerability is more of an issue for those further up the chain of command.'

Narcissus stared at him. 'If you really think that, then you are a fool, Centurion Macro. Your fate is tied to mine. If our enemies win the day, do you really think they will be satisfied by removing just the Emperor and his immediate circle? Look what happened when Sejanus fell. The streets were running with the blood of anyone who was even remotely associated with him. So spare me your delight in the greater misfortune of others.' He paused, as a thought struck him. 'There really ought to be a word for that quality since so many people seem to relish the misfortune of others.'

Cato cleared his throat. 'You sent for us for a reason.'

'I did. What did you make of the Emperor's announcement?'

'About the games? Or about the improvement of the supply of grain?'

Narcissus smiled. 'Both.'

'I don't see how he can possibly stage his naval spectacle. Where is he going to get so many gladiators from? I doubt there are ten thousand in the whole of Italia.'

'There aren't. Calling them gladiators is stretching a point. Some of them will be. But the rest will be criminals and the scrapings of the chain gangs from the mines and imperial estates. As long as the people get a spectacle they'll remember for as long as they live then they won't pay too much attention to the quality of the individual combats. We'll dress them up and place a weapon in their hands and let them get on with it, with freedom for the winners. That should provide sufficient incentive to get stuck in.'

'What about the ships?' asked Macro. 'How are you going to get warships up to the lake?'

'The engineers' barges are going to be made to look like biremes. How many people in Rome do you think can tell one end of a boat from another? It's all about appearances, Macro.'

'Not all,' said Cato. 'A spectacle does not feed its audience. What of the grain the Emperor mentioned? Where's that coming from?'

'That we don't yet know exactly,' Narcissus admitted. 'Septimus, you'd better fill them in.'

The imperial secretary nodded and was silent for a moment as he collected his thoughts. 'With that recent trouble in Egypt restricting the flow of grain, there was always going to be a shortage. That's where the guild of grain merchants comes in. If one source of grain begins to dry up, they find another province to import it from. As far as I understand it, they had compensated for the situation by offering tenders to suppliers in Gaul and Sicilia. The cargoes were landed in Ostia and carried up the Tiber to Rome, and then put up for sale in the guild's hall. The thing is, a handful of merchants bought up almost every shipment, bidding up well above the normal price range. There won't be another grain fleet arriving from Egypt until late in the spring. Meanwhile there's only a tiny trickle of grain reaching the market. Nowhere near enough to feed Rome.'

'So,' Narcissus intervened, 'the pressing issue is to find those who have been buying all the grain and then find out where they have been storing it. If there's been a plot to corner the market on grain, then I dare say the Emperor is not going to be too pleased when he discovers who is responsible. He might spare them from being thrown to the mob if they are public spirited enough to give their stocks to the Emperor to distribute to the public. In the meantime, we await a convoy of grain from Sicilia. I sent word to the governor of Sicilia a month ago to send us whatever grain he has sitting in the island's granaries. The first convoy should reach Ostia any day. When it does, the grain will be handed over directly to a cohort of the Praetorian Guard, for escort to Rome. That will assuage the mob's appetite for bloodshed and disorder temporarily. For now, we must discover who has been hoarding the grain.' Narcissus nodded at Septimus to continue.

Septimus stirred. 'It should have been an easy task, but the thing is when I questioned the merchants in whose name the shipments were purchased it turns out that they were acting on behalf of someone else and were paid generously to act as intermediaries.'

'For whom?' asked Macro.

'That's just it. They never met the final buyers, or buyer. They were funded in silver and told to deliver the shipment to a warehouse close to the Boarium. One rented out by Gaius Frontinus.'

Cato felt his pulse quicken. 'I know it. I've been there. That was where I lost Cestius.'

'Cestius?' Naricissus sounded surprised and he exchanged a brief look with Septimus.

'Do you know him?' asked Cato.

'Only by reputation. He leads one of the largest criminal gangs in the Subura, the Viminal Hill thugs, I believe.'

'That's right. But you also know him by sight. He was the man who led the attack on the Emperor that day we escorted him back from the camp.'

Narcissus thought a moment. 'The big man? The one you saved young Nero from?'

'That's him.'

'So that's Cestius,' Narcissus said deliberately. 'What has he got to do with this warehouse then?'

Cato explained how he had seen the man and followed him across Rome, and that he was known to at least one regular member of the grain merchant's guild. 'It's more than likely Cestius is behind the attempt to control the grain supply.'

Narcissus stroked his chin. 'But he'd need a fortune to do that. The street gangs do well enough, but it would take them several years at least to amass a fortune big enough to buy up the grain stocks. There's only one likely source for that kind of sum.'

Cato nodded. 'The stolen bullion.'

Septimus cleared his throat. 'Which means that Cestius is working with the Liberators.'

Narcissus glanced at him with a cold expression. 'Evidently. Cestius is another enemy we'll have to take care of in due course. In the meantime, you two will be dealing with Centurion Lurco. What is your plan?'

'Nothing elaborate,' said Macro. 'We follow him, wait until he's alone and then have a quiet word with him, if we get the chance. If that doesn't work, then we knock him on the head. Either way, we'll bring him back here and turn him over to Septimus. Then it's up to you to keep him out of circulation until our job's done.'

The imperial secretary stared at Macro for a moment before he replied in a cutting tone, 'Brilliantly conceived, I must say. It is a comfort to know that the army still employs strategists of the first water.'

'It'll work,' Macro replied sourly. 'That's all that matters.'

'See that it does.' Narcissus sighed. 'I fear that we are running out of time, gentlemen. There must be a reason why our enemies want Lurco to disappear. It has to be more than some kind of initiation test. They're getting ready to make their move, I know it. And the Liberators are not the only danger facing us. The Emperor's gladiator spectacle will distract the mob for a moment. Unless we feed them before it's too late then the people will turn on us like ravenous wolves and tear Rome to pieces.'

CHAPTER FIFTEEN

Dusk thickened over the capital and shrouded it in a thin mist as Centurion Lurco quit the Praetorian camp and entered the city. He was dressed in a thick blue cloak and only the soft leather boots that rose halfway up his calves indicated that he was a man of status. The bulge on his hip revealed that he was armed; lone footpads and small gangs of robbers presented a considerable danger in the darker alleys and byways of Rome.

Macro and Cato tailed him at a distance. After returning to the Praetorian camp following their meeting with Narcissus they had kept watch on the centurion's quarters, waiting for him to emerge. He came out once in the afternoon, in his military tunic, and made a brief visit to headquarters. Then, as the light faded, he stepped out in his cloak, ready to find his evening's entertainment. Cato and Macro fell into step fifty or so paces behind the officer. Like Lurco they were armed, and Macro carried a leather sap filled with sand and small pebbles.

Centurion Lurco made his way down the hill at a carefree pace, not once bothering to look behind him as he negotiated the dark streets. There were still plenty of people abroad, enough for Cato and Macro not to draw attention to themselves, and not so many that it was difficult to keep Lurco in view. He stayed away from the main thoroughfares as far as he could, to avoid the inconvenience of encountering any of the patrols and checkpoints of the urban cohorts.

As they tailed him into the Subura, Macro muttered to Cato, 'Can't imagine Lurco wanting to spend any time in this dump. That, or he's got cheap tastes, and friends who share them.'

'I'm sure there are plenty of young rakes who get their thrills from slumming it,' Cato replied. 'Unless he's heading somewhere else.'

A little further on, the centurion abruptly turned into a street to his right.

'Shit,' Macro hissed. 'He's on to us.'

They trotted forward to the junction before cautiously peering round the grimy corner of a tenement block. Lurco was a short distance ahead, striding on without any evident sign of concern. They let him open up a safe lead before resuming their pursuit.

'Why don't we take him now?' asked Macro. 'We're not far from the safe house.'

Cato shook his head. 'Let's see where he goes first. He might lead us to some interesting acquaintances.'

'Or he might just lead us to a bunch of delinquent piss-heads,' Macro countered. 'Or we might lose sight of him.'

'Not if we're careful. Besides, it wouldn't be a good idea to start a scene where we might draw a crowd. We'll wait and see who he meets, and then deal with him the moment we can catch him on his own.' Cato realised that he had spoken in a peremptory tone and glanced quickly at his friend to see if Macro had taken any offence. But Macro just nodded briskly, as if he had been given an order. Cato was mildly surprised by the little thrill of pleasure he felt at his friend's unquestioning obedience to his will, as well as his confidence in stating it. Perhaps they were both finally comfortable with his promotion over his former mentor. Former? Cato mused. No, not yet. There was still much that Macro could teach him.

'Watch it!' Macro nudged Cato sharply, pushing him to one side, just before he trod in a foul-smelling sprawl of rotting offal outside the door of a butcher's shop. 'Mind where you're stepping, lad. Bloody hell, do I have to hold your hand all the time?'

Cato chuckled.

'What's so funny?'

'Nothing. I was just thinking.'

Macro scowled. 'Which is why you nearly went arse over tit into that lot.'

Ahead of them the centurion had increased his lead and they had to hurry to catch up with him. The failing light made it hard to see Lurco clearly and they risked moving closer to him. Lurco continued steadily down the slope of the Viminal Hill before leaving the Subura district and climbing a street that led up on to the Quirinal Hill where some of the wealthiest inhabitants of Rome lived, their grand town houses interspersed with the more modest homes of lesser citizens and those who bought into the area simply to rub shoulders with their betters.

The last faint loom of dusk had given away to night and there were fewer people on the street now. Lurco turned into a road that ran between some of the larger residences. The plain walls, broken only by imposing doorways and narrow grilled window slits, were mis-leading. Behind the stout timbers of the doors fronting the thoroughfare there would be elaborate and finely decorated residences stretching a long way back from the street. The largest houses would also have ornate gardens, and perhaps even fountains.

At length Lurco stopped outside one of the more modest-looking entrances and paused to arrange his cloak before climbing the steps and rapping on the door. Cato pulled Macro into an arched doorway of a closed shop which afforded a clear view of the house, without exposing them to Lurco's view should he glance back down the street. They watched as Lurco knocked again and a moment later the iron grille in the door snapped open. There was a brief exchange that was too muted for Cato and Macro to make out any words, and then the door opened. Lurco entered and the door was shut firmly, followed by a dull scrape as an iron bolt shot home. The street was still, apart from a distant figure much further up the road, then he, too, was lost from view in the gathering darkness.

'What now?' asked Macro. 'Wait until he emerges again?'

'That's right. And see if we recognise any of the faces going in or coming out.'

Macro rubbed his hands together. 'Could take hours.'

'More than likely.'

'Bollocks. It's going to be a cold night.'

Cato nodded, biting back on the urge to tell Macro to stop stating the obvious. They stood in silence for a while and then Macro started to stamp his feet to try to keep them warm. Amplified by the archway, the sound of the nailed soles striking the flagstone threshold of the shop seemed deafening. Cato turned to him with a frown.

'Enough! You'll give us away.'

'Who to?' Macro gestured irritably towards the empty road.

Cato pressed his lips together for an instant and then responded as calmly as he could. 'It would be useful to know who owns that house. Why don't you scout round it while I watch the entrance? See if you can find someone who knows.'

Macro looked at him doubtfully. 'What if Lurco comes out while I'm gone?'

'He hasn't been there very long. I suspect he'll be a while yet. If he does emerge then I'll follow him and try and take him by myself and meet you back at the safe house. Just don't be too long yourself.'

'All right.' Macro eased himself away from the wall of the arch and stretched his back. With a brief glance both ways to make sure there was no one in sight, Macro stepped out into the road and then hurried across to the other side. He walked towards the entrance and did not pause as he passed by. A short distance beyond was a narrow alley that ran down the side of the house and he turned into it and disappeared from view.

Cato let out a sigh of relief. Macro was a fine soldier but clandestine duties that required patience did not number amongst his strengths. Cato squatted down in the shadows and settled his back against the door of the shop.

The alley was barely four feet wide and Macro guessed that it was little more than a service passage shared by the house Lurco had entered and its neighbour. The walls rose high on either side, leaving only a thin strip of gloom from the night sky. Although the ground was soiled underfoot Macro was acutely aware of the noise that his boots were making as he made his way down the alley and he tried to tread as softly as he could. He traced one hand along the wall, fingertips grazing over cracked plaster and patches of exposed bricks. Fifty paces or so along the alley he came to a small door and gently tried the latch but it was locked. Macro proceeded a little further and then heard some voices, a light-hearted blend of conversation and laughter. An instant later the notes of a flute added to the sound of the party. It came from a short distance ahead and Macro saw that the wall abruptly dropped to half its height as the main part of the house gave way to the gardens.

He hurried on and the sounds from the other side of the wall covered any noise from his boots. A short distance ahead Macro could see the tall cone of a poplar tree rising above the wall and he made towards it. If he could climb the wall, then the tree would give him some cover as he looked over the top, he reasoned. From there he could spy on Lurco and see whom he spoke to. However, the wall rose a good ten feet above the street and Macro hissed bitterly. Looking round he saw nothing that he could use to stand on. With a resigned grunt he reached under his cloak and took out his sword and tested the surface of the wall with the point. The plaster crumbled away freely and the bricks underneath were soft enough for Macro to chisel out a step. He worked quickly, creating several more up to a height where he should be able to reach the top.

Sheathing his sword, Macro pulled himself up and began to climb carefully, grimacing as his fingers strained for purchase in the hurriedly cut holds. He drew his knife and worked at the handholds, proceeding steadily towards the top of the wall. At length he could just reach up and grip the edge. With his knife sheathed, Macro heaved his body up, boots scraping to help lift his weight until his torso rested across the top of the wall. Macro paused for breath, his heart pounding from the exertions of the climb. The boughs of the poplar tree shielded him from the party guests in the garden and when he was ready, Macro swung his legs up and eased himself forward for a better view of the walled garden.

Low-cut shrubs and shaped bushes surrounded a paved area around a large oval pond. Here and there pieces of sculpture stood atop small marble columns. Even though it was a chilly night the guests of the house sat outside, warmed and illuminated by the braziers arranged on the paving stones around the pond. There were at least a hundred people at the party, Macro estimated. Mostly younger men, like Lurco, expensively dressed. In among them were a number of women in short tunics, the customary attire of prostitutes. Most wore lurid make-up, faces powdered white and eyes outlined with kohl, and their hair was carefully arranged in tresses and curls. Slaves moved among the throng with jars of heated wine that left thin tendrils of steam in their wake. Macro licked his lips at the sight and hoped there might be a chance of getting a quick jar in at the River of Wine once he and Cato had completed their night's work.

Macro edged a little further forward so that he might have a better view, keeping low to the top of the wall where one of the boughs of the poplar stretched over the alley. He searched the crowd for Lurco and easily picked him out in his blue cloak, standing with a group of men his own age, clustered about a brazier as they drank. The centurion was grinning as he and his companions listened to one of their number who had his back to Macro. The brazier threw his outline into sharp relief as he gestured with his hands and the others roared with laughter.

Having picked out Lurco, Macro methodically scrutinised the other guests and had almost satisfied himself that there were no faces he recognised when his gaze fixed on two women standing aside from the rest, talking animatedly in the faint red hue of the nearest brazier. Macro squinted, straining his eyes to make sure of what he was seeing. There was no question of it, the woman on the left was Agrippina. What the hell was she doing here? Macro watched her for a moment before turning his attention to her companion, a tall, slender woman with dark hair, unfussily pinned back into a bun. There was something familiar about her, but Macro could not place her and he frowned with the effort of trying to remember and then gave up. He had seen enough from his vantage point and still needed to discover the identity of the owner of the house.

Macro wriggled back and carefully swung his legs over the side of the wall before easing himself down. He tried to feel for the holds he had cut into the bricks earlier but his boots stubbornly refused to find them. With his arms tiring, Macro took a breath and let himself drop down into the alley. He landed awkwardly and fell back heavily on to his buttocks, jarring his spine.

'Fuck!'

Macro struggled to his feet and rubbed his back and then continued down the alley towards the rear of the house, where he knew the slave quarters would be. With a party in full swing there was a chance that the escorts of some of the guests might be waiting in the slave quarters that were always at the far end of the more opulent houses, kept at arms length from those they served. A short distance ahead the alley came to an end and Macro could hear a different set of voices now. Subdued conversation, lacking the high-spirited tone of the party guests. Macro adjusted his cloak to conceal his sword as best he could and then glanced round the corner of the wall. There was a wider thoroughfare here, passing between the rows of fine residences. Sure enough, there was an open gate at the rear of the house, illuminated by the flickering flames of torches mounted in iron brackets on either side. Several litters lined the street, their bearers hunched down in their cloaks beside the wall in an effort to keep warm as they waited for their masters to leave the party. Two burly men with clubs stood watch on the gate.

Taking a deep breath, Macro strolled out into the street and boldly approached the gate. The watchmen regarded him with vague interest. Macro raised a hand in greeting.

'Good evening!' He forced a smile. 'You got a party going on here?'

One of the guards stepped forward and hefted his club so that the thick shaft rested in his spare hand. 'Who wants to know?'

Macro drew up a short distance in front of him and frowned. 'That's an unfriendly tone, mate. Just asked a question.'

The watchman's face remained expressionless. 'Like I said, who wants to know?'

'Fair enough.' Macro shrugged and jabbed his thumb

at himself. 'Marcus Fabius Felix is the name. Personal bodyguard to one Aufidius Catonius Superbus, who managed to slip out of his father's house to join his friends at a party up on the Quirinal. Muggins here has been sent by his adoring father to bring young Aufidius home. So, have you got him here?'

'Don't know,' the watchman replied flatly. 'Don't much care either.'

'Now don't take that tone with me, friend.' Macro tried to sound hurt. 'I'm the one who should be feeling put out, having walked up and down these bloody streets for most of the afternoon and evening. This is the only party I've come across, so do us a favour and let me take the boy home.'

'Nothing doing, friend,' the watchmen replied with a flicker of a smile. 'So piss off.'

'Piss off?' Macro's eyes widened. 'There's no need for that. Just doing my job. Why don't you go and ask your master, whatever his name is, if my boy is here? At least do that for me, eh?'

'I ain't *your* slave,' the watchman growled. 'I ain't running at your beck and call. And the master won't want me to disturb him during a party.'

'Touchy type, is he?' Macro asked sympathetically.

For an instant the watchmen's expression betrayed a touch of anxiety. He clicked his tongue. 'Seneca's all right. It's that woman friend of his – the bitch. If anyone interrupts her night then she'll have the skin scourged off their backs quick as anything. Seneca will see to it. Obeys her like a dog.'

'That's tough.' Macro nodded. He cocked his head slightly to one side, as if in thought. 'All right then, I'll give this place a miss. I'll tell my master that I couldn't find the party.'

'Would be for the best, for all of us,' said the watchman, with relief. Then his face hardened again and he let his club swing loose. 'So, on your way.'

Macro nodded and stepped back into the middle of the street and walked off. He passed the back of two more houses before he cut back up another alley to rejoin Cato.

'Find out anything?' asked Cato.

'Enough,' Macro grinned. 'The house belongs to young Nero's tutor.'

'Seneca?' Cato breathed out deeply.

'Not only that, but I saw the Emperor's wife there among the guests.'

'You saw that? How?'

Macro explained how he had climbed the wall and then approached the watchmen on the rear gate.

'That would seem to rule out any link between Lurco and the Liberators,' Cato responded. 'Agrippina and her followers are no more likely to be in favour of a return to the Republic than Claudius.'

'Unless Lurco's spying on them for the Liberators,' Macro suggested.

'Then why would Sinius want him killed?'

Macro grimaced, cross with himself for not grasping the point at once. 'All right. Then maybe they want him dead because he is a follower of Agrippina.'

'Or maybe it's simply a coincidence that Lurco is there. Did you see him speak to her? Or Seneca?'

'No.'

'Hmmm.'

Both men were silent for a moment before Cato hissed with frustration. 'I can't see my way through all this. What the hell has Narcissus shoved us into this time? There's no question about there being a conspiracy . . . or perhaps more than one conspiracy.'

Macro groaned. 'Listen, Cato. This is making my head hurt. What do you mean, more than one conspiracy?'

Cato tried to put together the information they had been given by Narcissus at the start of their mission and all that they had uncovered since then. 'Something doesn't feel quite right about this. There's too much contradiction and too much that just doesn't make sense.' He paused and glanced towards his friend with a rueful smile. 'You're right about this line of work not being for us. Give me proper soldiering any day.'

Macro slapped him heartily on the back. 'I knew I'd make a professional of you! Come, let's tell Narcissus we've had enough of this bollocks and get back to where we belong. In the legions. Even if it means not getting a promotion. Has to be better than this, skulking around dark streets on a cold night, spying,' he concluded, his tone laced with disapproval that verged on disgust.

'I wish it was as simple as that. Narcissus won't let us go that easily. And you know it,' Cato said bitterly. 'We've no choice in the matter. We have to see this through to the end.' He hunched forward and gazed towards the entrance to the house. 'Meanwhile, we wait for Lurco to come out.'

The hours of the night crept past as they sat in the shadows of the archway. Cato felt the cold more keenly than his friend and his limbs trembled despite his best efforts to will them into stillness. He sat on the cold stone with as much of his cloak bundled up beneath him as possible and then wrapped his arms tightly about his knees. The street remained still and quiet, aside from the occasional passer-by and a covered wagon that trundled along the road in the direction of the Forum. Now and then there was a faint chorus of laughter or cheering from the revellers in the garden. Then, close to midnight, the door of the house opened and a dull shaft of light spilled across the street. A small party of young men and women emerged, loud and raucous, and staggered off. Cato stared at them for a moment, but none was wearing the distinctive blue cloak.

Macro stirred. 'What if Lurco is with a group of them when he comes out? What if they go on to somewhere else?'

'Then we follow them and wait again. At some point he's going to have to head back to the camp.'

'And so do we.'

'As long as we're back in time for morning assembly, there's no problem.'

'Other than being cold and bloody tired.'

Cato turned to him and smiled thinly. 'Nothing we're not used to.'

'Hurnnnn,' Macro growled irritably.

More of the party guests began to leave the house and their litters appeared out of the side alley, led by slaves bearing torches to light their way home. The two men in the archway across the street scrutinised the departing revellers with strained nerves.

'Bet you Lurco is the last bloody one to leave,' Macro grumbled. 'Trust our luck.'

'Shhh!' Cato hissed, craning forward. 'There he is.'

Two men stood on the steps at the entrance to the house. Lurco was conspicuous enough in his cloak, even without the hood being drawn back to reveal his face. The other man was wearing a plain black cloak, with the hood pulled far enough forward to conceal his features. They descended into the street and set off towards the Forum, in the direction of the archway where Cato and Macro were concealed.

Cato pressed himself against the wall of the arch and Macro crouched low by the door. Cato felt his heart pounding and stilled his breath in case the wisps of exhaled breath betrayed his presence. The boots of the approaching men echoed off the walls of the buildings on either side of the street. They talked loudly, in the way of men who have drunk deeply.

'Good party,' said Lurco. 'That Seneca knows how to entertain in style.'

'Style?' the centurion's companion snorted. 'The wine was good but the food was miserly, and I've seen better whores.'

'Ah, er, yes. I was actually talking of Seneca himself. Quite the raconteur.'

'Rubbish. Just another poser who thinks he's a cut above the rest of us because he can swear in Greek. And as for that harlot, Agrippina . . . I'm pretty broad minded, Lurco, but the damn woman is insatiable. Anything from a slave boy up to a raddled old fool like Seneca is fair game to her.'

There was a short pause as the pair passed Cato and Macro and then Lurco continued in a lower voice, 'I'd be careful about saying such things. You're talking treason, especially when you say it in front of an officer of the Praetorian Guard.'

'Pah, you're nothing but pretend soldiers. I've seen better men than you in the worst centuries of the Second Legion, and that's saying something . . .'

Their voices faded as they strode down the street. Macro seized Cato's arm and whispered urgently, 'That voice. You know who that was?'

Cato nodded. 'Vitellius.'

'What do we do? We can't risk having that bastard recognising us.'

'Come on.' Cato rose up. 'We mustn't lose them.'

Before Macro could protest, Cato set off after the two men, keeping to the shadows along the side of the street. With a muted curse Macro followed him. They kept their distance so that their footsteps would not be heard by those ahead of them. As Lurco and Vitellius headed out of the Quirinal district and reached a crossroads, Lurco slowed down and moved off to the wall of a house just before the junction. He hoisted up the hem of his cloak and fumbled under the tunic beneath.

'You go on, Vitellius. I'll catch you up.'

The other man glanced back and then nodded and turned the corner, leaving Lurco to sigh with relief as his piss spattered against the base of the wall.

'This'll do us,' Cato decided. 'Let's get him now, while he's on his own.'

Macro nodded and reached for his cosh as the two of them increased their pace, padding along the other side of the street until they were almost opposite Lurco. At the last moment they dashed across the cobbled way and Lurco turned dully at the sudden sound. Cato thrust his shoulders hard, slamming him against the wall. Lurco let out a pained grunt as the breath was driven from him. Macro swung his cosh across the back of the centurion's skull and his legs gave way and he collapsed into the puddle he had just created.

Cato was breathing hard and his heart was beating fast. It had been easier than he expected. Now they had to deliver Lurco into the hands of Septimus at the safe house. 'Let's get him up. Give me a hand.'

They reached down and pulled the unconscious centurion up between them, slinging one of his arms over each of their shoulders.

'Ready?' Cato asked softly.

'Yes.'

'Let's get away from here before Vitellius comes looking.'

They had gone no more than a few paces when a voice called out behind them.

'What the hell are you doing?'

Cato looked round sharply and saw Vitellius standing at the corner of the junction, no more than ten feet away. Even though it was night, the sky was clear and the loom of the stars gave just enough light to reveal their faces to each other.

Vitellius looked confused for an instant and then his jaw sagged a fraction before he called out in astonishment, 'You!'

CHAPTER SIXTEEN

Macro was the first to break the spell. He threw Lurco's arm off and spun round as he reached inside his cloak for the cosh. It was in his hand before he took his first pace towards Vitellius. The former tribune was too stunned to react, and further hampered by the wine he had consumed. Even so he ducked as Macro's cosh swept through the air and the impetus sent it thudding into the side of the building. Macro's knuckles cracked against the bricks and he let out a strangled cry of anger and pain as Vitellius stumbled back. Cato dropped Lurco and turned to help his friend but Macro charged on, thrusting his spare hand into Vitellius's chest and sending him sprawling on to the paving stones.

'Help!' Vitellius cried out. 'Help me!'

Macro fell on him, driving the wind from his lungs. At the same time he drew his bloodied cosh hand back and swung it viciously at the side of Vitellius's head. The latter sensed the movement and jerked round, taking the blow on his shoulder.

'Oh, sod it!' Macro growled as he dropped the cosh, balled his hand into a fist and smashed it down directly into the other man's cheek. Vitellius's head struck the ground beneath and he went limp, his arms dropping untidily across his chest. Macro drew his hand back to strike again but saw that Vitellius had been knocked cold. Macro struggled up, breathing hard. Cato stood on the other side of the fallen man, staring down.

'Great,' said Macro. 'Now what do we do?'

'He's seen us. He knows we're in Rome. We can't let him talk.'

'So.' Macro smiled cruelly, and drew his dagger out. 'I'd always hoped it would come to this.'

'What the hell are you doing?' Cato grasped his arm.

Macro turned to him with a surprised expression. 'We can get rid of him once and for all. You know what he's done, to us and others. I can't think of a man who is more deserving of a knife in the ribs and being left to bleed out in the gutter.'

'No.' Cato shook his head. 'That's not in our orders.'

'Then it's a bonus.' Macro pulled his hand free.

'No. Think about it, Macro. Witnesses saw him leave with Lurco. Narcissus is bound to hear of it. If he turns up dead, then Narcissus will know it was us.'

'So? He's no friend of Narcissus either.'

'That doesn't mean Narcissus won't use it against us. You don't go and kill the son of one of the most influential men in Rome without there being consequences.'

Macro was silent for a moment. 'Then let's just make him disappear. Drop him into the Great Sewer.'

'What if his body is found and recognised?'

Macro held up his dagger. 'I can make sure that he won't be recognised.'

'Put that away, Macro,' Cato said firmly. 'We have to take him with us.'

'Bollocks,' Macro grumbled. 'Won't be easy carrying 'em both.'

'We'll manage. Keep watch while I see to them.' Cato drew some thick twine and a few strips of cloth from the side bag under his cloak. He tied the hands of both men and then stuffed their mouths with the cloth. No one was about, and only the familiar sounds of the capital broke the silence. Cato helped lift Vitellius on to Macro's shoulders and then lifted Lurco, who was more slightly built than his companion.

'Ready?' asked Cato. 'Let's go.'

It was at least half a mile to the safe house and they kept to the side streets as they struggled under their burdens. At one point Vitellius began to stir and Macro was obliged to crack his head against a wall to keep him quiet.

'Don't get a taste for that,' Cato warned him as they continued up the slope of the hill into the Subura district. Just before they reached the safe house they ran into a rowdy group of young men and had to make up some story about their mates not being able to hold their drink. The two parties parted with good-humoured laughter. At last they staggered into the insula and dumped Vitellius in the vestibule before labouring upstairs with the centurion. Septimus opened the door for them, backing into the room which was illuminated by an oil lamp.

'Good work.' He nodded approvingly as he made to shut the door.

'Wait,' Cato gasped. 'One more . . . to come.'

'One more? What are you talking about?'

'Explain later . . . Come on, Macro.'

When they returned with Vitellius, the imperial agent stared at the second body in surprise, and then shock as he recognised his features.

'Are you mad? Good gods, do you know who this is? What the hell is he doing here?'

'He was with Lurco . . . when we took him,' Cato explained between breaths. 'We didn't have any choice.'

'You didn't have to bring him here. Why not leave him in the street?'

'He recognised us.'

'How?'

Cato exchanged a wary look with Macro before he replied. 'I take it that Narcissus has not told you about our past history.'

'Only what I needed to know,' Septimus replied stiffly. 'It is dangerous to possess too much knowledge in my line of work.'

'In that case, it's enough for you to know that we served with Vitellius in the Second Legion in Britannia. We didn't see eye to eye on a few issues.'

Macro chuckled. 'To put it fucking mildly.'

'In any case,' Cato continued, 'we can't afford to have him at liberty. He can link us to the disappearance of Lurco. Until our job is done, he has to be kept out of sight. He'll have to go with Lurco.'

'Or we could get rid of him,' Macro suggested and then raised a hand to placate Cato as his friend glared at him. 'Just trying to think through the options.'

Septimus sucked in an anxious breath. 'Narcissus is not going to like this. Matters are already slipping out of our control. Vitellius must be dealt with.'

There was a groan and the three men turned to see that Vitellius was stirring.

'He has to be blindfolded,' Cato said quietly to

Septimus. 'He's seen more than enough already. We don't want him to identify you.'

'Quite. Deal with it and put him in the other room while we talk to Lurco. We need to find out what he knows about the Liberators' plot.'

Macro took out his dagger and cut a strip from Vitellius's cloak which he wrapped twice round Vitellius's face before tying it off securely. Then he put his hands under the former tribune's shoulders and hauled him into the next room where he dumped him on the floor. The shock of the impact brought Vitellius to full consciousness and he mumbled into his gag as he writhed on the ground. Macro pressed his boot down on Vitellius's shoulder.

'Don't move,' he growled, 'and we might let you live. Cause any trouble and I swear, by all the gods, that I'll cut your throat. Understand?'

The other man stopped struggling and laid still, chest rising and falling. He nodded.

'There's a good patrician,' Macro said, with contempt. He turned away and returned to the other room where Cato and Septimus had propped the other captive up against the wall. Septimus pulled up his hood to conceal his features. Lurco was moaning faintly and Cato reached forward to pull the gag from his mouth. Lurco retched and an acidic waft of breath struck Cato's face. The centurion mumbled incoherently as his eyes flickered and Cato slapped him.

'Come on! Wake up!'

'Whharr . . . What?' Lurco blinked and jerked his head back against the wall with a sharp crack. He winced and let out a pained groan.

'Oh great,' Macro mumbled. 'All we need is for the idiot to get knocked out again.'

'Shhh!' Cato hissed irritably. He leant forward and roughly shook Lurco's shoulder. 'Lurco . . . Centurion Lurco!'

The man groaned and opened his eyes again, blinking as he struggled to focus. He glanced at the faces in front of him and his eyes widened in surprise. 'I know you. Of course I know you. Guardsmen Capito and Calidus. The new recruits.' He frowned as he tried to make out Septimus's face, but it was shadowed by the hood of his cloak and Lurco gave up and returned his attention to Cato and Macro.

'By the gods, I'll have you both crucified for this! Assaulting a superior officer and kidnapping him. You'll be shown no mercy.'

'Shut up,' Cato snapped, raising his fist threateningly. 'You're the one in trouble. Unless you answer our questions truthfully.'

For the first time Lurco looked uncertain, then scared. He swallowed anxiously and licked his lips before responding in a soft voice. 'Questions?'

'Don't play the innocent,' snapped Septimus. 'We know you're part of the conspiracy.'

Lurco's brow creased. 'What do you mean? What conspiracy?'

Septimus kicked him in the stomach, then, as Lurco gasped for breath, he stabbed a finger at him. 'No more warnings. We ask, you answer. Clear?'

'Yes . . .' Lurco whispered. 'Quite clear.'

'Right then. You were named by a traitor who recently fell into our hands. He gave you up before we finished with him. Said that you were one of the ringleaders of the plot to overthrow the Emperor.'

'It's a lie!' Lurco shook his head desperately. 'I'm not a traitor. For Jupiter's sake, I swore an oath of loyalty!'

'So did the man we questioned. Didn't stop him betraying Claudius. Nor you.'

'No. It's a mistake.'

'True enough,' Septimus replied and nodded to Macro. 'See what you can do to loosen his tongue, or his teeth.'

'My pleasure.' Macro smiled coldly and bunched his fists. He hooked his right into the centurion's cheek and Lurco's head jerked hard to the side. A fiery stab of pain shot down Macro's arm, adding to the existing pain following his earlier contact with the wall when he had felled Vitellius. Lurco let out a deep groan. He turned, dazed, to face his questioners again; their shadows, distorted and menacing, played over the far wall of the room. He spat out a bloody gobbet then spoke with quiet sincerity. 'I'm innocent, I tell you.'

'I see,' Septimus sneered. 'Then why were you named as a traitor?'

'I–I don't know. But I swear it's a lie.'

'Pah! You're the liar, Lurco. And a pretty poor one at that. I want the truth. Macro!'

Lurco's eyes snapped towards Macro, wide and pleading. This time Macro struck him with his left, and Lurco took it just above the ear as he tried to move his head out of the way. The centurion winced and his eyelids fluttered for a moment.

'Please . . . please. I'm innocent,' he mumbled.

Septimus regarded him in silence and then stretched up to his full height, narrowly missing one of the beams in the low ceiling. He regarded the centurion for a while and then scratched his nose. 'What do you think, lads? Is he being straight with us?'

'I don't think so,' Cato replied, playing along. 'Remember how long the other traitor lasted before he spilled his guts? It's just a question of how long we have to beat him before he gives up any information. Let's get on with it.'

'My pleasure,' Macro growled, edging forward, his fists raised.

'For pity's sake!' Lurco bleated. 'This is wrong. All wrong. I'm loyal to Claudius. I'm innocent. You have to believe me!'

'No we don't.' Macro pressed his hands together and cracked his knuckles, hoping that he wouldn't have to strike the man again with his bad hand.

'Look at it from our position,' Septimus continued in a more kindly tone. 'Why should we believe you and not the man who gave us your name?'

'Because I'm telling the truth. Ask your man again. Ask him why he's lying.'

'We can't, unfortunately. He died under questioning.'

Lurco went pale. When he spoke again his voice took on a pleading tone. 'Look, there's been a mistake. The man you interrogated, he must have got my name wrong.'

'No, no.' Septimus clicked his tongue. 'He was very specific. Centurion Lurco, Sixth Century, Third Cohort of the Praetorian Guard. That is you, isn't it? There's no mistake.'

'Then . . . then he must have been lying.'

Septimus exchanged an inquiring glace with Cato. 'What do you think?'

Cato pretended to reflect for a moment. 'It's possible. But then there's the other matter.'

'Oh?'

'That other business we discovered. The fact that Centurion Sinius wants him killed. That doesn't seem to make any sense. Very peculiar.'

'Yes.' Septimus nodded. 'Peculiar.'

Lurco looked from one to the other with growing apprehension. 'Sinius wants me dead? What's going on?'

'It's simple,' Macro said. 'Sinius gave us orders to kill you.'

'But we brought you here instead,' Cato continued. 'We already know that Sinius is part of the conspiracy. The thing that's puzzling us is why one conspirator would give orders for another conspirator to be murdered. Care to shed any light on that mystery?'

'I-I don't know anything about it.' Lurco raised his bound hands. 'You have to believe me. I beg you.'

Macro clicked his fingers and looked at Cato as if an idea had struck him. 'Perhaps the traitors are trying to cover their tracks? Dead men tell no tales, and all that.'

'But I'm not a traitor!' Lurco whined. 'I'm not part of any conspiracy!'

'Pipe down!' Macro snarled. 'Or you'll wake everyone in the bloody building.'

Lurco subsided.

Cato spoke again. 'If that's true, why do you think the conspirators want you dead? There has to be a reason. What is it that you know that makes you a danger to them?'

'I don't know. I swear I have no idea. Please believe me!'

The other three men stared at him in silence and the centurion cowered. Septimus took a deep breath and puffed his cheeks out. 'We need to talk. Put him next door with the other one.'

Macro and Cato grabbed the centurion by the arms and dragged him into the next room and placed him against the wall opposite Vitellius. They closed the door firmly behind them and then moved close to Septimus so that their words would not be overheard by the prisoners.

'We're none the wiser,' Septimus concluded bitterly. 'Why would the Liberators want him dead?'

'Perhaps they're just doing the imperial guard a favour,' Macro suggested with heavy irony. 'He's not the best officer I've ever encountered.'

'I think we can discount that,' Septimus replied, not knowing Macro well enough to be certain if he was being humorous.

Cato ran a hand through his scalp. 'If there's a reason why they want Lurco disposed of then it has to be because of something he knows, or because he is in the way of their plans. From what little we've got out of him, it seems he has no idea about the conspiracy.'

'Unless he's a bloody good actor,' Macro intervened.

'That's possible,' Cato conceded. 'But his fear seemed real enough. If he knows something that the Liberators think might threaten their plans, then it's clear to me that Lurco has no idea that he knows what he knows.'

Macro winced. 'Come again?'

'It doesn't matter,' Cato replied as he continued his train of thought. 'If they don't want him dead to keep him quiet, then the reason has to be that he is some kind of an obstacle. They want him replaced.'

'Replaced?' Septimus stared at him. 'Why would they want to replace him?'

Cato's mind grappled with the implications of his suggestion. If he was right then the danger to the Emperor was clear enough. 'Because he commands the Praetorian guardsmen who stand closest to the Emperor at the moment. If the Liberators can get one of their men to replace Lurco then they will be within striking range of the Emperor. Close enough to attempt to kill him. It makes sense. They've tried once already with that ambush on the imperial party the day of the Accession games. Next time they won't have to penetrate his line of bodyguards to stick the knife in.'

Septimus stared at Cato for a moment. 'You could be right . . .'

'Narcissus has to get Lurco and Vitellius out of Rome and keep them out of sight,' Cato went on. 'Then we wait to see who is appointed as the new centurion of the Sixth Century, and we watch him like a hawk. See who he talks to and make sure we're close enough to him to act whenever the century is escorting the Emperor.'

'That's taking quite a risk,' said Macro. 'I doubt that Narcissus will agree to it. Why not just arrest Lurco's replacement? And Sinius while we're at it?'

'Because they will lead us to the rest of the conspirators,' Septimus spoke before Cato could reply. 'And hopefully they'll lead us to what remains of the bullion stolen from the convoy as well.'

'That's right,' Cato agreed. He paused for a moment. 'But we have a more pressing issue to deal with before then – making sure that the grain Cestus has stockpiled is still at the warehouse near the Boarium. If we can confirm that then Narcissus can seize it and the Emperor can start feeding the mob. Once the people have food in their stomachs they'll be offering prayers to him rather than threats. That will knock the wind out of the Liberators' plans.'

'Very well,' said Septimus. 'We'll see to that tomorrow. Meet me at the entrance to the Boarium at noon. For now, you two had better get back to the camp and rest. I'll deal with our two friends.'

'Deal with?' Cato arched an eyebrow.

'They'll be taken somewhere we can keep an eye on them. I'll have them released once it's all over. They won't come to any harm.'

'More's the pity,' muttered Macro.

'How are you going to get them out of the city?'

'I've got a covered cart in a lock-up under the aqueduct at the end of the street.'

Cato nodded and he and Macro turned towards the door. Cato paused on the threshold. 'It just occurred to me. Sinius will want proof that the job's been done. I need something from Lurco.'

He entered the other room and came back a moment later with the centurion's equestrian ring. 'One more touch and that should convince Sinius.'

'Eh?' Macro glanced at him. 'What did you have in mind?'

'You'll see. Come on.'

Cato led the way out of the two-room apartment on to the landing. Just before he closed the door behind them, Septimus whispered, 'Until noon at the Boarium, then.'

Taking care to feel their way down the darkened

stairwell with its worn and creaking floorboards, Cato and Macro left the tenement block and emerged into the street.

'Back to the camp then!' Macro's tone was light hearted now they had completed their task. 'We should get a couple of hours' sleep before morning assembly.'

'There's one more thing to do first,' said Cato.

'What's that then?' Macro asked wearily.

'Something that's not particularly pleasant, but necessary.' Cato steeled himself to face the task, then gestured down the street. 'Let's go.'

CHAPTER SEVENTEEN

The men of the Sixth Century stood formed up, at ease, waiting for their commander to emerge from his quarters to take the morning parade. Centurion Lurco was late and the men would have fallen to muttering and shuffling their feet had they not been under the cold gaze of Optio Tigellinus as he paced steadily up and down the front rank, his staff tucked under his arm.

Cato could not help feeling conspicuous given that it was thanks to him and Macro that the century was standing in the cold, waiting in vain. By now the centurion, and Vitellius, should have left the city and be on the road to the remote villa where they would be held until Narcissus gave the order for their release.

'What the bloody hell is keeping him?' Fuscius whispered fiercely. 'Bet the bastard's in his cot sleeping off a skinful.'

'More than likely,' Macro replied quietly.

'Well, it ain't good enough. Officers should know better than to leave us out in the cold like this.'

'Legion officers would never get away with this,' Macro added. 'They're made of sterner stuff.'

Fuscius glanced at him and muttered in a sceptical tone, 'So you say.'

'I do.' Macro nodded. 'And I defy any man to say otherwise.'

'Who the hell is speaking?' Tigellinus roared as he strode back down the line towards them. Macro and Fuscius instantly shut their mouths and stared straight ahead. Tigellinus swept by, his eyes ablaze as he searched for any sign of the guilty parties. He carried on down to the end of the line, about-turned, and marched back.

'I didn't bloody imagine it. I definitely heard one, or more, of you dumb bastards muttering away like schoolboys on their first visit to a whorehouse! Who was it? I'll give you one chance to step forward, or the whole bloody century is on latrine duty!'

'Shit . . .' Macro spoke through gritted teeth. 'Always shit, one way or another.'

He drew a deep breath and stepped forward a pace.

'Macro!' Cato hissed. 'What the hell are you doing? Get back in line before he sees you.'

Macro ignored him and called out instead, 'Optio! I spoke.'

Tigellinus spun round and strode up to Macro, pushing through the first rank and stopping right in front of him, an enraged expression on his face.

'You? Guardsman Calidus. I expect more from a veteran of your experience. Or was your precious Second Legion no better than a bloody ladies' sewing circle? Eh?'

Cato winced. Under normal circumstances his friend would regard such a comment as fighting talk. The fact that he would have outranked Tigellinus if he had not been forced to go under cover would only fuel Macro's ire. But Macro kept his mouth firmly shut and did not respond to the provocation. Tigellinus paused briefly and then curled his lip as he continued.

'So much for the fighting spirit of the Second. You're on a charge, Calidus. I'll have you on latrine-cleaning duties for ten days. Next time you're on parade maybe you'll learn to keep your mouth shut.'

'Yes, Optio.'

'In line!' Tigellinus barked and Macro stepped back a pace.

The optio shot one last scowl at him, then turned on his heel and made his way back down the line.

'What the hell did you do that for?' Cato whispered out of the side of his mouth.

'He heard me. You know his type, Cato. Won't let a thing lie.'

'All the same, you haven't got time to waste shovelling shit.'

Macro shrugged slightly. 'Right now, I feel I'm wading through the stuff.'

They stood in silence a while longer, and some of the men of other centuries who had been dismissed from morning parade paused as they passed the end of the barracks to look on curiously.

'What are you gawping at?' Tigellinis shouted at them, and the guardsmen hurried on their way.

A tall, stocky officer strode past the end of the barracks in the direction of headquarters, glanced at the Sixth Century, and then paused midstride, changed direction and marched towards Tigellinus.

'What's all this, Optio?' Tribune Burrus called out. 'Why are your men still on parade?'

Tigellinus snapped his shoulders back and stood to

attention. 'Waiting for Centurion Lurco, sir.'

'Waiting?' Burrus frowned. 'What the fuck for? Send for him. Did you send a man for him?'

'Yes, sir. But the centurion was not in his quarters.'

'No? Then where the hell is he?'

The question was rhetorical and Tigellinus kept his mouth tightly closed.

Burrus shook his head. 'Right then, dismiss your men. Send someone to look for Lurco. I want him to report to me the moment he's found.' He raised his voice so that everyone in the Sixth Century would hear his words. 'I don't give a damn about rank when any man under my command fails in his duty. Centurion Lurco is in for the bollocking of a lifetime when I see him. Optio, carry on!'

'Yes, sir.' Tigellinus saluted, and waited for the tribune to stride off before he turned back to the men and drew a deep breath. 'Sixth Century . . . dismiss!'

The men turned to the side and then fell out, making for the barrack block, muttering in low voices as they speculated about the absence of the centurion. Cato and Macro returned to the section room with Fuscius and immediately the younger man closed the door. He turned round with an excited expression.

'This is a turn-up for the books, even for Lurco!'

Macro cocked an eyebrow. 'The centurion has form, then?'

'Oh yes. He's been the worse for wear before but he's never missed a parade. Where the hell has he got to?'

'Probably drunk himself insensible,' said Cato. 'He's going to be for the high jump whenever he turns up. Tribune Burrus doesn't look like the merciful type.'

'True enough.' Fuscius grinned as he placed his javelin

259

in the rack. His stomach rumbled plaintively as he stood back. Fuscius winced. 'By the gods, I'm hungry.'

'So are we all, lad,' Macro replied. 'But we do better than those down in the Subura. At least we get fed regular. Those poor bastards have to hunt for scraps. They'll be dropping like flies soon.'

Fucsius nodded thoughtfully. 'It ain't good. The Emperor's let us down badly. Won't be long until we start starving, alongside the mob. Then there'll be trouble.'

Cato looked at him. 'Trouble? You think there isn't enough trouble as it is?'

'The food riots?' Fuscius shook his head. 'That'll be as nothing compared to what will happen once people begin to starve to death in their thousands. I'm telling you, when that happens the streets are going to be running with blood. The Praetorian Guard will be the only thing that can prevent chaos. The only thing that stands between the Emperor and the mob. And when that happens either Claudius will have to promise us a sizeable fortune to keep us loyal, or . . .'

'Or what?' Macro prompted.

Fuscius shot a nervous glance towards the door to make sure that it was closed, and then continued in a subdued tone, 'Or we choose a new Emperor. One who can afford to pay for our loyalty.'

Macro exchanged a quick look with Cato before he cleared his throat. 'That's treason.'

'You've been in the legions too long, my friend.' Fuscius smiled. 'That's the way we do business in the Praetorian Guard.'

'And how would you know? You've barely served

long enough to know one end of a javelin from the other.'

'I listen to the others. I talk to people.' Fuscius nodded. 'I know what's going on. Claudius may be Emperor for now, but unless he does something to keep the Praetorian Guard sweet, there'll be those of us who might consider finding a new master.'

'Easier said than done,' said Cato. 'Britannicus is too young. So is Nero.'

'Nero may be young, but he's popular. You saw how the guards cheered him at the Accession games.'

'So, we just chop and change our emperors according to popular whim?'

Fuscius pursed his lips briefly. 'It's as good a reason as any. And you can be sure that any new emperor will do all he can to win the Praetorian Guard over as soon as possible. That suits me. And it'd suit you, too, if you were smart enough to realise it.'

Cato did not like the younger man's fickle under-standing of a soldier's duty. He had seen the unpalatable greed burning in Fuscius's eyes and felt an overwhelming desire to cut himself free from the venomous snakepit of Rome's politics. The mendacity and ruthless ambition that filled the hearts of those at the centre of power in the empire was unhindered by any strand of morality. Now that he and Macro had been sucked into this world he longed to return to regular army duties. The need to conceal his true identity and guard his back created a constant and exhausting tension and Cato had no desire to remain in Rome any longer than he could help it. He suddenly realised that marrying into Julia's family might well embroil him in the dangerous and devious world of the capital. Her father was a senator, a player in the often lethal game of politics. If he became part of that life, Cato realised that he would have to live on his wits all the time.

That was no life for a soldier, Cato reflected, then inwardly smiled with amusement at this ready identification of himself. Until recently he had harboured grave doubts about his ability as a fighting man and felt that he was merely playing the part of a warrior. That no longer troubled him. The hard experiences of years of soldiering had engraved the profession upon his soul, just as the weapons of his enemies had left their marks on his flesh so that all could see him for what he was – a soldier of Rome, through and through.

Even as he took comfort from this certainty, Cato felt a pang of anxiety as he wondered if he could balance that with being a husband to Julia, and one day a father to their children, should the gods bless them with any. Other men managed, but Cato wondered if he could cope with such a compromise. Equally, would Julia tolerate it? Would she be prepared to remain the loyal, loving wife while Cato campaigned alongside Macro to safeguard the frontiers of the empire?

He tried to shake off his doubts and concentrate his thoughts on his reply to Fuscius. It was possible that the younger man was testing him. Perhaps Fuscius was involved in the conspiracy in some way. Or had he over-heard something? More worrying still was the possibility that he simply reflected the views of many in the ranks of the Praetorian Guard.

'A new emperor,' Cato mused. 'And you reckon it'll be Nero.'

'Who else?'

'He's the most likely candidate to replace Claudius,' Cato conceded. 'Although, there's another possibility. Why should we bother with another emperor at all? Why not return to the days of the Republic? Of course, we'd be out of a job. What would be the point of the Guard without an emperor to protect?'

Fuscius stared at Cato for a moment. 'Whoever it is that rules Rome, you can be sure that they'll want protection. The senate will need looking after just as much as an emperor. And they'll be prepared to pay for it.'

Macro laughed. 'You're suggesting that the Praetorian Guard enters the protection racket.'

Fuscius shrugged. 'Call it what you like. The fact is, we're the real power behind the imperial throne, or whoever else we choose to support.'

'Do you really think that the army should seize power?' asked Cato.

A smile flickered across the young guardsman's face. 'Not at all. Just think of it as an unofficial check on the power of whoever rules Rome. For which service we will be handsomely rewarded.'

'Or else,' Macro added sardonically.

The latch on the door snapped up and the door swung open and all three men started guiltily as they turned to see Optio Tigellinus standing on the threshold of the room. He regarded them curiously.

'What's this? You look like a bunch of toga lifters caught in the act.' He let out a grunt of amusement before he jerked his thumb over his shoulder. 'Calidus, Capito, you're wanted at headquarters. Centurion Sinius sent for you. Better hop to it.'

'Yes, Optio.' Cato nodded. 'Any idea what he wants?'

'Not a clue.' Tigellinus smiled thinly. 'That's up to you to find out, my lad.'

Cato discreetly felt the slender bulge of the object in his belt purse. He had been expecting the summons.

Tigellinus began to untie the helmet strap under his chin as Cato and Macro made for the door. Just as they reached the threshold, the optio spoke again.

'Don't think that I haven't noticed how fond you two are of slipping out of the camp. You'd better not be doing anything that's going to cause me trouble, understand?'

Cato did not reply, but simply nodded, then gestured to Macro and they left the barracks and headed across the camp to headquarters.

'I understand that Centurion Lurco has gone missing.' Sinius cocked his head to one side as he regarded the two guardsmen standing in front of the desk in his office. 'He's nowhere to be found. The officer in charge of the watch on the main gate reports that he left the camp last night and he didn't return. Can I take it that we need not expect to see him again?'

'Yes, sir,' Cato replied.

'What happened to Lurco?'

Cato reached into his purse and drew out a small object and tossed it on to the desk where it landed with a soft thud. Centurion Sinius could not help briefly wrinkling his nose in distaste as he looked down at the severed finger, bearing the equestrian ring that belonged to Lurco. Cato watched his reaction closely. The finger had come from one of the fresher corpses washed out of the mouth of the Great Sewer. It had been short work to cut the finger off and ease Lurco's ring into place. The combination would have a convincing effect, Cato had reasoned, and would carry more weight than the simple claim that he and Macro had murdered the commander of their century. Sinius lifted the finger up for closer inspection of the crest on the ring and after a brief silence he nodded in satisfaction and laid it back on the desk. He looked up at Cato.

'Very good. I think you two may be the kind of men I can rely on after all. Your skills will be useful in the days to come. Very useful indeed.'

'And what about our money, sir?' asked Macro. 'Capito said you'd pay us another thousand denarii as soon as the job was done.'

'Of course there's a reward. You don't think that I would fail to honour our arrangement, I trust?'

'Trust is something of a luxury in this world,' Macro said. 'You pay me and I trust you. But try to swindle me and you'll end up joining Lurco . . . sir.'

The centurion glared at Macro and he spoke in a soft, chilling tone. 'You dare to threaten me? You know damn well what the penalty is for threatening a superior officer.'

'But at the moment you're not a superior officer.' Macro lifted his lip in a faint sneer. 'You're a fellow conspirator. Or, as some might think, a traitor. The only difference is that you think you're doing it for lofty ideals, whereas Capito and me are doing it for money.'

Cato watched his friend closely. Macro was playing his part well, just as they had agreed during the time it had taken to make their way across the camp to headquarters. It was important that he and Macro had a credible motive for becoming involved in the conspiracy.

Sinius nodded slowly. 'I see. Tell me, are neither of you prepared to act purely out of a sense of duty to Rome?' He shifted his gaze to Cato. 'What about you?'

Cato pursed his lips briefly. 'It's all very well to appeal to patriotism, sir, but the fact is that it makes precious little difference who runs the empire from the point of view of the likes of Calidus and me. Whether it's Emperor Claudius in power or you and your friends makes no odds to the people of Rome, or to us soldiers.' Cato paused. 'As long as there's an emperor, then there's a Praetorian Guard, and we do well enough out of the pay and perks. If you're planning to put your own man on the throne then we're still in a job, and we'll have picked up a nice little bonus for services rendered to you. However, if you're planning on doing away with the emperors and handing power back to the senate, then we stand to lose out, unless we're handsomely rewarded now. So, pardon me for looking out for number one. In any case, I don't suppose for an instant that your lot won't be passing up the chance to make your fortunes out of a change of regime. There are no pure motives in politics, are there, sir?'

'Ha! What are you, Capito? A soldier, or a student of political affairs?'

Cato eased his shoulders back and stood erect. 'I'm a soldier. One who has served long enough to know that his first loyalty is to himself and his comrades. The rest is merely eyewash for fools.'

There was a tense silence in the small office before Centurion Sinius smiled. 'It's reassuring to know that your only loyalty is to yourself. Men like you are a known quantity. As long as you are paid then you can be relied upon. Unless, of course, you encounter a more generous paymaster.'

'True.' Cato nodded. 'Which is why you and your friends will see to it that we're paid well if you want to keep us on your side. All the same, if you try to play any tricks on us, then I promise you won't live long to regret it.'

Sinius leaned back in his chair with a contemptuous expression. 'We understand each other well enough. Just do as you are told and take your reward, and when it's all over you keep quiet.'

'You needn't worry,' said Macro. 'We know how to keep our mouths shut.'

'Then see that you do.' Sinius picked the severed digit up between thumb and forefinger and dropped it into an old rag. He wrapped the soiled cloth round the noisome object and placed it in a small chest where he kept his styli and pens. Snapping the lid shut, Sinius glanced up at the other men. 'That's all for now.'

'Not quite all,' Macro growled. 'Our money.'

'Of course.' Sinius rose from his chair and crossed the office to a strongbox. He took a key on a chain from round his neck and fitted it into the lock. He reached in and drew out two leather pouches then closed the lid. He returned to his desk and set the pouches down with a soft clink. 'Your silver.'

Cato stared at the two bags, quickly estimating their likely contents. He looked up with a frown. 'How much is in there?'

'Two hundred denarii in each.'

'You said a thousand,' Cato snapped. 'Where's the rest?'

'You'll get it when the job is done, and only then.'

'It is done. Lurco has been dealt with.'

'Lurco is one step along the path. Your services are needed for a little longer.'

Cato sucked in a breath and spoke through clenched teeth. 'What else is there to do?'

'All in good time.' Sinius smiled. 'Suffice to say that it'll all be over within a month. Then you shall have the rest of your reward. You have my word on it.'

'Your word?' Cato sneered, reaching forward to take the purses and hand one to Macro. 'Listen, friend. In this world only money talks. You still owe us three hundred each. Now you'd better tell me what we have to do to earn it. If I'm going to put my neck out for you and your friends, then I want to know what you're asking of us.'

'No. You do as you are told, when you're told. That is all. The less you know, the better for all of us. Now go. Return to your barracks. You'll be given your instructions when we're ready to act.' Sinius cleared his throat and concluded in a loud curt voice, 'Dismissed!'

Cato and Macro stood to attention, saluted and then turned smartly to march from the office. Once the door was closed behind them Cato let out a sigh of relief and marched off down the corridor with Macro at his side.

'Things seem to be moving to a head,' Macro spoke softly. 'Within a month, he said.'

Cato nodded. 'And we're still no closer to discovering who Sinius is working for. We're going to have to watch him more closely from now on. Follow him, see who he speaks to. He has to meet with the other Liberators at some point. When he does, we need to be there.'

'Easier said than done,' Macro responded. 'They'll be

taking precautions. What if they only communicate by some kind of coded written message?'

Cato thought for a moment. 'That's possible . . . But if they are going to act soon then there's every chance they will have to speak face to face. We'll start following Sinius as soon as we've dealt with that business down at the Boarium.'

'All right,' Macro agreed. 'But before we meet Septimus there's another small matter that needs seeing to.'

'What's that?'

Macro hefted his pouch of silver. 'I'm not leaving this in the barracks where some thieving little toerag can get his hands on it. So before we go anywhere else, I think a little visit to one of the bankers in the Forum is called for.'

Cato slowed his stride to turn to his friend. 'What are you thinking? Do you mean to keep that money?'

Macro could not hide his surprise. 'Of course.'

'But you know damn well where the silver has come from.' Cato glanced round to make sure no one was close enough to overhear them. Apart from a handful of clerks chatting several paces ahead of them, the corridor was deserted. Cato lowered his voice even further. 'It belongs to the Emperor.'

'Not any more, it seems.'

'You think Narcissus is the kind of man who will accept that line of argument? He'll want it back, every coin that can possibly be recovered.'

'Which is every coin that he knows about. So I'm not going to mention this little lot. Nor are you,' Macro concluded firmly. 'Besides, lad, we've earned it, several times over. We'll just quietly bank this for now. If no one asks us for it, then there's no harm in hanging on to it. Agreed?'

Cato felt a surge of frustration briefly course through his veins. 'What if Sinius spills his guts when Narcissus moves to crush the plot? What if he tells Narcissus that we have the silver?'

Macro shrugged. 'Then we'll just have to make sure that we get to Sinius first when it's over.' His expression hardened as he glanced at Cato. 'If he's silenced before he can talk, then we might even get our hands on that chest he keeps in his office.'

The anxiety of a moment earlier returned as Cato hissed, 'You're playing with fire, Macro. Don't even think about it.'

'Why the hell not? I'm sick of doing Narcissus's dirty work for no reward. No fair reward at least. This is a chance for us to get ahead in life, lad. We'd be fools to duck the opportunity.'

Cato could see the dangerous gleam in his friend's eyes and knew it would be foolhardy to try to gainsay Macro in his present mood.

'We'll talk about it later, all right? I need time to think.'

Macro's eyes narrowed briefly, then he forced a slight smile. 'Very well, later.'

CHAPTER EIGHTEEN

'That's the place,' Cato muttered as he gestured towards the warehouse. Macro and Septimus were on either side of him as they strolled along the wharf. The same guard who had brusquely rebuffed Cato a few days earlier was sitting on a stool beside the gate. He held a small loaf in one hand and a wizened end of cured sausage in the other and his jaw worked steadily as he stared absent-mindedly at the barges moored along the quay opposite the line of warehouses. Despite the lack of grain there were still imports of olive oil, wine, fruit, as well as the usual flow of luxury foods for the richest tables in Rome. All of which fetched prices far beyond the reach of the teeming multitude of the capital's poorest inhabitants.

A short distance along the wharf from the warehouse of Gaius Frontinus a small crowd of ragged people stood watching the unloading of a barge. Several jars of wine had already been landed and now a chain gang was unloading large baskets of dried dates. The gang master was accompanied by a handful of men armed with cudgels who formed a loose cordon around the goods on the wharf and warily kept an eye on the surrounding crowd.

'Over there,' Cato said softly. 'We won't stand out in the crowd.'

They made their way over to the fringe of the silent gathering of men and women, some with children, and edged round until they could see the warehouse gate and the guard sitting in front of it. A moment before, Cato had not considered what the man was doing, but now he saw it for what it was, a cold-hearted display of cruelty as he ate while others starved.

'What are we going to do?' asked Septimus. 'We can't just walk in.'

'We could,' Macro growled. 'There's three of us and one of him.'

Septimus shook his head. 'If we force our way in, then word will get back to Cestius soon enough and the Liberators will know that we are on to them. We can't afford to scare them into hiding. It's just as important to smash the conspiracy as find the grain. Meanwhile we have to get in there and confirm that the grain is actually inside, and then get out without the alarm being raised.'

Cato scratched his cheek. 'Won't be easy. The warehouse is built round a courtyard. The wall facing the wharf is the lowest point. The rest of it is built up against the warehouses on either side and behind. There's no other way in. We have to go in through the gate, or over the wall. If we try and scale that, we're bound to be seen by the guard.'

Macro ran his eyes over the warehouse and nodded. 'You're right. So what do we do?'

Cato looked round the wharf for a moment before fixing his attention on the men unloading the barge, surrounded by the small crowd. 'We need a diversion. That's a job for you, Septimus. While Macro and I get inside the warehouse.'

He quickly explained his plan and then, while Septimus worked his way through the crowd towards the edge of the wharf, Cato and Macro moved off, back in the direction of the Boarium. They took care to keep close to the edge of the Tiber in order not to attract the guard's attention. There was a small danger that he might remember Cato's face, even though his coarse features and bovine expression hinted at a mind that was not readily accustomed to the retention of information. Once they had covered a safe distance they stopped and looked out across the moored barges to the leaden flow of the Tiber. Cato glanced towards the crowd and saw Septimus standing close to the gangway leading up from the barge. Cato discreetly raised a hand to give the signal.

Septimus edged forward and waited until one of the slaves carrying the baskets of dried fruit struggled up on to the wharf. Then he darted between two of the gang master's men and thrust his arms out into the slave's side. The latter tumbled over, his basket flying through the air until it hit the ground and dates exploded across the wharf. At once the waiting crowd surged forward and down, hands scrabbling to scoop up the dried fruit.

'Get off! Get back, you bastards!' the gang master bellowed in rage as he laid into them with his cudgel. He looked up at his men. 'What are you lot waiting for? Get 'em away from the goods!'

His men were startled into action and they began to lash out at those scrabbling around on the ground at their feet. In the struggle another basket was knocked over, spilling its contents. An excited cry went up as the starving mob closed in.

Cato glanced quickly over his shoulder and saw that

the guard outside the warehouse gate had stopped chewing and stood up to get a better view of the action. His lips lifted into a slight smile of amusement, and then he took a few paces away from his station to watch the frenzied violence as the mob and the gang master's men fought it out over the spilled barley.

'Come on!' Cato tugged Macro's sleeve and they turned to pad across the wharf to the warehouse wall. The guard had his back to them. He tore off another chunk of bread and continued to eat while watching the spectacle. Beyond the struggle Cato glimpsed Septimus backing away now that he had played his part in the plan. They reached the wall and Macro turned and clasped his hands together and braced himself against the rough bricks. Cato placed his right boot in Macro's hands and as his friend began to lift, Cato straightened his leg and reached up, fingers seeking purchase as he rose up the wall.

'Get me higher.'

Macro grunted with effort as he lifted Cato up and then groaned as Cato stood on his shoulder.

'I'm there,' Cato called down softly and then gritted his teeth as he pulled himself on to the wall and swung one of his legs up. His heart was pounding with the effort and he glanced quickly at the guard and was relieved to see him still watching the chaos on the wharf. Cato dropped down behind the wall and hurriedly unravelled the length of rope tied about his middle and hidden by a fold in his tunic. He tossed one end back over the wall and then grasped the other tightly, leant back and braced one foot against the wall. An instant later he felt Macro's weight drag at the rope. There was a scuffling sound and a muttered curse before Macro appeared on top of the wall. He hurriedly clambered over and dropped down inside the warehouse yard, dragging the rope over behind him.

For a moment both men stood breathing heavily, ears straining for any indication that they had been discovered. Cato looked round the interior of the warehouse yard. A paved area approximately a hundred feet by forty ran between the high walls of the massive building which enclosed the yard on three sides. Several doors faced the yard, all of them closed. There was no sign of life, and the yard felt oddly quiet after the din of the fight on the wharf. A handful of small handcarts stood against the wall. Cato took a deep breath and indicated the carts. 'At least getting out is going to be easier than getting in.'

'If you say so,' Macro replied. 'That depends on Septimus doing his job.'

'He did well enough to get us in. We can count on him. Come on.' Cato stepped towards the nearest door and saw that it was secured with a heavy iron bolt. A quick glance round the yard was enough to see that all the others were also bolted. Cato took up the lever and tested the bolt. With a lot of effort it began to move, giving a loud squeal as it did so. Cato stopped at once.

'Shit.'

'Easy there, lad,' said Macro. 'The noise outside will cover any that we make. And we can shift the bolts nice and slow.'

They took firm hold of the iron bolt and began to heave again. With a gentle rasp the bolt moved and a moment later slipped free of the receiving bracket. Fearing that the hinges might be as noisy as the door, Cato pulled it open carefully, just wide enough to admit himself and Macro. The light spilled across an empty stone floor and cast long shadows before the two men as they slowly entered, squinting into the shadows as their eyes adjusted to the gloom. It was a large space, eighty feet deep by half as much in width. Overhead the beams were high above the floor and a latticework of timbers supported a tiled roof. There were two narrow slits in the wall, high up, to provide light and ventilation, but not wide enough for even a child to squeeze through.

Cato bent down and scraped up some of the dust and grains from the floor. 'Looks like there has been wheat here.'

Macro nodded as he glanced around. 'If every chamber in this place is as big as this one, then there'd have been enough here to feed Rome for months. Let's try the next one.'

They worked their way round the warehouse yard, but every chamber was empty like the first. The only contents were a few coils of rope, blocks and tackle for unloading heavy items from the beds of wagons and a pile of torn and grimy sacking in the corner of the yard. In every chamber there was the same evidence that wheat had been stored there, and from the condition of the grain scattered on the floor, recently at that. When they closed the last of the doors Cato stepped back into the middle of the yard and folded his arms, frowning.

'Where has it gone?'

'Cestius must have thought this place was not safe,' Macro reflected. 'He must have figured that Narcissus and his agents would eventually discover where the grain was stockpiled. It's been moved on.'

'Without anyone noticing? You don't shift that much grain without drawing attention to it.'

'Unless you did a small amount at a time. Not enough for people to take notice.'

Cato thought briefly. It did not seem possible for Cestius to relocate his entire stock in limited movements in the time available. Even then there was another question that would need answering. 'Where would he put it all?'

'Another warehouse, perhaps?'

'Someone would have seen something.'

'In barges then, taken downriver to Ostia and stored there as soon as they bought each grain consignment.'

'It's possible. But then why are there signs of grain in every one of the storage chambers? It looks to me like they had all of it here before they moved it on. So why did they do it . . . ?' Cato chewed his lip. 'They must have been worried that it would be discovered. They're playing safe. After all, we discovered the location readily enough. In any case, I'm certain that the grain is still here in Rome.'

'Where then, smart-arse?'

'That's the question.' Cato looked round at the silent walls of the warehouse. 'It would have to be another place like this.'

'Cato, there must be scores of warehouses along the wharf on this side of the river alone. Not to mention those on the other side of the Tiber, and the warehouses behind the Forum, and the other markets in the city. We can't search them all.'

'Not without alerting the other side,' Cato conceded. 'As soon as they got wind that we were on to them they'd have to make their move and put whatever they're planning into effect.'

'So what do we do?'

Cato sighed. 'Tell Septimus to report back to Narcissus. What else? Now let's get out of here.'

They returned to the wall where one of the handcarts had been left a short distance to one side of the gate. Macro climbed up on to it and again lifted Cato up on to the wall. He cautiously peered over the top to where the guard had returned to his stool to continue his meal. Beyond, the fight over the spilt fruit had ended. The gang master and his thugs had re-established their cordon and the unloading of the barge had resumed. Several bodies lay on the ground about them, most moving feebly and a few lying still. Those who had managed to gather some of the dates had already fled the scene while the rest continued to watch the unloading of the barge, hoping for another chance to snatch something to eat. Cato looked for, and then saw, Septimus. The imperial agent raised a hand in acknowledgement and then made his way along the wharf to the gate. He stopped a short distance from the guard.

'Spare me some of that?' Septimus pointed to the bread and sausage resting in the man's lap.

'Fuck off.'

'Come on, friend. I'm hungry.'

'That's not my problem. And I'm not your friend, so like I said, fuck off.'

While Septimus took another step forward and asked again, more forcefully, Cato heaved himself up on to the wall and reached down to help Macro up. Then, making sure that the guard's attention was fixed on Septimus, they lowered themselves down the other side of the wall, straining the muscles in their shoulders and arms, and let go. Their boots crunched audibly on the filth and rubbish that had gathered at the foot of the wall. The guard started and looked round quickly. His eyes widened and in an instant he snatched up his club and was on his feet, his meal tumbling to the ground in front of the stool.

'I see! Thought you'd play a trick on me, eh? One comes from the front, while his pals take me from behind, eh?'

He lowered himself into a crouch, backed against the gate and swung his club to and fro. Cato could see that there were nails driven through the end of the club and could well imagine the damage those vicious points could do to a man's flesh. He raised a hand.

'Easy there. Our mistake. Come on, lads, this one's too tough for us. Let's be off.'

Septimus circled round the guard to join the others and then the three men backed away and turned to walk quickly along the wharf in the direction of the Boarium. The guard laughed nervously and blew a loud raspberry after them.

'Yes, piss off then, you wankers! If I see your faces round here again then you'll feel the kiss of my little Medusa here!' He thrust the head of his club after them.

'Bastard could do with a lesson in manners,' Macro grumbled, slowing his pace until Cato grasped his shoulder and urged him on.

'Not now. Let's get out of here before he remembers me.'

Septimus turned to Cato. 'Did you find anything?'

Cato briefly explained what they had seen and the

imperial agent's expression became anxious. 'Damn. We need that grain.'

'What about that convoy from Sicilia?' asked Macro. 'I thought that was going to save the situation for the Emperor.'

'It will, when it arrives. But the extra grain would have been good insurance in case there was a delay in the arrival of the convoy. Now it all hinges on its arrival. Pray to the gods that it arrives safely. The spectacle that Claudius is putting on up at the Albine Lake will only divert the mob for a short time.'

They walked on in silence for a moment before Cato gave a dry chuckle.

Septimus looked at him sharply. 'What?'

'I was just thinking about all the threats that Rome has faced over the years, and now it seems that hunger will succeed where barbarians, slave armies, ambitious politicians and tyrants have failed. If there's one great enemy of civilisation it is surely starvation. No empire, no matter how great, is ever more than a few meals away from collapse.' He glanced round at the others. 'Interesting, don't you think?'

Septimus glared at Cato and then caught Macro's eye. 'Your friend is not very helpful at times. Tell me, does his mind often wander like this?'

Macro nodded wearily. 'You can't imagine. Does my head in.'

Cato could not help smiling apologetically. 'Just an observation.'

'Well, keep your eyes and mind on the job,' Septimus chided. 'The Liberators are planning to do something soon. We have to be on our guard and look to the safety of the Emperor and his family. The enemy might have another chance to do something two days from now.'

'Why?' asked Cato. 'What's up?'

'The last section of the drain for the lake will be completed tomorrow. Claudius has decided to hold a celebratory feast for the engineers and a select audience before he gives the order for the sluices to open. It's not a public event, so there won't be too many people for your century to keep an eye on. But there's always the chance of trouble as the imperial retinue makes its way out of Rome, or comes back the same way.'

'We'll keep a close watch on the old boy,' said Macro. 'After that business in the Forum you can count on it.'

'I hope so,' Septimus replied as they reached the entrance to the Boarium. 'It's clear enough why the Liberators want the grain. That's the carrot they can offer to the mob once they've removed the Emperor. The question is, what are they going to use as the stick to beat Claudius? There's not much time left before they make their move, and we're still no wiser about their plan. You must concentrate on Sinius, find out who his contacts are. If we have the names of the ringleaders then we can strike first.'

'We'll do our best,' Cato reassured him. 'But Sinius isn't giving anything away. He's using us, but he's not taking us into his confidence. If we discover anything, we'll make sure we leave a note at the safe house at the first opportunity.'

'Very well.' Septimus bowed his head in farewell. 'I'd better make my report to Narcissus. He's not going to be happy.'

The three men parted and the imperial agent turned

abruptly and strode off through the Boarium in the direction of the imperial palace complex that loomed over the city from the crest of the Palatine Hill. Macro and Cato stared after him for a moment before Macro muttered, 'We're losing this one, aren't we?'

'What do you mean?'

'This fight . . . this job for Narcissus. We don't know where the grain is. We don't know what the enemy is planning. Shit, we don't even know who the enemy is, besides Sinius and Tigellinus.' Macro shook his head. 'I don't see any sign of a happy ending to this situation, Cato, my lad.'

'Oh, I wouldn't say that we're not making any progress,' Cato replied determinedly. 'We'll get there. You'll see.'

As they stepped into the section room they shared with Fuscius and Tigellinus, Cato caught the younger man admiring himself in a polished ornamental breastplate hanging with the rest of the kit from the pegs in the wall. There was a moment's bemusement before Cato saw the long staff crowned with a brass knob in Fuscius's left hand.

'Better not let Tigellinus catch you with that.'

'What?' Fuscius reacted instinctively and glanced towards the door with a worried expression, before he caught himself and smiled. 'It doesn't bother me. Not now. Tigellinus has no need of this any longer.' Fuscius held the staff up and looked at it proudly. 'This is mine.'

Macro laughed and turned to Cato. 'Sounds like the boy's balls have dropped at last. Fancy that.' He turned back to Fuscius. 'Seriously, I'd put that away before someone sees you with it.'

Irritation and a spark of anger flitted across the young man's face. Then Fuscius stood, stretched to his full height, and tilted his head back slightly as he addressed them.

'You'll have to stop speaking like that to me.'

'Oh?' The corner of Macro's mouth lifted in amusement. 'Why's that?'

'Because I am the new optio of the Sixth Century. The acting optio, anyway,' Fuscius added.

'You?' Macro could not hide his surprise, and not a little disapproval, as he regarded the other man. 'What about Tigellinus? What's happened to him?'

'Tigellinus?' Fuscius smiled. 'Until Centurion Lurco is found, Tigellinus has been promoted to acting centurion of the Sixth Century. Tribune Burrus made the decision. He said that he couldn't afford to have one of his units lacking a commander during the current crisis, and there'd be hell to pay for any man going absent without permission. When Lurco surfaces he's going to be broken to the ranks, and Tigellinus's appointment will be made permanent. Just as mine will.' Fuscius puffed out his chest. 'I'm the right man for the job, just as Tigellinus said when he chose me.' Fuscius's smile faded and he stared hard at Cato and Macro. 'That means that you two will call me optio from now on. Is that clear?'

'You?' Macro shook his head. 'You're the best man that Tigellinus could have picked? The most promising ranker in the century? I find that hard to believe.'

'Believe it!' Fuscius said fiercely. 'And I'll not warn you again, Guardsman Calidus. You will show me the respect due to my rank or I'll have you on a charge.'

'Yes, Optio.' Macro contained his smile. 'As you command.'

Fuscius strode up to him and glared at Macro for a moment, as if hoping to make the older man flinch. Macro met his gaze frankly and fearlessly, then with a brief snort of derision Fuscius strode out of the door, his staff of office clutched firmly in his hand.

Macro shook his head slowly. 'There goes a boy who thinks he's ready to take on a man's job . . . Reminds me of you, actually. That day you joined the Second Legion thinking that you were just going to stroll right into an officer's boots. You recall?'

Cato wasn't listening, he was deep in thought. He stirred as he became aware of the questioning tone in Macro's words.

'Sorry, I missed that.'

'Don't worry. Not important. What's on your mind?'

'Tigellinus. Acting Centurion Tigellinus that's what.' Cato's brow creased. 'The Sixth Century is tasked with protecting the Emperor and his family and the Liberators now have their man within striking distance of the imperial family. They've finally managed to penetrate the screen of bodyguards that surrounds Claudius.'

Macro pursed his lips and winced. 'You think Tigellinus will be the assassin?'

'What else? Why else have Lurco removed? They wanted to place Tigellinus close to the Emperor. That has to be it. And when the time is right, and the opportunity is there, Tigellinus will strike.'

'He won't get away with it,' said Macro. 'He'll be killed on the spot. Or taken and questioned.'

'That won't matter. With Claudius dead there will be chaos . . . confusion. That's when the rest of the conspirators will make their move. They'll use the Praetorian

Guard to move into the city and take control, and then announce a new regime, headed by the leadership of the Liberators. I'd stake my life on it,' Cato said grimly.

CHAPTER NINETEEN

As so often happens in April, a violent thunderstorm swept in from the west during the night and for the next two days and nights ominous dark clouds crowded the sky above Rome. The streets were shrouded in gloom, except for when brilliant bursts of lightning lit them up for an instant. Rain pelted down, hammering the tiled roofs, window shutters and paved streets. Rushing torrents swept down the streets and alleys of the capital, washing the dirt away and tumbling into the drains that fed the Great Sewer snaking beneath the heart of Rome before it joined the Tiber.

The population of the city sheltered indoors and for two days the streets were empty of the scavenging bands of the impoverished looking for scraps of food. The Emperor and his family did not venture out either. They remained in the palace and the men of Burrus's cohort of the Praetorian Guard took it in turns to march from the camp to the palace through the downpour, huddled in their cloaks. Despite the animal fat worked into the wool to render them waterproof, the rain found its way through and into the tunics beneath the armour, chilling the flesh of the guardsmen as they stood on duty, shivering, until they were relieved in turn and marched back to their barracks in the Praetorian camp.

There was no chance for Cato and Macro to check the safe house for any messages as the new acting centurion of the Sixth Century refused to allow any of his men to leave the camp when off duty. At his first morning parade as their new commander Tigellinus announced that the century's discipline had become lax under his predecessor. Henceforth, there would be an evening parade and extra drill, as well as their usual guard duty at the palace. The new optio was also relishing his promotion and bawled out his commands in emulation of Tigellinus. Tigellinus moved into Lurco's quarters and left Macro and Cato to cope with Fuscius, who now decided everything in the section room, from what time the lamp was extinguished at night to which pegs were reserved for the optio's use alone.

Macro did his best to keep his simmering irritation hidden. Cato, meanwhile, continued to ponder the mystery of the missing grain. He went over every detail of the search that he and Macro had conducted at the warehouse, as well as the information he had gleaned from the grain merchants' guild and the clerk at the offices of Gaius Frontinus. How could so much grain disappear into the city without any apparent trace? It was a maddening puzzle for Cato which vexed him as he polished his kit and spread his cloak and tunics out to dry on the small wooden rack that was set up close to the section room's compact brazier. Meanwhile, Macro dutifully headed out each evening to carry out his punishment in the latrines at the end of the block nearest the wall of the camp.

At last, on the third morning the storm blew away, leaving a clear blue sky in its wake and the sun soon began to heat the roofs and streets of Rome, sending tendrils of vapour twisting languidly into the air before they dispersed. The people began to emerge on to the streets, and once more the bodies of those who had starved to death or succumbed to an illness in their weakened state were carried out of the city gates in carts to be added to the many hundreds that had been placed in mass graves along the roads leading out of Rome.

Word arrived from the palace that the Emperor and his retinue would set out to inspect the engineering works and the preparations for the spectacle up at the Albine Lake. Burrus gave the command for the Fifth and Sixth centuries to form up and Tigellinus stormed through the barracks bellowing at his men to get their kit and form up ready to march. The soldiers of each section scrambled out, some still fastening chinstraps and buckling on their armour. When the last man was ready Tigellinus called them to attention and then inspected the ranks, pulling his men up on every minor infraction while Fuscius noted the crime and punishment on a waxed tablet. When the inspection was complete Tigellinus moved back and faced his new command, his fists resting on his hips.

'No doubt some of you are still wondering what's become of Lurco. As far as you're concerned he's dead. As far as he's concerned he might as well be, once Tribune Burrus gets his hands on him.' Tigellinus paused while some of the men chuckled. Then he drew a deep breath and continued, 'I'm your centurion now. I set the standard and I will command the best century in the entire Praetorian Guard. That means I will be hard on you. I will have discipline. I will have smartly turned-out soldiers and I will have heroes, if the need arises. Any man who falls short of my requirements had better be ready to transfer out of the Guard to some lesser formation. If such a man chooses to stay then I will break him. Is that clear?'

'Yes, sir!' the men responded unevenly.

'I didn't bloody hear you!' Tigellinus bellowed. 'You sound like a bloody rabble! I said, is that clear?'

'Yes, sir!' the soldiers shouted in one voice that echoed back off the wall of the opposite barrack block.

'That's better.' Tigellinus nodded. 'You've already proved to the Emperor that you are good in a fight. He has honoured us by making this unit his personal escort. I mean to keep that honour for the foreseeable future, gentlemen. Whenever the Emperor leaves the palace I want my men to be guarding him. I want us to remain his first and last line of defence. We will be the shield and sword at his side. He will continue to put his faith in us, to trust us with his life, and the lives of his family. I need hardly remind you how grateful emperors can be to those who give them good service. Do your duty and we'll all do well out of this. Don't let me down.' He ran his eyes along the ranks of his men and then turned to Fuscius. 'That's all. Have the men form up by the main gate, ready to march, Optio.'

'Yes, sir!' Fuscius stood to attention, and remained there until Tigellinus had left the small parade ground. Then he called out, 'Sixth Century, left face!'

The two lines turned and stood ready for the next order.

'March!'

As the column moved forward, Macro spoke quietly to Cato, now marching ahead of him. 'What do you make of that?'

'You know what I think,' Cato answered. 'We keep our eyes and ears open and watch like a hawk.'

The men of the Fifth and Sixth centuries marched up to where Tribune Burrus was waiting, mounted on an immaculately groomed black horse. When the column stood ready he waved a hand towards the gate and the leading rank moved off. They entered Rome and marched down to the palace where the imperial retinue joined the column before it marched back out of the city and headed towards the lake, over ten miles from the capital. The Emperor was attended by fewer advisers than usual, Cato noticed. There was Narcissus, but no sign of Pallas or the Empress, or the two boys.

The rain-washed countryside smelt fresh and the warmth heralded the coming of spring. The first buds were emerging on the branches of many of the fruit trees lining the route. The litters carrying the imperial party were between the two centuries of Praetorians and from the rear Cato could just make them out when he craned his neck to look over the gleaming helmets and javelin tips rippling ahead of him. As the column passed between small villages, the inhabitants came to watch their Emperor pass by and offered a cheer as Claudius raised a hand in greeting. On either side of the litters marched the German bodyguards, their barbarian appearance unnerving the more timorous villagers.

They reached the lake in the early afternoon and the men were allowed to fall out of line and rest while the Emperor and his advisers inspected the preparations for the Naumachia. The imperial grandstand was nearly complete, constructed on an artificial mound that had been raised at the edge of the lake. Along the shore carpenters were hard at work preparing the barges and river craft that had been hauled up from the Tiber to serve as the two fleets that would battle it out on the waters of the lake. Makeshift masts rose from the decks of the vessels with spars, sails and rigging that were more decorative than functional. Rowing benches were fixed along the sides and stout rams attached to the bows of each boat. From a distance they might pass for the warships of the Roman navy, but on a much reduced scale. A quarter of a mile away from the activity on the shore of the lake stood the stockades where those who were to fight were to be held for the duration of the spectacle.

'Unbelievable,' Macro commented ruefully as he and Cato surveyed the scene from a rocky outcrop a short distance from where the men of the escort relaxed on the verdant grass either side of the road leading back to Rome. 'I've never seen anything like it. It looks more like the preparations for a major campaign than a bloody gladiator show.'

'I don't recall there being quite as much effort being put into the invasion of Britannia,' Cato responded with an ironic grin. 'But then Claudius was only out to win a new province for the empire. Now he's out to win the heart of the mob, an objective of far more strategic importance at present – assuming he lives long enough to appease their taste for gladiator fights, not to mention their hunger. I'd say the odds are stacking up against Claudius.'

They turned their attention to the imperial party as the official in charge of organising the spectacle made his report to the Emperor. Even at a distance of over a hundred paces Cato could see that Claudius was giving the man his full attention. Every now and then his head twitched violently as he limped alongside the official.

'Not such an enviable thing being the Emperor, is it?' Cato said in a reflective tone. 'Enemies on all sides, and those closest to him are by far the more dangerous.'

'You talk utter bollocks at times, Cato,' Macro responded. 'You think our lives are any less at risk than Claudius's? I don't think so, and I have the scars to prove it, and so do you. In any case, there are one or two perks that go with the job of being the absolute ruler of the greatest empire in the world. I think I might just get used to the occupational hazards.'

'It's one thing to face a man with a sword in a straight fight. Quite another to walk into a room full of people, knowing that many of them would as happily stab you in the back as offer you a greeting and promise undying loyalty. Speaking of which, where's Tigellinus?' Cato scanned the imperial party, anxiously looking for the centurion.

'He's over there, with Burrus and the others.' Macro pointed towards the handful of men clustered around Tribune Burrus who was still in the saddle. Cato saw the tall figure of the centurion and let out a quiet sigh of relief. Macro heard the soft escape of breath and looked at his friend.

'When do you think Tigellinus is going to make his move?'

Cato thought for a moment. 'He might make an attempt at the first chance he gets, provided he has no regard for his own life. But from what I've seen of the man, I doubt he'll throw it away if there is any hope of saving it. If I were Tigellinus I'd bide my time until I was close to the Emperor, and with as few others surrounding him as possible. Then I might have a chance to escape after striking the blow. So, when the Sixth Century is close to the Emperor, we stay closer still to Tigellinus.'

The Emperor completed his tour of the preparations and returned to his litter. As the imperial retinue began to make its way along the shore to the engineering works at the end of the lake nearest the Tiber, the optio called the men back into formation. The guards swiftly marched to take up their positions around the Emperor and then fell into step with the slaves carrying the heavy gilded litter. The party wound its way along the edge of the lake until it reached the first of the stepped dams that led down towards the tributory of the Tiber, three miles away.

The imperial column halted. A small party of engineers in plain tunics approached and bowed in front of the litter. Claudius swung his legs over the side and hobbled over to the youthful-looking man leading the engineers.

'My dear Ap-apollodorus!' Claudius greeted him. 'How is the work progressing? Nearly completed, I trust? I expect the storm has put you behind schedule.'

The engineer gave a deep bow, as did his companions. 'No, sire. The works were completed according to schedule. And I have prepared something interesting to amuse the mob when the Naumachia begins.'

'Oh?' Claudius cocked an eyebrow. 'And what would that be?'

'I'd prefer it to remain a surprise, sire. I'm certain you will be impressed.'

Claudius frowned briefly, and then his expression

relaxed. 'Very well, young man. But you are certain the weather has caused no delays? Be honest n-now.'

'I would not let a bit of rain and wind cause me to break my word to you.'

'Good man!' Claudius beamed and clasped the engineer's forearm. 'I wish all m-my officials were as eff-efficient as you.'

The Emperor turned to Narcissus, standing a short distance behind him. 'You and Pallas could learn much from this young f-fell-fellow.'

The imperial secretary forced a smile. 'It would be a shame to take such a promising talent under my wing and rob you of the skills of an accomplished engineer, sire. Apollodorus's undoubted talents are better deployed in the field, rather than the palace – although Pallas might benefit from his expertise.'

'Pallas?' The Emperor thought for a moment and then nodded. 'Yes, yes. He does seem to be r-r-rather off form these days. Tired and distracted.' Claudius smiled indulgently. 'I imagine the fellow's in love. It tends to be a wearisome process.'

'Yes, sire. Perhaps Pallas should be sent to Capri for a rest. I would be glad to oversee his staff during his absence.'

'I'm sure you would.' Claudius smiled. 'Then again, perhaps you also need a rest, my friend.'

'Not at all, sire.' Narcissus stood as erect as he could. 'My place is at your side. I live only to serve you.'

'How fortunate I am to have such servants. C-come, Narcissus! Let us learn something of the art of engineering from our d-d-dear Appollod-d-dorus here.'

The engineer bowed his head again, and then began

to talk through the procedure he had devised to drain the Albine Lake. Cato listened as best he could to the engineer's lecture but his eyes were fixed on Tigellinus. The centurion stood at the head of the century, no more than fifty feet from the Emperor. His hand was resting on the pommel of his sword, his fingers drumming against the sword handle. Between him and Claudius stood a loose screen of German bodyguards. The Emperor was safe for the moment, Cato decided.

Apollodorus gestured down the vale leading to the river. 'As the Emperor can see, I have ordered the construction of a series of dams, each with a sluice, so that we can control the flow of water as we drain the area around the lake. If we had simply cut a channel from the lake to the river, as I believe your adviser, Pallas, originally suggested, then we might well have caused the Tiber to overflow and flood the centre of Rome as the main body of water reached the city.'

Narcissus chuckled. 'Not one of my friend's finer moments, alas. Still, Pallas has his talents, whatever they may be.'

'Quite right.' Claudius nodded. 'My wife, the Empress, rates him highly indeed.'

Macro whispered. 'Oh, I'm sure she does.'

'Shhh!' Cato hissed.

The engineer led the way down the track that had been cut into the slope of the vale. Every half mile or so was another dam, behind which the water flowing out of the lake filled an expanse of the vale. Late in the afternoon the procession finally reached the last and biggest of the dams. At its foot a small stream flowed round a curve in the vale, the sides of which were appreciably steeper than up by the lake. The stream was fed by a culvert dug round the end of the dam. A handful of workmen stood off to one side, loading unused timber on to a wagon. They briefly bowed towards the Emperor and then continued with their task.

Apollodorus paused at the base of the dam where long, thick lengths of timber braced the stakes driven vertically into the ground. A number of ropes had been tied round the central buttress timbers and led up to the sides of the vale where they were fed through large pulleys, secured to stakes.

Narcissus looked up warily at the dam towering some fifty feet above him. 'Are we quite safe here?'

'Perfectly!' Apollodorus smiled confidently. He stepped forward and slapped one of the buttress timbers. 'It will take a hundred men pulling on the ropes to dislodge each of these. When the time comes, that is exactly what will happen, once we've cleared the route that the flow will take down to the tributary leading into the Tiber. For now, nothing short of an earthquake will shift these. Once the water behind this dam has drained, we'll move up the vale, draining each pool in turn until we reach the lake. That way we can control the flow of water and there'll be only the slightest of rises in the level of the Tiber for a short time.' He stood back and looked up at the dam with undisguised pride in his achievement. Then, conscious of the Emperor once again, Apollodorus turned to him hurriedly. 'The celebration to mark the completion of the project is ready, sire. Just round the bend in the vale there, on the bank of the river. If you would do me the honour?'

'What? Oh, yes. Yes, of course!' Claudius smiled. 'It

would be m-m-my pleasure, young man. Lead the way!'

Narcissus stepped forward. 'Sire, it is late in the day. It is already unlikely that we will return to the city by nightfall. It would be wise to set off for Rome without delay.'

'Nonsense!' Claudius frowned. 'What? Are you afraid of the dark? In any c-case, this man has done a wonderful j-jo-job. The least we can do is celebrate his success.'

Narcissus bowed his head. 'As you wish, sire.'

The Emperor patted Apollodorus on the back. 'Lead on, my boy! L-lead on!'

The vale curved gently to the right before giving out on to an expanse of open ground. Two hundred paces beyond, the river gleamed in the sunshine as it flowed towards Rome. Several tables had been arranged together and covered with an expanse of red cloth. On the table sat a huge cake, artfully constructed to resemble the dam they had just seen. Thirty or forty of Apollodorus's staff stood waiting beyond the table and bowed their heads at the Emperor's approach.

Claudius smiled in delight as he reached the table and inspected the cake. 'Excellent! Most excellent! I trust it tastes as good as it looks?'

'It should, sire. The best cooks scoured Rome for ingredients to prepare it.'

'This looks delicious. I'll be the first to taste it, if I may?'

'Of course, sire.' Apollonius clicked his fingers and a slave ran forward with a spoon for the Emperor. Claudius paused a moment and then dipped it into the blue jelly behind the dam and turned to his retinue. 'Tribune Burrus. One of your men please.' Claudius turned to the

297

engineer. 'I m-me-mean no offence, but I have to be sure.'

'I understand, sire.'

Burrus turned in his saddle to survey the men of the Sixth Century. Before he could speak, Tigellinus stepped forward. 'I volunteer, sir!'

Burrus opened his mouth, as if to speak, then shrugged and nodded. Cato felt his muscles tense as the centurion paced forward, between two of the German bodyguards. He stopped a short distance from the Emperor and there was a brief pause before Claudius offered the spoon up to his mouth. Tigellinus leant forward and consumed the mouthful. His jaws worked briefly and then he swallowed. There was another pause before Claudius arched his eyebrows. 'Well?'

'Bloody tasty, sir!' Tigellinus barked.

'No ill effects?'

'None, sir.'

'Very well.' Claudius waved him away and Tigellinus backed off through the cordon of German body-guards. Cato let out a pent-up breath and felt his body relax.

'We'll have some of this delicious cake and then return to R-r-rome,' the Emperor announced. 'Tribune, you may order your men to stand down while I eat.'

'Praetorian Guard!' Burrus called out. 'Fall out!'

The guardsmen, on reduced rations, looked on envi-ously, having moved off a short distance to allow Claudius and his small retinue to pick at the cake and indulge in small talk. Cato noted with a smile that Narcissus was doing his best to insert himself between his master and the engineer and respond to the words of the Emperor with his customary obsequiousness while frowning frostily at every comment made by Apollodorus.

Macro was staring wistfully at the cake. 'I could murder some of that.'

'It looks far too rich,' Cato responded dismissively. 'Probably give you indigestion.'

'I could live with it.' Macro tore his gaze away and looked at his friend. 'I was a bit worried there, when our friend Tigellinus stepped up to test the food.'

'Me too. Seems I was right. Whatever his plan is, it doesn't involve suicide.'

'Except by indigestion.' Macro turned to look for the centurion as he and Cato leant on their shields. Tigellinus had moved a short distance off and had unfastened his chinstraps and removed his helmet. He mopped his brow and then began to unbuckle his breastplate. He glanced briefly back up the vale with a strained expression. Easing his armour on to the ground, Tigellinus stretched his shoulders, raising his arms into the air.

Macro turned back to look at the small party of dignitaries crowded around the cake, scooping away at the choice ingredients. His stomach grumbled loudly enough for Cato to hear and the two exchanged a smile. Cato opened his mouth to comment, but before he could speak a dull crash reverberated through the air. Everyone turned in the direction of the sound. A moment later there was another crash that merged into a cacophony of splintering timber and falling rocks. Then a rushing roar that swelled up and filled the air. A sudden breeze stirred at the end of the vale, and strengthened.

'What the fuck is that?' Macro turned towards the din.

But Cato knew instantly what the sound was and his

stomach knotted in icy terror. He glanced towards the Emperor, staring up the vale, a spoon heaped with jelly halfway to his mouth. As Cato turned back he saw a dark liquid mass, gleaming and foaming, sweep round the bend in the vale, smashing down the stunted trees that clung to the steep slopes, dislodging boulders and mounds of earth, carrying all before it. The vast body of water that had been held back by the final dam roared out of the vale, directly towards the imperial party and its escort.

CHAPTER TWENTY

At first no one moved. Every man was too horrified by the sight of the churning wall of water sweeping towards them. Tigellinus acted first. He cupped a hand to his mouth and yelled, 'Run! Run for your lives!'

The cry broke the spell and the imperial retinue, the engineers and the Praetorian guardsmen began to flee, some heading directly away from the water, while most tried to escape to the side where the ground rose slightly. Cato threw down his shield and spear and snatched at his chinstraps. Macro did likewise, already moving away from the wave.

'Wait!' Cato called to him. 'We must save the Emperor!'

Macro paused, then nodded and they turned towards the table and the cake. Claudius was stumbling towards the river as fast as his limp would allow, casting terrified glances back over his shoulder as the wave approached. Tigellinus was racing across the ground after him and Cato saw, with a stab of fear, that the centurion might reach the Emperor first. He struck out, sprinting as fast as his legs would carry him, still weighed down by his scaled armour vest. Macro ran after him. A strong breeze rippled the folds of the Emperor's toga and the loose strands of his hair as the wave thrust a cushion of air ahead of it. The hissing roar of the pounding water seemed deafening to Cato as he ran at an angle towards Claudius. To his left he could see that Tigellinus was gaining ground and would reach the Emperor first. His dagger was grasped in his hand, point held low and level as he single-mindedly sprinted towards his prey.

The air felt cool at Cato's back and he risked one last glance towards the wave and saw that it was no more than fifty feet behind him, an ugly churning mass of spray and brown water carrying brush and trees with it. There was a cry of terror and despair away to his right as the first of the Praetorians went down, and then the voice was instantly silenced as the man was submerged in the tumult.

Ahead, Tigellinus was no more than ten feet from the Emperor, and then he stumbled, the toe of his boot stubbing against a rock. He fell down, the dagger spilling from his fingers. Cato ran on, calling out, 'Sire!'

Claudius looked back at Cato, wide eyed, then past him, aghast. Cato grabbed the Emperor's arm with one hand and wrenched at the toga with the other. At once the Emperor struggled and lashed out with his spare hand. 'Help! Murder!'

'No, sire! The toga will weigh you down!' Cato shouted, ripping the thick woollen material from the Emperor's shoulder. He heard Macro cry out a short distance behind, but before he could turn to look, the wave struck. There was an instant when he felt a surge around his calves, and Cato stepped in front of the Emperor, trying to shield him with his body. The full force of the water slammed into his back, instantly wrenching him off his feet. Cato tried to stay upright, kicking down to get purchase on the ground as he was swept along. He held tightly to the Emperor, pushing Claudius up. The water surged around his head, flowing over him and roaring in his ears before he surfaced, snatching a breath.

Something struck him in the ribs, a winding blow that drove the air from his lungs in an explosive cough and water instantly flooded his mouth before he could shut it. Then he was under again, still holding the Emperor and feeling him struggling wildly in his grasp. Cato felt something solid close by and risked letting go of Claudius with one hand as he groped. He felt the branch of a tree. He clamped his fingers round the rough bark and pulled himself and the Emperor towards it. His head burst through the surface once more and Cato took a breath. Around him was a chaotic mass of spray and water and debris, with the heads of men and flailing limbs all about. Cato thought he saw Macro a short distance away, but water closed over the head before he could be sure. Claudius came up, spluttering at his side.

'Sire!' Cato yelled into his face. 'Grab the branch!'

Claudius turned his head to Cato. 'I can't! I'm being dragged down! S-s-save yourself, young man. I'm done for!'

Cato saw that his toga was still caught round his chest and debris in the surging water was pulling at the cloth and dragging the Emperor with it. Cato grabbed at the fabric and wrenched it as hard as he could, working it free. It slipped down a little, yet Claudius was still being pulled under and let out a despairing cry before the water closed over his face again. He came up and Cato shouted, 'Kick it free! Kick it free, or you'll die!'

'Yes . . . yes,' Claudius spluttered. 'Kick it free.'

While he thrashed at the material with his legs, Cato used his spare hand to try to pull the toga away from the Emperor's body. The wool was like a live thing, squirming in the chaotic current, the folds wrapping around Cato's hand and arm. With one last pull it came off and both men came up, heads and shoulders clear of the water as they gripped the branch. The water around them was no longer raging quite so much and Cato could see for the first time that they had been swept some distance from the end of the vale. Around them were the remains of the tables, and Cato saw Tigellinus, some fifty feet away, trying to haul himself on to one of the tabletops, which was spinning round in the fast current.

'Cato!'

He turned and saw a commotion in the water where Macro was trying to swim towards the branch. Then, between them, another figure came up coughing and hacking, his arms flailing to keep him above water. Cato saw that it was Tribune Burrus.

'Over here, sir! Here!' Cato waved his arm and Burrus began to kick out towards him. The tribune reached the branch and wrapped his arms over it, gasping for breath. Cato looked round and saw that Macro would join them in a moment. Then he noticed something strange a short distance ahead of them. The leading edge of the wave just seemed to have disappeared, leaving a sharp line no more than fifty feet away.

'Oh shit,' Cato muttered. 'The river . . .'

The tree, and the men clinging to it, were being swept towards the steep riverbank and down into the river. Cato put his arm round the Emperor and clung tightly to the branch. He saw that Macro had grasped the end of a smaller branch a short distance away. Cato filled his lungs and cried out above the din of the rushing water, 'Hold on tight! We're going into the river!'

The end of the branch abruptly shot out into thin air for an instant. Then it tipped over the edge. Once again water closed over Cato and he felt his legs being scraped by rocks and debris as the branch dragged those hanging on to it under the raging surface of the river. The water roared in Cato's ears and his lungs began to burn. The Emperor seemed to writhe against him, but it was impossible to tell if he was struggling or simply being battered about by the current. Then there was a swirl in the water and the branch broke the surface. Cato snatched a deep breath.

'Sire, are you all right? Sire!'

The Emperor retched and spluttered and rested his head on the branch as his body was wracked by a coughing fit.

Cato looked round and saw that Burrus was still clinging on, but could not locate Macro. Cato turned his head from side to side, anxiously scanning the surface of the river. There were several men visible, struggling to stay afloat or striking towards the bank. Tigellinus was sprawled across the tabletop some distance away. Now that the river had absorbed most of the water unleashed by the collapse of the dam, the worst had passed, Cato realised. Except there was no sign of Macro. Then he saw a glistening hummock in the water some twenty feet away. It began to roll over and Cato realised it was a body, and then, stricken by fear, he recognised Macro's features as his face briefly cleared the surface before submerging again.

'Tribune!' Cato called out. 'Tribune Burrus, sir!'

Burrus looked up with a dazed expression, his single eye blinking.

'Look after the Emperor, sir! Do you understand?'

'Yes . . .' Burrus nodded, concentrating his thoughts with some effort. Cato turned to Claudius. 'Hold on, sire. We'll get you out of this.'

Then he released his grip on the branch and thrust himself out towards one of the other tables that was slowly turning round in the current close to where Macro was floating. Cato pulled his chest on to the table and kicked out with his legs, striking out towards his friend who showed little sign of life. As he came within reach, Cato threw out his arm, his fingers struggling for purchase in the folds of Macro's tunic. He tightened his grip and pulled Macro on to the table. A thin trail of blood etched its way down Macro's forehead and Cato saw a cut on his head.

'Macro!' He shook his shoulder violently. 'Macro! Open your eyes.'

His friend's head rolled limply back on to the planks of the table and his jaw sagged open. Cato slapped him hard. 'Open your bloody eyes!'

There was no response and Cato slapped him again, harder. This time Macro's head jerked up and his eyes blinked open. His jaw clenched defiantly. 'Which one of you bastards hit me, eh?'

Then the water in his lungs caused him to cough and retch agonisingly and it took him a while to recover sufficiently to register Cato's presence. He smiled weakly. 'What the hell happened to you, lad? You look a right state.'

Cato could not help smiling back in delight. 'Me? You should see yourself.'

'What . . . what happened?' Macro grimaced. 'Feels like some bastard's dropped a rock on my head.'

'You must have hit your head on the branch when we went into the river.'

'River?' Macro raised his head and looked round in confusion. Then he started as he recalled the final moments before the wave struck. 'The Emperor!'

'He's safe. Over there.' Cato pointed towards the branch where Burrus had shifted position to be at Claudius's side. It was close to the riverbank and a moment later it snagged on some obstruction under the surface and swung in towards the bank. Cato gave vent to a short sigh of relief and then punched Macro lightly. 'Come on. Let's get out of here.'

Cato started kicking, working the table round so that it pointed towards the riverbank. Then he and Macro kicked out, heading away from the middle of the current. It took a while in the swift flow before they felt the bed of the river beneath their boots and eased the table into the narrow strip of reeds growing along the water's edge. There they abandoned the table and waded through the reeds until they reached firm ground and slumped on to the grassy bank beyond the reeds. Macro cradled his head in his hands and groaned while Cato remained on hands and knees, head hung low as he breathed in deeply, coughing up the last of the water in his lungs and spitting to clear his mouth. His heart was beating fast and he was trembling uncontrollably. The air was cold and made his soaked body feel colder still, but Cato knew that the trembling was due to the frantic exertion since the wave struck him. That and the delayed shock and terror over what had happened.

He struggled to his feet and scanned the surrounding landscape. Looking upriver he could see the end of the vale, some half a mile away. An earthen streak scarred the pasture between the vale and the bank of the river. Uprooted trees lay scattered across the ground and several figures stood or sat amid the mud, staring about them. More stood at the fringes of where the wave had swept past. There was no sign of the imperial litters, or the tables on which the cake had stood. A few hundred paces upstream Cato could see Burrus supporting the Emperor as they made their way back upriver. There was no sign of Tigellinus in any direction.

Cato squatted down beside Macro. 'How do you feel?'

'Sore.' Macro puffed his cheeks. 'I must have taken quite a crack to the head . . . I was holding on to that branch – we went over something and dropped down. That's the last I can recall until some bastard smacked me round the chops.' He glanced up. 'That was you, I take it.'

'What are friends for?' Cato offered his hand and helped Macro on to his feet. 'Come on, let's get back to what's left of the century.'

They began to walk towards the figures scattered about the flood plain, some of whom were looking for survivors caught in the debris or tending to the injured.

'What the hell happened?' asked Macro.

'That's obvious. The dam gave way.'

'How? How is that possible? You heard the engineer. It would take a hundred men to cause the dam to collapse.'

Cato thought for a moment. 'Evidently not. It collapsed by itself, or someone helped it to.'

'Shoddy bloody Greek workmanship – that's what caused it.'

'You really think so? Just when the Emperor happened to be standing right in the path of the wave when it struck? Quite a coincidence.'

'It happens. The gods will play their games.'

'So will some traitors. Did you see Tigellinus? It was as if he was the only one among us who wasn't surprised by the wave.'

They continued in silence for a while before Macro cleared his throat. 'All right then, so if the Liberators are responsible for this, how the hell did they manage it?'

'I don't know. Not yet. But I want a good look at what's left of the dam.'

By the time they joined the other survivors, the remaining German guards had formed up round the Emperor. Their drenched locks of hair, streaked with mud, and their soiled tunics and armour made them look even more barbaric than normal and the Praetorian guardsmen and the civilians kept their distance. Someone had found a stool for the Emperor and Claudius sat on it numbly, surveying the scene. The survivors had instinctively made for the high ground to one side of the end of the vale, in case of another disaster. Narcissus was leaning in towards the Emperor, offering words of comfort while a terrified-looking Apollodorus stood a short distance off, between two of the German bodyguards.

'You two!'

Cato turned sharply to see Tribune Burrus striding towards them. He and Macro stood to attention and saluted the commander of their cohort. Burrus studied

Cato's features briefly and then nodded. 'You're the one who helped me to save the Emperor, aren't you?'

Cato thought quickly. It was tempting to take the credit for his part in rescuing Claudius, but it would be dangerous to risk drawing any attention to himself, or Macro. Particularly if word got back to the Liberators who would be certain to suspect their motives.

'I was holding on to the same branch. That is all. I believe you were the one most responsible for saving him, sir.'

Burrus's eyes narrowed, as if he suspected some kind of a trick. Then he nodded slowly. 'Very well. All the same, I shall make sure that your part in this does not go unrewarded.'

Cato nodded his gratitude.

'Your centurion's missing. Have you seen him?' the tribune asked.

'He was close to us in the river. I lost sight of him afterwards.'

'A pity. A good man that. Quick off the mark to try to save the Emperor when the wave struck. Lucky I was there to succeed where he failed, eh?'

'Indeed, sir.'

'His optio's in charge now.' Burrus nodded towards Fuscius who had somehow managed to hang on to his staff and was busy searching among the bedraggled survivors for men from the Sixth Century. 'You'd best report to Fuscius directly.'

'Not yet, Tribune,' Narcissus called out as he made his way over to the three guardsmen. 'I want to have a closer look at the dam. I want these two to help me, in case there's any further danger.'

'Further danger?' Burrus looked surprised by the suggestion, then shrugged. 'Very well, they're yours.'

The imperial secretary nodded towards the Emperor and lowered his voice. 'Look after him. He's badly shaken.'

'Of course.'

Narcissus glanced at Cato and Macro with the blank expression of one accustomed to seeing the broad mass of humanity as a single class of servants. 'Follow me!'

They strode off across the grass, skirting the slick expanse of mud that sprawled across the land between the vale and the river. When they entered the vale, they had to progress carefully across the slippery ground and negotiate the tangled remains of trees and shrubs. As soon as they were out of the sight of the survivors, Narcissus turned to Cato and Macro.

'That was no accident. That was a blatant attempt on the Emperor's life, and mine.'

Macro snorted. 'Not to mention a few hundred guardsmen and civilians. But I suppose we don't count for much, eh?'

'Not in the grand scheme of things, no,' Narcissus replied coldly. 'For now I'm happy for that Greek engineer to think it was an accident. He's scared out of his wits and might divulge some information that might be useful. Now or later.'

'Later?' Cato glanced at him.

'If by some slip of the tongue he tells me something that leaves me with a hold over him, that's a useful by-product of the situation.'

Macro shook his head. 'By the gods, you never miss a trick, do you?'

'I try not to. That's why I'm still alive and at the side of the Emperor. Not many of my predecessors can claim to have survived in that position for a fraction of the time that I have.'

'And now Pallas is trying to push you out,' Macro noted and clicked his tongue. 'Puts you on the spot, eh?'

'I've bested sharper men than Pallas,' Narcissus replied dismissively. 'He won't concern me for much longer.'

'Oh?'

Narcissus shot him a quick look and then stepped round a large boulder. He looked ahead and pointed. 'That's where we'll find some answers, I hope.'

Cato and Macro followed his direction and saw the remains of the dam. A line of rocks stretched across the narrow bottom of the vale and water still trickled from between them. More rocks and shattered timbers lay strewn about the ground in front of the foundations of the dam. The three men picked their way forward and stopped a short distance below the main breach.

'I'm trying to recall how it looked before,' said Narcissus. 'I should have paid more attention to that bore, Apollodorus. Weren't there some big sticks supporting the middle?'

'Sticks?' Cato smiled. 'I think he called them buttresses.'

Narcissus looked at him and frowned briefly. 'Buttresses then. I remember he said that they would need plenty of men to shift them when the time came to drain the water behind the dam.'

'That's right.' Cato nodded.

'So what happened? Where did all these men suddenly come from? There wasn't anyone near the dam.'

'Yes . . . Yes there was,' Cato replied. 'You remember that party by a wagon close to the base of the dam.'

Macro nodded. 'Yes. Can't have been more than ten of them though. They wouldn't have been able to shift those timbers. Not by themselves.'

'No. You're right,' Cato conceded.

They picked their way across the muddy debris. Then Narcissus pointed down the vale. 'Isn't that one of them? One of those buttresses? Or at least what's left of it.'

Cato and Macro turned to look. A hundred paces away, to the side of the vale, what looked like a shattered tree trunk stood up at an angle, wedged between two huge boulders. Cato could see that it was too straight and regular to be the remains of a tree. 'Worth a look,' he said.

'Why?' asked Macro, not liking the look of the mud-encrusted tangles of vegetation that lay between them and the shattered buttress.

'For the dam to collapse, both of the main supports would have to give way first, right?'

'So?'

'So, aren't you curious about how they did give way?'

Macro gave him a surly look. 'I could be more curious.'

Cato ignored him and began to clamber across the ruined landscape towards the two boulders. After a moment the other two followed. Cato was examining the thick length of timber when they caught up with him. Some of the buttress was buried in the mud and another six feet or so protruded into the air before ending in a confusion of shattered splinters. Cato was tracing his fingers across what was left of a regular line at the edge of the splinters.

'Do you see here?' He moved aside to give them a clear view. Macro stood on tiptoe and squinted.

'Looks like it's been sawn.' He reached up and traced his fingers along the mark. 'Quite some way into the timber.'

Cato nodded. 'I'd wager that we'd find the same on the other buttress if we could find it, as well as some of the lesser supports. Weaken enough of them and you'd no longer need hundreds of men to put enough pressure on the timbers to cause them to give way, or shatter under the strain, like this one.' He patted the timber. 'Just shift some of the supports and the pressure of the water behind the dam will do the rest.'

Narcissus nodded. 'As I said, this was no accident, and here is the proof.'

'There is something else,' Cato said. 'When we saw the wave, did you notice how everyone was rooted to the spot?'

'Yes. What of it?'

'One man wasn't. Centurion Tigellinus made a run at Claudius before anyone else gathered their wits enough to react. And he had taken off his heaviest pieces of kit to make sure he wasn't weighed down.'

Narcissus's brow furrowed slightly as he recalled the event. 'Yes, he was quick off the mark. I might have assumed he was going to protect the Emperor, were it not for the fact that he had replaced Lurco.' He looked at Cato. 'Are you saying Tigellinus knew about the dam? That that was why they got rid of Lurco, because this was what they had been planning?'

'Perhaps.' Cato looked unsure. 'But how could they know that the Emperor was planning to visit the drainage works? The decision to replace Lurco was made before Claudius decided to come here today.'

'It's a big project and has taken years to complete,' Macro observed. 'There's every chance that he would come to see the final stages for himself.'

'More than a chance,' Narcissus interrupted. 'Apollodorus didn't put on that celebration by himself. It was Pallas's idea. He organised the celebration and commissioned that cake.'

'So Pallas is behind this?' Macro frowned. 'Pallas is working for the Liberators?'

'I don't know,' Narcissus admitted. 'It's possible. But I doubt it. Pallas has nothing to gain from a return to the Republic. In fact he has as much to lose as I have. I doubt that he was behind this attempt on Claudius's life.'

'Why not?' asked Cato. 'If Claudius drowns then Nero is the most likely successor.'

'That's true,' Narcissus conceded 'But there were enough people in the palace who knew that the Emperor would be here. Any one of them could be working for the Liberators. However it happened, the Liberators got wind of his visit to the project and decided to bring forward their plan for Tigellinus to assassinate the Emperor. They sabotaged the supports for the dam and Tigellinus knew what was going to happen and made ready to strike in the moment of confusion as the wave came towards us.'

'It's a bit far fetched,' Macro protested. 'Tigellinus would be putting his life at risk. For that matter, so would those men who were involved in weakening the dam. One wrong step there and the whole thing would have come down on them.'

'Just shows how determined our enemy has become,' Narcissus said grimly.

'They want an assassin close to the Emperor. Whatever plans they have for Tigellinus, the chances are that there would be precious little hope of him escaping having committed the deed. In fact, this business with the dam probably gave him the best possibility to strike and get away with it that he was likely to get.'

Cato nodded. 'I think you're right. The trouble is, if this was just an opportunistic attempt, then the initial plan is still ready to go ahead, as long as Tigellinus has survived, or they have another man ready to step into his boots if he hasn't. We still have to be on our guard. Are you going to tell the Emperor?'

Narcissus hesitated. 'Not yet. I want to have this investigated. I have to be certain of the facts before I go to Claudius.'

'Fair enough. There is one thing though. Apollodorus had no hand in this. The wave came as much of a surprise to him as the rest of us. You should put his mind at rest before you have him look at the evidence.'

Narcissus considered the suggestion. 'Perhaps later on, after he's been questioned. For now I'm content for people to think that it was an unfortunate accident. That's clearly what the Liberators want us to think, and I don't want them running scared just yet. They're making their move. They failed this time. They will try again if they think we aren't wise to their conspiracy. The more risks they take, the better the chances we have of identifying and eliminating them.'

'And the better chance they have of eliminating the Emperor,' Macro retorted.

'Then we shall all have to be more alert to potential dangers, shan't we?' Narcissus said sharply. He paused and forced himself to continue in a more measured tone. 'This is my chance to deal with the Liberators once and for all. I should have crushed them many years ago when I had the chance,' he added bitterly. He continued swiftly, 'If we force them to go to ground now, then they will bide their time and wait for another opportunity to strike. In the meantime the Emperor will be under constant threat and my agents and I will be stretched to the limit to respond to every possible sign of danger. Better to finish it now, don't you think?'

Macro looked at him and shrugged. 'It's your decision. It's not really my job to ferret out conspirators. It's up to you to protect the Emperor.'

'No.' Narcissus tapped his finger on Macro's chest. 'It's up to all of us. All those whose duty it is to protect the Emperor, and Rome. You swore an oath.'

Macro's fist shot up and closed tightly round the imperial secretary's hand. 'And I'll swear another oath if you ever poke me like that again. Got it?'

The two men stared at each other, until Macro clenched his fist hard and Narcissus's gaze faltered as he winced. He wrenched his hand free and flexed his fingers painfully. 'You'll regret that.'

'I've regretted a lot of things in my life,' Macro responded dismissively. 'Didn't stop me from doing them in the first place.'

Cato was growing impatient with the mutual hostility of his companions. 'Enough!' he said sharply. 'We should rejoin the Emperor. Narcissus, you need to see him safely back to the palace before the Liberators start spreading rumours that he has been killed.'

The imperial secretary shot one last scowl at Macro before he nodded. 'You're right. Besides, his escort is in poor shape to resist an attack. We need to be on the road before night falls.'

'Quite.' Cato gestured to them. 'Let's go.'

They set off, eager to quit the silent desolation of the vale. As Cato led the way he could not help wondering at the determination of the enemy. If they were prepared to risk their own lives so willingly in order to achieve their aims, then they were as deadly an enemy as he and Macro had ever faced. The next time they struck they had better be more zealous in their efforts than ever.

CHAPTER TWENTY-ONE

'Fourteen drowned, another ten injured and twelve still missing, including the centurion,' said Fuscius as he slumped down on to his cot in the section room. He shook his head. 'The lads didn't stand a chance when the water hit us . . .' The young optio closed his eyes and his voice dropped to barely more than a whisper. 'I was certain I'd die when I went under.'

Cato was sitting on the cot opposite and leant forward. 'I think we all were. Something like that is never going to be on the training programme, is it?'

His attempt at gentle levity fell on deaf ears. Fuscius stared at the ground between his boots. 'The Fifth Century suffered even more losses than we did . . . I thought joining the Praetorian Guard was supposed to be a cushy number. First the bloody riot and now this. It's like we're cursed.'

Macro gave a harsh laugh. 'What? You think being a soldier ain't supposed to be dangerous? Lad, you should have seen some of the pickles that Capito and I have been in over the years. Much worse than this. And we're still here to talk about it. None of it was to do with curses. So you just raise a cup to the comrades you've lost, honour their memories and get on with the soldiering. That's all you can, and should, do. You don't sit there, wallowing in your own misery, muttering about curses. Especially when you're an optio. Until Tigellinus returns, or is replaced, you're in command of the century. So you'd better pull yourself together.'

Fuscius looked up and stared at Macro. At first his expression was neutral, but then his eyes narrowed in suspicion. 'This has all happened since you two arrived.'

'Us?'

'That's right. Before then everything was nice and easy. Now we've been battered by the mob, Lurco's disappeared and half the Sixth Century has been lost in a freak flood.' He paused. 'From where I'm sitting it looks like more than a coincidence. Which begs the question, what have you two done that has caused the wrath of the gods to be heaped on your comrades, eh?'

'You're talking bollocks, lad. Capito and I have been doing our duty. Nothing more or less. Same as you. Same as the rest of the lads. The gods have got nothing to do with this.'

'So, the dam just collapsed all by itself then? A freak accident? Do us a favour, Calidus. That was an act of the gods if ever there was one.'

'Act of the gods, my arse! Some bastard—'

'Calidus!' Cato snapped. 'That's enough. The optio's had a tough time of it. If he's going to take command, then he needs rest. So leave him be.'

Macro turned to Cato with an enraged expression. 'You heard him. The little shaver thinks this is down to us.'

Cato raised his eyebrows meaningfully.

'Oh . . . yes, I see . . .' Macro swallowed his anger and turned back to Fuscius. He cleared his throat. 'My, er, apologies, Optio. I was out of line.'

'Fair enough.' Fuscius nodded slowly. 'Let's let it lie, eh? I do need to rest. Maybe Tigellinus will turn up. If not, then I'll need to be fresh come the morning.'

'That's right, Optio.' Cato nodded. 'We'll see to it you're not disturbed. Better still, Calidus and I will clear off for a bit and give you some peace.'

Macro shot Cato an angry look but his friend glared back and jerked a thumb towards the door. They rose from their cots and quietly left the room as the young optio lowered himself on to his coarse mattress and curled up on his side. As Cato closed the door behind them, Macro hissed angrily, 'That little oik needs to be put in his place. How dare he speak to us like that?'

'Keep your mind on the job,' Cato replied quietly. 'You nearly gave the game away just then. As far as anyone else is concerned, the collapse of the dam was an accident, remember? Until Narcissus says otherwise.'

'You really think that story is going to convince people for much longer?'

'No,' Cato replied wearily. 'But it might buy us some time before the other side takes extra care in covering their tracks. Right now we need all the help we can get.' Cato nodded towards the door. 'Let's talk, but not here. Just in case. Let's go down to the mess.'

The large room at the end of the barracks on the ground floor was almost empty. Besides Cato and Macro there were only a handful of men in one corner, half-heartedly playing at dice. They looked up and nodded a greeting and then returned to their game. Choosing a table on the opposite side of the mess, the two friends sat down. Macro sighed impatiently.

'Well, here we are. What do you want to talk about?'

Cato did not reply at once. He stared down at the heavily scored surface of the table and then ran a finger slowly along the grooves where some bored guardsman had carved his initials some years earlier. 'I'm trying to work out where we've got to in all this.'

'Good luck, lad. I'll confess it's getting too complicated for my head. These bloody Liberators seem to be getting their dirty hands in everywhere. They've got men in key positions in the Praetorian Guard. They've used their contacts in the grain merchants' guild to buy up the grain supply and now they've managed to sabotage that dam. They're everywhere, I tell you, Cato. Like bloody sewer rats.'

Cato frowned at Macro's last words for a moment, as if trying to recall something, and then he gave up with a shake of his head. 'You're right, and that doesn't seem right to me. How can the Liberators have so many people working for them and still keep to the shadows? It doesn't make sense. The more people they have in play, the harder it gets to keep the whole thing secret. If anyone stands a chance of infiltrating such a conspiracy and destroying it then it's Narcissus. And yet he seems to know no more than we do. That's something of a first in our dealings with him.'

Macro grunted with feeling.

'There's something else that doesn't seem to add up,' Cato continued. 'Why weren't the Empress or Pallas at the lake today?'

'I think we know the answer to that one well enough.'

Macro grinned. 'They had better things to occupy themselves with.'

'Leaving that aside, don't you find it just a little too convenient that they happen not to be with Claudius on the day he is almost killed?'

'It's certainly a lucky escape,' Macro agreed. 'But what are you implying? You think they had something to do with today's little adventure? That doesn't make sense, lad. Earlier on you were saying that Tigellinus was in on it. We know that he's part of the Liberators' conspiracy. In which case, how can he be working for Pallas and the Empress? Not unless they are all in it together. But how could that work? The Liberators are hardly likely to make common cause with the wife of the Emperor. They want her removed from the scene just as much as they do Claudius. And not just her, but the rest of the imperial family and all their most trusted advisers, like Pallas and our boy Narcissus.' Macro shook his head. 'The fact that Pallas and Agrippina weren't there today has to be a coincidence.'

'You may be right,' said Cato. 'But if you were the Liberators, wouldn't you want to remove the imperial family in one go? Why risk Tigellinus and those men who sabotaged the dam only to have to go through it all again with the rest of the imperial family? With the Emperor dead the security around the rest of them would become far tighter; the Liberators would find it much harder to finish the job.'

Macro reflected on this for a moment. 'Perhaps they're getting desperate. They've already failed in one attempt to assassinate the imperial family. Perhaps they're taking their chances as and when they can.'

'That might be,' Cato conceded. 'But there's another possibility. What if we are dealing with more than one conspiracy here? What if the Liberators are plotting to eliminate the imperial family, while at the same time Pallas and Agrippina are also plotting to do away with Claudius and clear the path to the throne for Nero?'

Macro shook his head. 'That still doesn't explain this afternoon. If Pallas was responsible, then how do you explain Tigellinus's part in it?'

Cato puffed irritably. 'I can't. Not yet. Unless he's some kind of double agent . . . What if he were?' Cato's mind suddenly raced ahead with the suggestion. 'Now that would make sense of things. The question then becomes which side is he really working for and which side is he misleading?' He recalled what he knew of the recently promoted centurion. 'He returned to Rome from exile about the same time as Agrippina. Perhaps he's working in her interests. He could be posing as a servant of the Liberators to use them to help Agrippina and Pallas . . .' A sudden flash of inspiration fired Cato's mind. 'Yes! That would make some sense of what happened this afternoon. The Empress and Pallas intend to wait until the Liberators have removed Claudius and then seize power. When she has what she wants and Nero sits on the throne, she can use the intelligence gathered by Tigellinus to move against the Liberators.' He paused and smiled. 'Clever, very clever.'

'You're looking very pleased with yourself,' Macro said drily. 'Maybe you're right but that doesn't help us to discover how the Liberators are intending to do away with Claudius.'

'I know.' Cato's expression resumed its earlier

weariness. 'All the same, I must let Narcissus know about my suspicions as soon as possible. If I'm right, then the threat to Claudius is greater than Narcissus knows.'

'After today's dowsing, I think Narcissus might just be thinking that already.'

Cato laughed. The sensation felt as if a burden had been lifted from his mind. He realised how exhausted he was. Aside from the strength-sapping struggle against the body of water that swept him away and down the river, Cato was covered with scratches and bruises from the battering he had endured in the process. He needed rest badly, and looking at Macro he could see that his friend did too.

'The hour's late. We should get some sleep.'

Macro nodded and they rose stiffly and made their way out of the mess. They exchanged nods with the men still playing dice and then closed the door behind them. Outside a long colonnade led to the stairs up to the second storey. They had passed the centurion's quarters and office and then the first of the section rooms when they saw a figure by the foot of the stairs pace slowly towards them. The man's features were indiscernible. He stopped ten feet away, blocking their path. Cato strained his eyes and could just make out that the man was covered in mud. He wore a tunic and boots and his dagger scabbard was empty. His sword hung against his left hip, as was the custom for officers. Cato swore a silent oath and stood to attention.

'Centurion Tigellinus. Sir, I thought we had lost you.'

'Tigellinus?' Macro began, then snapped to attention beside Cato.

The other man was breathing heavily, and there was a

pause as he stared back. Then his lips parted in a faint grin.

'Back from the dead, that's what I am. Bloody river swept me on for miles before I grounded on some stinking mudbank. By the time I got out and made my way back to the lake, the rest of you had gone and it was dark. So I marched back here.' He took a step forward and stared at Cato. 'So what happened?'

'Sir?'

'The Emperor, did he survive?'

'Yes, sir.'

There was no expression in the centurion's mud-streaked face and he remained silent for a moment. When he spoke again his voice was unnaturally calm and measured. 'Was it you that saved the Emperor's life?'

'No, sir. It was Tribune Burrus.' Cato lowered his voice and spoke deliberately. 'Although you might easily have reached the Emperor first, had you not stumbled.'

'Yes, I would have reached him,' Tigellinus replied flatly. 'Was the Emperor injured?'

'No, sir. Just badly shaken by the incident. The survivors of the escort took him to the palace before returning to the Praetorian camp.'

'I see.' Tigellinus was silent for a moment, his expression unreadable. Then he cleared his throat. 'How many casualties among our lads?'

'Over a third of the century, sir. Though some of them are marked down as missing, including you.'

'Then Fuscius is in command?'

'Yes, sir.'

'Where is he?'

'Sleeping it off, sir. Do you want us to wake him and send him to you?'

Tigellinus thought a moment and shook his head. 'No need. Just tell him that I've returned and he's back to normal duties when the morning trumpet sounds.'

'Yes, sir.'

The centurion regarded Cato and Macro in silence until Macro coughed lightly.

'Is there anything else, sir?'

'I'm not sure. Is there anything else that you two want to tell me?'

'Sir?' Macro responded innocently.

'I wonder, did you have any specific orders to carry out today?'

'Orders, sir?' Cato intervened. 'I don't understand.'

'Don't play the fool with me, Capito. You, Calidus and I are sufficiently well acquainted with Centurion Sinius and his friends to know what we are all about. So you don't have to pretend otherwise. I'll ask you again. Did Sinius give you any orders today?' Tigellinus leant forward slightly, his intent gaze flicking between Cato and Macro. 'Well?'

Cato felt his heartbeat quicken and feared that his inner turmoil might be read in his face. He strove to keep a steady and neutral expression as he stared back at the centurion with unwavering eyes. It was tempting to deny everything and play dumb. But it was clear that Tigellinus knew about their connection to the Liberators, probably from his dealings with Centurion Sinius, or perhaps another conspirator higher up the chain of command. Equally clearly he suspected that their orders were being withheld from him.

With a sudden flare of insight Cato realised that Tigellinus was as fearful as he was. If his masters had given separate orders to either Cato or Macro, or both, then it was clear that they did not trust him enough to share that information. Worse, they might actually distrust Tigellinus enough to order a separate attempt on the Emperor's life in case Tigellinus failed. Cato had to make his response quickly, before the centurion turned his attention to Macro. He made his decision. If the Liberators were on the verge of attempting to overthrow the Emperor then it was important to disrupt their plans.

'Yes, sir,' Cato replied in a wary tone. 'Sinius told me of your orders, and said that I was to carry the assassination through if you failed for any reason.'

Tigellinus drew a long, deep breath and exhaled through clenched teeth. 'I see. And you did not think to tell me this?'

'Centurion Sinius told me to watch you and act if I needed to. He did not say that I should make you aware of my orders. I assumed that you either knew already, or that you weren't supposed to know of my part in the attempt.'

Tigellinus stared at Cato for a moment and then switched his gaze to Macro. 'And you? What did you know of this, Calidus?'

'Nothing, sir,' Macro answered truthfully.

Tigellinus turned back to Cato. 'Why is that, I wonder?'

Cato shrugged. 'A secret shared is a risk doubled, sir. Perhaps that's why Sinius told only me to keep a watch on you.'

'Perhaps,' Tigellinus mused. 'At least I know where

I stand in the eyes of our good friends, the Liberators.'

'Sir, I don't know if I should have told you this. Sinius didn't expressly say that I shouldn't. But perhaps it would be best if he did not know we had spoken.'

Tigellinus's face slid into a crafty expression. 'I shan't say anything, for now, Capito. But in future, if Sinius tells you anything, then you tell me. Is that clear?'

'I'm not certain that would be wise, sir.'

'I'm sure it wouldn't. But if I were to tell Sinius that you spilled the beans so easily then I doubt he would consider you a reliable, or inexpendable, member of the conspiracy. You understand? In future, when he speaks to you, you speak to me. If you don't then I shall make your life difficult, not to mention dangerous. Clear?'

'Yes, sir.' Cato nodded. 'As you wish.'

'Quite. Now, out of my way. I have to get this bloody mud off me and my kit.'

Cato and Macro stepped aside and a foul odour wafted into the air between them as Tigellinus strode by. They watched him reach the end of the colonnade, enter his quarters and shut the door with a crash.

Macro turned to Cato with a cold stare. 'What was that all about? You never said anything about Sinius's orders.'

'That's because he never said anything to me.'

'What?' Macro frowned then jerked his thumb in the direction of the centurion's quarters. 'Then why tell him different?'

Cato looked both ways along the colonnade to ensure that no one would overhear their muted conversation. 'What else could I do? If I said no then Tigellinus might realise that I had been out to save the Emperor rather than kill him. I had to make it look as if we were on the same side.' Cato paused to let his friend think through his explanation, before continuing. 'In any case, it helps our cause if Tigellinus is now suspicious of Centurion Sinius and the other Liberators. Divide and rule. It also helps that he thinks he has some kind of power over us. Such men are more likely to be indiscreet when they take so much for granted.'

'And it makes me look like a bit of a dickhead,' Macro responded sourly. 'Like I'm not trusted.'

'Not at all. The Liberators are playing a dangerous game. They have to operate in complete secrecy. It would make sense to keep the smallest number of people in the know, and even then only to tell them as little information as is required for them to play their part. Do you see?'

'Of course I bloody well do,' Macro fumed. 'I just don't like being put on the spot like that.'

'That's part of our job, for now. We have to think on our toes, Macro.' Cato searched his friend's face for some sign of understanding. 'Things are coming to a head. Once we see this through then we can get back to soldiering.'

'Assuming Narcissus keeps his word.'

'True enough,' Cato conceded.

'And assuming that we survive this little game of secret agents.'

'As long as we watch each other's back and be careful what we say, then the odds are that we will.'

'Care to place any money on that?'

'As much as you like.' Cato smiled, spat on the palm of his hand and held it out. 'Where should the money go if you win?'

'Bah!' Macro growled and slapped Cato's hand aside. 'Piss off. I've had enough of your games for tonight. I'm turning in.'

Macro made for the stairs and began to climb. After a pause, Cato followed. Back in the section room Fuscius had turned on to his back and was snoring lightly. The other men removed their boots and lowered themselves onto their cots without another word. As usual Macro was asleep within moments and added his deeper, more guttural snores to those of Fuscius. Cato folded his arms behind his head and stared up at the ceiling, trying hard to ignore the din. He tried to focus his mind on the twists and turns of the conspiracy that he and Macro had been struggling to unravel for the last two months, with limited success.

Before long Cato's mind began to wander, lighting upon one aspect of the conspiracy after another. Then, without warning, his mind filled with the feral expression on Cestius's face as he thrust Britannicus aside during the food riot and made to strike at Nero. Cato frowned at the memory. Something about it did not fit with the other aspects of the conspiracy. He strained his mind to make the connection but was too tired to concentrate effectively. At length he shut his eyes and a vivid memory of the moment the wave struck filled his mind. He had been certain that he would die. That they would all die, swept away and drowned by the deluge. But the gods had been merciful. He still lived, as did Macro, the Emperor and most of the men caught by the wave. The conspirators had failed to kill Claudius, just as they had failed back in the Forum. One thing was certain. They would try again, and soon.

CHAPTER TWENTY-TWO

The next day the two depleted centuries of Burrus's cohort were brought up to strength by men from the other units of the Praetorian Guard. The tribune himself was awarded a grass crown by the Emperor for saving the life of another Roman citizen. The ceremony was performed in the courtyard of the palace with all the men under the tribune's command formed up on three sides to face the Emperor as he expressed his gratitude. Standing to attention on the left flank of the Sixth Century, Cato had a good view of the imperial party surrounding Claudius as they tried with various degrees of success to look as if they were enjoying the Emperor's laboured rhetoric.

Immediately behind Claudius were his family. Agrippina struck a suitably maternal pose between Britannicus and Nero, her hands resting on their shoulders. While she lightly caressed her natural son, Cato noted that her fingers worked rather more firmly on the shoulder of Britannicus, edging gradually towards the exposed flesh of his neck. At one stage he winced and looked up at her sharply and was rewarded with a vicious glare. When she at last dropped her arm to the side, Britannicus took the opportunity to shuffle out of his stepmother's reach.

Over Agrippina's shoulder Cato could see Pallas, head slightly tilted upwards as if savouring the Emperor's words. At his side stood Narcissus, looking gloomy, his face and arms bearing the scratches and bruises he had received as he tumbled through the wave released by the sabotaged dam. He stared rigidly at the ranks of the Praetorian Guard and then turned to regard Pallas with a poorly disguised expression of utter loathing.

Beyond the coterie of imperial freedmen and a handful of citizen advisers stood several favoured senators and the prefect of the Praetorian Guard, Geta. He stood with an impressive soldierly bearing, straight backed, chest out. His breastplate gleamed brightly and the purple sash tied about his waist was neat and precise. The ends of the sash hung in decorative loops from where they had been tucked behind the topmost fold of the sash. Fine leather boots fitted his calves like an extra layer of skin, and gilded tassels hung from the tops, just below the knee. Cato could not help smiling faintly. Glorious as Geta looked, Cato knew that he would be regarded with simmering derision by Macro who was inclined to see such finery as superfluous and unmanly.

Cato's amused expression faded as he reflected on the sinister reality that lay behind the ordered display of hierarchy and unity. Among those standing so calmly behind the Emperor were traitors plotting to murder him, while others planned the deaths of the entire imperial family. Cutting across the treason were the rivalries between Nero and Britannicus, Narcissus and Pallas and, no doubt, the professional rivalry between the Praetorian prefect and the newly decorated Tribune Burrus.

Cato could not help feeling a depressed cynicism at

the façade of order, duty and loyalty presented to the people of Rome. They shared the same flesh and blood as the commoners but their lives were bound up in a constant struggle for influence, power and riches that was nakedly self-serving when the pomp and dignity were stripped away. The leaden sense of despair that it engendered weighed down upon Cato as he thought that this was how it was, is and would be for as long as those few with power were more concerned with accruing it for themselves rather than using it to better the lot of those they ruled.

He found himself wondering if it might not be better for Rome if the Liberators succeeded in sweeping away the Emperor, his family and all the wasteful trappings of the imperial household. He had never known what life was like under the Republic. There were no more than a handful of men and women still left in Rome who did, and their memories of that age were dim and unreliable. The passions of those who had murdered the tyrant Caesar were as distant as legends now. The Liberators' claim to be their successors was as hollow as the loyalty professed by those who now stood behind the Emperor. Despots all, Cato thought sourly. The only difference between them was that some were struggling to gain power while others struggled to retain it. They were indifferent to the rest of humanity, unless the retention of their position forced some show of common feeling.

Macro was right, Cato decided. It would be better to be far from Rome with its treachery and its luxurious caprices that softened men and made them into scoundrels or fools. Better to be back in the ranks of the legions where a man's worth was defined by the rigid and honest standards of military life. Even as he thought it, Cato wondered whether his yearning for the certainties of a soldier's life outweighed his yearning for the love of Julia, and a life spent with her, which might well entail living in Rome. He sensed that he knew the answer to that and hurriedly pushed all thought of making a choice aside as the award ceremony concluded and the newly crowned Tribune Burrus turned to his men and gave the order for the cohort to return to the camp.

The following day the cohort marched out to the Albine Lake as the final preparations were made for the coming spectacle. The change of season was evident in the new growth bursting from trees, shrubs and vines in the countryside through which the cohort marched. The men had been issued with marching yokes to carry their mess kits, spare clothing and meagre rations. For the duration of the spectacle the cohort was to camp close to the newly erected imperial compound where Claudius and his guests would be accommodated in luxury.

The weather had turned decisively and warm sunshine bathed the Praetorians marching along the road. As good weather will, especially after a cold, drab winter, it raised the spirits of the men and they talked and sang lustily as they marched. Their officers relaxed the usual discipline of the Praetorian Guard and indulged their mens' good humour so that the column took on the ambience of a friendly procession rather than a manouevre conducted by the elite formation of the Roman army. Even Macro, a soldier to the very core of his being, was content as they advanced in broken step. He felt good to leave Rome behind and savour the familiar grinding chorus of nailed boots, the weight of a yoke braced against his padded shoulder and the cheery camaraderie of the rankers. The road crossed rolling countryside and afforded pleasing vistas over the farmland with its newly sown crops. One field contained a small flock of sheep with several newborn lambs whose wool gleamed like freshly laundered togas.

'This is the life, eh?' Macro grinned at Cato. 'Proper soldering.'

Cato adjusted his yoke once more. He had never had Macro's experience of being a common legionary and had therefore never quite mastered the art of carrying the heavy yoke with any degree of comfort over long distances. Already he was beginning to wonder what had possessed him yesterday when he had been so adamant in his desire to return to what his friend so fondly termed proper soldiering. He bunched his padding up under the wooden shaft as best he could before he replied to his friend. 'Ah yes! Blisters and tired muscles. What more could a man ask for, I wonder.'

Macro was well used to Cato's assumed dour accept-ance of the strains of marching and laughed. 'Come on, lad. Admit it, you're as pleased to be out and about as I am. No more skulking about in Rome for a few days at least. And it'll be good to spend some nights under the stars with grass at our backs, a fire to warm us, and a jug of wine to share. May not be much food in our bellies, but there's no shortage of wine thank the gods. Now that would be a tragedy. Man can live by bread alone, but who would want to, eh?'

'I don't know,' Cato grunted under the burden of his

yoke. 'I would give up a month's pay for a decent haunch of mutton and a freshly baked loaf of bread right now.' He glanced wistfully at the grazing sheep and lambs.

'Don't even think about it!' said Fuscius, marching beside the column where he had overheard the exchange and noted Cato's look. 'That lot are protected by order of the Emperor. All available livestock for ten miles around the city has been commandeered by the Emperor.'

'What for?' asked Macro.

'There's one man who ignores the gazette.' Fuscius laughed. 'Claudius wants to make sure that he has the biggest audience he can find for the spectacle. One way to guarantee that is to offer the mob food as well as entertainment. They'll come all right.'

When the cohort reached the lake, Cato was astonished by the work that had been carried out in the few days since he had last seen the site. The pens built for the combatants were already filling with men and as the cohort marched up he could see a long line of prisoners, in ankle chains, being led to the site from the south. A unit of auxiliaries stood guard over the pens. The imperial pavilion had been completed and dominated the shoreline. Although constructed from timber, it had been painted in white so that from a distance it looked like a small palace constructed from the finest marble. The main viewing stand was built over the water and supported by heavy piles driven into the bed of the lake. At the side of the pavilion was a stand where the Emperor would be able to review the fighters as they paraded past and boarded the small ships of the two fleets.

The carpenters had completed their work on the vessels which were drawn up at either end of the pavilion, some twenty on each side. The beams of the barges had been built up to support decks that covered the rowing benches fitted into what had been the holds. Decorative fantails curved over the sterns while eye motifs had been painted at the bows, either side of the iron-tipped rams. It was hard to believe that the vessels had enjoyed a previous life as humble barges plying their trade along the Tiber. Out on the lake several of the small ships were going through their drills as a detachment of sailors from the imperial navy hurriedly trained the crews in the rudiments of rowing and steering.

Further along the shore, surrounded by a guarded palisade, were the stores of bread, meat and wine to be distributed to the people. Much of this had been taken from the vast storerooms beneath the imperial palace in a desperate bid to stave off the starvation of the mob long enough for the grain convoy from Sicilia to arrive. On the far side of the lake there were already some small groups of people clustered around makeshift shelters and smoke from campfires trailed into the air against the backdrop of the hills beyond.

A palace official guided the cohort to the site prepared for their camp, a short distance from the prisoner pens. As the centurions and officers bellowed the order to down packs, Macro stretched his shoulders and rocked his head from side to side to ease his neck muscles. Then he paused and sniffed the air and wrinkled his nose.

'What is that stench?'

Cato pointed towards the prisoner pens. 'Over there. Can't see any latrine trenches. They're having to shit inside the pens.'

Both men paused to stare at the palisade before Macro

muttered, 'That's no way for a fighting man to have to live.'

'They're not fighting men. Remember what Narcissus said: mostly criminals and any other dregs that could be scraped together to fill out the ranks on each side.'

Macro was silent for a moment. 'Even so, they'll be fighting soon enough and shouldn't be treated like animals.'

'You two!' Fuscius cried out. 'No dawdling! Get over to the wagons and fetch a tent for the section!'

A line of wagons had been parked at the far end of the campsite and the men of the cohort were busy unloading bundles of goatskin, tent poles, guy ropes and ground pegs. As Macro and Cato trudged over towards the wagons between the lines marked out for each century's tents, Macro chuckled. 'Seems the optio's found his voice again. Bawling us out like a veteran. Or trying to at least. Funny, he reminds me of you back in the early days.'

'Me?' Cato looked at him with raised eyebrows.

'Sure. Shrill, overkeen and making up with pickiness what you lacked in experience.'

'I was like that?'

'Near enough.' Macro smiled. 'But you came good, eventually. So will our boy, Fuscius, you'll see.'

'Maybe.' Cato glanced at the optio and continued in a low voice. 'If he's smart enough to keep his nose out of any conspiracy.'

'Do you think he's involved?'

'I don't know.' Cato thought a moment. 'He was as unlikely a choice for preferment as Tigellinus, so I think I'll reserve judgement for now.'

Macro shook his head. 'You're seeing conspirators everywhere, my lad. I wonder how long it'll be before you start suspecting me.'

Cato smiled. 'On that day, I think I'll just go and quietly open my veins. If there's one thing in this world that I know the true worth of, it's our friendship. It's seen us through—'

Macro smiled awkwardly and raised a hand to silence his friend. 'Stick a boot in it, Cato, or you'll make me fucking cry.'

During the night the slaves and servants of the imperial household arrived to prepare the pavilion for the imperial family and their guests. They worked by the light of braziers and lamps to ensure that all the furnishings and banqueting tables and couches were ready for the Emperor's arrival the following noon. A steady trickle of torches advancing round the far side of the lake indicated the arrival of the slaves sent to find good vantage points for their wealthy masters still in bed back in Rome. The opposite shore was nearly half a mile away and ranged along its length the campfires and torches glowed against the dark hills, and their reflections glinted and glittered across the surface of the water. After the rest of the men in their section had retired to the tent to sleep, Cato and Macro shared a wineskin and watched the numbers swell on the far shore.

'I doubt that there will ever be a spectacle on this scale again,' mused Macro. 'I've never seen or heard of the like.'

'That's because there's never been such a need for one,' Cato suggested. 'Desperate times call for spectacular diversions. If anything goes wrong with the show, or the mob isn't entertained sufficiently then Claudius's days are numbered. Either the mob will tear him to pieces or the Liberators will stab him in the back, or the deed will be done by someone even closer to him.' Cato was silent for a moment. He reached for another piece of wood to toss on to the dying campfire. 'Shit . . .'

'What's the matter?'

'Hardly a great state of affairs, is it? We risk our lives and shed our blood keeping the barbarians back from the frontiers of Rome only for these fools to put it all in jeopardy.'

'So? What do you think you can do about it?'

Cato was silent, then looked cautiously into his friend's eyes. 'Not much, I admit. But it seems to me that right now Claudius is the best hope for Rome. That's why we must do all we can to keep him safe.'

'Claudius?' Macro shook his head. 'I think you've had too much wine, my lad.'

Cato leant forward. 'Listen, Macro, I'm not drunk . . . I'm serious. We've seen enough of the world to know that Rome, for all its faults, is not the worst of empires. Where Rome rules there is order and prosperity and – though I know you don't place much store by it – culture. There are libraries, theatres and art. And there is a degree of religious tolerance. Unlike those nests of arrogance and bigotry in Britannia and Judaea.' Cato shuddered as he recalled the Druids and Judaean fanatics he and Macro had faced in battle. 'Rome is the best hope for mankind.'

'I doubt that's a view shared by those we have crushed on the battlefield and made into slaves.' Macro stared into the small flames licking up from the charred wood and ash of the fire. 'You're an idealist, Cato. A romantic. There is no more to it than a test of strength. We conquer because that is what Rome does, and we are good at it.'

'There is more to it than brute strength . . .' Cato began, then he paused. 'All right, there is that. But Rome has more, much more, to offer than simply the sword. Or it might have, but for some of the emperors. I've seen them at close hand. Tiberius and that monster, Gaius. Each of them has wielded power with carelessness and cruelty. Claudius, for all his faults, has tried to be better. The question is, do you think young Britannicus, or Nero, will continue his good work?'

'I hadn't even thought about it.' Macro yawned. 'As long as they can pay to maintain the legions and leave the campaigning up to the professionals, then that's all that concerns me.'

Cato stared at him. 'I don't believe you. You think I don't know what stirs your heart?'

Macro turned to face him. 'Even if I felt some of what you do about all this, then I'm old enough to know that it is a waste of time to even think about it any more. Will you change the world? Will I? No. That's not for us. It never was, never will be. Not for men of our class. Do you not think that I once felt as you do?' Macro paused, and continued in a kindly tone, 'It is like a sweet delirium and age is the cure. Now, I'm tired. I'm going to sleep. You should rest too.'

Macro eased himself up, half-empty wineskin in hand, and nodded to Cato before walking across to the flap of the section tent and disappearing inside. Cato drew up his knees and wrapped his arms round them as he stared into the wavering glow of the fire. Macro's blunt outlook on life angered and frustrated in him equal measure, as ever. Cato's heart was young enough to harbour boundless dreams and desires to shape his future, and he demanded that others should think as he did. If they did not then it was through lack of vision or inclination. Yet, even as he felt the heat of ambition in his heart, Cato's mind coldly considered his friend's point of view. There was wisdom in Macro's words, but when wisdom is proffered from the position of greater age and experience it is seldom palatable.

The night air was chilly and Cato trembled as he hunched his body to try to stay warm. Beyond the fire he could make out the mass of the imperial pavilion, its white paint dimly luminous in the starlight. He wondered what preoccupied the minds of men like Claudius, and his heirs. Men not doomed to the obscurity that was the fate of the masses. For all his ambitions and dreams, Cato well knew that a hundred, a thousand, years hence men would still talk of Claudius, while the names of Macro and Cato, and countless others, would be buried and forgotten in the dust of history. He stared at the outline of the imperial pavilion with simmering resentment for a long time, as the last heat from the fire faded away.

'Well,' he muttered to himself at length, then stood up. 'You're a cheery bugger, aren't you?'

As he made his way towards the tent, Cato saw a figure moving along the far side of the tent line. As he passed one of the braziers lit to warm the sentries, Cato recognised the features of Tigellinus. He exchanged a salute with one of the men on watch. So, Cato mused, there's another man whose troubled mind was denying him sleep. He watched a moment longer as the centurion continued into the night, in the direction of the prisoner pens, and then Cato ducked inside the goatskin section tent, felt his way carefully to his bedroll and lay down to sleep.

CHAPTER TWENTY-THREE

Throughout the morning the people of Rome continued to stream down the Appian Way towards the lake. Most were families on foot, ragged and gaunt looking, with infants strapped to their mothers inside slings of soiled cloth. In among them were hawkers carrying bundles of goods or hauling handcarts laden with cushions, fans and wineskins. The usual sellers of snacks and round loaves of bread were conspicuously absent. There were only a handful of mules and ponies used to draw the carts and they were as starved as the people, ribs showing through their hides like silky cloth laid over iron bars. Most of Rome's draught animals had already been butchered for food. Even their bones and skins had been boiled up to add to a watery broth. In among the stream of starving humanity came the better off, still adequately fed, and chatting animatedly among themselves as their slave escorts cleared a path for them with stout clubs and wooden staffs.

As they reached the shores of the lake the multitude was carefully marshalled between lines of tables where they were handed their food ration from the stockpile brought up from the storerooms of the imperial palace. In among the plain loaves of bread and strips of cured meat were luxuries that hardly any of the common people had ever heard of, let alone seen. Honeyed cakes, lark's tongue pies, haunches of smoked venison, jars of the finest garum and pots of preserved fruit plucked in distant provinces and shipped to Rome at vast expense. Some of the recipients of the Emperor's largesse looked at the fine food in blank incomprehension before sniffing and sampling them. Most then attempted to trade them for something more recognisable.

Clutching their rations, the people then continued on, round the lake, to find a place to sit and watch the coming spectacle. The space along the shore rapidly filled up and then the slope behind so that to Cato and Macro, watching a short distance to one side of the imperial pavilion, the opposite shore seemed to be one seething landscape of humanity speckled with colour.

'By the gods,' Macro marvelled. 'I have never seen so many people. All Rome must be here, surely.'

Cato shrugged. It was hard to conceive of the number of people on the far shore. He knew that the Great Circus could hold over two hundred thousand spectators, and if the population of Rome was nearly a million souls, as he had been told, then surely most of them were here today. The streets of the capital must seem like those of a ghost town, the stillness and quiet broken only by the odd figure or voice of those too infirm to travel to the lake, or too dishonest to pass up the chance to break into empty houses and shops. Only the rich could afford to leave armed slaves behind to safeguard their property. Cato turned to look towards the diminishing reserves of food stockpiled a short distance behind the imperial pavilion and calculated that they would be exhausted by the second day of the spectacle. After that only the Sicilian grain ships stood between Emperor Claudius and a ravenous mob.

If Claudius was toppled, the Liberators would step forward with the vast supply of grain that they had hidden away somewhere in, or near, Rome. Having starved the mob into violence in the first place, the Liberators would then play the part of public-spirited benefactors. The thought made the blood burn in Cato's veins. He pushed his anger aside and forced himself to concentrate. In the Liberators' place, where would he store so much grain?

'Heads up, lads!' Fuscius called out. 'Banquet's over. Stand to!'

The imperial party had been dining under a large open-sided tent and the last notes of music from the flutes and harps of a Greek ensemble died away as Claudius led his family and advisers past the other guests who had hurriedly risen to their feet. They emerged into the bright sunshine and the men of Burrus's cohort snapped smartly to attention, javelins and shields held firmly in each hand. Three centuries stood lined up either side of the short route from the banqueting tent to the garlanded entrance of the pavilion, beyond which a wide staircase led up to the viewing platform. The German bodyguards were already in place, positioned around the imperial box where Claudius and his family would sit on cushioned chairs.

The Sixth Century, still enjoying the particular gratitude of Claudius, had the honour of guarding the outside of the pavilion while the rest of the cohort was to be held back a short distance in case they were needed to assist the auxiliaries guarding the food stockpile and prisoner pens.

Once the Emperor and his entourage had entered the pavilion, Burrus marched the other five centuries away and Centurion Tigellinus began to dispose his men around the perimeter of the pavilion. Cato and Macro were posted to a shaded spot just below the reviewing stand.

'Here we go,' said Macro, gesturing towards the prisoner pens. 'The show's about to start.'

Cato turned his head and saw the first batch of prisoners being led out through one of the gates. They were herded down to the ships by the shore and there half of them were issued helmets, shields, swords and armour from the back of a wagon. The other half were directed up the wooden ramp to the first ship's deck and then ordered below to man the oars.

'Look at that kit,' Macro remarked. 'They must have emptied the Temple of Mars for that lot. Celt, Greek, Numidian. Some of that stuff must date back to before the civil war.'

Once the prisoners had been armed they boarded the vessel and loosely formed up on deck to await their officers. The two fleets were distinguished by the colour of the pennants flying from the top of each mast. The fight had been billed as a re-enactment of the battle of Salamis where the Greek warships had taken on a much larger Persian fleet and won the day. The ships chosen to represent the Persians carried light blue pennants, while those playing the part of the Greeks carried scarlet colours. One by one the other ships were similarly manned and then finally, two hours after midday, the admirals in command of the two fleets and the ships' officers were assembled before the reviewing stand. Most of them were professional gladiators, chosen to provide the discipline and leadership needed to lead the vast number of barely trained criminals and slaves who had been forced to take part in the spectacle. Looking over them Cato could see that they were in fine condition and some carried scars from previous combat. Tigellinus called out the four sections of men that he had been holding in reserve to form a line between the fighters and the reviewing stand.

The gladiators and the Praetorians stood facing each other in silence, until Narcissus emerged on the reviewing stand and crossed to the rail to look out over the raised faces of the men who would lead thousands of men to their deaths on the lake.

Narcissus was silent for a moment before he began his address in a harsh tone. 'In a moment the Emperor will be before you to acknowledge your salute, before the Naumachia begins. I would prefer that you were all chosen men, the very best that could do honour to the spectacle that you are privileged to take part in. But you are not. You are all that could be scraped together in the time available. Little better than the scum on those ships that you will be commanding. That said, I demand the best from you. As do they.' He pointed towards the far shore. 'Put on a good show. Make sure that you and your men fight well and those that survive may be rewarded.'

As the imperial secretary had been speaking, Cato noticed that some of the gladiators and the other fighters looked confused and some turned to mutter angrily to each other.

'Silence there!' Narcissus yelled. 'Stand still, and show respect for your Emperor!'

He turned and nodded to the bucinators standing either side of the doorway that led on to the reviewing platform. They raised their instruments, pursed their lips and blew several strident notes, rising in pitch. As the signal faded, Claudius stepped into the bright sunshine. The golden wreath on his unkempt snow-white hair gleamed brilliantly. The impression of his finely embroidered toga was marred somewhat by the splatters of sauce that ran down the front of it. He held a gold cup in his hand and made his way unsteadily to the rail. Narcissus bowed before him and backed to the side.

'Gladiators!' Narcissus called out. 'Greet your Emperor!'

There was a pause before the men mumbled an uneven salute whose words were barely distinguishable. Claudius, bemused by the wine he had consumed, could not help laughing and as the salute died away he shook his head.

'Come, you men. You c-c-can do better than that, surely?' The Emperor raised his free hand. 'On three! Ready? One, t-t-two, three!'

'Hail, Caesar!' the fighters bellowed in one voice. 'We salute you, those who are about to die!'

Claudius shook his head as he saw that some of the men had not joined in. He raised his cup and slurred, 'Or not, as the case may be. On that I gi-give you my word.'

The gladiators glanced at one another as they digested what the Emperor had just said. Claudius turned to Narcissus and muttered.

'Get 'em on the ships and start the ba–battle, before any more time is w–w–wasted.'

'As you command, sire.'

The Emperor turned and lurched back towards the

350

interior of the pavilion, wine slopping from his cup. As soon as he was gone Narcissus hurried to the rail.

'To your ships! Prepare for battle!'

Cato was watching the fighters closely. Several were talking animatedly and the rest were clustering round, shouting their support.

'There's trouble.'

'What are they saying?' asked Macro. 'Can't quite make it out.'

Cato caught the odd word but not enough to make any sense and he shook his head. Above them Narcissus's voice rang out again, shrill and angry.

'Get to your ships or I swear I will crucify every last one of you who survives the fight!'

The fighters parted and one of the gladiators stepped forward, thumbs tucked into his belt as he gazed defiantly at the imperial secretary. 'Nothing doing. We all heard the Emperor, as you did. It was clear enough what he said. We're pardoned. The fight is off.'

Macro turned to Cato with a surprised expression, and Cato shook his head uncomprehendingly.

'What did you say?' Narcissus asked in astonishment.

'The Naumachia. It's off. That's what the Emperor said.'

'Are you mad? What are you talking about?'

The gladiator frowned. 'It was clear enough to us. He said we weren't to die. He gave his word. You heard it from his own lips. The Emperor's word is law. There was a rumour going through the pens last night that the spectacle was off. Looks like it was true after all.'

'He meant nothing of the sort, you fool! Now get to your ships!'

The gladiator turned to look at his nearest supporters and there was a muted exchange before he turned back to Naricissus and folded his arms. 'We are pardoned men. The Emperor said as much. We demand to be set free at once.'

'You demand?' Narcissus choked. 'How dare you, slave!' The imperial secretary leant over the rail and shouted down to Tigellinus. 'Centurion, kill that man, and any others who refuse to obey their orders.'

There was a brief pause and the air filled with tension as the gladiators and the other fighters reached for the handles of their swords. Centurion Tigellinus stepped in front of his line of men and looked up at Narcissus. 'Sir?'

Narcissus stabbed a finger at him. 'Do as you are ordered, or you'll share his fate. Do it!'

Tigellinus stepped back into line, raised his shield and drew his sword. He sucked in a nervous breath and called out the order. 'Sixth Century! Advance javelins!'

There was a loud stamp as the guardsmen planted one foot forward and then lowered the tips of their javelins at an angle towards the gladiators. Cato looked over the men opposite and calculated that there must be at least eighty of them, more or less even odds if the situation got out of hand. Beside him Macro fixed his stare on their leader and growled, 'I had hoped never to fight slaves again. Gladiators least of all.'

'A sestertius to a denarius that this lot were trained at the school in Rome,' Cato muttered.

Macro glanced at him. The Great School was famed throughout the empire for the quality of the gladiators it turned out. Macro sucked in a deep breath. 'Then we're in trouble.'

Centurion Tigellinus must have shared their anxiety and turned to order one of the men to run to Tribune Burrus to request reinforcements. As the guardsman hurried off, Tigellinus raised his shield and turned it to face the gladiators. 'Sixth Century, at the walk, advance!'

The line of Praetorians rippled forward, their ceremonial armour gleaming on top of their spotless white tunics. It had been some time since Cato and Macro had fought as part of a battle line, rather than in command of one, and Cato concentrated on keeping the length of his pace the same as the men on either side of him. Before him the leader of the gladiators stretched out a hand towards Narcissus.

'Tell the Praetorians to halt! Or it'll be the blood of your men that's shed. And the Emperor will hold you responsible, freedman.' His voiced dripped with contempt as he uttered the last word.

Cato glanced back quickly and saw Narcissus glaring down on the scene, his lips pressed together in a narrow line.

'Gladiators!' their leader bellowed. 'Draw your weapons!'

The air filled with the sharp rasp and rattle of blades being ripped from their scabbards and Cato raised his oval shield higher so that it protected his torso and the lower part of his face. The gladiators were less than twenty paces away. Behind them a palisade stretched from the shore to the pens. A handful of auxiliary troops in a watchtower beyond the palisade had witnessed the confrontation and one was now calling down to his colleagues to alert them. There would be no escape for the gladiators in that direction, Cato decided. Indeed, there would be no escape for them in any direction. They could only stand their ground and die, or make for the ships. Those who had already boarded crowded on to the foredecks to watch and Cato prayed that they would not be fired by the indignant zeal that had caused their leaders to defy Narcissus. Fortunately, they were far enough away not to have heard the Emperor's offhand remark and the bitter exchange it had provoked.

The leader of the gladiators lowered himself into a crouch and held his buckler forward of his body, ready to punch it into the face of the first enemy that dared to oppose him. His sword was drawn back, ready to stab. The other men quickly followed his example, spreading out to give themselves space to move. Cato could not help wondering at the difference in fighting styles between the gladiators and the Praetorians. One side trained to fight as individuals, experts in the techniques required for the individual duels that defined their lives. Ranged against them were the elite soldiers of Rome, drilled to fight in disciplined battle lines, each man just one part of a machine.

Tigellinus called out to them, 'Save yourselves! Give up that man and you will be spared.'

'Fuck you!' a voice screamed back.

Their leader's lips parted in a feral grin and he slapped his cuirass with the flat of his sword. 'Come and get me!'

CHAPTER TWENTY-FOUR

'So be it,' Tigellinus responded coldly. 'Sixth Century, halt! Ready javelins!'

Cato and Macro drew up with the rest of the men, and then adjusted their grip and hefted the javelins back and tensed their muscles ready to hurl the missiles when the centurion gave the order. Cato had lived through this moment in previous battles and waited for the enemy to flinch and waver. Instead the gladiators held their ground, unmoving, their eyes fixed unblinking on the Praetorians, their muscles poised to dodge the first strike of their opponents.

'Try for their leader,' said Macro. 'If he goes down, the rest may give up.'

Cato nodded.

'Release!' Tigellinus yelled.

Cato hurled his arm forward, throwing his weight through the line of the javelin's flight and releasing his grasp at the last instant. The dark shaft arced up into the air with the others javelins of Tigellinus's century. They rose up between the two bodies of men and then seemed to slow at the top of their arc before plunging down. The gladiators had developed sharp reflexes as part of their training and darted aside as the javelins landed among them. Only a handful of men were struck down, one skewered through the top of his skull, the point passing down his neck and deep into his body. Cato saw the man stagger on the impact, then hold still before he pitched forward and was lost from view. Two more were mortally wounded as the deadly iron lengths of the javelin heads ripped through their torsos. The last, standing directly in front of Cato, howled as the javelin slammed through his boot and pinned his foot to the ground. The remainder, incredibly, had escaped harm.

'Bloody hell,' said Macro. 'They're good. Never seen men move so damned fast.'

'Draw swords!' Tigellinus yelled.

Cato grasped the handle of his weapon, taking care to lock his fingers firmly round the leather grip, knowing full well that it was fatal for a fighter's sword to slip in his hand during battle. He pulled the weapon from his scabbard and held it level, the side of the blade resting against the trim of his shield with no more than six inches protruding beyond the shield. On either side of him the rest of the guardsmen continued to advance on the gladiators, sword points glinting.

Their leader, unharmed by the Praetorians' javelins, swiftly sheathed his blade and snatched at one of the shafts angled into the ground. He yelled to his followers. 'Come on, lads, give them some of their own medicine!'

He hurled the javelin towards the guardsmen, now less than twenty paces away. He could hardly miss the line of shields and gleaming helmets bearing down on him. The javelin punched through the shield of the man next to Macro, bursting through his shield arm and lodging hard against the guardsman's mailed chest, before the weight of the shaft dragged his shield and arm down. He let out a roar of pain as his pace faltered and he dropped out of line, sheathing his sword, and then wrenched his shield arm free in a welter of blood.

'Close up!' Macro ordered instinctively. 'Close the line!'

Several of the gladiators followed their leader's example and four more of the guardsmen went down before Tigellinus could react to the danger and prevent the loss of more of his men.

'Charge!' he cried desperately. 'Charge!'

Macro's mouth opened wide as he let out a deafening roar of battle rage, then he lowered his head and pounded forward. Cato gritted his teeth and stayed close to Macro's flank. Ahead of them the gladiators braced themselves for the impact. Those with javelins still in hand grasped the shafts tightly, ready to use the weapons as spears. There was a rolling clatter of thuds and grunts, broken by the sharp ringing rattle of blades clashing as the Praetorians surged in among their foes.

Macro made straight for a barrel-chested German with shaggy hair tied back from his face. The man raised his heavy round shield and held a falcata out to the side, ready to strike. He bared his teeth in a snarl and leaped forward. The shields crashed together forcefully, but the greater momentum was with Macro. He threw his weight in behind his shield for good measure, causing the German to stumble back a couple of paces. Even so he was trained to recover swiftly and savagely parried Macro's thrust, sending the point wide. Good as his responses and technique were, it was his training for individual combat that did for him. His attention was fixed on Macro and it was only at the last instant that he recognised the threat from Cato, coming from the other side. Cato punched his shield in, catching the German hard on the shoulder and knocking him off balance. He went down, his wide back bent over one knee. Cato struck without hesitation, ramming his blade deep between the shoulder blades, ripping through muscle and shattering the man's ribs and spine. He wrenched the blade free, with a spray of hot blood, and instantly turned to guard against any attack.

'Good kill, lad,' Macro acknowledged.

The skirmish raged around them, the gladiators holding their own as they fended off the Praetorians' blows with their shields or parried them away with deft flicks of their wrists. As Cato watched he caught sight of the leader as the man slammed his buckler into a guardsman's helmet, snapping his head aside. Then the gladiator followed through with a powerful thrust into the exposed throat, ripping the blade free at once as he stepped back, lowering his body into a crouch, looking round for his next opponent. There were other Praetorians on the ground, Cato noted, and only two gladiators. Only the armour and larger shields of the Praetorians were saving them from suffering even more casualties in the uneven fight.

'We're losing this,' Macro observed. 'We'd better do something. We have to take charge.'

Cato nodded, keeping his eyes on the fight. It would draw attention to them, and there would be those who might wonder at their easy assumption of command – if they survived the skirmish.

Macro snatched a deep breath and bellowed, 'Praetorians! On me! On me!'

Cato echoed the cry. The nearest of their comrades began to edge towards them and quickly a small ring formed, shield to shield, as the guardsmen sought the protection of the formation.

'Hold your position!' Macro called. 'There'll be help any moment! Hold on!'

Tigellinus had echoed the cry and a second ring of Praetorians had formed a short distance away. The rest fought back to back or were locked in a series of individual combats across the open ground. Cato kept his shield up as he stood beside Macro. Glancing to the other side he saw Fuscius breathing heavily. The optio's eyes were wide and his teeth were bared in a snarl. Despite the fierceness of his expression his arms were trembling and the end of his sword wavered as he pointed it at his foes.

'We're safe enough,' Cato said to him. 'If we keep together and hold the formation.'

Fuscius glanced at him quickly and then looked back, nodding vigorously.

The gladiators surrounded the ring, but there was no co-ordinated attempt to charge home. Instead each man seemed to have chosen a particular soldier as his opponent and either stood sizing them up or darted forward to attempt to slip their weapon round the shield. Some made feints and then tried to strike. In all cases the presence of the soldiers on either flank of their chosen target foiled their attempts. This was not the kind of fight they had been trained for and their frustration was evident. There was a lull in their attacks. Cato sensed the opportunity to make a fresh appeal to them to end the fight.

'You cannot win!' he called out. 'There'll be more soldiers here any moment. You'll be cut to pieces if you resist. Lower your swords!'

'We die either way, brothers!' the leader called out.

'Out there fighting to entertain Romans, or here and now, fighting Romans! Fight on!'

With a bellow of rage the gladiator charged at the man just beyond Fuscius and punched high with his shield, forcing the Praetorian to raise his shield to counter the blow. At the same time he drew his arm back and swung it in a hooking arc, under and round the bottom of the guardsman's shield, then up in a vicious thrust into the Praetorian's groin. So hard was the blow that it drove the air from the man's lungs and almost lifted him off his feet as the blade punched up into his vital organs. With a savage cry of triumph the gladiator ripped his sword free and leaped back, then punched the gore-stained blade into the air.

'Kill them! Kill them all, my brothers!'

There was a chorus of roars and shouting from his companions as they closed round the two rings of Praetorians and hacked and slashed at the shields and helmets.

'We have to take their leader down,' Macro grunted as he parried a sword thrust. 'If he falls, they may lose heart.'

Cato risked a glance back, past the pavilion, and saw the nearest of the other Praetorian centuries hurriedly forming up. A trumpet sounding the alarm from beyond the palisade announced that the auxiliaries were also making ready to intervene. However, there was still time enough time for the gladiators to cut Tigellinus and his men to pieces. Up on the reviewing stand the Emperor had re-emerged, goblet still in hand. He glared angrily down on the scene.

'What is this? Who gave the order for the fight to start?'

Cato cleared his throat. 'Let's do it then.'

Macro nodded and braced himself in a crouch, weight on the balls of his feet. 'Ready, lad?'

'Ready.'

'Now! Disengage.' Macro stepped back into the ring, closely followed by Cato. At once Macro called out another order. 'Close up!'

Fuscius and the man to Macro's right edged towards each other while Cato and Macro sidestepped round until they were lined up with the gladiators' leader. Cato moved forward, pushing between two of his comrades. 'Make way there! Make way.'

The guardsmen shuffled aside to let them in and Macro stared intently at the man no more than eight feet away. 'We'll take him when he next strikes. On my command.'

Cato tightened his grip on his sword and felt his blood surging through his veins, making his muscles tingle with the familiar tension of battle. The gladiator fixed his eyes on Macro who grinned and beckoned with his sword hand. 'Go on then! Try me, if you dare!' Macro moved his shield arm to the side to expose his chest, taunting his opponent.

The gladiator's brow creased and he roared, 'Then die, you bastard!'

He sprang forward, sword angled up at Macro's throat. Macro kept his shield low and swung his sword up to parry the blow. At the last moment the gladiator did a cut over and redirected his attack at the angle between Macro's helmet and his shoulder. The same instant Cato leaped forward, slamming his shield into the gladiator's side as his sword hacked down into the other man's extended sword arm. The edge cut deep into muscle before jarring against bone. The arm spasmed and the fingers exploded away from the sword handle so that the weapon clattered clumsily off the double layer of mail on Macro's shoulder. The man stumbled back, blood gushing from his wound as he let out an animal howl of rage and pain. His followers parted around him, pulling back from the Romans, staring aghast at their leader. His sword arm hung uselessly at his side. He cast his buckler to the ground and clamped his shield hand over the wound, trying to stem the flow of blood.

'Come on,' Macro muttered to Cato. 'Let's finish this.'

They stepped forward warily, watching for danger, but the gladiators kept their distance. Their leader had slumped down on to his knees, eyes clenched as he fought to contain the agony of his injury. Macro stood over him while Cato faced the others, his shield up, ready to deal with any man who sprang to the gladiator's aid.

'Your leader is beaten!' Macro called out. 'He is finished! Sheath your weapons if you don't want to die with him here!'

There was a pause as the other men waited for a response from their leader. Macro ground his teeth in fury before he snarled, 'Do it! Do as I say, or there will be no mercy for you!'

The first of the gladiators hesitantly returned his blade to its scabbard. Another followed his lead, then more as the rest drew away from the Praetorians and did as Macro ordered. Their wounded leader remained on his knees, gazing around him fiercely. 'Fight, damn you! Fight back. You were promised freedom by the Emperor. Now fight for it, or it will be taken from you!'

'The man's a bloody l-l-liar!' Claudius shouted drunkenly. 'I said no such thing! The cheek of the fellow!

Kill him. K-ki-kill any of them who refuse to lower their swords. Quickly.' He gestured to the far side of the lake and the sound of a slow mocking clap carried across the water. 'Don't test their patience any longer.'

The leader of the gladiators saw that his cause was lost. He glanced up at Macro and spoke quietly. 'Make it quick.'

Macro nodded. The gladiator reached out with his good arm and clasped it round the back of Macro's knee and tipped his head back and to the side to expose his neck and collarbone. Macro knew that the warriors of the arena were trained how to die with no show of fear, and only the faint tremor in the man's hand as it clutched the back of his knee betrayed his real feelings. Leaning his shield against his side, Macro raised his sword, then felt for the slight notch behind the man's collarbone. Then he eased the tip of the sword against the flesh, not hard enough to break the skin.

'Ready?'

The gladiator nodded and closed his eyes.

'On three,' Macro said calmly. 'One . . .'

He punched the sword down with all his strength, thrusting the blade through the gladiator's vital organs, into the heart. The impact caused him to gasp, his jaw jerking down as his eyes opened and bulged. Macro gave the sword a twist and then yanked it out, the blood welling up from the open mouth of the wound in a swift torrent. The gladiator swayed a moment and then toppled on to his back, staring up at the sky as he gasped one last time and died. There was a brief stillness around the scene and Cato heard the shout of orders and the tramp of boots as Tribune Burrus led the rest of the cohort towards them. The sound drew the attention of some of the other fighters and they backed away towards the palisade. A handful of others followed suit, then more, until only a few men remained under arms, glaring defiantly at the Praetorians.

'Sixth Century!' Tigellinus called out. 'Form line!'

The men hurried into place. Macro paused to use the hem of the gladiator's tunic to wipe the blood off his blade, then he and Cato joined the others. Several bodies lay stretched out on the ground, most of them Praetorians, and the wounded among them moaned with pain.

'Last chance,' Tigellinus called out to the men who still defied the order to put aside their weapons. 'Sheath your blades, or die.'

'Then die it is!' one of the men, a tall muscular easterner, cried out. His dark lips drew back in a snarl and he charged at the Praetorians. There was a brief flurry of blows as he struck out at one of his foes, driving him back from the line. Then the Praetorians on either side turned on the gladiator. He managed to parry the first stroke before being stabbed in the side. He pulled himself off the blade with a groan and was at once struck from the other side, and then from the front. A few more savage blows cut him to the ground where he slumped, chest heaving as he bled out.

The brutal end to his show of defiance unnerved the last men still standing with swords in their hands and they returned them to their scabbards and backed away. Behind them, the auxiliaries appeared along the walkway behind the palisade, javelins held at the ready.

'Just in time,' Macro commented sourly.

A moment later Tribune Burrus reached the scene and deployed his men on either side of the Sixth Century, hemming in the gladiators. He strode up to the reviewing platform and saluted the Emperor. 'Your orders, sire?'

Claudius's expression was cold and merciless and the fingers of one hand drummed on the rail while his other hand tightly clenched the goblet.

'There is only one f-fate for those who defy the Emperor. I would have you all slaughtered here and now . . . were it not for that rabble over there.' Claudius nodded at those who covered the hills on the far side of the lake. The disgruntled clapping had reached a crescendo. 'As it is,' he continued, 'you will die out there, on the water, if there is any justice. B–b–burrus!'

'Sire?'

'Get these scum on to their ships at once.'

'Yes, sire.'

With a last scowl, Claudius turned away from the rail and made his way back into the pavilion. Burrus strode through the ranks of his men and approached the gladiators. Placing his hands on his hips he glared at them.

'You heard the Emperor. When you get on those ships I'd be sure to put up a good fight if I were you. Impress the mob enough and some of you may walk away from this alive. Off you go.'

The gladiators began to shuffle towards the waiting ships.

'MOVE!' Burrus yelled at them. 'You've buggered about long enough already! Run, you bastards, before I have my men shove their javelins up your arses.'

The men picked up the pace and trotted down towards the shore. One of them held back and approached the tribune tentatively.

'Well?' Burrus barked at him.

'Sir, the leader of our fleet is dead.' The gladiator indicated the man Macro had killed. 'We have no commander.'

'You do now.' Burrus thrust a finger at him. 'The job's yours. Get out of my sight.'

The gladiator bowed nervously and then ran off to the largest of the ships flying red pennants from their masts. When the last of the men had boarded their vessels, the gangways were hauled aboard and then the fighting men crowded to the rear in order to raise the bows high enough for the men at the oars to be able to back the ships away from the shore. To Macro and Cato, who had served with the navy during a campaign against a nest of pirates, the manoeuvres of the scratch fleets of Persians and Greeks appeared clumsy. Even so, at the sight of the ships making their way to their start lines, the crowd on the far side of the lake rose to their feet and the slow clapping stopped.

With the gladiators no longer presenting any danger to the Emperor, Tribune Burrus stood his cohort down and the Sixth Century took up their positions around the pavilion. The bodies of the dead were removed by the auxiliaries while the wounded were hurriedly tended to by the imperial physician who did not want to miss the spectacle taking place on the lake.

As the two battle lines formed half a mile apart, across the width of the lake, Centurion Tigellinus made the rounds of his men. Cato and Macro stood to attention as he approached. Tigellinus regarded them closely for a moment before he spoke.

'That was quick thinking back there,' he said quietly. 'When you called on the men to form up.'

'Seemed like the best thing to do in the situation, sir,' Macro replied.

'I see. It was as if you were used to issuing commands. A man who did not know better might think you had been an officer once. An optio perhaps, or even a centurion.'

Macro's gaze did not waver as he responded. 'Thank you, sir.'

'I did not mean it as a compliment, Calidus. It was an observation. Tell me, how is it that two rankers are able to behave so like men used to command?'

There was no mistaking the suspicion in the centurion's face.

Macro pursed his lips calmly. 'There's not much to tell, sir. When you've served in as many campaigns as I have, you learn to do what circumstances demand. There's been more than one occasion when my centurion's been knocked on the head in a battle, the optio too. Then someone has to step up and take charge. I've done it a few times, so has Capito here. So would any veteran worth his salt, sir.'

Tigellinus considered his reply, and nodded. 'Fair enough. Then it's as well that you're on my side. When the time comes, a few good men may well change the destiny of Rome.' The centurion stepped closer and glanced from one man to the other. 'There's more to you two than I thought. That had better be a good thing.'

Cato frowned. 'Sir?'

'I've a few inquiries to make. If you two turn out to be anything other than what you claim you are, then you'll be joining Lurco as soon as it can be arranged.'

He did not wait for a reply but turned on his heel and

strode away. Cato let out a long anxious breath. 'We're in the deepest of shit, my friend.'

'Bollocks we are,' Macro replied. 'Our cover story is sound enough. By the time he can discover anything about us, the job will be over and we'll be far from Rome. As long as Narcissus lives up to his promise.'

'Like I said, we're in the shit.' Cato stared at the retreating back of Tigellinus and added, 'I hope you're right about him.'

They were interrupted by the blare of trumpets from the other side of the pavilion and turned to look out across the lake. Two barges were anchored between the two fleets and a large rock-filled basket was suspended between them. As soon as the signal was given, the men on the barges cut the basket loose and it splashed into the water.

Macro frowned. 'What's that all about?'

As they continued to watch, there was a disturbance in the water a short distance from the two barges. Three gleaming spikes emerged from the lake, followed by a shaft and then a hand and an arm. As the water cascaded off the rising object, Macro shook his head in wonder. 'What the hell is that?'

Cato smiled. 'That is Apollodorus's little crowd-pleasing opener, I think.'

Now it was clear what the object was – a huge likeness of Neptune, painted gold, and as the counterweight sank to the bottom of the lake, the impressive device that the engineer had promised Claudius stood a good twenty feet tall, water lapping at the feet as if the structure was standing on the surface. A great cheer rose up from the far shore and a flickering shimmer rippled along the slopes overlooking the lake as the crowd waved coloured strips of cloth to emphasise their approval.

'Oh, that's good!' Macro grinned in delight. 'Very clever.'

Meanwhile the crews of the two barges were rowing frantically for the shore, anxious to get clear of the two fleets before they clashed. Another blast from the trumpets provided the signal for the Naumachia to begin. There was a brief defiant cheer from each of the two fleets of twenty vessels and then the steady sound of drumbeats from the timekeepers on each ship. The oars stroked the water in a clumsy rhythm as the small warships gradually gained speed. Some were faster than others and the lines quickly became ragged, made more chaotic still by the inability of a handful to steer a straight course.

'Not the most impressive display of nautical skills I've ever seen,' commented Cato. 'Even the greenest crew in the fleet would run rings round that lot.'

'Yes, yes,' Macro responded irritably. 'Why don't you stop coming the seasoned veteran with me and just enjoy the show, eh?'

Cato glanced at his friend. 'The calm reserve of old hands . . .'

'Shhh!'

The leading ships were within missile range of each other and now Cato could make out a thin waft of smoke from the decks of each vessel. An instant later an arrow from one of the blue-pennanted ships traced a fiery arc across the open water, leaving a fine smoky trail behind to briefly mark its passage. The arrow plunged into the lake a good fifty feet short of the bow of the nearest enemy ship.

'So much for eastern archery,' Macro chuckled. 'That was way off.'

The failure of the first shot to reach the target did not stop the inexperienced archers on both vessels from loosing off more arrows and the surface of the lake was peppered with tiny splashes as the two ships closed on each other. There was no attempt to manoeuvre into a better position to use the ram and the two crashed into each other, glancing off as they struck bow to bow. The makeshift mast of the Greek ship snapped close to the deck and pitched forward, rigging snaking behind it, toppling on to the fighters crowded on the foredeck. An excited cheer came from the far shore. As the men struggled to free themselves from the rigging, their opponents hurled grappling hooks across and hauled the ships together before the first men scrambled aboard. From the shore the distant glint of swords and armour told little of which side had the upper hand.

More ships clumsily made their way into the fray and those that had been slowest to get off the mark now reaped the benefit of being able to pick a target to ram in the beam. The first such attack was crudely handled and the speed was too slow for the ram to break through the hull. The crew backpaddled a short distance to try again, only to be caught by one of their foes full on. Slivers of wood from shattered oars burst into the air as the small ship reeled under the impact, pitching men into the water. A handful of those in armour managed to remain briefly on the surface before the weight dragged them under. The shocking impact of the ramming ship also proved to be its undoing as the brazier used for lighting the fire arrows tipped over, spilling burning embers across the deck which quickly set fire to the tarred rigging. Soon the vessel was ablaze and flames, fanned by the gentle breeze blowing down the lake, spread to the ship that had been rammed. The fighting ceased as the men of both sides made to save themselves, desperately stripping off armour before grabbing anything that might give them buoyancy and jumping over the side.

'Poor devils,' Cato muttered as the vast audience cried out with delight.

Within two hours of the signal for the battle to begin the surface of the lake was littered with debris from the ships. One vessel had sunk and three more were on fire. The rest were locked in a series of duels and tangled melees, to the cheers of the crowd as they tucked into the food issued to them earlier in the day by the Emperor's officials. Watching them, and hearing the occasional loud comments from the pavilion, Cato conceded that the spectacle was succeeding admirably as a diversion from the difficulties besetting the capital. If the entertainment and provisioning could be eked out for another day or two then the Naumachia had succeeded in its purpose.

The sound of hoofbeats drew his attention away from the lake and he turned to see an imperial courier galloping along the shore from the direction of the road leading back to the capital. The rider was bent low over his mount, urging it on as the foam spattered back from either side of the bit in its mouth. He reined in sharply in front of the pavilion and swung himself down from the saddle before running towards the stairs leading up to the Emperor's box.

'What's his hurry, I wonder.' Macro rubbed his cheek. 'Bad news?'

'When was the last time there was any good news?' Cato replied.

They turned back to watch the fight, but Cato could not help wondering what tidings the courier had brought to the Emperor in such haste. The light was beginning to fade as the sun slipped below the horizon. The trumpets sounded again, and according to their strict instructions the surviving ships of both fleets began to disengage and limp back towards the shore on which the pavilion stood. The small ships divided either side of the pavilion and it was possible to count them and see that the Persians had won the upper hand on this first day of the spectacle. One by one the ships beached and the weary crews and fighters stumbled down the gangways and were swiftly disarmed and herded away to their pens by vigilant auxiliary troops.

Macro nudged Cato and pointed briefly. 'Look there, isn't that Septimus?'

Cato looked in the direction Macro had indicated and saw four men loaded down with wineskins under the direction of an individual in the plain purple tunic of one of the servants on the palace staff. A quick glance was enough to confirm the man's identity.

'It's him.'

'Then what's he doing here?'

'Has to be something to do with Narcissus.'

Macro glanced wearily at Cato. 'I worked that out for myself, thank you.'

They watched as the party moved from one group of Praetorians to the next, working their way towards Cato and Macro. As they approached, Septimus indicated the wineskins and called out, 'A token of his imperial majesty's gratitude to his loyal soldiers!'

Septimus clicked his fingers and one of the men began to unsling one of the wineskins. Septimus moved closer to the two soldiers and continued to smile pleasantly as he spoke in an urgent undertone.

'Narcissus sent me as soon as the courier had passed on his message. It was the only way to get a message to you without attracting attention. Say nothing. Just take the wine and listen.' Septimus glanced round to make sure that there was no one else close enough to hear, then continued in a whisper, 'There is news from Ostia. The grain fleet from Sicilia was lost in a storm. Only two ships survived, and they were forced to dump most of their cargo over the side.'

Macro whistled softly. 'That's buggered things up.'

'You don't say,' Septimus responded drily. 'The Emperor was counting on that grain to keep order in Rome once the Naumachia is over. And now . . .'

He left the sentence unfinished and Cato could readily imagine the chaos that would break loose on the streets of the capital once the people discovered that nothing could save them from starvation. Cato reached for the wineskin that one of the slaves was holding out to him. He spoke to Septimus in a low voice. 'What does Narcissus intend to do?'

'There's not much he can do. It will be up to the Praetorian Guard to keep order on the streets at any cost. Prefect Geta has suggested that he returns to Rome and calls out the rest of the Guard to start preparing the defence of the imperial palace, the senate house and the temples. Claudius will remain here tonight and watch the games in the morning before he and the rest of the imperial family slip away.'

'What does Narcissus want us to do?' asked Macro.

'Nothing yet. Just be ready to act when he sends word.'

'There is something that we can do,' said Cato. 'Something that we have to do now.'

'Oh?'

'Find that grain that's missing from the warehouse.' Cato stared fixedly into Septimus's eyes. 'You tell Narcissus we must find it. The Praetorian Guard won't be able to hold back the mob for long. Only that grain can save the Emperor now.'

CHAPTER TWENTY-FIVE

The next day, once the spectators' attention was fixed on the renewal of the fighting on the lake, the Emperor discreetly departed, accompanied by only the Empress, Nero and Britannicus. Most of his retinue remained in the pavilion to cover his absence. Tribune Burrus left the First Century of his cohort behind to guard the pavilion and to add to the deception. The rest of his men formed a column behind the empty prisoner pens and took a little-used path between the foothills before joining the main road leading to Rome. They reached the city gate early in the afternoon and saw at once the measures being put in place by Prefect Geta. The men of the urban cohorts who usually stood guard over the gate and collected the tolls had been sent to patrol the streets and their places were taken by Praetorians.

Inside the city wall the streets were quiet and almost deserted since most of the inhabitants of Rome were enjoying the entertainment at the Albine Lake. Sections of men from the urban cohorts occupied the main cross-roads. As the column crossed the Forum and approached the imperial palace, Cato noted that the doors to the temples were closed and wooden barricades comprised of sharpened stakes had been placed about the entrances.

Behind the barricades stood more men from the Guard. Similar defences had been erected to protect the palace gates. Once the imperial family and its escort had been safely escorted inside, the gates of the palace were closed behind them and the locking bar was heaved into its receiver brackets for good measure.

'Place looks like a fortress,' Macro said quietly as he looked round at the preparations being made for the defence of the palace complex. Wagons had been positioned behind the wall either side of the gate and covered over with planks to provide a fighting step. Stocks of javelins lay in bundles on the ground beneath the wagons.

Cato shrugged. 'Maybe, but the Praetorians can't hope to cover every way in. The walls are easy enough to climb over in many places. It's just a show of force. The prefect's hoping to intimidate the common people when they return from the lake.'

'They'll behave, once they see soldiers everywhere,' Macro replied confidently.

'You think so?'

'Of course. They'd be mad to go up against the Praetorians and the urban cohorts. They'd be slaughtered.'

'But they will be mad. Hunger will drive them to it, and they will have nothing to lose. In any case, the Praetorians will also be without food soon. They'll be weakened, and perhaps even tempted to make common cause with the mob.' Cato lowered his voice. 'When that happens, the people who control the grain will become the real power in Rome.'

He looked around at the preparations to defend the palace, and saw more guardsmen higher up the Palatine

Hill, posted on the balconies and the garden terraces. The sight provoked an unsettling thought.

'This may look like a fortress, but it could equally be used as a prison, or a trap.'

Macro turned to him. 'What do you mean?'

'The imperial family are surrounded by Prefect Geta's troops. The senate house has been sealed up and I'll bet there will be a curfew imposed on the streets until the crisis is resolved, one way or another. Anything could happen to the Emperor and his family and Geta would be able to tell the outside world whatever story he liked. And once that hidden grain is released to the mob, they'd be grateful to whoever saved them from starvation. By the time Geta lifts the curfew, Rome might well have a new emperor, or no emperor at all.'

Macro thought for a moment before he responded. 'You're jumping at shadows again, lad. This is happening because the grain convoy from Sicilia was lost in that storm. The Liberators can't have foreseen that.'

'No, but they are prepared to take advantage of the opportunity it presents to them. Trust me, Macro, if they intend to strike, they'll do it soon. Very soon.'

Cato looked over to where Tribune Burrus was conferring with his officers. Beyond them Prefect Geta appeared from a small entrance beneath the wide flight of stairs that ascended to the lofty portico of the palace's main entrance. Burrus and the others stood to attention as they became aware of his approach. Geta issued a rapid series of commands and then returned to the palace as the group split up. Tigellinus strode across the courtyard to his century and called for their attention.

'Men, the prefect says there will be trouble on the

streets of the capital in the coming days. The riot we saw earlier was merely a taste of what we can expect. The food supply in the city is all but exhausted. There is barely enough left in the palace to feed us on half rations for more than two days. From tonight, rations will be cut to a third.'

There was a groan from some of the men, and a handful of angry mutters before Tigellinus snatched a deep breath and roared at his men, 'Silence in the bloody ranks! I don't like to go short any more than you do, but we have orders to carry out, and our duty is to protect the Emperor. The Sixth Century will take up position in the imperial accommodation suite. Apart from those barbarian thugs of the German bodyguard, we are the last line of defence.' He paused to let his words sink in. 'You will be vigilant. You will carry out your orders without question. Without question, gentlemen. This is an uncertain time, a dangerous time. When it is over, the only thing that will matter to us is that we did our duty. Optio Fuscius will take you to your stations. The cohort will be relieved at dawn. That is all.'

Tigellinus handed a set of waxed tablets to his optio and stood aside as Fuscius stepped forward and puffed out his chest to give the order. 'Sixth Century, follow me!'

As the guardsman marched past their centurion, Tigellinus briefly fell into step alongside Cato and Macro. 'Be ready to act on my order. Whatever that order may be. Is that clear?'

'Yes, sir,' Cato muttered, and Tigellinus stepped away from the column and watched the rest of his men file past.

The optio led the way up the wide stairs and through the main entrance into the palace. There was evidence of the prefect's preparations on all sides: checkpoints at the entrance to every audience chamber and banqueting suite, and at the doors to the slave and servants' quarters. Some entrances had been closed off and the doors barricaded by heavy items of furniture. The imperial accommodation was at the highest point of the Palatine Hill, overlooking the Forum. It comprised a range of sleeping chambers, studies and terraced gardens. There was one entrance to the suite from within the palace but a determined man could scale the walls from below and Fuscius positioned men to guard against such a threat. The optio consulted the waxed tablets that Tigellinus had handed him and pointed to Macro.

'Calidus! You and Capito here, on the balcony outside the Emperor's study.'

Macro nodded and he and Cato climbed the steps up on to the colonnaded balcony. Fuscius waved the rest of the men on to the largest of the terraced gardens. As they marched off, Macro turned to Cato.

'What was Tigellinus's little pep talk all about? The only thing that matters is that we obey orders.' Macro puffed his cheeks. 'Looks like you might be right about what's going on. The Emperor's in danger.'

At that moment there were footsteps inside the study and Macro and Cato quickly stood to attention, backs against the pillars on either side of the door leading from the balcony into the study. Out of the corner of his eye, Cato saw Claudius limp over to his desk and sit down on a padded stool. Two of his German bodyguards silently took their places on either side and a short distance behind their master. In front of the desk stood Prefect Geta, Narcissus and Pallas, together with Agrippina. Narcissus glanced towards the men guarding the access from the balcony and for an instant there was a look of surprise in his thin features, before he forced his face to assume its customary neutral expression.

Claudius flicked a finger at Geta. 'Make your r-report, Prefect.'

'Sire, I have six cohorts in the palace precinct. Three on duty until the morrow and three resting. The other cohorts have taken control of the city gates, the Forum and the senate house. I have ordered that the senate's proceedings be halted until the crisis has passed.'

'Oh?' Claudius looked at him sharply. 'In whose name did you give such an order?'

'Yours, sire. You were still on your way back to the city at the time. I thought it best to act at once rather than risk any delay. For the safety of the senators.'

Claudius considered this and nodded. 'Very well, but I will not have my officers take such d-d-decisions in my name again. Is that clear?'

'Yes, sire. My apologies.'

There was an awkward pause before Claudius spoke again. 'So, gentlemen, what are we to do? There are a m-million people in Rome, and almost nothing to f-f-feed them with. I trust that orders have been sent to every town and village for at least a hundred m-miles to send what food they can?'

Narcissus nodded. 'Yes, sire. I sent out messengers the moment I heard about the loss of the convoy. They carry orders to requisition whatever food and transport is available to supply Rome.'

'On my authority as well, I dare say.'

'Yes, sire,' Narcissus replied. 'As the prefect stated, there was no time to waste.'

'I see.' Claudius sniffed. 'It would appear that the government of R–r–rome can continue perfectly well in my absence.'

There was another awkward silence before Claudius spoke again. 'Anyway, even if food is requisitioned, it will not arrive in sufficient quantities to save the m–mob from starvation. Is that not true?'

'Alas, yes, sire,' said Narcissus. 'That is why you and your family should leave Rome until the danger has passed.'

'Leave Rome?'

'Yes, sire. As soon as possible. Before the mob returns from the Naumachia and discovers what has become of the grain fleet. Once they hear the news, there will be panic and a breakdown of order. The imperial family will be in danger.'

'Nonsense,' Geta interrupted. 'My men will see that you are adequately protected.'

'You command nine thousand soldiers,' Narcissus replied. 'You are outnumbered a hundred to one. Even the Praetorian Guard cannot defy such odds.'

'We're game. Let 'em try to break in here and see what happens.'

'If they get over the walls of the palace, then it's obvious what will happen. They will butcher everyone they find. Regardless of rank. That is why the imperial family must be moved to a place of safety. Outside the city.'

Pallas shook his head. 'Out of the question. The

Emperor must remain here, to set an example to his people. To share their suffering during the present difficulties, figuratively speaking. If you leave Rome, sire, they will say that you are abandoning them to their fate. You will lose their respect, their love and their loyalty. Such a loss may take years to recover, if it ever does. As one of your closest advisers, I strongly urge you to remain in the palace, under the protection of Prefect Geta and his fine soldiers. With them at hand, I cannot believe you and your family would be in any danger.'

Narcissus took half a step towards the Emperor. 'Sire, I must protest.'

'Enough!' Claudius raised a hand. 'Still your tongue, N-narcissus. I must think.' Claudius scratched his unruly white hair. He was silent for a moment before he looked up at his wife. 'And what do you think, my d-dear? What should I do?'

Agrippina tripped lightly round the desk and knelt before him, taking his hands in hers. 'My dearest husband, Pallas is right. The people look to you. You cannot flee when they need you most.'

'The Emperor is not fleeing,' Narcissus interrupted. 'He is merely exercising prudence for the good of Rome. What would it profit the empire to put his life, and those of his family, at risk?'

Agrippina turned and scowled at Narcissus. 'Is it the Emperor's life you wish to protect, or your own?'

Cato watched as Narcissus sucked in a breath and coolly addressed his reply to the Empress. 'I have devoted my life to the service of the Emperor, my lady. His continued safety has filled my waking thoughts. My motives are selfless.' Narcissus paused and then gestured towards

Pallas. 'I cannot think what impulse motivates my colleague here to place the Emperor in jeopardy. Pallas, my friend, why would you so willingly undermine all that I have striven to do to make our master safe from his enemies?'

The other imperial freedman gave Narcissus an icy glare before he responded in an even tone. 'We are merely advisers to his imperial majesty. I consider it unseemly to offer my opinion in such a forceful manner as you do. The Emperor will make his own decision.'

'Well said!' Agrippina smiled. She turned to her husband and looked up into his face with an adoring expression. 'It is for you to say, my dearest love. Should we stay and brave the peril that faces our people, or should we do the sensible thing, as good Narcissus suggests, and flee the city until the danger has passed?'

Claudius looked down at her fondly and cupped her cheek in his hand. Agrippina turned her head slightly to kiss his hand and then close her lips over his finger. The Emperor's eyes fluttered for a moment before he withdrew his hand.

'I have decided. We shall st-st-stay in Rome. It is the right thing to do. At least for tonight.'

Cato saw Narcissus's shoulders sag a little at the words. Pallas did his best not to smirk and Geta clasped his hands behind his back, the thumb of his sword hand vigorously working the flesh of the other hand.

'Fine words, my husband,' said Agrippina as she stood up. 'Brave words. But bravery alone will not sustain a man. You have not eaten all day. Come, you'll need your strength. Let us eat together, in my bedchamber. I'll send for some food. Your favourite dish perhaps?'

'Mushrooms!' Claudius grinned. 'You are good to me, Agrippina.'

He eased himself on to his feet and straightened his back as he faced the other men in the room. 'I have spoken my m-mind. Let it be known that the Emperor will remain in Rome.'

Geta, Pallas and Narcissus bowed their heads and stood aside as Claudius and his wife, hand in hand, made their way out of the study. Geta followed them out. The two imperial freedmen were the last to leave, as social protocol demanded. As the prefect of the Praetorian Guard left the room, Pallas turned to Narcissus with a look of cold amusement. 'If I were you I'd take my own advice and get out of Rome, while you can.'

'What, and leave the Emperor's life in the hands of you and your friends?' Narcissus spoke loudly enough for Cato and Macro to catch his remarks.

'Friends?'

'The Liberators. That's who you are working for. You and Geta. What have they promised you as a reward?'

Pallas shook his head mockingly. 'You're barking up the wrong tree, my friend. I have nothing to do with the Liberators. For what it's worth, I pledge my life on that.'

'Liar.'

'No.' Pallas stood in front of Narcissus and thrust his finger into his chest. 'You will live to see the truth of it, but I would not count on living much longer than that.' He paused and ran his eyes over the imperial secretary. 'It has been a pleasure to have worked alongside you these past years, Narcissus. For the most part, at least. We have served Claudius well, but no emperor lasts forever. The only issue is who will succeed Claudius. You have made your choice of who to serve, and I have made mine. Farewell, Narcissus.' He held out his hand, but the imperial secretary did not move. Pallas shook his head sadly. 'I would prefer that we parted as friends. It's too bad. Goodbye.'

Pallas turned away and strode from the room. Narcissus watched him leave, with undisguised hatred. When the sound of his rival's footsteps had faded away, he turned to the balcony and approached Macro and Cato.

'You heard?'

Cato nodded. 'Every word.'

'They mean to murder Claudius, I am certain of it. The fool has played into their hands,' Narcissus said bitterly. 'That little bitch has him wrapped around her finger. Him and that bastard, Pallas. We have to act quickly.' He stopped and looked at them with a puzzled expression. 'How did you two come to be posted here?'

'Fuscius had a duty roster,' Macro explained. 'Tigellinus handed it to him.'

'Tigellinus?' The imperial secretary stared at him anxiously. 'He means to place his men as close to the Emperor as possible. Has he given you any instructions?'

'He told us to be ready to act.'

'That's all?'

Cato nodded.

Narcissus rubbed his jaw anxiously. 'The Liberators have men in place close to the Emperor. The prefect and some of his officers are in on the plot and they have taken control of the palace. I'd say they will act soon. Tonight perhaps. Certainly no later than noon tomorrow.'

'Why then?' asked Macro.

'Because the spectacle is over. Most of the mob will remain by the lake tonight. They will set off for Rome at first light and reach the city at midday. Unless there is food here to feed them, there will be nothing to stop them venting their rage. It's my guess that the Liberators will have taken control by then. The Emperor will be dead, and then they'll produce all the grain that they have amassed in secret. The mob will be grateful enough to whoever feeds it.' Narcissus looked at them with a cynical smile. 'Once the people have been won over, the Liberators will start to remove anyone who was loyal to the previous regime. In which case, I'm as good as dead already. Me, and Britannicus.'

'Why not the others?' asked Cato. 'Won't they want to dispose of Agrippina and Nero as well?'

'Why would they?' Narcissus asked bitterly. 'My guess is that they're in on the plot. Why else would Agrippina have persuaded the Emperor to remain in the palace? Now they have Claudius where they want him.'

Cato was thinking. 'That doesn't make sense. Agrippina can't be part of the Liberators' plot.'

'Why not?'

'She was there when the Liberators attacked the imperial party in the Forum. They tried and nearly succeeded in killing her son.' As Cato recalled the incident, there were some details that still defied explanation, but he continued with his original line of thought. 'And afterwards, Nero spoke to me. He said he would reward me when he became Emperor. He seemed quite certain about it.'

'So?'

'If he believes he is going to be Emperor, then

Agrippina must have planted the idea in his head. You said it yourself, she is using him to further her own ambitions. In which case, why would she conspire with the Liberators?'

'He's got a point,' said Macro.

Narcissus hissed with frustration. 'All right. Then if she's not part of the Liberators' plot, why is she trying to keep Claudius in Rome, where he's in greatest danger? There's only one good reason for that. She's running her own conspiracy. She's working with Pallas to remove the Emperor and place her son on the throne. It's no secret that she has been doing her best to bend Claudius to her will. Firstly by seducing him, then persuading him into marriage, then the adoption of her son and finally making Nero heir to the throne.'

'Now that makes more sense.' Macro nodded. 'So we're dealing with two conspiracies, not one. The Liberators want to remove the entire imperial family, while Agrippina wants to replace the Emperor with her son. That I can get my head round.'

It made sense, thought Cato, but for one small nagging detail. 'You're right. She and Pallas have a motive, and the means, if they can get their strike in before the Liberators and disarm them. But there's something that still doesn't fit. Something that I've not been able to explain.'

'Speak up then, man,' Narcissus hissed. 'We haven't got much time. We have to act. What's the problem?'

'It's about that day in the Forum when the Liberators attacked the imperial party. Their leader, Cestius, pushed Britannicus aside just before he went for Nero.'

'What of it?'

'Why would the Liberators pass up the chance to kill one of the Emperor's sons? It would have been the work of a moment to strike Britannicus down before turning on Nero. Why did Cestius spare Britannicus?'

'I don't know,' Narcissus said irritably. 'Perhaps Cestius didn't recognise him. There's no time for this now, Cato. We can go through it all later. Right now we have to save the Emperor. We need to protect him. I don't know how far the conspiracy has spread through the ranks of the Praetorians. We know about Geta, Sinius, Tigellinus, and I have the names of a few other suspects but that's all. There could be many more. The only troops that we can rely on are the German bodyguards. I'll have them all roused and placed close enough to the Emperor to prevent any assassin getting through to him.'

'That won't be enough to save him. The Liberators, and Pallas – assuming you're right about him and the Empress – are not the only threat. We have to keep the mob under control, or they'll succeed where the conspirators have failed.'

'To do that we need to feed the mob,' Narcissus responded tersely, 'and I can't just make grain appear.'

'No,' Cato conceded.

Macro sniffed. 'Either way, we're in deep shit. Just like I said. The situation stinks.'

Cato stared at his friend. 'That's it,' he muttered. 'It has to be.'

'What are you on about, lad?'

'Cestius. You remember when we first ran into him, and his men. At the inn?'

'Yes. What of it?'

'Do you remember how they smelled?'

Macro nodded. 'Like shit.'

'Exactly. Just like shit,' Cato said with an excited gleam in his eyes. 'And where would you go to stink like that? A sewer, that's where. To be precise, the Great Sewer that runs right under the heart of the city before it flows into the Tiber.'

'Very interesting. So what if Cestius and his pals have been mucking about among the turds? How does that help us?'

'Think about it, Macro. Where does the Great Sewer empty out into the Tiber?'

'Not far from the Boarium. In fact close to that warehouse of Gaius Frontinus.'

'Right next to it as it happens.' Cato could not help smiling at the cleverness of the conspirators. 'Surely you see it now.'

Macro looked at Cato, then glanced at Narcissus. 'What's he talking about?'

Narcissus stroked his jaw. 'I think I can guess.'

'There's no other answer,' said Cato. 'We know that the grain was taken to the warehouse. Sometime between its purchase and when we searched the place, the grain was moved to another location. I've been trying to think how they managed it without attracting any attention to themselves. Now I know. They must have access to the sewer. They used the sewer to move the grain unseen. That's probably why Cestius and his men were at the inn that night, to celebrate the completion of the job.' He turned to Narcissus, eyes fired with excitement. 'We have to go back to the warehouse. I need some men we can trust. We can't use the Praetorians. It'll have to be the Germans. Give me fifty men, and torches, and we'll find that grain.'

'I don't know if I can spare them. They're needed here.'

'If we don't secure that grain, it won't matter where they are.'

The imperial secretary struggled to make a decision. Then he nodded. 'All right, but you can take twenty men. No more. You'll need one of their officers.' Narcissus thought quickly. 'Centurion Plautus can be trusted.' The imperial secretary looked up at the sky above the city. The light was fading fast and a pastel red hue stained the horizon. 'You'd better go quickly. And take Septimus with you. Leave your kit here.' Narcissus wagged his finger at Cato and Macro. 'You'd better be right about this. If anything happens to the Emperor because there weren't enough men to guard him properly then it'll be on your head, Cato.'

'Thanks for the kind words of encouragement,' Cato replied sourly. 'There's one more thing. How are we going to get out of the palace without raising the alarm?'

Narcissus could not help a small smile. 'There's a way. You didn't think the emperors would have built a place like this without a secret exit, did you? It comes out close to the Great Circus. Caligula used it from time to time when he wanted to go to the races incognito. It was kept a secret from the Praetorians in case they tried to keep an eye on him during his peregrinations.'

Macro chuckled. 'Didn't do him much good then.'

'You'd better take us to this passage,' said Cato. 'And have your Germans meet us there, armed and ready.' He nodded towards the sunset. 'I think we're in for a long and bloody night. Only the gods know what the dawn will bring.'

CHAPTER TWENTY-SIX

'Next time keep a civil tongue in your head.' Cato smiled pleasantly as he gently prodded the warehouse guard under the chin with the tip of his sword.

The man looked confused, as well as scared. 'Sorry, sir. I-I don't understand.'

'You don't remember me, do you?' Cato frowned, robbed of his brief moment of pleasure. There was nothing to be gained from taking a small revenge on a man who had completely forgotten his offence in the first place. 'Never mind. Tell me, has anyone entered or left the warehouse since you have been on watch?'

The man glanced round at the group of big men who had stolen up on him in soft-soled boots while he dozed and then picked him up and pinned him to the wall of the warehouse of Gaius Frontinus. He swallowed nervously as his eyes turned back to Cato.

'Best to be honest, if you want to live,' Cato said softly, pricking the man's skin slightly.

'Just one m-man, sir.'

'Reckon that's Cestius,' said Macro at Cato's side. 'What did he look like? Big bloke? Small?'

The watchman looked Cato up and down. 'About your size, sir.'

'Not Cestius then.' Cato eased his sword off the man's neck. 'How long ago?'

'No more than an hour, I'd say.'

'And no one else?'

'Yes, sir. I'm sure of it.'

'Right, then you're coming with us. Macro, open the gate.'

Macro nodded and stepped over to the heavy iron bolt and eased it free of the receiver as quietly as he could. Thanks to the curfew there was no one on the wharf but Cato was wary of alerting anyone inside the warehouse to their presence. Macro eased the gate open just wide enough to admit himself and the rest of the men in single file. Cato allowed Septimus, the centurion and five of his Germans to pass through before he nudged the watchman towards the gap.

'Don't make a noise or try to get away from me, understand?'

The man nodded vigorously and Cato steered him inside. The warehouse yard looked just as deserted as it had a few days earlier. A crescent moon provided some dim illumination and by its light the centurion and his men quickly searched each of the storerooms. They were as deserted as before. There was no sign of any life.

'Look for a hatch or some kind of drain cover,' Cato ordered. 'It has to be here somewhere.'

The centurion and his men searched again before the officer reported back to Cato. 'Nothing.'

'Damn.' Cato released his grip on the watchman. 'Have one of your Germans keep an eye on him. He's not to utter a sound. If he tries to raise the alarm, or makes a run for it, tell your man to cut his throat.'

The centurion nodded and called one of the bodyguards over to issue his orders in a mixture of broken Latin and their own harsh guttural tongue. Cato turned to Macro and Septimus.

'There has to be some kind of access to the sewer system here. We have to look until we find it.'

'Or we don't,' said Macro. 'Or we run out of time. Face it, Cato, this is a long shot.'

'No it isn't,' Cato replied determinedly. 'It has to be here. Keep searching.'

He strode away from the others and began a circuit of the yard, examining the ground under the carts carefully. Septimus came up to him and spoke in a hushed tone. 'What if there's a false wall?'

'What do you mean?'

'Supposing Cestius and his men knocked through a wall into a neighbouring warehouse, and then made up a false wall to disguise the gap?'

'No, that wouldn't work. If they did that they'd have had to have hired another warehouse and we'd know about it. Besides, that wouldn't explain the stink of Cestius and his men.'

'You're assuming that it was to do with the sewer. There could be other explanations.'

Cato stopped to look at Narcissus's agent. 'Such as?'

Septimus tried to think for a moment and then shrugged.

Cato nodded. 'Quite. Now, if you've finished, let's continue the search.'

Septimus went off in the opposite direction and Cato continued to work his way round the yard. There was no sign of any disguised hole on the front wall and he was starting to edge his way along the inside wall when the pile of sacking in the far corner caught his eye. A faint ray of hope glimmered in Cato's heart and he made his way over to it. He knelt down and began to pull the sacks aside. Macro joined him.

'Having fun?'

'Just give me a hand.'

They worked methodically, clearing them away, and then, just before they reached the angle in the wall, Macro paused, looked down, and hurriedly pulled away several more sacks. 'Over here. I've found it.'

Cato dropped the sack in his hand and went to crouch by his friend. There amid the cobbles at Macro's feet was a small wooden handle. Macro tried to clear some more of the sacking away but it would not move. Grumbling, he grasped a loose corner and pulled hard. There was a tearing sound, a length of the coarse material ripped free and Macro stumbled back with a curse.

Cato knelt down for a closer look. 'Clever. They've stuck the sacking down on to the hatch to help conceal it.'

He grasped the handle and gave it an experimental pull. The hatch was heavy and Cato applied his other hand. An area four feet square began to rise. Cato turned to Macro. 'Help me.'

With Macro helping at the corner, they raised the hatch and eased it back against the rear wall of the courtyard. A wide ladder fixed to one side led down into pitch blackness. There was no sign of movement, but there was a faint sound of trickling water, and a waft of foul air.

Cato turned and called as loudly as he dared, 'Septimus, over here. Plautus, bring your men.'

The others padded over and stood looking down at

the opening. Cato gave the order for the torches to be lit. Plautus took out the tinder box from his side bag and began to strike sparks on to the thin sheets of charred linen. As soon as the first glimmer of a flame appeared he fed it with some dried moss until the flame was large enough to use. He gestured to one of the men carrying the bundled torches. 'Let me have one.'

He carefully dipped the tallow-impregnated cloth on the end of the wooden shaft towards the flame and held it there until the torch produced bright yellow tongues of light. Plautus rose to his feet.

'Let's light the rest of them.'

One by one the torches flared into life and Cato took one. He ordered Plautus to leave the warehouse guard gagged and bound and then cautiously lowered himself on to the top rung of the ladder. He descended a few more rungs and by the light of the flame he could see that Cestius and his men had shored up the sides of the shaft with stout timbers. Ten feet down, the shaft opened up and Cato held the torch out to examine his surroundings. Old brickwork curved away on both sides and below there was a dull gleam of moving water. The ladder descended another six feet and then he reached the bottom. He was standing on a narrow paved walkway to one side of a small tunnel. It was just possible to stand erect under the curved ceiling. At his side a glistening flow headed steadily towards the Great Sewer. The air was thick with the stench of human waste and Cato wrinkled his nose in disgust.

'What can you see?' Macro called down.

'There's a tunnel. Leads towards the sewer in one direction. The other seems to head towards the Aventine district. Bring the rest of the men down. I think we've found what we're looking for.'

As the other men descended the ladder, Cato made his way a short distance upstream, examining the walls and the walkway. Most of the brickwork was covered in a layer of slime, but there were extensive patches that had been scraped away, and the same was true of the walkway which looked as if it had been heavily used recently enough for the stone to be dry to the touch, with scant evidence of new growth. Behind him the sounds of the Germans muttering in disgusted tones filled the tunnel.

'Nice spot you've discovered here,' Macro grumbled as he and Septimus joined Cato. 'Very fragrant.'

Cato ignored the comment and stared along the tunnel. There was no movement within the loom cast by his torch, aside from the flow of sewage and the scampering of a pair of rats as they scuttled away from the men who had invaded their realm. There was a splash and a scrabbling sound from the dark as they ran off.

'Do you think any of them are still here?' Septimus asked nervously as he stared into the gloom.

'One at least.' Cato stood up. He turned back to Centurion Plautus. 'Tell your men that we go on from here in silence. Not a sound, understand?'

'Yes, sir.'

Cato could not help a slight smile at being addressed as a superior. Narcissus had told the centurion to obey him and Macro when he had briefly introduced the two Praetorians, dressed in plain white tunics and carrying no sign of their rank. Now it seemed that Plautus recognised and accepted Cato's authority without having to be told anything of his real identity and rank. He glanced back and saw that all the men were ready to follow him. The flickering glow of the torches illuminated the damp walls of the tunnels and the flow of sewage gleamed as turds and rubbish drifted by. Cato held his torch forward at an angle and then gestured with his spare hand. 'Let's go,' he called softly.

He crept forward, leaning over slightly as the roof of the tunnel became lower and the flame licked off the brickwork overhead. The sewer led straight for fifty paces before bending to the right. Cato calculated that they were nearly at the edge of the warehouse area and heading in the direction of the Aventine district, one of the poorest districts of the city. Another hundred paces on they came to a junction where a smaller tunnel, no more than four feet high, led off to the left. Cato raised his hand to halt the men behind him then examined the tunnel. There was no walkway and no sign of disturbance in the growths on either side of the tunnel. He waved the men forward again.

They passed more junctions but there was no sign that Cestius and his men had deviated from the walkway. After quarter of a mile of slow progress the sewer opened up into a chamber. Two large tunnels entered from each side, while directly opposite was a small cataract. Filthy foam bubbled across the surface of the chamber and the churned-up sewage made the stench more overpowering than ever. One of the Germans coughed violently and then bent over and threw up.

'That's going to help.' Macro frowned. He looked round. 'What now? Which way do we go? Left or right?'

Cato glanced from side to side for a moment before he

consulted Septimus. 'I reckon we must be close to the Aventine.'

The imperial agent thought for a moment and then nodded. 'I think you're right.'

'In which case, the left tunnel would take us towards the Palatine, and the other one into the Aventine district. Where would Cestius be most likely to hide the grain?'

'I doubt he would want to hide it near the palace. There are several secret tunnels beneath it, as you know. He wouldn't want to risk running into any of those. The other tunnel is our best bet.'

'I agree. Let's have a look. Macro, you come too.' Cato turned to the centurion. 'Stay here while we scout ahead. I'll send Septimus back for you if it looks like we're on the right track.'

'Yes, sir. But don't be too long, eh?' Plautus sniffed. 'The air here is fucking horrible.'

Cato grinned and clapped the man on the shoulder before he entered the right tunnel, followed by Macro and Septimus. Thankfully there was another walkway on the side that saved them from having to wade upstream through the flow of sewage. Cato kept his torch up and paused every so often to examine the sides of the tunnel and the paving stones at their feet. They had gone no further than fifty feet when he stopped and turned round to face the others.

'This isn't the right way.'

'How can you tell?' asked Macro.

'There's no sign that anyone's used this route for a while. Look at the walls. They're untouched. Same with the walkway.' He used the edge of his boot to scrape some of the grime from the stone beneath. 'We've missed something. Come on, we have to go back.'

Back in the chamber Cato looked round again, then his gaze fixed on the cataract. He worked his way around the edge of the chamber to examine it more closely. The channel above the pool was perhaps six feet high, and dropped eight feet into the pool. Tendrils of some kind of growth hung down amid the flow cascading from above. Cato held his torch up to the steady torrent, grimacing as some of it splashed on to him. It was impossible to see through the flow. He bit his lip. There was only one way to find out for sure if his suspicion was correct.

Cato drew the torch back and held it low as he bent forward to shield it from above, flinching as he felt the heat of the flame. Then he sucked in a breath and edged forward along the narrow walkway leading under the cataract. At once his head and shoulders were pounded by water and lumps of solid matter. Then he was lost from the view of his comrades.

Macro's mouth opened in alarm. 'What the fuck is he doing?'

Septimus and the bodyguards stared towards the cataract in silence, waiting for a sign of Cato. For a while none of them moved, and the only noise was the crashing rush of fluid over the cataract, amplified by the brick walls of the chamber. Macro could not wait any longer to find out what had become of his friend and hurried round the edge of the chamber. He paused momentarily at the edge of the cataract but before he could steel himself to duck beneath the flow, something moved out from under the curtain of foul water and Cato, minus his torch, burst through spluttering, his eyes clenched shut. As soon as he was out of the flow he straightened up and opened his eyes with a grin.

'Found it.'

Macro looked him over. 'You look like . . . well, you know what you look like. So what's there?' He jerked his thumb at the cataract. 'Besides the obvious.'

'Best if you see for yourself.' Cato leant past him and beckoned to Septimus and Plautus. 'Bring 'em over!'

'See for myself?' Macro shook his head. 'You are joking.'

'It's nothing we haven't been in before,' Cato quipped. 'At least it isn't deep this time. Come on, follow me. Just be sure to keep your feet on the edge if you don't want to slip and end up in the pool there. And shield your torch. The rest of you wait here for a moment.'

Cato led the way and with a reluctant sigh Macro followed him with gritted teeth. The sewage closed over his head briefly and then he was through and he found himself in a brick-lined tunnel stretching back behind the cataract. Cato bent down to retrieve the torch he had left on the ground. Macro mopped his brow and took a few paces further in and looked down the tunnel. The floor was paved and there was a channel in the middle, flanked by two stepped walkways, but the channel was dry.

'What is this place?' Macro wondered. 'If Cestius and his lads put it together then they're a damned sight better organised than I thought.'

'I doubt they had anything to do with it,' Cato responded. 'I had a brief look further along. There's a feed tunnel off to the right and a bit further on this comes to a dead end. My guess is this section of the sewer was abandoned. At least until Cestius and his gang started to use it.'

'What makes you think they have?'

'This.' Cato held up his spare hand and opened it to reveal a few grains of wheat. 'I found it just inside the tunnel leading off this one. They brought the grain this way sure enough.'

'Then that's a pity. It's sure to have been spoiled by going under that river of shit back there.'

'No. That's not how they did it,' Cato's eyes gleamed. 'Come and see.'

He led Macro back to the cataract and pointed up at the ceiling. For the first time, Macro noticed a wooden board secured to the brickwork by a bolt at each corner close to the cataract. The other end had a chain attached to a hook mounted in the ceiling. Cato handed his torch to Macro and lifted the chain off the hook and eased the board towards the cataract. As he did so, a long stout wooden shaft clattered to the floor, narrowly missing his boots.

'Aha! I thought there would be something.' Cato nodded. 'Right then, the next part should make it all clear to you. Watch.'

Bracing his boots, Cato pushed the board out into the flow, straining as he pushed it out and up. The flow of the sewage was deflected away from the ledge and now the two of them could see the startled expressions of the other men. 'Get that post!' said Cato. 'Wedge it up under the board. Quickly. I don't know how long I can hold this up.'

Macro grabbed the post and stood beside Cato as he placed one end under the board and then scraped the other end into a small niche in the floor that seemed to have been cut into the stone deliberately. 'There.'

They stood back and watched as the flow poured over the edge of the board, well clear of the ledge running under the cataract. Septimus appeared round the corner of the tunnel, then Plautus and the first of the Germans.

'Can't tell you how glad I am you came up with that.' Septimus nodded at the board. 'Otherwise . . .' he gestured towards them with a grimace.

'It wasn't down to me,' said Cato. 'It's something that Cestius and his friends came up with, so they could get the grain through without exposing it to the sewage. Simple, but very effective.' He turned to Plautus. 'I think we're very close to them now. Have your men draw their swords. We'll also put out some of the torches. Calidus, Septimus and I will feel our way ahead. You follow on, slowly. We can't afford to give ourselves away until we know what lies ahead.'

Plautus nodded. 'We'll be ready to go in as soon as you give the word, sir.'

'Good.' Cato held his torch out into the flow to douse the flames and then handed it to one of the Germans before he turned towards the tunnel. He took a calming breath and the three of them set off, the padding of their soft-soled boots drowned out by the sound of the cataract until they had gone a good fifty feet further. The light from the torches faded behind them. Cato trailed his fingertips against the side of the tunnel until they came to an opening. He slowed down. 'Here. To the right.'

'Can't see a bloody thing,' Macro grumbled from the darkness. 'Daft idea not to bring at least one of the torches.'

'Too risky,' Cato replied. 'We've no idea what lies ahead. Best not to risk alerting Cestius.'

'We're sure to outnumber him. Those German lads might not be the sharpest arrows in the quiver but they're tough. We've got nothing to fear from Cestius. Not unless he's got a small army tucked away down here.'

'He might have, for all we know. But I'm more worried about him getting away. I need to speak to him, if I can.'

'Why?' asked Septimus.

'I need some answers,' Cato replied bluntly. 'We're wasting time. Let's move.'

They set off down the side tunnel, feeling their way in the darkness with one hand on the wall, while they probed ahead with the toes of their boots. The floor of the tunnel was dry and the only sounds were the occasional scrape of their footsteps, the sound of their breathing and the scuttling of rats. Twice Cato thought that he could hear something ahead of them but by the time he stopped and whispered for the others to be still the sound had gone. The pace was slow and Cato worried that the Germans might start to follow them in their eagerness to finish the job and get out of the tunnels back into the open air. He glanced back frequently and was gratified to see the faintest glimmer of a torch only once. Centurion Plautus clearly had his men in hand.

Which is more than Cato could say for his imagination. Every sound seemed grossly magnified so that he was torn between anxiety over the amount of noise he and the other two men were making and fear that the sounds were covering up any danger that may lurk ahead in the blackness.

'I don't like this,' Septimus muttered. 'What if there's nothing here?'

'Then there's no grain to feed the mob. The mob gets angry and kills the Emperor and you and Narcissus are out of a job, sunshine,' Macro replied in a low growl. 'Bear that in mind, and keep your mouth closed, eh?'

Cato came to a halt. Macro brushed up against his back before he could stop and there was a final shuffle of Septimus's boots before there was quiet. 'Listen.'

At first Macro could not separate out any noise that might be of significance. Then there was the unmistakable sound of laughter from ahead, a brief snatch and then quiet again.

Cato turned in the direction of his companions, invisible in the pitch black of the tunnel. 'Septimus, you stay here.'

'What? Alone?' The fear in his voice was clear. 'Why?'

'Calidus and I are going on ahead. When Plautus and his Germans catch up I don't want them going any further unless I give the word. You tell him to stop and wait.'

There was a pause before Septimus's voice quavered. 'All right. But don't be too long.'

Cato reached back and tugged Macro's tunic and they edged forward even more slowly than they had advanced so far. A short distance further on they heard voices, more laughter and the shrill cry of a woman. Then there was the faintest hue of light ahead, revealing the dark outline of the tunnel as it turned to the left. The two men kept moving and soon they could see enough to light their way and no longer needed the reassurance of touching the wall. Cato lowered his hand to his sword handle and carefully drew the weapon. He heard a light dry rasp as Macro followed suit. Cato lowered himself into a crouch. His pulse quickened and his mouth felt dry. He slowed down and stopped as he came to the corner. The sound of voices, many of them, filled the tunnel now and Cato turned back and held up a hand to halt Macro who was just visible in the gloom. Then he edged a step forward and slowly looked round the corner.

The tunnel gave out on to what looked like a huge storeroom, illuminated by the flames of several braziers and torches guttering in brackets fixed to the walls. In front of the tunnel the ground was a jumble of rocks. At first Cato thought that the space must have been constructed, then he realised that it was a natural cave that had been enlarged by human hands. The walls seemed to have been cut from the rock in places to expand the size. Guttering torches in iron brackets provided enough illumination to make out the details. Great mounds of grain sacks had been piled at the far end and extended well over half the length of the cave, some hundred paces long by forty across. To one side a wide ladder climbed up to a ledge, beyond which there was a brick-lined passage that sloped upwards into the shadows.

At the near end of the cave were several tables and benches at which sat thirty or forty men. There were a handful of women too, in short tunics that reached just below their buttocks. Their faces were powdered white and dark kohl had been crudely applied around their eyes. To one side was a table longer than the rest. At its head sat Cestius, with a plump red-haired girl sitting on his lap, the fingers of one hand playing with his curls as he squeezed the breast that sagged loosely out of her tunic. The toughest-looking men of his gang sat close by, drinking and laughing with their leader.

Cato gestured to Macro to join him.

'What do they think they're celebrating?' Macro whispered once he had taken in the scene.

'What do you think? They're sitting on top of a mountain of grain in a city on the verge of starvation. They're going to make a killing. Or someone is, and they'll take their cut.'

They continued to watch in silence for a moment before Macro spoke again. 'I reckon we can take 'em. Most of them are armed with daggers. There's a few swords, clubs and axes about the place. They look tough enough, but they've had a skinful of wine and that'll take the edge off their ability to fight.'

Cato scrutinised the men in the cave. He agreed with his friend's assessment, but they would still be out-numbered by Cestius and his gang. It would be prudent to make sure that Narcissus knew about the grain and the cave, in case the fight went against them.

'All right, we'll do it. But we'll send one of the men back to report to Narcissus. Just in case.'

Macro shrugged. 'If you think it's necessary. Thanks to those bastards I've had to spend the night wading through shit. I don't feel like being very merciful.'

'Nevertheless, we'll send a man back.'

They eased their way back from the corner and Cato pointed back down the tunnel to where a slight glow indicated the position of Septimus and the German bodyguards. 'Bring 'em up, but make sure they do it nice and quiet, and put their torches out. We're outnumbered and we'll need the advantage of surprise.'

Macro nodded, then turned to make his way back down the tunnel. Cato watched him briefly and then returned to the corner. He stared at Cestius, determined to take the gang leader alive. That would not be easy, Cato reflected. Cestius was a powerfully built killer who was sure to fight to the death if he could. Even so, only Cestius could answer the question that had plagued Cato ever since they had clashed in the ambush at the Forum.

The approach of Macro and the rest of the men was heralded by the light scrape of footsteps and Cato turned just in time to see the last glow of orange from the tunnel flicker out as the final torch was extinguished. The men emerged from the darkness and Macro gestured to them to fan out on either side. The Germans crept silently by and eased themselves into places of concealment behind the rocks. As quietly as they could, they drew their swords and crouched, waiting for the order to attack. Cato drew back into the mouth of the tunnel and hurriedly outlined the report for Narcissus. The German assigned for the task nodded as Plautus translated, then handed the man his tinder box and one of the extinguished torches. The German turned to make his way back into the darkness. A moment later there was a faint flare as he struck sparks, then again, before a brief pause and then a steady glow swelled in the gloom. It quickly faded away as the man made his way off into the tunnel.

Cato crept forward to join Macro who was squatting behind a large rock in the middle of the line of Germans. Cato drew a deep breath to steady his nerves and then tightened his grip on the handle of his sword. 'Ready?'

'As I'll ever be. Let's have 'em.'

Cato tensed his limbs, glanced left and right to see that the rest of the men were watching him intently. Then he snatched a breath and shouted, 'Follow me!'

CHAPTER TWENTY-SEVEN

As the cry echoed off the walls of the cave Cato leaped over the rocks in front of him and sprinted towards the men and women at the tables. Macro let out a deafening roar that was instantly drowned out by the savage cries of the Germans as they charged. The laughter and drunken talk of Cestius and his men ceased abruptly as they stared at the bearded intruders racing towards them, swords drawn, bellowing barbaric war cries. For a moment Cestius and his men were too stunned to move. Then the spell was broken as Cestius turfed the woman off his lap and sprang to his feet, ripping out his short sword as he did so.

'Don't just fucking sit there! Pick up yer tools and get 'em!' he shouted.

Cato was charging towards Cestius, visible over the heads of his men, when a stocky man with dark features and hairy arms stepped into his path, swinging up a heavy club pierced with nails. Gritting his teeth, the man swung the club in a savage arc towards Cato's head. The end of the club, with its lethal spikes, whistled through the air and Cato ducked low as the weapon passed inches from his scalp with a whoosh. The man grunted as the shaft of the weapon struck his other shoulder, hard. Cato thrust his sword up at an angle and the point ripped through the man's tunic and sliced open the muscles packed over his ribs. Instead of recoiling in surprise and pain, as Cato expected him to, the man just roared with anger, his senses numbed by drink. He swung the club in a vicious backhand. This time Cato stumbled back out of range and the head of the club swept past his face, and on into the head of one of the man's companions who was staggering drunkenly forward to get into the fight. The full weight of the club struck home and with a sound like an egg being thrown against a wall, the points of the club pierced skin and bone and drove deep into the man's brain. His head snapped to the side and then he collapsed, dragging the club down with him.

With an angry curse his comrade wrenched violently at the handle of the club, trying to free it, but all he succeeded in doing was waggling his victim's head about obscenely. The man's jaw worked furiously and his eyes bulged as blood and brain matter spattered from his wounds. Cato pounced forward and stabbed the man armed with the club deep in the guts. He wrenched his sword free, thrust him aside and moved on, scanning the battling figures for Cestius. The flames of the braziers threw wild shadows as the men fought and the air was filled with thuds and the clatter and ringing of blades. It was hard to make out the features of any man in these conditions, and only the beards and bulk of the Germans singled out one side from the other. To his left Cato could hear Macro somewhere close at hand, bellowing at his enemies as he laid about him with his sword.

Cato caught a glint of metal to his right and spun round to see a man charging him with a dagger held high.

411

His face was distorted by a savage battle cry and his unkempt beard bristled. Cato swung his sword up and knocked the blow aside.

'Fool!' he yelled at the man. 'I'm on your side!'

The man he took for a German growled a surly apology in Latin and then his eyes widened at the same instant that Cato realised his mistake. The wine had taken the edge off the other man's reactions and Cato struck first, punching the hilt of his sword into his opponent's nose which gave with a dull crack. Blood streaming down his face, the man stumbled back, tripped over a bench and fell, knocked cold as his skull struck the edge of one of the tables. Cato moved on, thrusting between men locked in savage duels, searching for Cestius. There was a sudden flurry of rags as someone slammed into his chest with a shrill screech. Cato absorbed the blow and looked down to see a short fat woman with tangled black hair pummelling his chest with her clenched fists. The moment she realised he was looking down at her, she raked his cheek with her fingernails. Cato felt a burning sensation as she drew blood and he instinctively rammed his knee up and into her chest and then kicked hard. She flew back and slammed into one of the gang members with a deep grunt, then stood fixed in place by the sword that had pierced her back and burst out of her abdomen and through her grubby brown tunic. The man thrust her body forward with his left hand as he ripped his sword free, then punched the bloodied blade at Cato's face. What he lacked in swordsmanship he made up for in brute strength and Cato's attempt to parry the blow only just deflected it from his face. Even so the edge of the blade cut into the top of his ear.

'Bastard!' Cato cried out in rage. He gritted his teeth and launched himself forward, balling his left hand into a fist. The blow caught his opponent on the jaw. It was a solid punch and would have dazed a normal man. But those who followed Cestius were chosen for their strength and toughness. They were men from the slums of Rome where you either learned to talk with your fists or you were beaten down into the gutter. His head snapped back but then he straightened and laughed at Cato. His expression abruptly changed to one of puzzled surprise as he looked down and saw that Cato's sword had pierced him in the side, just below the ribs. Cato twisted the blade one way, then the other, working it into the man's vital organs. Each twist brought a deep agonised groan to the man's lips. Then Cato ripped the blade out in a dark gush of blood.

The agony of his mortal wound only seemed to enrage the man further and he threw himself at Cato and both fell on top of a table, the impact knocking their swords from their hands. The man's face was inches from Cato's; his sour breath stank of cheap wine and roasted meat. One hand was groping its way up Cato's chest and he realised that the man was reaching for his throat. Cato grabbed the hand and tried to force it aside, but his opponent was too strong for him and Cato felt the fingers pinch viciously into his neck. He was dimly aware of a hot dampness across his stomach and chest as the man's blood flowed from his wound. Cato clawed at the man's hand but it clenched more tightly still, and he felt his eyes bulge and a dark red veil begin to close in over his vision.

★

Some twenty feet away Macro was wrestling with another of Cestius's men, each grasping the wrist of the other's sword hand in a deadly test of strength. Their eyes met and the gang member half growled and half chuckled as he strained his muscles and felt Macro's arms begin to give.

'That the best you can do?' the man sneered.

'Not quite the best,' Macro spat back. 'Try this!'

He drew his head back and with a savage jerk head-butted the other man in the face. It was a tactic he had used several times before in battles and skirmishes, but rarely without a helmet on. As their skulls cracked loudly together, the other man's jaw snapped shut under the impact, his teeth biting deeply into his tongue. Macro felt a piercingly sharp pain across his forehead. His head reeled sickeningly.

'Fuck, that hurts . . .' he groaned. Then, sensing that his opponent's grip had eased off, Macro thrust him back, ripped his sword arm free and thrust the blade into his opponent's throat. The gangster collapsed to his knees, blood pumping from his wound. Macro kicked him to the ground. He looked about him. The fight had spread out across the floor of the cave and several bodies lay on the ground or sprawled across the tables and benches. Cestius was exchanging vicious sword blows with one of the Germans while Septimus finished off a wiry man with a thrust to his heart. Macro felt a stab of anxiety as he failed to see any sign of his friend. Then he noticed two figures struggling on top of a table a short distance away. The man on top was one of Cestius's gang members. Macro could just make out that the individual beneath was tall and thin and his gangling legs were kicking out desperately as he tried to free himself.

'Not again,' Macro muttered to himself as he raced across to save Cato. As he pushed past one of Plautus's men Macro saw Cestius smash his sword down into the skull of the German warrior, cutting through bone and brains. Cestius wrenched his sword free with a vicious yank and then retreated a pace to quickly survey the skirmish. With a bitter frown he turned to run towards the base of the ladder leading up to the tunnel.

'Shit.' Macro gritted his teeth in frustration. He was still ten feet from Cato and now a handful of struggling figures had blocked his path. Cato must be saved, but equally Cestius could not be allowed to escape. Then Macro saw Centurion Plautus cut down a man on the other side of the table where Cato was pinned down.

'Plautus!' Macro yelled.

The centurion's head whipped round and Macro thrust his hand towards Cato. 'Help him!'

Plautus glanced towards the table and nodded and at once Macro pushed his way free of the melee and ran after Cestius. The gang leader had cleared the area where the tables and benches stood and crossed the open floor of the cave. He reached the bottom of the ladder, sheathed his sword and jumped on to the second rung. His hands grasped one of the stout cross timbers above and he began to scale the ladder with nimble agility and was well out of reach by the time Macro reached the foot of the ladder. Cestius's boots were scrambling over the ledge above the top rung as Macro began to climb after him. He had ascended six feet when he felt the ladder lurch under his grip. He clung on instinctively and looked up. Cestius loomed overhead. He was pushing the ladder out, away from the ledge. For an instant Macro thought that the ladder's angle was not steep enough to enable Cestius to topple it, but then the man raised his boot and kicked it away with all his might. The ladder swayed back and seemed to steady for a moment before slowly falling back into the cave, carrying Macro with it.

The red mist had almost closed across Cato's eyes as he stared up into the face of the man throttling him. A froth of bloody spittle had formed at his lips from his bitten tongue and it dripped down on to Cato's chin. The pressure on Cato's throat was excruciating and with the last reserves of his strength Cato lashed out with his knees and boots and punched his left hand into the side of the man's face as hard as he could, again and again. Even as he struggled, some small part of his mind seemed to look down on him with deep regret at the ignominy of dying in the cave, killed by a lowly street villain, while he stank of shit. Hardly a fitting end for the decorated soldier who aspired to marry the daughter of a senator. At that, his heart filled with longing for Julia and a determination not to die here in this cave. Tensing his neck muscles and pressing down as hard as he could with his jaw, Cato stopped clawing at the man's hand and jabbed his fingers into his eyes as hard as he could.

His opponent bellowed with rage and pain, spattering Cato's face with blood, but he did not loosen his grip. The pressure that threatened to burst Cato's head became greater than ever for a brief moment, and he clenched his eyes shut. Then it was gone, and the weight pressing down on his chest abruptly eased. Blinking his eyes open, Cato saw his attacker in the thick hairy arms of Plautus. With a savage twist the officer broke the man's neck with a loud crunching crack and then threw the body down with a triumphant 'Ha!' before he heaved Cato off the table and back on to his feet.

Cato nodded his thanks and then winced. He reached up to his throat and touched it tenderly. It took a moment for the dark mist to clear from his vision and for the nauseating dizziness to pass. As soon as Plautus could see that he was able to fend for himself, he turned away and charged back into the melee.

A quick glance round the cave was enough for Cato to see that Cestius's men were losing the fight. Most of them were down, as well as several of the Germans and two of the women. Another three had backed off into one corner and were clutching each other in terror as they watched. One woman, stockier and braver than her companions, stood bare chested, a sword in one hand and a dagger in the other as she screamed shrilly at the two grinning Germans moving in on her. Cato recognised her as the woman who had been sitting in Cestius's lap a short time before. One of the Germans contemptuously lowered his sword and bared his own chest as he approached her. Her screaming stopped and she sprang forward, breasts swaying, and stabbed at him. The German moved nimbly aside with a deep laugh and made to swat her bottom as she blundered by. Instead, she turned neatly and stuck the sword into his side and then swung her other hand and slammed the dagger through his throat. The German's laughter died on his lips and then turned to a hoarse gurgle as he clawed at the blood coursing from his neck.

'Barbarian scum!' she screeched. 'Die, you pig!'

Those were her last words, as the other German ran

her through with a brutal thrust that carried her off her feet before she dropped back on to the ground as the sword blade ripped free from her guts.

Cato tore his eyes away and looked for Cestius. The gang leader was not among those still on their feet. Then he noticed Macro rising up from the ground over to one side of the cave, struggling to get himself free of the ladder that had fallen on him. There was a movement from above on the ledge and Cato saw the unmistakable outline of Cestius against the glow of a torch flickering at the entrance to the tunnel. Then the man turned and snatched the torch out of its bracket before he made off into the tunnel. Cato quickly gave orders to Plautus to remain in the cave and guard the entrances until more men could be sent to secure the grain.

By the time Cato had joined his friend, Macro was back on his feet, wrestling the ladder back into place. He glanced round as he heard Cato's footsteps and noted the raw scratches and finger marks around Cato's throat.

'You still fit to fight, lad?'

'Yes,' Cato croaked and winced with agony. He pointed up the ladder.

'Aye.' Macro nodded. 'Let's get after the bastard.'

With Macro leading the way, they climbed the ladder and stepped up on to the ledge. A faint orange loom from Cestius's torch was still visible in the tunnel and they ran on, their footsteps echoing off the walls of the tunnel. After a few paces the tunnel began to slope up, continuing in a straight line so that they could see Cestius some distance ahead, outlined by the glow of the torch that he held up and out in front of him. Then the tunnel began to bend to the right and flatten out and for a moment they lost sight of their prey and ran on blindly. Fortunately the tunnel had been well used and the floor was smooth and unobstructed. Rounding the corner they caught sight of Cestius again as he approached a small doorway at the end of the tunnel. The gang leader paused and glanced back. As soon as he heard the footsteps behind him he ducked through the doorway and then there was a sharp grating sound as the door began to close.

'Shit!' Macro grunted, pushing his legs harder, Cato panting a short distance behind him. Ahead the aged hinges of the door squealed with protest as the bottom of the door scraped across the fine gravel that had gathered on the stone lintel in the years that the door had been left open. Cestius's face could be seen by the light of his torch, strained and desperate as he heaved his muscled shoulder against the door. He had already half closed it and now the door seemed to be moving more easily as Macro and Cato sprinted towards him. There was a gap of barely six inches as Macro slammed into the edge of the door, nudging it back a short way. Cato threw himself against the aged wood at Macro's side, and scrambled for purchase on the ground with his boots. The tunnel filled with the sounds of the three men straining on both sides of the door and for a moment Cestius seemed to be giving ground. Then he let out a sharp hiss of air and heaved with all his strength and the door began to close again.

Macro reached for the handle of his dagger and snatched it out. The gap was already less than a foot but he thrust his arm through, turned it in and stabbed at where he guessed Cestius must be. The blade caught in a fold of material and Macro punched it home, tearing into the flesh beneath. There was a bellow of pain from the other side of the door and the pressure slackened.

'Heave! Heave the bastard!' Macro yelled and thrust again, missed, and then snatched his hand back to press on the door. It gave way, gradually. 'We've got him!'

Suddenly the door fell back and Macro tumbled forward on to his knees. Instinctively he threw his weight to one side, crashing against the side of the tunnel, as he anticipated a blow from Cestius. But the gang leader was on the run again, sprinting across the low chamber on the other side of the door. The air smelled of damp and mould and by the flare of Cestius's torch Cato could see that the stone walls were covered with slimy growths. Macro jumped back on to his feet as Cato ran past him and they chased after Cestius under a low arch on the far side of the chamber and out into a space beyond. It was a long, low storeroom filled with discarded piles of timber, iron hoops, damp heaps of old leather covered in mould and what looked to be broken chariot wheels. Cestius was weaving through the piles of junk, making towards a squared-off doorway at the end of the storeroom. With a grunt Macro squeezed under the arch and straightened up alongside Cato. He cast a quick, curious glance round at his surroundings as they set off after Cestius. A pathway of sorts had been cleared through the junk and with a fleeting moment of satisfaction Cato saw that they were gaining on their prey. Cestius was only some forty feet ahead of them when he ran through the entrance to the storeroom and began to climb a narrow flight of stairs, rising at a sharp angle. Cato and Macro were breathing hard as they reached the steps and ran up them, taking them two at a time.

At the top they emerged into a huge vaulted chamber that stretched out in a shallow curve on either side. The chamber was nearly a hundred feet wide and the far wall was pierced by wide arches that reached up some twenty or so feet. The floor of the chamber was covered in sand which extended out beyond the arches into a vast open space that stretched out into the darkness. Cestius sprinted towards the nearest arch, kicking up divots of sand in his wake.

'Come on!' Cato urged.

They ran on, hearts pounding and muscles burning with the effort. They passed through the arch and out into starlight.

'Bloody hell!' Macro panted. 'We're in the Great Circus.'

On either side of them the sand stretched away towards the dark mass of the spectator seating on either side. Ahead of them rose the central island with its assorted statues and officials' platforms. When the chariot races took place, this vast space was filled with the deafening roar of two hundred thousand voices, madly cheering on their favourite teams. Now there was an uncanny and immense stillness, and Cato felt his flesh tingle as he continued to pursue Cestius across the smoothly raked sand of the racetrack.

'We have to catch him before he reaches the far end,' Macro called to him. 'If he gets out of the public entrance and on to the streets we'll lose him.'

Cato nodded and pushed his tiring limbs on. Then, just as Cestius drew parallel with the raised platform of the imperial box, he stumbled and fell headlong. The torch shot out of his hand and hit the ground in a flurry of sparks. He was down only briefly before he clambered to his feet and snatched up the torch, but it was long enough for Cato and Macro to catch up to him, drawing their swords as they did so. Cato edged to one side, and Macro the other, crouching low and ready to strike as they drew ragged breaths of the cool night air. Cestius could see that the route to the public entrance was blocked and he backed away, towards the base of the imperial box, his sword drawn.

'Give up,' said Cato. 'You can't escape now.'

'No?' Cestius licked his dry lips. 'Let's see if you two have got what it takes to beat me, eh?'

'By the gods, you're full of it,' Macro growled. 'Shove an enema up your arse and they'll be carrying you to your funeral in a bloody thimble.' He patted his sword against the palm of his left hand. 'Come on then, you arrogant shit.'

'Stop.' Cato held up his hand. 'I want him alive. Cestius, throw down your sword.'

'No chance!' Cestius snarled and quickly stepped forward, sweeping the torch round in an arc so that it flared fiercely as it roared past Cato and Macro, forcing them back a pace. He suddenly frowned. 'I know you . . . The Praetorians at the inn. And . . .'

His rapid recollection was interrupted by distant cries from the starting gates where they had emerged from the storerooms. A handful of figures were trotting across the sand towards them. Staff and officials who worked in the Circus, Cato guessed, come to investigate the disturbance. Cato pointed towards them with his spare hand.

'You can't escape. If you fight us you will die. If you give up, you may be spared.'

'I'm no fool, Praetorian. I know what fate awaits me.' Cestius crouched low, sword and torch held out, ready to fight. 'I'll not give in meekly. If you want me then you're going to have to kill me first . . . before I kill you!'

He sprang forward, sweeping his torch out towards Macro and then turned swiftly on Cato to make a thrust with his sword. While Macro fell back before the fiery arc, Cato held his ground and parried the attack, and then responded with a feint that forced Cestius to recover his blade and hold it close, ready to counter Cato's attack. Instead, Cato held his sword up and stared at his opponent, noticing the dark patch of blood on the right shoulder of Cestius's tunic, where Macro had stabbed him as they had struggled for control of the door at the end of the tunnel. The point of the big man's sword quivered as his injury caused his arm to tremble. Cato stepped forward and feinted to the right, then cut under Cestius's blade and stabbed to the left. It was a simple attack, intended to test the other man's responses rather than draw blood. With a desperate motion Cestius knocked the sword aside and backed away, closer to the base of the imperial box which was a scant few feet behind him. Cato made to attack again, and this time Macro went in from the other side. Cestius warded them off with a flurry from his torch and sword, and then his heel struck the solid wall behind him. There was no room to manoeuvre any longer and Cato sensed that he would react in the only way left to him now, a wild attack.

'Careful, Macro.'

'Don't worry, I know his kind,' Macro replied without taking his eyes off Cestius.

The staff of the Circus were much closer now and one of them called out, 'Oi! What do you three jokers think you're playing at? You're not allowed in here. Take your bloody fight somewhere else.'

'Shut your mouth!' Macro yelled. 'We're Praetorians.' He gestured with his sword. 'That one's a criminal and a traitor we've been hunting. Now you either help us take him down, or you answer to the Emperor.'

'He's lying!' Cestius called out. 'They're thieves. Tried to rob me before chasing me in here. Save me and I'll make it worth your while.'

The officials drew up just short of the confrontation, not sure who to believe. With himself and Macro reeking of sewage and wearing heavily soiled tunics, Cato feared that the burden of proof rested on their shoulders. They could not risk any delay. He snatched a deep breath and shouted, 'Now, Macro! Take him!'

With a roar Macro sprinted in, sword held up and ready to strike, while Cato charged from the side. Cestius tried to parry Macro's sword with his torch but the blazing length was punched aside and down into the sand. Macro rushed on, slamming into Cestius with his shoulder and sending him crashing back against the wall. An instant later Cato cut down into Cestius's sword arm, slicing through the muscled flesh and down to the bone, severing tendons so that the other man's fingers released the sword. Cato's momentum carried him on; he thudded into Cestius's side and his sword punched home into the giant's guts with a wet thud. Cestius let out an explosive grunt and his body stiffened for a moment before he sagged and

424

his legs gave way, and he sank on to the sand. Macro and Cato drew back and regarded him cautiously, but Cato could see by the light of the torch still burning where it lay on the ground that Cestius's wound was mortal.

He reached down to pick up the gang leader's sword and toss it to one side, out of reach, before sheathing his own weapon. Macro kept his sword to hand and moved round to confront the other men who looked on in silence. 'You lot, stay back!'

They needed no prompting and Cato left Macro to keep a watch on them while he concentrated his attention on Cestius. The big man was slumped against the wall, legs stretched out in front of him, his hands clasped over the wound in his side. His eyes were tightly clenched for a moment before he opened them and smiled bitterly at Cato.

'Told you you'd have to kill me,' he said softly. He closed his eyes again.

'Cestius.' Cato leant forward and shook his shoulder. 'Cestius!'

The giant's eyes flickered open. 'Can't you let a man die in peace?'

'No,' Cato replied harshly. 'Not until you answer some questions.'

'Fuck you.'

Cato drew his dagger and held it up for Cestius to see. 'I can make this painful if you refuse to talk, or quick and painless if you co-operate.'

'I'm dying. What difference does it make?'

Cato smiled coldly. 'Do you really want to find out?'

There was a brief silence between the two men before Cestius shook his head faintly.

'Right, then.' Cato lowered the dagger. 'First, who paid you to hoard the grain?'

'A Praetorian centurion. Sinius.'

Cato nodded. 'What was the arrangement?'

'He paid me in silver. I laundered the money through my gang and used the proceeds to buy the grain. I used some of the merchants as fronts. The grain cargoes were stored in a warehouse, and then my lads moved it to the cave.' Cestius smiled thinly. 'As you know. We were to take a big cut when Sinius gave the word to start selling the grain. That was the deal.'

Cato nodded. 'Did Sinius tell you who he was working for?'

'Not my business to inquire into the reasons for anything. Not these days. More trouble than it's worth. Not that it stopped Sinius blabbing away that it was for a noble cause. All for the good of Rome.' Cestius sneered, and then his features contorted and he let out a long, keening moan. Cato squatted down beside him, fearing that he might die before he had given up all the information that he wanted. At length Cestius's pained expression faded and he licked his lips and fixed his gaze on Cato once again.

'Did you meet any of the other conspirators?'

Cestius was silent for a moment before he responded. 'Not among the Liberators.'

Cato leant forward. 'Then who else?'

Cestius ignored the question and asked one of his own. 'Who are you working for, Praetorian? Not the Liberators. I know that. Your master is in the imperial household, I'd guess.'

Cato said nothing.

'Which means Pallas . . . or Narcissus.'

'I have one more question,' Cato said. 'About the day your gang attacked the imperial party in the Forum. How did you know we were going to be there?'

'It was planned from the outset. I was paid to have my lads provoke the food riot . . .' Cestius began to breathe raggedly. 'Once it was in full swing we were to stand by to ambush the Emperor and his escort . . . Would have killed our targets too, if you and your friend there hadn't got in the way.'

Cato felt his heart quicken. 'Targets? The Emperor and his family?'

Cestius shook his head. 'The Empress and her son.'

'Just them?' Cato felt a cold tingle at the base of his neck.

'Yes.'

'No one else? Are you certain?'

'He was quite clear about it . . . Just Agrippina and Nero.'

'Who? Who gave you the order?'

Cestius winced and sucked in a long shallow breath. Cato reached forward and shook his shoulder roughly.

'Who paid you to do it? Tell me!'

Cestius licked his dry lips again and this time there was blood in his spittle. A thick dark drop trickled down his chin as he replied. 'A man from the palace. I've done jobs for him before. Made people disappear. Put the frighteners on others. Kind of thing I do well.' Cestius smiled with pride.

'Enemies of the Emperor?'

'Not always.'

'What was his name?' Cato demanded.

'Don't know. Wasn't part of the arrangement. He just paid me to do what his master needed done, and not ask questions.'

Cato hissed with frustration. 'Well, what did he look like? The man who gave you your instructions?'

Cestius shrugged. 'Just a man. Your build. Few years older . . .'

'What else?' Cato snapped. 'Any scars, anything to make him stand out?'

'Yes . . . A mark, a tattoo here.' Cestius reached up and touched his neck just below the ear.

Cato felt his blood grow cold and he heard Macro swear softly. 'What kind of tattoo?'

Cestius thought briefly. 'Only saw it clearly one time. Once, when we met in the public baths. A crescent moon and star . . .'

Cato knew at once where he had seen the distinctive mark before, the day they had arrived in Rome.

'That's Septimus – has to be,' Macro muttered to Cato. 'Septimus? What the hell is going on?'

Cato's mind was filled with a jumble of recollected images and lines of thought that had seemed confusing or came to a dead end. Now they fell into place, one by one. There was a conspiracy lurking in the shadows even deeper than that being hatched by the Liberators. A monstrous scheme that left Cato marvelling at its brilliant deviousness even as it repulsed him and made him aware for the first time of the scale of the deception that both he and Macro, among many others, had been enduring for years. He stood up quickly and turned to his friend.

'We have to get back to the palace at once. We must find Narcissus.'

'Narcissus?'

By the dying flickers of the torch in the sand, Cato looked at his friend intently. 'We've been duped. There's more than one plot against the Emperor. I suspected there might be. But there's something else. We have to go, Macro. Now.'

Cestius chuckled.

'What's so damned funny?' asked Macro.

'Just agreeing with your friend there. Now would be a good time to act.'

Cato rounded on him. 'Why?'

'Last word I had from Sinius was that I should be ready to move the grain back to the warehouse first thing tomorrow.'

'Tomorrow?' Cato's brow creased. 'Then whatever the Liberators are planning is going to happen tonight . . .' His guts were seized by an icy dread. 'Shit, they're going to try to kill the Emperor tonight. We have to go, now!'

As Cato turned towards the public entrance there was a plaintive groan as Cestius stirred and raised a bloodied hand. 'Wait! You promised me a quick death, Praetorian.'

'So I did.' Cato turned back and briefly stared down at the gang leader before tossing his dagger down into the sand behind him. 'There. You've used one on other men, striking them from the shadows. Now use it on yourself, if you have the guts.'

Cato began to run towards the public entrance and Macro followed him across the sand.

'Oi! Oi, you!' One of the Circus staff called after them. 'You can't leave him here! Oi! I'm talking to you!'

The man ran a few paces after the two figures receding into the gloom and then stopped. There was a short grunt from the direction of the imperial box and then a long expiring sigh. By the time he turned to see what had happened, the mortally wounded giant had slumped over on to his side and lay still, the handle of a dagger protruding from his chest.

CHAPTER TWENTY-EIGHT

By the flickering glow of the same oil lamp they had used to light their way out of the imperial palace Cato and Macro emerged from the secret tunnel leading towards the Circus Maximus. Macro shook his head as he considered the situation.

'I don't get it. Why would Narcissus want Nero and Agrippina killed?'

Cato cautiously tried the door that Narcissus had led them to two hours earlier. It was still unlocked and he eased it open and peered out into the chamber where the fuel was stored for the palace's main bathhouse. Neatly stacked logs lined the walls. Cato waited a moment but there was no sound or sign of movement, so he beckoned to Macro to follow him. 'Think about it, Macro. After all, you should know the answer.'

'Don't play cute,' Macro grumbled. 'Just tell me.'

'It was you who saw Agrippina and Pallas together, remember?'

'How could I forget? The wife of our Emperor in the paws of some greasy little Greek freedman is hardly an edifying sight.'

'Quite.' Cato smiled. 'Nevertheless, there's no avoiding the truth. Agrippina has taken Pallas as a lover. His fortune is linked to hers, and that of her son. Pallas is positioning himself for the day when Claudius puts in his application for divinity. If, as looks likely, Nero becomes the new Emperor then Pallas would be in a very powerful position as the lover of Agrippina.'

'Obviously,' Macro sighed.

'So where do you think that leaves Narcissus?'

Macro paused midstride. 'Wait, are you saying he'd dare to make an attempt on the son of the empress?'

'Why not? It's the most sensible thing to do. If he just killed Pallas, then Agrippina would be sure to find herself a new lover soon enough and then Narcissus is back to square one. If he kills Nero, then Britannicus will have no rival for the throne and Agrippina's influence will diminish, and Pallas's fortunes along with hers. Of course, the tricky part is to remove Nero in such a way that there is no suspicion that Narcissus might be behind the assassination. So he used Cestius and his gang. That's why Cestius spared Britannicus. He was under orders to kill only Nero and possibly his mother. Narcissus was there with us so that it would look like he was in just as much danger as everyone else.'

Macro was silent for a moment as they trod warily across the chamber towards the narrow door leading into the service corridor beyond. 'By the gods, Narcissus and his friends play some pretty deadly games with each other.'

Cato shrugged. 'Welcome to life in the imperial palace. Conspiracy, treachery and murder are the diet of those who run the place.' He turned to Macro with a rueful smile. 'Now you can see why I was lucky to be sent to join the legions. I doubt I'd have survived for long if I had gone into the imperial service, like my father. At least in the army you know who your enemies are . . . most of the time.'

Macro snorted. 'Most of the time, but not in the Praetorian Guard. They're a bunch of pretty puppets playing at soldiering and politics in equal measure.'

Cato nodded. 'And that is what makes them so dangerous to the emperors. Tiberius nearly lost his crown thanks to the Praetorians, and Caligula lost his life. The odds are that Claudius and a good many of his successors are going to go the same way.'

'Unless the Liberators get what they want.'

Cato shot his friend a quick look. 'I suppose. Anyway, we'd best be quiet from here on.' He lifted the latch on the door and eased it open. The service corridor was empty, and the only light was from a single torch guttering at the foot of the stairs leading up into the heart of the palace. Cato blew the lamp out and placed it by the door before he and Macro padded down the corridor, passing the doors to several more chambers. The staircase led up to one of the palace's kitchens where the shelves that were usually filled with luxuries were now mostly bare.

'It's quiet,' said Macro. 'Haven't seen or heard a soul so far.'

They passed out of the kitchens into one of the main thoroughfares and made for the private quarters of the imperial family.

'I don't like this,' Cato said softly. 'We should have run into someone by now. Some of the Praetorians, or the slaves at least.'

At last, as they approached the doors to the private suites of the Emperor and his family, they saw some of the guards. Eight Praetorians stood on watch by the light of a brazier. As Cato and Macro emerged from the gloom they saw a figure step forward and recognised Fuscius.

'Stop there!' the optio barked. 'Identify yourselves.'

Cato muttered to his friend, 'Time to drop the cover story, I think.'

'High bloody time,' Macro agreed with feeling.

As they stepped into the pool of light cast by the brazier, Fuscius swore softly. 'Calidus and Capito! What have you two been up to? You're covered in filth.' His eyes widened as he was struck by a more salient thought. 'You're supposed to be on guard! You've deserted your posts.'

'Quiet!' Cato snapped. 'Optio, what's going on? Where are the rest of the Praetorians?'

Fuscius opened his mouth in astonishment at being addressed in this curt manner by a ranker. He puffed out his chest as he took a deep breath to bawl the two men out.

'There's no time for lengthy explanations,' Cato said curtly. 'All you need to know is that my name is not Capito. I'm Prefect Cato and this is Centurion Macro. Why are there so few men in the palace?'

'Hold it.' Fuscius stared at them. 'What's going on?'

'We've uncovered a plot to kill the Emperor. We've been investigating a plot involving some officers of the Praetorian Guard.'

'Bollocks. I don't believe it. You two are on a charge.'

'Shut your mouth,' Macro said firmly. 'Or it'll be you on a charge, sunshine, at the very least, should anything happen to the Emperor. Now tell the prefect what's going on. Where are the rest of the Praetorians?'

Fuscius swallowed nervously before he replied. 'All

right, all right then . . . they've been ordered out of the palace to guard the perimeter of the imperial quarter. Only Tribune Burrus and two centuries remain in the palace.'

'Who gave the order?' Cato demanded.

'Prefect Geta. Less than half an hour ago, I'd say. Same time that he ordered the German bodyguards to be confined to quarters.'

Cato felt his blood go cold. 'Where is Tigellinus?'

Fuscius glanced from one to the other briefly, his mouth working helplessly. Then he shook his head. 'The centurion's not here.'

'Where is he then?' Cato demanded.

'He went off with Prefect Geta and another officer, Centurion Sinius, and a squad of men.'

Cato stabbed his finger into the scale armour on the optio's chest. 'Where did they go?'

'I don't know. They were making for the gardens. Doing the rounds of the sentries, I think the prefect said.'

Cato exchanged an anxious glance with Macro before he addressed Fuscius again. 'Where's the tribune?'

'He set up a command post in the entrance hall, sir.'

'Then you go to him at once. Tell him to bring every man he can to the imperial quarters immediately. Tell Burrus that the Emperor's life depends on it. We'll take these men with us.' Cato saw the optio was on the verge of indecision again and he took a step towards the man and grasped him by the shoulders. 'Get a grip on yourself, Fuscius! You have your orders, now go!' Cato gave him a firm shove away from the entrance and Fuscius hurried away towards the main entrance of the palace, the clatter of his nailed boots echoing off the high walls.

Turning back, Cato faced the remaining Praetorians. Their expressions were as shocked and surprised as the optio's. He needed them to accept his authority and obey his orders without question. Cato drew a calming breath as he looked at them. 'I meant what I said about the danger to the Emperor. There are traitors in our ranks. Men who would break their sacred oath. The only hope we have of stopping them is if you obey my orders, and those of Centurion Macro, without question. Is that clear?' He looked at each man in turn, daring them to defy him. There were no dissenters and Cato nodded.

'Very well. Draw your swords and follow us.' He gestured to Macro, and with a light scrape of his blade, Cato drew his sword and trotted through the entrance of the imperial quarters with Macro at his side. With a chorus of steely rasps the Praetorians drew their weapons and fell in behind the two officers.

As they ran down the long corridor connecting the main part of the palace to the more private and comfortable suites occupied by Claudius and his family, Cato hurriedly thought through the layout of this part of the palace complex. There would still be some men of the Sixth Century at their stations, and perhaps a handful of the German bodyguards who had been with the Emperor when their comrades had been quietly removed from the scene. Therefore the logical route for the assassins to take would be through the terraced gardens and then a final assault through the colonnade that ran along the side of the gardens. It would take them longer than the direct route, but it would avoid having to bluff, or fight, their way through each checkpoint. There was still a chance that they might reach the Emperor first.

Two flights of stairs led up to the highest level of the palace where the sleeping quarters and the gardens overlooked the heart of the city. As they climbed breathlessly up the final set of stairs, Cato heard a cry of alarm, then a shout and the unmistakable clatter of sword blades.

'On me!' he called, taking the last three stairs in a frantic leap. The corridor was lit by oil lamps and was some ten feet wide, with doors opening off each side. It stretched the full length of the top level of the palace, and the Emperor's sleeping chamber and private study were halfway along on the left. The sound of voices and the clash of blades were louder now. As Cato, Macro and the Praetorians sprinted along the marbled floor, a door opened just ahead of them and Britannicus stepped out, bleary eyed. His sleep-clouded mind cleared in an instant as he saw the soldiers pounding towards him, swords drawn.

'Get back inside!' Cato shouted as he slithered to a halt. He turned to the nearest of the Praetorians. 'You! Stay with the Emperor's son. Lock the door and guard him with your life.'

Without waiting for the man's response, Cato ran on again. The sounds of the fighting echoed dully off the corridor walls and then, when they were no more than twenty feet from the Emperor's study, the door burst open and a German fell out, crashing on to the floor. A Praetorian leaped out after him, stabbing down on his sword with his full weight. The blade tore through the German's stomach and the point burst through his back and struck the marble beneath with a loud crack. The German bellowed with agony and then his face contorted into a snarl as he grabbed the other man's head in both hands and bit off his nose.

Cato thrust his blade into the Praetorian's spine as he reached the door and the man gasped, dropping his sword, before he slumped over the body of the German. Rushing inside, Cato saw that he had been right. The shutters that had been drawn across the doors leading out on to the portico and the gardens had been smashed open and the splintered remains hung on the hinges. The main lampstand that stood beside the Emperor's desk had been knocked over in the fight and the only illumination in the room came from a single lamp holder still casting its wan glow from a small table in one corner.

The room seemed to be filled with leaping shadows as men fought like furies. Cato held his sword out and glanced round, and saw the Emperor back into the wall behind his desk. In front of him stood Narcissus, a dagger held out as he shielded Claudius with his body. A huge German stood to one side a short distance before his master, sweeping the air with a long sword as he screamed out his war cry. There were two more Germans fighting in the room, together with a palace slave. Against them were ranged eight Praetorians, two of whom wore the breastplates of officers. A German, two slaves and two Praetorians were already down on the floor, moaning from their wounds.

Macro reacted to the confused scene first. 'Form up on the Emperor, lads!'

He led the way, rushing round the side of the room towards Claudius and Narcissus pressed up against the wall behind their German protector. Cato accepted the sense of Macro's order at once and joined the other men.

'Stop them!' a voice cried out. 'Kill the Emperor! Kill the tyrant!'

Cato recognised the voice – Sinius.

Leaving two of their number locked in combat with the bodyguards in the middle of the study the traitors surged towards the Emperor, rushing round the desk, and one man vaulted over it. The German managed one more swing of his sword, cutting down one of his attackers before the rest swarmed over him, hacking and stabbing with their short swords. He staggered under the impact and then collapsed on to his knees, arms stretched wide as he struggled, even in death, to shield his master. His sacrifice delayed the assassins for only a heartbeat, but it was long enough for Macro to reach the far wall. With a bellow he charged headlong into the men who had killed the German, punching his sword into the face of the first man in his path. As the skull shattered with a wet crack, Macro slammed into the next two men, sending them flying back, one falling at the feet of Narcissus who promptly stabbed him in the back with his dagger, the other stumbling back among his companions.

Cato was close behind his friend and swerved aside to place himself between the traitors and the Emperor as one of the officers thrust his way past the press of bodies caused by Macro's wild charge. In the gloom Cato could just make out Prefect Geta's determined expression as he raised his sword and made to strike at Claudius. Cato threw his blade up to deflect the blow and sparks sprang from the expertly forged metal as the weapons struck. He felt the impact of the savage blow travel down his arm and his fingers were momentarily numbed. The prefect's sword cut through the air to one side of the Emperor and clattered against the wall, gouging a chunk out of the ornately painted plaster. Claudius flinched as a chip of plaster struck him on the cheek. Before Geta could recover his sword to attack again, Cato threw himself forward and slammed his left forearm into the prefect's chest, throwing him off balance. The Praetorians following on behind Macro and Cato forced themselves between the Emperor and the traitors and the room filled with the desperate grunts and cries of the two sides, together with the scrape of blades as they fought hand to hand.

'Hold 'em back!' Macro bellowed as he fell into place beside Cato.

For a moment the struggle continued and then the first of the traitors retreated, clutching his spare hand to a wound in his sword arm. With no way through to the Emperor, the others backed off one by one. Geta turned to them in fury.

'Fools! If you don't kill him now, you are as good as dead. It's too late to retreat. Strike! Strike a blow for liberty while you still can!'

Geta lashed out with his sword in a series of vicious cuts which Cato parried as best he could until Macro launched himself forward, hammering his sword against the prefect's, forcing the other man back.

One of the Praetorians made to move forward and help Macro but Cato grabbed his shoulder. 'Stay where you are! Every man is to hold position. Protect the Emperor until help gets here.'

The two sides drew apart and the din of the fighting was replaced by heavy breathing as the Praetorians and the traitors watched each other warily. Geta glared at the Emperor, then swallowed nervously before he took a half step towards Claudius and the men guarding him. Before he could call on his men to attempt another strike against the Emperor, the sound of shouting and footsteps echoed along the corridor outside the study.

'That's Tribune Burrus,' Cato spoke out to the traitors. 'Throw down your weapons and surrender.'

'Surrender and we all die!' Geta responded loudly. 'There will be no mercy if we fail now.'

His followers hovered indecisively for an instant before one turned and ran back through the broken shutters. Another made to follow him and then others fled, leaving Geta and Sinius alone. Beyond them, Cato was aware of a third officer, in the shadows by the broken shutters.

'Cowards!' Geta yelled bitterly. 'Cowards all!'

Sinius grabbed his arm and pulled his superior back. 'There's nothing we can achieve here, sir! We must go.'

'Go where?' Geta asked.

'There may be another chance, sir. Come!' Sinius roughly pulled the Praetorian prefect away and then bundled him out of the room towards the gardens. Cato lowered his sword and looked round the room. The wounded were moaning on the floor. Two of the men lay still. Those on either side of him were breathing heavily from their desperate run through the palace and the brief skirmish in the Emperor's study. The Emperor himself was unhurt but there was no mistaking the terror in his eyes.

'You men stay here,' Cato ordered the Praetorians. 'Macro, with me!'

He tightened his grip on his sword as they strode briskly across the room towards the smashed shutters. They stepped out of the study cautiously, just in case any of the traitors were waiting for them in the colonnade outside. The light of the crescent moon bathed the garden in dark shades of grey and the figures of the traitors were easy enough to see as they fled down the shingle paths through the neat shrubberies and flower beds. Macro started after the nearest of the men but Cato grabbed his arm.

'No. Leave him. Those are the ones we want.' He pointed his sword at the three officers running towards the steps leading down to the lower terrace of the garden where there was access to the servants' quarters beneath the imperial suites. If Geta and the others could reach them, they might lose their pursuers in the labyrinth of service corridors and storerooms before escaping into the city's streets. Cato and Macro set off after the officers, sprinting down from the colonnade towards the steps. They lost sight of their prey momentarily between two lines of neatly trimmed box hedges and then saw them, a short distance ahead. Geta and his companions dashed down the stairs and headed across a paved area towards the dark entrance to the servants' quarters. An instant later there was a faint glow there that outlined the stone arch and then the flicker of a torch and the sound of voices.

The three men stopped as they realised there was no escape in that direction. They turned and ran the opposite way, along the balcony that looked directly down on to the Forum. At the far end lay a secluded rose garden surrounded by tall hedges. Cato and Macro chased after them while the first soldiers spilled out from the servants' entrance. Higher up there were shouts as more men began to search the upper terrace for the traitors. Burrus's voice carried through the night air as he issued his orders. The three officers hurried round the corner of the rose garden out of sight. Cato stopped and cupped a hand to his mouth.

'Over here. They're over here! Hurry!'

He and Macro continued their pursuit, rushing headlong round the edge of the neatly trimmed bushes only to see an empty stretch of path before them, lined with pine trees on one side which filled the air with their rich scent. Cato held up his hand to stop his friend and they stood, hearts pounding, as they strained their eyes to see in the gloom.

'Where did they go?' hissed Macro. 'They have to be close. Best be careful, lad.'

They paced forward warily, senses tuned to detect the slightest sign of movement or sound in the trees on either side of the path. The voices of Burrus's men rang out across the garden and then Cato saw a party of soldiers appear at the far end of the path. He took a breath and called out.

'Geta! You're trapped. There's nowhere to run. Give yourself up!'

There was no response from close at hand, but the soldiers at the far end of the path began to trot towards Cato. Suddenly, not twenty feet ahead, there was a deep groan and a body slumped out of the shadows and fell across the path, a sword clattering dully to the ground beside the man.

'What are you doing?' Geta's voice rose up in alarm only to be cut off abruptly. There was a rustling between the trees behind the body and then a stifled cry.

'Shit.' Macro started forward. 'The bastards are doing themselves in.'

Cato ran after him. Before they could reach the body,

a figure stepped out on to the path, sword in hand, and faced Macro and Cato. As he stepped away from the tree, Cato saw who it was.

'Tigellinus.'

They halted, a safe distance beyond sword's length, and raised their weapons, ready to fight if the centurion chose to resist. Behind him the soldiers approached at the run.

'You three!' a voice called out. 'Drop your swords!'

Tigellinus glanced briefly over his shoulder before he tossed his weapon on to the path. The Praetorians slowed to a stop and their leader carefully stooped to pick up Tigellinus's sword before he gestured towards Cato and Macro. 'You too!'

'What?' Macro growled. 'We're on the same side, man! We're the ones who sent for Burrus.'

'We'll see soon enough,' the Praetorian replied. 'Now drop those swords, before me and my lads make you.'

Macro took a step towards them.

'Do as he says,' Cato intervened, throwing his weapon at the feet of the soldiers.

Macro hesitated a moment, then shrugged and followed suit.

Once the weapons had been collected and the Praetorians had surrounded Cato, Macro and Tigellinus, the leader of the soldiers prodded the body on the path with his boot and then squinted into the shadows where a second corpse lay.

'What's going on here, then?'

Tigellinus cleared his throat. 'You address me as "sir" when you speak to me, Centurion Tigellinus, commander of the Sixth Century, Third Cohort.'

'Bollocks,' Macro spat. 'You're nothing but a bloody traitor, like your two friends here.'

'Friends?' Tigellinus responded in a surprised tone. 'I think you are mistaken. I saw these men running from the Emperor's study. I chased after them and caught up with them here. There was a fight, and I slew them by my own hand.'

Macro was dumbfounded and took a moment to speak. 'That's a bloody lie! It was me and Cato who were chasing 'em, and you too, you traitor!'

'I haven't the slightest idea what you are talking about,' Tigellinus said smoothly.

'Right, that's enough!' the leader of the Praetorians snapped. 'Shut your mouths, all three of you. Tribune Burrus will soon have the truth out of you, make no mistake.' He detailed four of his men to pick up the bodies before turning back to his prisoners. 'Let's go!'

CHAPTER TWENTY-NINE

Emperor Claudius eased himself down on to the padded throne in the small audience chamber he used for his routine business. Through the arched windows running along one of the walls the first glimmer of the coming dawn illuminated the city's skyline and the first bird calls of the day carried into the palace. Neither the pink tinge in the sky nor the light-hearted chorus of the sparrows touched the hearts or minds of those gathered in the chamber.

The room was lined with German bodyguards hastily summoned from their quarters where Prefect Geta had confined them a few hours before. The bodies of the prefect and Centurion Sinius lay in the centre of the room. Sinius had a wound to his throat while Geta had been stabbed in the heart. The surviving members of their party stood behind the bodies, their hands bound in front of them, their expressions fearful. Centurion Tigellinus stood a small distance apart, flanked by two of the Germans. Cato and Macro, still in their soiled tunics, were also under guard. The Empress, Nero and Britannicus sat on stools to one side of the Emperor's throne and on the other side were the Emperor's closest advisers, Narcissus and Pallas, together with Tribune Burrus.

Claudius's gaze slowly travelled round the occupants

of the chamber and Cato could see that he was still badly shaken by the attempt on his life. A small nick in his cheek had bled unchecked for a while and a streak of dried blood ran down his jowl and had stained a small patch at the top of his white tunic. He leant forward, resting his elbow on his knee as his fingers nervously stroked his jaw. At length he eased himself back and cleared his throat.

'By the gods, someone is going to p-pay for this.' He thrust his finger at the two corpses. 'That is the f-f-fate of anyone connected with this conspiracy. I want their heads mounted in the Forum for all to see. I want their f-families sent into exile. Their sympathisers will be sent to the lions in the ar-arena.' He swallowed and coughed as he choked on his rage. The coughing continued for a moment, and his head twitched violently as he struggled to regain control. At length the fit passed and he glowered at the bodies in silence, until the silence became unbearable. Narcissus bit his lip and then took a quiet step forward to draw his master's attention.

'Sire? Perhaps it would be best to begin with Tribune Burrus's report,' Narcissus suggested.

Claudius thought a moment and then nodded. 'Yes . . . Yes. Good. Well, Tribune? Explain yourself. Keep it to the p-point.'

All eyes were on Burrus as he strode forward and faced the Emperor directly. As usual he was immaculately turned out and his crested helmet was tucked under his arm. He bowed his head curtly before he began.

'I called the men out as soon as Optio Fuscius told me what was going on, sire. I took the first available section and gathered more men as we made for the imperial suite.

By the time we got to your study the traitors had fled, so I sent the men out to search the gardens. That's where they found the bodies, and those three.' He indicated Tigellinus, Cato and Macro. 'They were making all sorts of claims so I ordered that they be held under guard while I made sure that you and your family were safe, sire, and that there was no sign of any further traitors hiding in the gardens or in the imperial suite. As soon as I discovered Prefect Geta's part in the plot I gave instructions for his orders to be revoked. The Germans were sent for and the rest of the Praetorians assigned to guard the palace were recalled from outside and repositioned to protect the imperial palace and prevent anyone from entering or leaving without your permission. That's when I received your summons to come here, sire,' Burrus concluded with a brief nod.

Claudius nodded and pursed his lips. He pointed to Cato and Macro. 'And you two? What's your st-story? I seem to recognise you. Have I seen you before?'

'Yes, sire,' Cato answered. 'During the campaign in Britannia, and here in the palace some years before. And we were there, at your side, when the imperial party was attacked in the Forum. And when the dam collapsed below the Albine Lake.'

'Oh?' Claudius narrowed his eyes. 'I see you wear the tunics of Praetorians, but you look like beggars from the F-f-f-forum. What was your part in the night's events, eh? Are you part of the conspiracy?'

'No, sire. Centurion Macro and I led the party that saved you in your study.'

'Did you now? . . . Centurion Macro, you say? And who are you then, young man?'

'Prefect Cato, sir. Before that, a centurion in the Second Legion.'

'But you wear the tunic of the Praetorians, like those t-traitors lying there on the floor. Burrus, are these two yours?'

'Yes, sire.' Burrus frowned. 'They joined the Guard several weeks ago. Promoted from the legions. At least that was their story. They went by the names of Capito and Calidus. Now they claim to be Prefect Cato and Centurion Macro.'

'So then.' Claudius turned back to Cato and Macro. 'What were two legionary officers doing in the P-p-praetorian Guard, under false names? Unless you were part of the plot against me.'

Narcissus stepped forward with a light cough. 'Sire, I can vouch for these men. They are indeed officers from the legions. It was I who summoned them to Rome to carry out a mission, in your service, sire.'

'Mission? What m-mission?'

'You recall the matter of the theft of the silver bullion, sire?'

'Of course. I'm old, not st-stupid.'

'Indeed, sire.' Narcissus bowed his head. 'Then you will remember that I reported discovering a connection between the theft of the silver and certain members of the Praetorian Guard. Men who I suspected were linked to the Liberators.'

Claudius nodded. 'Continue.'

'In order to pursue my investigation I needed some men on the inside, sire. Cato and Macro have served you well before and such is their loyalty to you that they willingly agreed to risk their lives and go under cover in an effort to penetrate the conspiracy.'

'Agreed?' Macro whispered. 'That's pushing it.'

'Their mission was dangerous,' Narcissus continued. 'But between their efforts and those of my most trusted agents, we were able to identify the ringleaders of the conspiracy, as well as uncovering the full scope of the plot, sire. We discovered that the traitors were behind the grain shortage. They intended to provoke civil disorder by deliberately starving your people. Luckily the Liberators' grain hoard has been located and it is now under the protection of one of the urban cohorts, sire.' Narcissus paused and coughed. 'I gave the order in your name, if you'll forgive me.'

The Emperor's eyes lit up and he leant forward. 'This grain is safe, you say? Then we must start feeding the m-m-mob as soon as p-possible.'

'I have already given the orders to begin moving the grain to the palace, sire, so that you may take credit for restoring the grain dole.'

'Very good!' Claudius smiled in relief. Then he waved a hand. 'Go on.'

Narcissus paused a moment as he looked meaningfully at Centurion Tigellinus. 'Although two of the officers who led the plot are dead, and the other would-be assassins are also dead, or captured, there are still others involved in the conspiracy against you. Or, more precisely, the two conspiracies.'

Claudius frowned. 'Two? Explain yourself.'

Narcissus gestured towards Cato and Macro. 'My agents discovered the existence of a parallel plot, sire. The Liberators were not the only traitors working towards your downfall. The collapse of the dam and the attempt to disrupt the Naumachia were the handiwork of other conspirators. Those who hoped to turn the Liberators' efforts to their own ends . . .' Narcissus turned towards Tigellinus and paced slowly round him so that he could look back, in the direction of Pallas, before he resumed. 'It was only with tonight's attempt on your life that I began to grasp the scope of their plans. It was their intention to do what they could to help the Liberators murder you, sire. And then make use of the chaos to replace you with their choice of Emperor.'

Cato saw the blood drain from Pallas's face as the imperial secretary outlined his thoughts. Pallas glanced quickly at Agrippina before he got control of himself and stared rigidly at his rival, Narcissus.

'Who are these other traitors then?' the Emperor demanded. 'Who do they intend to r-replace me with?'

Narcissus turned and bowed his head towards Nero. 'Your adopted son.'

Claudius sucked in his breath and turned towards Nero. 'Is this true?'

The boy's jaw sagged and he shook his head. Before he could speak, Agrippina jumped to her feet with a furious expression and stabbed a finger at Narcissus. 'He's a liar! Like all these Greek freedmen you choose to surround yourself with.'

Pallas winced.

'How dare you accuse my son?' Agrippina said furiously. 'How dare you?'

'I did not accuse him of taking part in the conspiracy,' Narcissus responded loudly enough to override her protest. 'I said that there were others who wished to use Nero to replace the Emperor. Presumably so that they could manipulate him for their own ends.'

'Who are these traitors?' Claudius repeated, his mind concentrating sufficiently to eclipse his stammer. 'Name them.'

'I can't, sire. Not yet. Not quite,' Narcissus apologised, even as he looked at both Pallas and Agrippina. 'But I know the identity of one man close to the heart of the second conspiracy. Notably this officer.' He pointed at Centurion Tigellinus. 'My agents, Cato and Macro, caught him with the bodies of the two officers who led the attempt on your life, Prefect Geta and Centurion Sinius. He was with them then, and he fled with them, and it is clear that he killed them in order to cover up his part in the plot. Naturally, the centurion protested his innocence, and claimed to have chased them down and engaged them in combat before killing them.'

'That is the truth, sire,' Tigellinus cut in calmly.

'No, it is a lie,' Narcissus responded. 'As will be proved when you are handed over to my interrogators who will find out exactly who your accomplices are. They have something of a knack for getting answers out of traitors.'

Tigellinus looked at Agrippina and she glanced at Pallas and discreetly made a gesture to urge his intervention. Pallas licked his lips anxiously and then stepped forward.

'Sire, this man, Centurion Tigellinus, is innocent. I swear it.'

'Oh?' Narcissus could not help a small smile. 'And how can you be so certain?'

'He is working for me,' Pallas replied. 'He has been from the start.'

Claudius looked confused. 'This traitor is your agent?'

'He is no traitor, sire,' Pallas replied. 'I too had discovered that the Liberators were plotting to bring you down. Like Narcissus I decided to place a man inside the conspiracy to find out who was behind it. Is this not true, Centurion?'

'That's right.' Tigellinus nodded steadily. 'That was the plan.'

'Even though we did our best to infiltrate the conspiracy, we were unable to achieve as much as my esteemed colleague and his team.' Pallas bowed his head politely towards Narcissus who responded to the words of praise with an icy, hate-filled glare. 'Tigellinus was still in the process of gathering intelligence tonight when your enemies struck, sire. However, he did manage at least to warn the Empress and Prince Nero before they could be attacked.'

Claudius held up a hand to still Pallas's tongue, and turned to his wife. 'Is this true?'

Agrippina nodded. 'He entered my sleeping chamber to tell me and Nero to go and hide. He said he would try to save you.'

Claudius stared at her. 'Nero was in your room? In your bed?'

'He could not sleep,' Agrippina replied steadily. 'The poor boy had a headache and I was comforting him.'

'I see.' Claudius turned to Pallas. 'And how did you come to know this?'

'Sire?'

'That Tigellinus managed to warn my wife?'

'She told me, as we were waiting for you here, a moment ago.'

'Very well.' The Emperor scratched his chin. 'I think

I'll hear the rest of it from the centurion's lips. Speak up, Tigellinus. What happened next?'

'I left the Empress, sire, and ran to catch up with the traitors, but they had already burst into your study to attack you. I heard sounds of fighting then saw the traitors fleeing. I recognised Geta and Sinius and pursued them. I brought them to bay at the far end of the garden. They were forced to fight and, by the grace of Jupiter, I overcame them. That's when Capito and – I beg your pardon, sire – that's when the agents of Narcissus turned up, together with the Praetorians. Too late to be of assistance, alas,' he added in a regretful tone.

'So you say,' Narcissus intervened. 'But the truth is that you murdered these two officers to prevent them from implicating you. Far from investigating the Liberators' conspiracy, you were actually doing everything you could to further it so that your masters could seize power in the name of Prince Nero, after the Emperor was killed. It's clear that you warned the Empress to hide in order to preserve her and her son, and had no intention of doing anything to save the Emperor.'

Tigellinus shrugged. 'It's a nice story, freedman. But it's still just a story.'

'Oh, it's more than a story,' Narcissus sneered. 'It's no coincidence that the Empress, the Prince . . . and Pallas were not with the Emperor the day when the dam was sabotaged.'

'Was it sabotaged? I had no idea.'

'Then why did you attempt to kill Claudius when the water rushed down upon us?'

Tigellinus frowned. 'I did no such thing.'

'Yes you did.' Narcissus turned to Cato. 'Isn't that

right, Prefect Cato? If you had not intervened and reached the Emperor first, he would have been murdered. Is that not so?'

Cato was acutely aware of every eye upon him and felt his heart quicken with anxiety. Even though the truth was that Tigellinus, Pallas and Agrippina had been plotting the death of the Emperor, he was shrewd enough to see that they were covering their tracks adroitly. So far Narcissus had cleverly avoided accusing Pallas and Agrippina directly and had focused his accusations on Tigellinus. Under torture the centurion would inevitably confess their involvement and Narcissus's case against them would be complete. But what if the imperial secretary failed to bring them down? Cato knew that if that happened, he and Macro would be sure to join Narcissus on their list of enemies – a danger that Cato could not ignore. He cleared his throat.

'It was peculiar that the centurion was alone in not being surprised by the wave. He had stripped off his armour and was the first to react. That is why I placed myself between him and the Emperor.'

'I was as surprised as anyone else,' Tigellinus countered. 'Should I be blamed for reacting to the danger more swiftly than you? Have you considered that your preventing me from coming to the Emperor's aid might have actually increased the risk to his life?'

'I was tasked with protecting the Emperor,' said Cato. 'Your actions were suspicious, to say the least. And, as the imperial secretary has pointed out, it was very convenient for you that those with most to gain from the Emperor's death were not on the scene.'

'I am not responsible for the whereabouts of members

of the imperial household,' Tigellinius said dismissively. 'Whereas I am responsible for the safety of the Emperor and went to his aid the moment I perceived the danger to his life.'

'Enough of your lies!' Narcissus broke in. 'Let's put this matter in the hands of the interrogators. They'll get to the bottom of things soon enough. Sire, may I give the order?'

Before Claudius could consider the question, Agrippina hurried to his side and knelt beside him. 'My dearest Claudius, we cannot let this good man suffer just because one of your servants suspects him of some kind of involvement in this awful plot by the Liberators.' Her voice was low and sweet and she cast a pitying look at Tigellinus. 'It would be a poor reward for saving my life and that of my son. Besides, Pallas has vouched for him.'

Claudius smiled at her. 'Yes, but Narcissus has not, and I have learned to trust his judgement over the years.'

Agrippina took his hand and pressed it to the thin folds of material covering her breast. Claudius's smile took on a distinct leer. She spoke again, in a lower, softer voice that was almost a purr. 'Narcissus has worked tirelessly for you. I know that. But tired men make mistakes, my love. It's only to be expected. The poor man is overwrought and is so used to seeing conspiracies that sometimes the simple truth escapes him. You've heard his accusations, and you have heard Tigellinus's explanations of his conduct. I believe him.'

Claudius twisted round to cup her cheek with his spare hand, while keeping the other on her breast. 'My dear, you are t-t-too good. Too innocent of the ways of men.'

Cato saw the panic etched on Narcissus's face. The

imperial secretary took a step towards his Emperor. 'Sire, I suggest that we leave my interrogators to settle the matter. If Tigellinus is innocent we shall know soon enough. Better that he suffers a little than permit a traitor to go free.'

'Please, Claudius, there's been enough blood shed tonight,' said Agrippina, then she moved her head slightly so that she could kiss the palm of his hand. As Cato watched, he saw her tongue dart out and flick over the Emperor's skin and Claudius gave a little shudder of pleasure.

'You're right, my love.' He smiled, then looked up at the others gathered in the audience chamber. 'The plot against me has been crushed. The ringleaders are dead. All that m-m-matters now is to start feeding the people of Rome again. Pallas, you can take charge of that.'

'With pleasure, sire.' Pallas bowed low.

Claudius turned to Narcissus. 'You have done well, my friend. Once again you have defeated my enemies and I am in your d-debt. But the Empress is right. We must not lash out in a blind panic. The centurion was carrying out Pallas's instructions. I am indeed fortunate to have two such devoted servants...' He paused and looked at Cato and Macro. 'I owe my thanks to you...' His brow creased.

'Cato, sir,' Cato filled in. 'Prefect Cato and Centurion Macro.'

'Cato and Macro. Fine work. You shall be rewarded. It is thanks to you that R-rome can be fed once more.' He rose from his throne and approached them with a grateful smile. Then he stopped at arm's length and sniffed the air and grimaced. 'Yes, well. Good j-job. Better go and, er, get yourselves bathed and find some fresh t-t-tunics.'

'Yes, sire,' Cato and Macro replied with a smart bow of their heads.

Claudius forced another smile before shuffling back out of range of the odour emanating from their filthy tunics. He took Agrippina's hand again and beamed dotingly at her. 'Come, my love. It has been an eventful night. We could b-b-both do with a rest, eh?'

The Empress raised her plucked eyebrows suggestively. Claudius led her towards the rear door of the audience chamber. Then he paused and looked back at the prisoners who had been standing silently, hoping that they might have been overlooked. 'Oh, and have those men executed. Their heads are to be mounted next to their leaders'. See to it, Pallas.'

'Yes, sire.'

Claudius turned back to his wife and continued towards the door with his awkward gait. Britannicus and Nero followed a short distance behind. The rest of the men in the chamber stood in silence until the Emperor and his family had left. Then they began to talk in muted tones. The Germans marched the prisoners away to their deaths while others removed the bodies of Geta and Sinius. Tigellinus turned to Cato and Macro with a smirk. 'I hope for your sake that our paths don't cross again.'

'Don't worry,' Macro responded. 'We'll be quitting the Praetorians as soon as we can. Back to the proper army for us.'

'Lucky you. Less pay, fewer prospects and the squalor of the frontier. I am positively consumed with envy.'

Macro grabbed the centurion's tunic and pulled him close. 'I know what you are,' he said in a soft voice, dripping with menace. 'You may have fooled the Emperor but we know the truth, Cato and me. If our paths do ever cross again, I swear I'll kill you first and ask questions later.'

'That would be rather pointless,' Tigellinus observed as he reached up and pulled his tunic out of Macro's fingers. 'Now, if you'll excuse me, I find your stench offensive.' He backed away to a safe distance and took his place beside Pallas. The freedman could not help a triumphant grin as he faced Narcissus.

'It's not over,' the imperial secretary said firmly. 'You've won this round, but you won't be able to fool the Emperor for ever.'

'I won't have to. How much longer do you suppose Claudius will live? Five years? Three? One?' Pallas plucked at the hem of his tunic. 'My boy is next in line to the purple. Britannicus is a spent force. Face it, you picked the wrong horse, Narcissus. I have Nero, I have his mother and the Emperor has given me the job of handing out the grain. I should think that makes me the most popular man in a starving city, don't you? Meanwhile, what do you have? The Emperor's gratitude, that's what. How long do you think that's going to work in your favour when Agrippina has her claws stuck into the old boy? Whatever your undoubted talents, I doubt that seducing a randy old man is among them.' Pallas patted the imperial secretary on the shoulder. 'Enjoy this moment, my old friend. There won't be any more opportunities. You have my word on it. Come, Tigellinus.' He beckoned to the centurion and headed towards the door of the chamber. 'We must have a little talk about your future.'

Only Narcissus, Cato and Macro remained in the chamber. The imperial secretary stood and stared at the Emperor's throne with a bitter, weary expression. Macro tugged his friend's arm and spoke softly. 'Come on, we're done here. It's over.'

'Over?' Cato shook his head. 'How can you say that?'

'The people will get their grain. The Emperor's survived an assassination attempt. We're still alive.' Macro shrugged. 'That's as good a result as you can hope for in my book. Now, I could use a bath, a drink and some sleep. So could you. Let's go, lad.'

'Go? Go where? Back to the camp? Isn't that going to be difficult now that our cover story has been exposed?'

'Where else can we go? We don't have any home outside of the barracks, Cato.'

Cato thought a moment, and nodded. Now that the plot had been foiled, they should be safe enough at the camp under their real names. For a few days at least, until some better arrangement could be made. Cato took one last look at the dejected imperial secretary. There was still one matter to be resolved.

'Narcissus . . . We'll talk later.'

'Yes,' Narcissus replied vaguely. Then he turned to face Cato with a calculating look. 'Talk about what?'

'The Liberators,' Cato replied deliberately. 'That, and your promise to find us postings back to the army, with confirmation of my promotion.'

'I see. Yes.' Narcissus nodded slowly. 'We'll speak later then.'

CHAPTER THIRTY

'Lurco and Vitellius were not particularly grateful when I gave orders for their release,' said Narcissus, smiling faintly. 'Vitellius swore that he would have his revenge on you two, apparently.'

'Then perhaps you shouldn't have bothered with Vitellius,' Macro responded without a trace of humour. 'It would have been better if you had arranged for him to be dropped into a nice deep well. I doubt he'd have been missed by many people. Come to that, if you want the job done, you only have to ask.'

'I'll bear it in mind,' Narcissus replied. 'Were it not for the fact that Vitellius hates Pallas even more than me, I might be tempted to take you up on your offer. As it is, he may yet be of some use to me. Frankly, I need every ally I can get at present.'

Cato briefly wondered if the imperial secretary was looking for sympathy. It had been five days since the attempt on the Emperor's life. Claudius had spent most of the time with his young wife and left his subordinates to run his affairs. While Pallas had taken charge of distributing the grain supply, Tribune Burrus had been appointed prefect of the Praetorian Guard. The other prefect was pensioned off and there were no plans to replace him. Henceforth, there would be one commander of the

Praetorians, with all the dangers that entailed. The Empress had seen to it that Centurion Tigellinus was promoted to replace Burrus. It was clear to Cato that the balance of power had shifted from Narcissus to Pallas and his associates.

Narcissus had been silent for a moment, as if awaiting a response to his predicament. When none came he frowned slightly and leant forward, resting his elbows on his desk, and arched his fingers together as he regarded the two officers sitting in front of him.

'As you will recall, the Emperor promised you a reward for your services in uncovering the Liberators' plot. Given that Agrippina is busy wrapping Claudius round her little finger, it would be best to claim that reward now, before she entices him into changing his mind. Rome is likely to become as dangerous a place for you as it is for me in the days to come.'

'I doubt that,' Macro commented. 'We're not party to the games you and Pallas are playing.'

'Oh, but you are. Very much so. You and Cato came close to exposing Pallas and Agrippina's plot. Tigellinus was lucky to escape with his life. I doubt that they will be very forgiving as far as you two are concerned. In which case it would be wise to remove you both from Rome and find you safer employment. Pallas's star is rising, and at present I find it hard to believe that Nero will not succeed Claudius. In which case, Britannicus is a lost cause. There is not much I can do to save him now. Indeed, I may not be able to do much to save myself, but I'll do what I can for you. It is the very least that you deserve after all that you have done in the service of your Emperor.'

Cato shook his head. 'Spare us the sanctimonious air of self-sacrifice, Narcissus. If you want to keep us safe then it's only because you think you might have cause to use Macro and me again one day. That being the case, we'll take our reward, and on our terms.'

'Your terms?' Narcissus's eyebrows rose. 'And what terms would those be?'

'You will see to it that my promotion to the rank of prefect is confirmed, and you will provide us both with commands worthy of our ranks. We've earned it, over and over, and we will have what is due to us,' Cato concluded firmly.

The imperial secretary stared at Cato. 'You have a pretty high and mighty opinion of yourself. What makes you think I will bow to your demands?'

'It is in our mutual interest,' Cato responded. 'While you still have some influence over the Emperor, Macro and I can profit from it.'

'And what's in it for me?'

Cato regarded the man coldly for a moment before he replied. 'If you give us what we want then Macro and I will keep quiet about your attempt to have Nero murdered.'

Macro stirred and looked at his friend in surprise, but kept his silence as he waited for Cato to explain.

'I don't know what you are talking about,' Narcissus responded flatly. 'I suggest you withdraw your groundless accusation.'

'Groundless?' Cato chuckled. 'I don't think so. I had it from the mouth of Cestius, before he died. You paid him to kill Nero.'

'I did no such thing.'

'He took his orders from Septimus who answers directly to you. It comes to the same thing.'

'I'm afraid not. Cestius is dead. You have no evidence.'

'Not unless we can persuade Septimus to confirm what Cestius told us. Not just about the attempt to kill Nero, but also about other tasks he performed for you.'

'What tasks would those be?'

Cato stared at the imperial secretary. 'Those associated with the threat posed by the Liberators for several years now.'

Narcissus met Cato's eyes without betraying his thoughts in the smallest degree. 'Go on.'

'Very well.' Cato nodded, gathering his suspicions and conclusions together. 'Let's talk about the Liberators. They've been a thorn in Claudius's side ever since he became Emperor. More precisely, ever since you began to wield power behind the scenes.'

'Most interesting. So what?'

'There have always been conspiracies against emperors. But never anything as enduring and as secretive as the Liberators. Which is odd, given how they have failed to achieve much, until recently.' Cato paused. 'I've given it a lot of thought in the last few days. It occurs to me that if the Liberators didn't exist, then it might be a good idea to invent them.'

Macro frowned. 'What are you talking about? How can that be a good idea?'

Cato turned to his friend. 'Think about it. There are plenty of people who would happily see the back of the emperors. They might even consider hatching their own plots against Claudius. But what if there was a secret organisation dedicated to his downfall? Not so secret that no one ever heard of them, of course. Wouldn't they attract the attention of almost every aspiring assassin? Far better to join other like-minded people than go it alone.'

Macro pursed his lips. 'I suppose.'

'Then what could be more logical than to use the Liberators as a front to draw out those who harbour a grudge against Claudius? It's just the kind of scheme that a man tasked with running the Emperor's spy network might come up with, don't you think?'

Macro shook his head. 'That's a step too far. Even for Narcissus. That would be playing with fire.'

'Yes, it would be risky, but while it worked it would provide an invaluable means of identifying traitors, and then arranging for their quiet disposal, or recruitment as double agents.'

Narcissus sat back in his chair. 'All very interesting, but you have no proof that any such scheme ever existed.'

'Of course not. That's how it would have to work. The Liberators would need a high degree of autonomy if they were to believe that their conspiracy was real. Only there was something that you didn't anticipate.' Cato shook his head slightly. 'You didn't think that the organisation might take on a life of its own. You lost control of them, didn't you?'

Narcissus did not respond, and there was a tense silence until Narcissus cleared his throat.

'As I said, you have no proof to back up your wild speculations.'

'I will have, once Septimus is interrogated. He was your middle man. He shared everything that you knew about the Liberators. He was more than a middle man, he is your right-hand man.'

Narcissus smiled. 'As it happens, he is even more than that, Cato. Septimus is my son. Do you really think he would betray me? That's why I placed him in that position. I can rely on him, at least.'

'Your son?' Cato was taken by surprise. Then he nodded. 'That makes sense. But even a son might sell his father out, with the right . . . persuasion. I wouldn't count on Septimus holding his tongue.'

'Then you should not rely on him being taken alive for interrogation. Either he would take his own life, or it could be arranged for another to do the deed for him.'

Cato felt his stomach turn in disgust. 'You wouldn't do that.'

'I would. Do you think a man from my background could achieve what I have without abandoning every principle save that of self-interest? Well?'

For a moment Cato's composed mask slipped as he muttered, 'By the gods, you are a monster . . .'

Narcissus shook his head. 'I am the servant of the Emperor, tasked with keeping him on the throne at any price. That is all.'

There was a brief silence before the imperial servant continued. 'I know that you may despise me for what I am about to say.'

'No,' Macro interjected. 'We despise you already.'

Narcissus shot him an icy look. 'Be that as it may, you have to understand the stakes before you condemn me. I am all that stands between the order of the Empire and chaos. That is the nature of my world. There is no room for all those fine values that you soldiers think are so important.' His lips lifted in a sneer. 'I think you'd better go back to the army. Your sense of morality is too dangerous to you here in Rome, and it threatens all that I stand for . . .'

Cato closed his eyes and fought down the bile that filled his guts. When he opened them again he refused to meet Narcissus's gaze and turned instead to Macro. 'I think I felt cleaner when I was standing up to my neck in shit back in the Great Sewer. He's right, Macro. We should get out of here. Get out of Rome. Get back to the army.'

His friend nodded, rising to his feet. 'Like I always said. Let's go.'

Cato stood up, then looked at Narcissus for the last time. 'You'll see to it that we get our commands. Do that and we'll not speak of what we know. Not to anyone.'

'That is the deal,' Narcissus agreed. 'And since you wish for it so fervently, I shall be delighted to have you sent back to . . . Britannia. I'm sure the natives will be delighted at the prospect of your return.'

'Suits me,' Cato replied, then with a quick look at Macro he turned and led the way out of the imperial secretary's office, feeling sick to the core of his being. Both men were silent until they had left the palace behind them and emerged into the crowded thoroughfare of the Sacred Way, the route that ran through the heart of Rome.

'Do you think he will keep his side of the bargain?' asked Macro.

'He will. It serves his ends to get us far from here as soon as possible. After that, he'll have no time to spare us any attention. He'll be too busy dealing with Pallas.' Cato thought for a moment. 'I doubt he'll survive for long. I think he's finally met his match.'

'Then good riddance.'

Cato looked at his friend and laughed humourlessly. 'Narcissus falls, Pallas rises and all is as before. That's how it will be.'

'So? By then we shall be far away. Back where we belong.'

'Britannia?'

'Why not? That's where the fighting is best at the moment.' Macro clapped his hands together at the prospect. 'Think on it, lad. Battles to be won, booty to be had as far from that slimy reptile Narcissus as possible. And we still have that small fortune Sinius gave us. What could be better?'

Cato stopped and stared at his friend. 'You intend to keep that?'

'Why not? You can't say that I've not earned it. You too.'

Cato thought for a moment. 'If anyone found out we had kept the silver, then we'd be in deep trouble.'

'Who's alive to tell the tale?' Macro smiled. 'Sinius is dead, so is Geta.'

'What about Tigellinus?'

'He might know something about it. But if he says anything, it'll only prove that he knew more about the Liberators than he's said so far. He'll keep his mouth shut.' Macro looked at Cato pleadingly. 'Come on, lad. After all that we've been through, it's only fair. It's not as if Claudius is going to miss a handful of coins.'

'Handful?' Cato wrestled with the idea for a moment, before the spectre of Narcissus and his devious machinations appeared in his mind's eye. He nodded. 'Why not?'

'Good lad!' Macro gave a relieved grin and clapped him on the shoulder. 'I knew you'd see the sense of it.'

'Good sense doesn't come into it,' Cato said quietly.

They reached the road leading back up to the Praetorian camp and stopped. Since their true identities had been revealed, they had been granted accommodation at headquarters, although they were regarded with cool formality by the other officers.

'You go ahead,' said Cato. 'There's something I have to do.'

Macro gave a lopsided smile, half tender, half nervous for his friend. 'She's back in Rome, then.'

'I heard this morning.' Cato felt dread welling up in his heart again at the prospect of seeing Julia. It had been over a year since they had last seen each other. In that time there had been a handful of letters exchanged. Though her words had been tender and reassuring, Cato could not help fearing that they were no guarantee that her heart was still his. 'I told myself I would see her as soon as we were finished with Narcissus.'

'So, go on, then. What are you waiting for?'

Cato's brow creased as he stood still, as if rooted to the spot. 'I don't know . . . I really don't know.'

'What is there to know, except the truth of how things stand between you?' Macro punched his shoulder. 'You can only discover that by going to see her.'

'Yes. You're right. I'll go. Now.'

'Want me to hold your hand?'

Cato looked at him sharply. 'Fuck off, thank you.'

Macro laughed heartily and winked at Cato before turning away and striding up the road leading to the camp as if he had not a care in the world. Cato watched him enviously for a moment and then continued on his way, pushing through the crowd as he made for the house of Senator Sempronius on the Quirinal Hill.

It was late in the morning when he stepped up from the street on to the steps to the entrance of the house. The heavy wooden doors were open and the last of the senator's clients were sitting on benches in the atrium, waiting to present their petitions to their patron. A slave approached Cato to ask him his business.

'I'm here to speak to Julia Sempronia.'

'Yes, master. What name shall I give her?'

Cato sucked in a deep breath to calm his nerves. 'Prefect Quintus Licinius Cato.'

The slave nodded and turned away on his errand. For an instant Cato was tempted to call the man back and cancel the instruction, but the slave was already at the far end of the atrium and Cato did not want to shout after him. It was too late for that. He stood, his right hand twitching against his thigh. He looked round, not really taking in the details of the house.

Then he froze.

Overhead the sky was clear and larks swooped high above, but Cato had no eyes for them and no ears for their shrill song. Instead he stared across the atrium at a slender young woman in a plain, long, light-blue tunic. She was standing in the opposite doorway, her dark hair tied back in a simple ponytail. She stared back at him. Then she began to walk steadily across the tiled floor, round the shallow pool in the centre of the atrium, her pace slowing as she approached him. Cato tried desperately to read her expression, for any hint of the despair or joy that the next moment might bring.

'Julia Sempronia.' He bowed his head formally, not knowing why he did it and feeling foolish.

'Cato,' she replied softly. 'Cato . . . My Cato.'

Then with a patter of her slippered feet she rushed into his arms and held him tight and Cato felt a warm wave of relief sweep through his chest. He pressed his cheek down against her hair and closed his eyes as her scent, almost forgotten, rushed back amid a confusion of memories and emotions.

Julia drew back and he opened his eyes to see her staring into his face. She reached a hand up to touch his lips, then moved her fingers lightly and uncertainly to trace the line of his scar. Then he saw a tear gleaming at the corner of her eye, where it swelled like a tiny translucent pearl before it rolled down her cheek.

Cato felt his heart torn in two as he regarded her. Much as he loved and desired Julia, Cato wanted to leave Rome at the first opportunity and get far away from its deadly cross-currents of deceit and treachery. He and Macro would be leaving to rejoin the army campaigning in Britannia. Nothing could sway Cato from that. Those were the terms that Julia would have to accept if she still wanted to have him.

'What's wrong, my love?' Her brow furrowed anxiously.

Cato took her hands in his. 'We must talk.'

AUTHOR'S NOTE

Being set mainly in Rome, *Praetorian* is something of a departure from the usual battlefield adventures of Cato and Macro. The last occasion they were in the city was when they were waiting for the outcome of an investigation into the death of a superior officer. Then they were living on the last of their savings, forced into taking rooms in a crumbling tenement block in one of the slum districts. It was only a brief interlude, however, and they were soon sent off to join a naval campaign against a gang of pirates. At the time I was quite taken with Rome as a setting for the story and wished that Cato and Macro could have spent more time in the capital. It's a fascinating setting to write about. With a population of around a million, Rome was a vast city even by modern standards. It is worth pointing out that during the early Renaissance the population of Rome was no more than fifteen thousand − living amid the ruins of a civilization that dwarfed their own. It was not until the nineteenth century that the population of Rome returned to the levels it had enjoyed under the Caesars. That is eloquent proof of the fact that human history is not a tale of steady progress towards greater knowledge and achievement.

Even so, daily life in ancient Rome was no picnic. The streets were filled with refuse and sewage and the stench would have been unbearable to a modern nose. Poor sanitation was only one of the dangers. With no regular police force on the beat, the streets were ridden with crime. Cut-purses and roving gangs of thieves haunted the narrow alleys winding off the main thorough-fares. Even if you avoided that threat you still had to face the danger of a complete lack of building regulations. With such a huge population squeezed into a relatively small area, the value of building land was at a premium. Accordingly, a mass of cheaply constructed tenement blocks rose up on Rome's hills, and in the valleys between the hills. Many were as high as six storeys and all of them posed significant fire risks as well as being in danger of collapse, burying alive those unfortunate enough to dwell within, as well as any unlucky passers-by.

The vast majority of the population lived in grinding poverty in these high-piled, filthy, crime-ridden slums. Perhaps half the infants born in these slums survived beyond the age of five and did well to live to the ripe old age of fifty. As with all great cities, food had to be trans-ported in from the countryside and therefore commanded relatively high prices which many could not afford. It had long been realised that a starving mob was not conducive to social stability and so the Senate and, later on the emperors, put in place a system of food subsidies and handouts. Having seen to the stomach of the mob, Rome's rulers proceeded to occupy their minds with entertainments. Something like a third of the days in every year were given over to chariot races, gladiator spectacles and public festivals. It was by such means that the emperors kept the mob in check. It was, however, always a parlous mechanism for social control and vulnerable to the fluctuations in supply of grain depicted in *Praetorian*.

It was a different story for the rich, of course. Those who could afford it bought houses on the hills where breezes made the stench more tolerable and helped to clear away the brown smog that frequently cloaked the capital. Attended by slaves, they could live off the best and most exotic foods that were imported into the city. They enjoyed the best seats at the Great Circus and in the theatres, as well as the complete gamut of pleasures of the flesh.

This then was the Rome in which Cato and Macro arrived to carry out their undercover mission for Narcissus. Although they had fought on the frontiers of the empire, the presence of Rome was always in the back of their minds as the embodiment of all the values that they were fighting for. The city was very much the centre of the Roman world. Not only was it the seat of government, it was also home to the temples of the empire's gods, and the hub of a vast economy that spanned the known world. In a race as hidebound by tradition as the Romans were, the fount of those traditions would always be regarded as sacred and its soldiers would be willing to face any peril in defence of the honour of Rome and all that it stood for.

This makes the reality of life in the great city such an interesting contrast to the abstract principle for which men like Cato and Macro fought and died. The ideals on which Rome had been built had largely perished along with the Republic and by the mid-first century the authority of the emperors was absolute. Sure enough there were still people who professed a yearning for the old days but they were usually sensible enough to keep their political views to themselves. The Senate, once the scene of debates and deeds that shaped the known world, was reduced to little more than an exclusive club who rubber-stamped imperial edicts. The power that had once been theirs had been transferred to the coterie of advisers who surrounded the emperor. To rub salt in the wound, these advisers were frequently men from inferior social classes. In the palace itself, there were deep divisions between the emperor's subordinates who jostled for influence over the emperor. Influence led to power and the chance to make vast fortunes, as the likes of Narcissus and Pallas duly did. If the stakes were high for the emperor's advisers, they were higher still for members of his family. The casualty rate amongst those closest to the emperor made the dangers facing those soldiers guarding the frontiers rather mild by comparison. For a brilliantly racy portrait of the lethal nature of life in the imperial palace I'd heartily recommend reading Graves's *I, Claudius*, or watch the excellent BBC television series.

Read on for exciting
bonus material
from Simon Scarrow

ROME TODAY

In preparing to write *Praetorian*, I paid my customary visit to the ground on which the novel is set. Ostia, the scene of the opening chapters, is a fine place to get some sense of the scale and appearance of the ancient world. Of course, it requires a degree of imagination to overlay the monochrome remains with the vibrant colours that would have existed in the first century, but there is still a tangible atmosphere of Roman-ness about the ruins.

Modern Rome offers many windows into the past, though a lot of what is there post-dates the age of Claudius. The heart of the city is still the Roman Forum, and the Via Sacra – the most venerable of the Roman thoroughfares – still stretches for a good distance and it is possible to retrace the steps of Julius Caesar, Pompey and Cicero. Having read Tom Holland's excellent account of the death of the Roman republic, *Rubicon*, it made the hairs on the back of my neck rise to stand in the same place where these extraordinary individuals played out their deadly political games. Towering over the remains of the great public buildings surrounding the Forum is the Palatine Hill with the remains of palaces sprawling over the slopes and crest. The view from the top still gives a tangible sense of the vista enjoyed by those who lived and worked in the imperial palace. For a close look at some of the most striking artefacts of ancient Rome a visit to the museum on the Capitoline Hill, where the temple of Jupiter once stood, is well recommended. At every turn you will come face to face with sculptures which are familiar enough from the mass of illustrated books that have been written about Rome. There is, however, no substitute for seeing them in the flesh – as it were.

Further afield, one can still cross the Tiber over bridges dating back to the days of Cato and Macro. Sections of the city wall and some gates still remain, as well as a length of the wall of the Praetorian Camp. The Great Sewer – the Cloaca Maxima – still exists and, indeed, stretches of it are still in use. For all sorts of health and safety reasons it is very difficult to get access to it, so I was not too sorry to miss out on that particular pleasure.

EMPEROR CLAUDIUS AND THE PRAETORIAN GUARD

Born in 10 BC, Claudius was one of the longer-living members of the imperial family. His father and brothers were fated to die young, unaided by natural causes. In the dangerous world of the imperial household, Claudius was overlooked by his potential rivals as well as the more senior members of the family owing to his physical impediments and supposed mental deficiencies. Emperor Augustus and his wife Livia found him an embarrassment and did all that they could to ensure that he was kept far from public view so as not to reflect badly on them. His own mother considered him to be a monster only partially formed by nature, according to Suetonius, who also describes him as having a pronounced limp, chronic stammer and tendency to dribble when over-excited.

While Claudius was no fool, it is hard to square the historical record with Graves's interpretation of him as a wily survivor. Claudius was fortunate, if that is the word, to be regarded as a harmless idiot, and there is some reason to believe that those who classified him as such had good cause. He was certainly easily gulled by those who surrounded him, most notably his wives and freed-men. Suetonius describes him as a fairly inconsistent character just as inclined to make a complete fool of himself as earn anyone's respect. He also had a cruel streak, most visible when he was witnessing a gladiator fight and keen to see the expression on the face of a man as he died. Given that Claudius lacked the charisma, intelligence and respect demonstrated by most candidates for emperor it rather raises the question of how he got the job.

To answer that we need to be aware of another component of the power structure in ancient Rome. While the emperors might have wielded supreme authority over the empire, they were only mortals at the end of the day. As such, they needed protection from those who might take exception to their right to rule. The very first emperor, Augustus, realised the need for a military unit to act as his bodyguard and weapon of last resort in the case of social disorder in Rome. Accordingly, he adapted the army tradition of providing a special unit to protect the commanders of the legions and created a permanent force based in Rome. To avoid any temptation to abuse the potential power that went with being commander of the Praetorian Guard, Augustus resorted to the tried and tested practice of dividing the command between two prefects. To further ensure that these posts were not filled by men of influence, he bypassed the aristocracy and chose the commanders from the ranks of the equites, the second tier of the Roman class system.

This arrangement seemed to answer the security needs of the early emperors. During the reign of only the second emperor, Tiberius, things went awry, however. The Praetorian prefects happened to be father and son, and the latter, Aelius Sejanus, had an ambitious streak in him a mile wide. Using his position, he inveigled himself into the emperor's affection by posing as a tireless and loyal servant. Secretly, he was planning the gradual removal of the emperor's heirs with the long-term goal of marrying into the imperial family and taking the throne for himself. Naturally, such an audacious scheme was bound to be detected by someone at some stage, so Sejanus ensured that he was the gatekeeper of the emperor. All communication with Tiberius was routed through Sejanus. This was made easier when Tiberius left Rome to live on the island of Capri where he could indulge himself in whatever sexual perversions he desired, far from the view of the Roman public. Tiberius was content to leave the running of his affairs to his apparently good and faithful servant back in Rome. Ultimately, Sejanus's enemies managed to sneak a warning message through to Tiberius who then took immediate steps to remove Sejanus from command, and have him, his family and his supporters massacred.

After this episode, Tiberius took a good deal more care to be *au fait* with the activities of the commanders of the Praetorian Guard. Unfortunately, one of his heirs, Gaius – more familiarly known by his cognomen Caligula – had grown rather impatient of waiting for his uncle to die and hatched a plot with Prefect Macro (no connection to the hero of my novels) to speed Tiberius on his way. The unfortunate Macro did not have much chance to claim his reward before he was done away with and replaced by a dour and proud officer named Cassius Chaerea. Caligula was barely a year into his reign when he slipped into madness and convinced himself that he was a god with limitless power. As gods do, he was inclined to treat mortals as his playthings, and took particular pleasure in tormenting Prefect Chaerea. Whenever the emperor was asked for the day's password he would come up with a line like 'kiss me quick', which Chaerea was duty bound to pass on to his men – the cause of much hilarity for Caligula, but much embarrassment for the proud soldier. Eventually Chaerea cast professionalism aside and threw in his lot with a group of plotters who had resolved to kill Caligula before he got round to executing them on trumped-up treason charges, so that he could confiscate their property (a revenue-raising expedient that might be of considerable use if applied today . . .). On the appointed day, Caligula and his wife and child were butchered on the way to the Circus Maximus. The assassins, led by Chaerea, were resolved to kill every member of the imperial family and return Rome to its republican heritage.

One member of the family, the emperor's uncle, Claudius, ran for cover the instant that he heard about the murder of Caligula. With their master disposed of, the Praetorian Guards in the imperial palace quickly decided to snatch what loot they could in the ensuing panic. One such Praetorian happened to wander into a room that opened out on to a balcony overlooking Rome. Finding nothing of interest he was about to leave when he noticed two feet protruding from the base of a curtain by the balcony. Whipping it aside he was surprised to find Claudius cowering behind the curtain. At once Claudius fell to his knees and begged for mercy, hugging the Praetorian's legs. At first the soldier had not a clue what he should do about his discovery. Dragging Claudius to his feet he went to find a superior to decide on the fate of the dead emperor's uncle. That officer had no orders covering the situation and so Claudius was taken by litter up to the Praetorian Camp.

Meanwhile, the plotters had managed to talk the leaders of the Senate into ordering the Urban Cohorts (the nearest thing Rome had to a police force) to take control of the Forum and the Capitoline Hill. With the emperor dead, the senators had begun to debate the restoration of the republic when word arrived that Claudius was alive and well up at the Praetorian Camp. Hoping to lure him out of the Camp and then kill him, the senators asked Claudius if he would come to the Senate house to add his thoughts to the debate. Claudius replied that he was not allowed to leave the Camp. The danger was clear enough and the solution to his difficulty was equally obvious. Claudius asked to address the Praetorian Guard and made them an offer. If they were prepared to acclaim him emperor and swear an oath of allegiance to him then he would ensure that every man would receive a 'gift' equivalent to five years' pay. Now that kind of offer doesn't happen every day and the Praetorians, who had shortly before been facing the possibility of being out of a well-paid and comfortable job, leapt at the opportunity. When Claudius did emerge from the Camp, at the head of thousands of well-armed and highly motivated soldiers who had acclaimed him as their emperor, who was going to argue with his appointment?

The lesson of that day was apparent to everyone with an interest in who ruled Rome. An emperor would only ever last as long as he enjoyed the loyalty of the Praetorian Guards. Fortunately, the rank and file had little interest in politics and could be kept sweet with regular gifts and the provision of entertainment. Throughout his reign Claudius made sure that the palms of his Praetorians were regularly greased. The emperors who came after him followed suit, and those that didn't were often swiftly and fatally reminded of the dangers of not keeping the Praetorians sweet, as Galba discovered in AD 69 when he refused to pay up on his accession to the imperial throne. For their part, the prefects of the Praetorian Guard had discovered a taste for politics and, in the centuries that followed, a large number of them paid for it with their lives. Ultimately, the mercenary self-interest of the Praetorian Guard was exposed following their murder of Commodus, when they auctioned the throne, in public, to the highest bidder. Like the short stabbing sword of the Roman legions – the gladius – the Praetorian Guard was a double-edged weapon, and every bit as dangerous.

AN INTERVIEW
WITH SIMON SCARROW

How do you begin your research for each book? What discovery has particularly surprised you in the course of your research for *Praetorian*?

The starting place for the Roman novels is usually the original histories, letters and so on of ancient writers like Cicero or Tacitus. They give great accounts of the cut and thrust of Roman politics, as well as the various campaigns and wars that the legions fought. Quite often an idea for a story will occur while I am working through one of these texts. Alternatively, I like to travel to the places where I think a novel could be set and scout round for any ruins, museums or settings that could help form the backdrop of a novel. I find it very easy to imagine how things might have been back in the past and make detailed notes of the feel of a place. For *Praetorian*, I made a visit to Rome and explored the streets with a modern guide book in one hand and an ancient Roman city plan in the other, and tried to superimpose how I imagined Rome might have looked over the modern buildings and streets.

The most interesting discovery I made was the reference in Suetonius to the naval battle Claudius staged to entertain the Roman people. Here was a public entertainment on the most lavish scale featuring thousands of combatants and dozens of ships. In reality, it took place on the Fucine Lake, some distance from Rome. I wanted to depict the fight, but needed it to be set nearer to Rome and so I switched the setting to the Albine Lake, much closer to the capital. Otherwise, I follow the historical event as closely as possible.

What do you find most fascinating about this period in Roman history?

The first century fascinates me because it is the era in which Rome finally succumbed to an imperial regime. The first emperor, Augustus, had taken power following a long and bloody series of factional wars and struggled to establish a hereditary line of emperors to give stability to Rome. His immediate successors, however, were cruel and/or crazy and their poor form endangered the legacy of Augustus. The emperors faced conspiracies organised by die-hard republicans, as well as other plots hatched within the imperial household. At the same time, the emperors were always conscious of the need to curry favour with the mob and this led to ever more excessive forms of public entertainment and foreign campaigns intended to add to the prestige of the incumbent. This is why Cato and Macro are kept so busy and why I won't be short of plots for a good while yet.

Your Roman novels have had a number of different settings including Britain and Egypt. What has been your favourite location for your novels? Why did you decide to return to the heart of Rome for *Praetorian*?

One of the most useful characteristics of the age in which my novels are set is the fact that hardly a year goes by without Rome doing great harm to someone, somewhere, around the Mediterranean. This means that my two heroes can find themselves in a variety of settings and it is an opportunity for readers to discover more about the Roman empire, and the wide range of enemies they faced, from the woad-painted Celts in the north to the robed Arab desert tribes of the eastern frontier.

Of all the countries I have been fortunate to visit while researching my novels the most atmospheric was Jordan. There is such a huge variety of scenery, from the lush greenery of the hills in spring to the barren, blood-red sands of Wadi Rum. Both the Greeks and the Romans left their mark on Jordan and the ruins of Jerash, Umm Qais and Petra are spectacular. But, without doubt, the most striking location I explored was the ruin of the small fort at Q'sar Bashir. It is remarkably well preserved amid a wasteland of stony desert many miles from the nearest town. I was so struck by the solitude, silence and stillness of the place that I knew I had to write about it, and so it became the inspiration for the fort that Macro and Cato have to defend in *The Eagle in the Sand*.

In this latest book the lads have returned to Rome since their work in the eastern provinces is over – for now. Having fully expected a well-deserved rest they find themselves immersed in an undercover operation on the orders of the ever-scheming Narcissus. The last time Macro and Cato had been in the capital for any length of time was during the period before they were sent to fight the pirate fleet in *The Eagle's Prophecy*. I had a lot of fun reconstructing Rome in that novel and since then I had been keen to get my heroes back to the city, and deep into the heart of the powerplay that surrounds Emperor Claudius. It would be a big challenge for two soldiers who are used to fighting the enemies of Rome on the frontier to have to contend with the plotters striking from the shadows.

This would be a completely new kind of test for Macro and Cato, I realised. Instead of the wide open battlefields they would be fighting in narrow alleys and dank tunnels, and they would be living right amongst their enemies. Also, it would be a chance to provide a worm's eye view of the imperial family and their coterie at work. Characters such as Nero are too often portrayed in popular fiction and film as fully matured psychopaths and this would be a chance to present one of the most infamous emperors as the more gentle and sensitive teenager he might have been.

Finally, having set up the threat to Rome's grain supply in both *The Gladiator* and *The Legion*, it was time to follow that strand through and see what the effects would have been in the capital. With its vast population (nigh on a million people according to some estimates), Rome was a veritable parasite, sucking in the resources of empire. The flipside of this was that the city was very vulnerable to any threat to the logistical network that kept the city supplied with food. As the saying goes, no matter how grand a civilization is, it is never more than three meals away from a revolution. With the disruption to the grain supply from Egypt, there would have been a severe shortage of affordable grain and much discontent as a result. Perfect conditions for the Liberators to exploit in their bid to topple Emperor Claudius, I thought.

Praetorian is your eleventh novel about Cato and Macro. How do you think that the characters have evolved during the series?

Cato and Macro are now like old friends and it is always a pleasure to meet up with them again when I settle down to write a new adventure. Because they are fully rounded characters, their dialogue flows nicely and their keen awareness of each other's foibles means that there is a constant friendly banter that tips over into moody sniping from time to time. Some readers tell me that they are more like father and son than friends. I think there's a degree of truth in that, and perhaps at other times they are like brothers. I prefer to see them as two aspects of my own character. Cato sounds to me pretty much how I used to be as a student – idealistic, fascinated by new sights and knowledge and very self-conscious and self-critical. Conversely, Macro is rather like how I have become as the years have passed – somewhat jaded, less interested in fine causes and more keen on the simple pleasures in life. Most of all, impatient and unwilling to suffer fools (amongst many other demographics) gladly. So, their relationship is a dialogue of the ages really, and that makes it ageless and a lot of fun to play around with.

Of course, being in the military they have to deal with the realities of rank and for a long time Macro was comfortable being the senior officer of the two. For his part, Cato was happy to be Macro's side-kick and learn his trade from an older, more experienced soldier. Inevitably, Cato had to outgrow this role and move out from under Macro's wing to prove himself. So it has been fascinating to watch them adjust to the new arrangement now that Cato is Macro's superior. *Praetorian* provides a short breathing space before they return to the army to continue the campaign in Britain, where Cato will assume the rank and responsibilities of a prefect while Macro serves as a centurion.

In your Roman novels you write about two fictional heroes in a factual historical setting, but in your Revolution quartet about Wellington and Bonaparte your main protagonists were real people. How easy do you find it to blend fact and fiction in your novels?

The Revolution novels were much harder to write because my main characters have been put under such close scrutiny for the best part of two hundred years. One of the first things I discovered when I began my research for the series is that there are over a hundred thousand historical texts dealing with Napoleon alone. There are a somewhat smaller number that focus on Wellington. This meant that I had to be as accurate as possible and only bend the facts discreetly when I had to make the story run smoothly. I am delighted that so many people have written to me to compliment me on the accuracy of the story. Almost as delighted as I am to hear that they have enjoyed the books immensely. There is one 'armless' little mistake that I freely own up to and that is not having Somerset lose a limb at Waterloo. There had been more than enough suffering to write about at that point, and it would have distracted readers' attention from the resolution of the relationship between the two main characters.

As far as the Roman series goes, the main characters *are* fictional, but I have researched the details of the lives of the men of the Roman army and navy as thoroughly as possible to ensure that my representation is accurate. The same goes for the settings for their adventures and I have the mosquito bites and sunburn to prove it. In addition, Macro and Cato are often in the thick of real military operations, such as the invasion of Britain in AD 43 and the earthquake that struck Crete in AD 49. Writing stories from the point of view of the common soldiers, rather than from the lofty perspective of Caesar, Cicero and Tacitus, provides readers with a fresh insight into the ancient world and I make no apology for the fact that I am writing fiction. After all, what readers want first and foremost is a good story, rather than an excuse for a lecture on the ancient world seasoned with superfluous Latin and barely digestible information dumps. For me, research is there to serve the story, not the other way round. If people learn more about the ancient world from reading my novels then I regard that as a bonus.

What inspired you to start writing? Did you always want to be a writer?

I first became a storyteller when I was nine years old. Back then, I was at a boarding school (Vernon Holme, about as lovely a place to be a child as you could wish) and, after lights out, each boy took his turn in making up a story. I enjoyed doing this and became quite good at it. Good enough to get the job full-time. It was great fun to think up characters, plot and setting and the tales were often quite bizarre and fantastical. I loved the way in which my audience got wrapped up in the tale. As the years passed, I began to set some of the stories down in spare exercise books and used others for homework exercises. That was always my favourite task in English lessons. In fact, one of my best ever pieces of work was the script for a radio play set during the revolt of Spartacus.

At the same time I was not alone in being a storyteller in the Scarrow household. Both of my brothers, Scott and Alex, were also keen on making up tales and we would often discuss ideas and build up stories over the dinner table. Sometimes we would think of them in terms of novels, but we also came up with a host of ideas for films as well. At one stage I had an idea for a science-fiction film and went as far as building a full-scale set for a starship bridge complete with banks of lights, switches and computer screens (I shudder to think what the electric bill came to when it landed on my parents' doormat), as well as several highly detailed miniature craft for special effects shots. Alas, A levels got in the way of a directing career and I ended up at the University of East Anglia. I continued to write short stories in my spare time and, having graduated in the middle of a recession, I decided that I would write my first novel while I waited for a job to come up. It was a post-apocalyptic tale set in the Bahamas and while it provided a useful training experience it was not good enough for publication. So I continued with two more novels, a comedy and a detective story, before realising that I was writing what I thought other people wanted to read, rather than what I wanted. At the time I was a big fan of the Hornblower and Sharpe novels, as well as the Roman crime novels of Lindsey Davis. It occurred to me that what I really wanted to read was a military series set in the Roman era. Not being able to find anything like that in the bookshops I started to write my own. Mainly for my own satisfaction. When I showed some of the material to my colleagues at the college where I was then working, they were keen and kind enough to encourage me to continue and a year or so later the first of Macro and Cato's adventures had been written. I found an agent who found an editor and so began my career as an author.

Which of your novels is your favourite or your proudest achievement?

It's almost impossible to pick a favourite. There are many aspects in each of the books that I am very proud of. Particularly those moments in the Roman novels where Macro and Cato do something or say something that I could have never anticipated. Indeed, sometimes they even give me quite a shock. The scene in *The Eagle's Prophecy* when Macro encounters his long-lost mother was as much of a surprise to me as it was to him! What is particularly gratifying about this is that the characters have become real enough to act independently of my plans for them. That feels like a true achievement to me. Far better than writing about characters who are merely puppets inserted into a novel to move the plot along.

If I had to pick one book to stand as my proudest achievement it would probably be *Young Bloods*, the first novel in my Napoleon and Wellington series. That is because it was a new direction and I knew it would be a huge challenge to write something that would be an epic account of the most significant era in modern history. To be honest, I was not sure that I could handle the material. A vast amount of research was needed, as well as finding a way to get under the skins of two giants of history. *Young Bloods* proved that I could do this, and it gave me the confidence to complete the rest of the series, as well as tackle other historical periods.

Which other writers do you most admire? Is there a book you wish you had written?

I was an avid reader of historical fiction as a child and I dare say my list of favourite authors will sound very familiar. C.S. Forester, Rosemary Sutcliff, Henry Treace, Alfred Duggan and a host of others. Later on I hugely enjoyed the work of Bernard Cornwell, Patrick O'Brian and Lindsey Davis and at the moment I admire the sheer brio of writers like C.C. Humphreys and Robert Low.

As for a book I wish I had written, well, that's easy. *The Da Vinci Code* would do very nicely as a pension fund. I suspect, however, that the real thrust of the question is to discover if there is a book that I would be proud to have written. The answer is no. Not through any sense of hubris. Simply because part of the pleasure of discovering a good book is the feeling that the other author is doing a far better job of it than you could. Conversely, the only time I wish I could have written someone else's book is when they have made a complete hash of a good idea. Luckily, the filtering process of submission to agents and publishers tends to mean that such work is very much in the minority of those books that make it into print.

Also by Simon Scarrow

The Legion

When the actions of a rebel gladiator in Egypt threaten the stability of the Roman Empire, Prefect Cato and Centurion Macro know he must be stopped. The locals are holding the Romans responsible for the attacks Ajax and his crew have been making along the Egyptian coast and, with the southern frontier under raid by the Nubians, Egypt is dangerously volatile.

Tasked by Egypt's governor with tracking and defeating the renegade, Cato and Macro are soon hot on Ajax's trail. Joining with the Twenty-Second Legion, they are determined to destroy the enemy. But will the strength of a psychotically fatalist gladiator and his new-found Nubian allies, hell-bent on destruction, defeat the Roman warriors?

978 0 7553 5376 7

headline

Now you can buy any of these other bestselling
books by **Simon Scarrow** from your bookshop
or *direct from his publisher*.

The *Roman* Series	
Under the Eagle	£7.99
The Eagle's Conquest	£7.99
When the Eagle Hunts	£7.99
The Eagle and the Wolves	£7.99
The Eagle's Prey	£7.99
The Eagle's Prophecy	£7.99
The Eagle in the Sand	£7.99
Centurion	£7.99
The Gladiator	£7.99
The Legion	£7.99
The *Wellington and Napoleon* Quartet	
Young Bloods	£7.99
The Generals	£7.99
Fire and Sword	£7.99
The Fields of Death	£7.99

TO ORDER SIMPLY CALL THIS NUMBER

01235 400 414

FREE P&P AND UK DELIVERY
(Overseas and Ireland £3.50 per book)

or visit our website: www.headline.co.uk

Prices and availability subject to change without notice

Embark on a journey with Cato and Macro and find out about their other exploits across the Roman Empire.

www.catoandmacro.com/the-books